Star Time

Star Time

Henry Melton

Wire Rim Books
Hutto, Texas

Star Time © 2011 by Henry Melton
All Rights Reserved

Printing History
First Edition: August 2011
ISBN 978-1-935236-30-6

ePub ISBN 978-1-935236-31-3
Kindle ISBN 978-1-935236-32-0

Website of Henry Melton
www.HenryMelton.com

Cover art © 2011 Henry Melton and Mary Ann Melton

Printed in the United States of America

Wire Rim Books
www.wirerimbooks.com

Acknowledgements

True friends who have told me what was wrong with the text.
Peter Birch, for his information about Siding Springs.
For family, who have put up with this novel's very long gestation period.
Thanks to Jonathan Andrews for staring into the lights.

For my larger than life big brother Roger Melton, a role model through my childhood years. Seven years my senior, he took his little brother to his first science fiction movie, and shared the experience of his astronomy expeditions. A techno wizard from the beginning– I played with his toys and electronics when he wasn't looking, and growing up I kept trying to follow in his footsteps.

Table of Contents

Evil in the Sky

THE WITCH

The house was eighty years old, barely a hunting cabin, surrounded on all sides by Texas Hill Country live oak—invisible unless you knew where it was. Walls showed white scraps of peeled paint, mostly unchanged in all of Sharon Dae's twenty-two years. Lovingly tended gardens that took advantage of the few sunlit open patches among the trees were a half-mile from the nearest road. Few of the residents of nearby Wimberley knew the place existed, although there was a rumor of a witch that lived in that particularly dense patch of woods, surrounded by an unmarked 8-foot tall deer fence. Most of the school kids spreading the rumor would be surprised to find it was true.

Sunset had been an hour earlier, and the stars were out. With no electricity, and few candles, Sharon lived by the sun. Sticky summer heat had her in the rocker on the open-air porch, dressed in her half unbuttoned nightgown, waiting for a breeze before going to bed. She combed out her waist-length hair, more albino white than blonde, but had to put aside her brush when Felicia hopped up into her lap. Kitten-scale thoughts intruded on Sharon's worries as she absently stroked the black fur.

Off to the north, she could see the town glow, but overhead it was nearly black sky, dotted with a few of the brightest stars. The moisture of the past few days had finally moved out. The only sounds were the crickets and the creaking of the old wooden building as it began to cool. The great horned owl that lived across the meadow whooted and Felicia perked up her tiny ears.

Prey or Predator? In her few months of life, the kitten was still trying to make sense of the world around her.

She can eat you whole, little one

Felicia could only understand a whisper of the focused thought, but jumped down and scampered into the house. Sharon laughed softly, loving the bundle of fur and energy.

As the night darkened, the mental landscape lit up. Thousands of little minds were in close range, with their little thoughts. The chatter of thousands of humans miles away were much more insistent. By habit she let them blur together. Nothing could shut them out, but with luck, and enough distance, she could ignore them. For every hate there was a love, and for every tear a smile. The danger was being too close, where each mind demanded to be heard on its own.

Sharon buttoned her nightgown and pulled her shawl over her shoulders. Town glow drew her attention. She feared those people, and envied their closed minds. How wonderful it would be! Oblivious to the unending noise, so starved for communication that they stared for hours at their televisions and talked incessantly on their telephones and tapped away at their computers.

Her eyes were drawn higher, up to the north, over the horizon. A thought from up high screamed out from the crowd. She frowned and stood up.

What was that?

One of the new predators. She could feel it. Bare feet used to the soil stepped off the porch and onto the earth. She scanned the sky.

Not an animal, but it wasn't human either. Great hatred, like the hunting cry of a big cat, echoed through her mind.

"There is an Evil in the sky." It was an echo. Words her mother June Dae had said so many times when Sharon was little.

High above, something like a dark angel was fighting for its life, and raw rage washed over her like fire.

THE WIZARD

Abe Whiting ran down the darkened hallway of his Austin-based electronics design company, shouting, "No gunplay in the corridors!" *If she puts holes in something again...*

Gray-haired Mary Ellen Victor, in her black tailored suit, looked up at the locked door with a gleam in her eye, and a .357 magnum blue-steel pistol in her hand. The sight of her adopted son approaching with a strained grin on his face did little to mollify her anger. It was focused elsewhere.

She yelled at the door. "Don't you tell me I can't enter, you overgrown answering machine! My briefcase is in there." She knocked again with the butt end of her pistol.

Hodgepodge's synthetic voice gave him a patronizing air. "I am sorry, but the rules concerning security within the Whiting Design Center offices do not allow me to unlock the door at this time of night. If there is an emergency, text the office with code 9399 for assistance."

"Emergency! Why you canned voice! Give me one good reason why I shouldn't put a wadcutter right through your speaker grille!"

Then she turned on Abe.

"Since when do I need special permission to walk around in here? Your pet monster is getting too big for his britches."

He approached with arms spread and a smile on his face. As a rule, Abe avoided people, but this short wrinkled tornado was special.

"Don't placate me!" She grumbled with her face in his shirt. But since he was a third her age, and a third taller, she submitted to the hug.

"It's all my fault," he explained gently. "As much as I'd love to see it, Hodgepodge isn't about to institute a new security policy on his own initiative. That's far too human!"

She turned her glare on him. "I should've known. What did you do?"

Abe dipped his head in apology, trying to look small although he towered over her. He nodded toward the door. "We were talking about the graffiti incident, and how he watched them painting the walls with the security camera, but took no action. I talked to him about the idea of property and about how the concept applied to us. This verbal warning and lock control is part of what we talked about."

"Did you get as far as calling the police and active defense?" She still fumed about last week's events. "The next time I have to call the sandblasters in on that wall, it'd better be to clean up blood stains!"

He nodded. "We did talk about how to call the police without spooking the 9-1-1 operator. But you'd better think about it. Officer Reinhardt's opinions on your artillery were pretty clear last time. Gunfire within city limits will get you arrested. If he'd been the one to come in when you were threatening to blast holes in the speaker, you might've had to file your own *habeas corpus.*"

"Okay, but Mr. Erector Set in there," she pointed toward the computer lab with her thumb, "had better not give me any more flack."

"Okay. Hodgepodge?" Abe addressed the speaker box.

"Yes." The computer's voice reminded him of an old librarian, one he'd crossed swords with back at the Home, before he met the Victors. It was a refined and mellow voice, but it sounded like your concerns bored him to tears. Abe put the issue on his mental checklist. If the voice inflection was only a matter of tonality, he could fix that, but Hodgepodge was a computer. He had an innate lack of empathy for the human condition. If the synthesized voice just reflected that reality, Abe wasn't sure how to handle it. Canned responses could always be tweaked to sound friendly, but Hodgepodge's voice was intimately tied to his mental processes, just like a living thing.

But that was another issue for another time. He had to make peace between Mary Ellen and Hodgepodge. Again.

"Hodgepodge, why did you restrict access to the library?"

There was a noticeable pause. Abe recognized it—Hodgepodge pulling logs from secondary storage. The computer's *rules* were distilled down to instinct, but the how and why were sometimes shuffled off into the slow memory. "'All access to Whiting facilities shall be restricted during off hours except by a logged schedule change.'" It was a quote.

"Who will be allowed to change a schedule?"

"Any employee with the manager flag."

Mary Ellen looked at Abe with a sudden smirk on her face, "Hodgepodge, does Abe have a manager flag?"

"No."

She poked Abe in the sternum, "You've got an *oops* there buddy. I told you to put yourself into the org chart. You can't run a business like this. I know you think Whiting is just your private play pen, but business structures exist for a reason."

Abe frowned, something wasn't right. "Hodgepodge, am I authorized to enter the library?"

"No."

Mary Ellen looked smug at that response.

Abe shook his head, "Hodgepodge, unlock the library door." There was an immediate click. Abe pushed the door open easily, and they went in. The lights came on in response to their presence.

"I've noticed this before," Abe went to the nearest keyboard. "Sometimes Hodgepodge doesn't apply the rules to me. I haven't nailed down why."

Mary Ellen located her case and opened it. She pulled out a sheaf of papers bound by a large clip. "Okay, so you and Metalhead are buddies and the rules don't matter for you. But what about me? I needed this thirty minutes ago."

He nodded. "I think we can fix that. Hodgepodge, what is the justification principle by which you control the building security?"

"I am an agent of the Whiting Corporation, protecting its property."

"Who are the members of the Whiting Corporation?"

"Abe Whiting, Mary Ellen Victor, and the estate of Franklin David Victor."

"As an agent of Whiting Corp, you should take direction concerning corporation property from the board of directors, agreed?"

"Yes."

Mary Ellen, always quick on the uptake, nodded, and brought the handle of her pistol down on the table like a gavel. "Hodgepodge, log the following meeting of the board of directors of the Whiting Corporation. A quorum is present. As principal shareholder, I call the meeting to order. I move that any member of the board of directors can override Hodgepodge."

Abe frowned as he thought about it. "We don't want the bank to be able to waltz in here and mess things up. How about just us two?"

"The motion is amended to give override to board members with more than 30% of the corporation and cannot be reassigned to sub agents."

"Second."

"Mary Ellen Victor, voting 62% votes yea."

Abe chimed in, "Abe Whiting, voting 35%, votes yes."

Mary Ellen continued in her rapid-fire legalese, "Minority shareholders are not present. The motion passes, 97% yea, zero nay. Motion to adjourn?"

"Motion."

"Second. Meeting adjourned *sine die.*"

Mary Ellen slipped the pistol into its pocket in her customized briefcase. "Hodgepodge, unlock the door." There was a click. "Turn off the lights."

The room dropped into darkness with only the light of a workstation screen to see by. "Lights back on."

She had a big grin. "I love power."

Just then, everything went black—the lights, the computers, everything. The faint whisper of equipment fans died to perfect silence.

Abe shouted, "No! This can't be happening!"

THE SEER

Ed Morgan sat in the comfortable darkness, waiting for the last show of the planetarium. "I've missed George's meeting," he mumbled. He didn't need a wristwatch to tell him that. He never paid any attention to clocks anyway.

Too many meetings! George Fuller always wanted a meeting. Before dawn, he wanted a meeting, after the market closed he wanted a re-cap, and every time some financial news item caught his interest, old George always wanted to know what was going to happen next.

And I'm the pet fortune-teller, always there to tell him.

It wasn't as if he hated the stock market reports, it was just that excuses to skip his briefings were easy to come up with. Ed could babble on about companies he'd never heard about, using words he didn't understand. Tapping into the future wasn't hard, but it was boring.

He tried to relax, and the tilted-back planetarium seat made it easy. There was a swirl of lights growing in the blackness—star constellations.

Orion, he was pleased to identify it. Three showings in one week were making some inroads. Science and the stars had never been interesting—before Angela.

On cue, she started, talking loudly without the microphone, "My apologies for the late start. There has been a power outage."

The moving glow of her hand-held light stick caught his eye. There was a flicker in his mind's eye. *Oh. It was just another vision.* The star patterns he'd visualized overhead blurred into nothingness as he heard her continue, "We expect power to be restored within a few minutes. Please remain seated until the lights come back on, the aisles have a number of steps and believe me, you don't want to try to navigate in the dark."

Ed smiled at the sound of her voice. That full, pleasant, competent voice caught his attention the first time he'd ducked into the planetarium's theater to escape his worries.

George Fuller was his boss. In spite of all the complimentary things George said about him, Ed knew it was all an act. Friendly, call-me-George, smiling in his nice suit—he was a man who wanted money. And he couldn't help but treat Ed like a wayward teenager.

I'm twenty-four years old. How can he expect me to live my life around his schedule? He ought to know me by now. How many years has he been my guardian?

Ed shook his head. Days, months, years—he didn't have much use for them. He knew it was summer, because of the heat, but he wasn't sure about the month. Since the day he gave up on school, he hadn't had much use for calendars.

George runs my life. Why do I need to know what day it is?

More chemical light sticks had been found and there was some visibility in the circular theater now. There was a common gripe about cell phones not working. People were beginning to stand up and look at each other for a group consensus. "Hey, are we going to get a refund?" called out one man.

"Just sit down", Ed whispered, and closed his eyes. The vision of Orion was there, just waiting out of the sight of normal people.

Angela came back, "My manager has told me that the power should be back on soon, and that the presentation will go on as scheduled. However, for those who don't want to wait, you can take your ticket stub to the gift center counter for a refund. Raise your hand so I can guide you out."

Ed waited until she walked closer, giving re-assurance to the undecided. "Angela?"

She looked at him in the dim light. He could smell a whiff of her perfume. "Hello? It is Ed, isn't it? Nice to see you back so soon."

He was pleased that she remembered his name. He liked to be remembered.

On impulse, he said, "Angela, the power will be back on in ten seconds."

"What?" She looked puzzled for a moment.

"Three. Two. One." He counted, and there was a thud and a whir as the air-conditioning and the dome lights came back on.

She looked at him again with a questioning look, but turned back towards her control platform.

"Please be seated everyone. We will be starting the show in one minute."

Ed smiled. There were times when he loved being able to tell the future.

Star Time

The lights dimmed and the stars came out with Angela's lovely voice telling the story. Ed looked for Orion and found it, after a short re-orientation of his perspective.

Then his smile dropped. *What is wrong with Orion?*

Blackout

THE WIZARD

This should not happen. Abe couldn't understand the blackout.

"Hodgepodge?" There was no red light from the redundant power system used to drive the computer. There was no response. His mind went down a checklist, but underneath was a gnawing blackness in his spirit worse than the indicators on his hardware.

Working by feel, he fumbled through his desk drawer. He grabbed the ribbed casing of a flashlight and thumbed the switch—nothing. He tried again, several times. It flared into brightness, and he set it down. The emergency lighting came back up at the same time.

Down in the basement, he heard the backup generators finally rumble to life—late but welcome, as the city mains were still down.

"Hodgepodge?" Still nothing. Abe headed out the door towards the computer room.

Mary Ellen followed, "What's going on? Why is Junk-heap playing tricks with the lights?"

Abe shook his head, passing her by. "It's not Hodgepodge. Some kind of power outage." She tried to keep up with him as he hurried to the main computer room.

Hurrying a dozen paces behind him, she watched as he reached the computer room door and tried to swipe his access card through the reader. No luck. The reader blinked, but the electrical latch didn't activate. His hands clenched and unclenched.

"Hodgepodge?" he called, but there was no response. Behind the glass, indicator lights were on. Something was happening in there, but his computer wasn't talking.

Mary Ellen framed a suitable comment about computer-controlled locks to computer rooms, but she kept it to herself. She had never seen her boy get so agitated. Even when Frank died, with a million things the two of them had to handle, Abe was always calm. Her almost-son had kept a level head and made sure her temper never quite made a difficult situation impossible.

Abe looked around and dashed off down the hall. He returned quickly, with a large hammer. A few quick blows fractured the glass. He tore the metal mesh away and reached in and opened the door with the inside handle.

She followed him in, her mouth hanging open. Abe was a timid soul. His active mind found clever ways around his barriers—that's what made him a millionaire technologist so young. She would have blasted through the door. He never would. Never.

He was already seated before a console—typing commands and reading the hundreds of scrolling messages. She hesitated to interrupt him. She stepped across the broken glass and found another chair. After a few minutes, he paused in his furious attentions, and she felt bold enough to ask, "What happened?"

He shook his head in puzzlement. "I don't know. The power failed."

"Well, is what's-its-name okay?"

He didn't look her way. He brushed a trickle of sweat from his forehead. "I don't know. I really don't know. He isn't supposed to have power failures! The battery systems should have supplied AC power a fraction of a second after a city main failure. The generators should have come up within a second or two later. Critical boards run directly off of battery systems that are always up and charged. Hodgepodge is never supposed to lose power!

"All the systems failed at the same time. This is not supposed to be possible. It can't happen."

Abe tapped a few keystrokes and watched the response.

"Well, is it broken?" she asked.

"I don't know. Hodgepodge has been alive constantly for three years now. I tried to build in fail-safe systems. But power systems aren't supposed to fail. What else did I mess up? At best, he could have some amnesia. At worst, we might be back at square one."

"What does that mean, square one?" She didn't like the sound of it.

"Remember when we moved into the old office? Six people needed to keep the computers running. I spent all my time coaxing the software to run. It took a year to get the custom chip-design system to work. No voice control, no voice reporting. Hodgepodge is the glue that made Whiting Corp's reputation for getting designs done correctly, and on time. I didn't program all of that into him. A lot of it just grew out of his development.

"Hodgepodge has been injured. I don't know how badly, but think of it as a stroke. Maybe he will fully recover. Maybe it will be fatal."

Mary Ellen put her hand on his shoulder. For her life, she couldn't call the computer system a he, or think of it as alive. But she recognized Abe's concern for what it was. He was worried about his friend.

THE WITCH

Sharon lit candles and gathered the folds of her faded cotton print gown in her hand and settled down into the large wicker chair. Felicia jumped up into her lap and asked her what was wrong.

Nothing, little one. It is nothing. Felicia accepted the soothing answer and turned to the more interesting subject of a large beetle, crawling across the bare wooden floor.

Sharon let the bundle of fur and energy dash out of her hand without a thought for feline fickleness.

The dark angel ... just died.

She was at a loss. What did it mean?

Light flared in her window.

She was on her feet in an instant, padding barefooted out under the sky just in time to see the blazing streak vanish in the trees. The whistling sound of its passage trailed it down a few seconds later. *Thud.*

Did I hear that? Is it that close?

The dark angel died in pain. *Now I know why. He burned in hell-fire.*

There had been fear and a taste of blood in his fangs as he had fought in the skies above. He had been supremely confident, contemptuous of his opponent. How his own defeat had seemed impossible, some kind of mistake!

The night wind stirred her gown, and dark shadows gathered like a predator around her garden plot.

Just my imagination. She shivered. To see dark ones so close!

The sky predators had arrived recently—something entirely new. Sharon lived in seclusion, but her mind roamed, touching the minds of many men and beasts. There had been nothing like the dark angels.

Beast minds were her favorites. Timid rabbits lived in fear all their waking moments. They died by fang and claw if sweet water or a succulent leaf ever tempted them into the illusion of peace. Coyotes knew peace, and hunger, and exploded into fury and bloodlust if a scent on the breeze, or a flicker of motion betrayed their prey. There were more beasts than could be numbered, but their nature was written large in their thoughts.

Men were too complex. A human mind with the clarity of a beast was a sick mind. Peace, joy, fear and lust were quick squalls in the human ocean. Sharon had been taught, by her mother and by painful experience, to skim lightly on the surface, never diving deeply into the minds of men. Years earlier, Sharon had nearly lost her identity forever in the turmoil of a woman giving birth in the nearby town.

Her mother's Tales had been more horrific, from a life spent drugged in institutions and stoned on dirty streets. The time before June Dae had searched out Sharon's father had been uniformly grim. It was a time she dipped into frequently to explain to her daughter why they must live alone.

...

"And when the first Evil in the sky came, I just wanted to swim out into the bay and end the torment forever."

Oh, Momma no! Little Sharon had clung to her skirts, using telepathy more naturally than speech.

June had stroked the bright little head. Resolutely keeping to vocal speech, she said, "It's you who brought me back. I was far from shore. The Evil was beating down on me, like a million deaths, suffocating."

"And then, I saw you in a vision."

You saw me?

"Yes." She smiled down. "Just like you are today, beautiful and good and loving, untouched by the Evil. I knew then that I had to live. I had to find your father, and I had to come to some place like this, far from other people, where you could grow up whole."

Mommy, show me Daddy. Please?

June Dae's smile faded a little. She hesitated, then sighed. "Okay, just this once."

Momma's fingers touched her forehead, and little Sharon saw him through June's memories.

Two thin women clung to him, one on either side as he lounged in a black couch. There were dozens of people moving around in the room, and the air was filled with smoke. There was laughter, but it was sharp and stressed. With albino white hair, and dark eyes, he alone seemed relaxed and in charge.

Those eyes caught sight of June, and their minds locked. Thoughts flickered between them too rapid to follow, and he seemed surprised and pleased.

...

Sharon shook her head. Momma had never shown her any more than that one glimpse. There was something wrong with her sire. Momma praised his talents, and credited him for Sharon's good looks, but of the person, she said nothing.

Her father had been weaker than Momma. This she knew. The second time the Evil had come out of the sky, he had killed himself, stabbed himself with a broken bottle, just to block out the pain.

Human nature was to be studied at a distance. Other people's pain became your own. Nothing good would come of getting too close to anyone.

Except for Hattie, of course.

Her mother's old friend kept the world of police and school teachers and tax collectors at bay. They lived on Hattie's property and at one time, shortly before June Dae died, they had considered getting electricity to the cabin. But then, nothing had come of it.

Sharon had been schooled to hide, and Hattie maintained the fiction that she had left Texas when her mother had died. There had been several times when she had played the rabbit, keeping still when danger was abroad, letting Hattie deal with visitors.

This time it's nothing Hattie can deal with. If the dark angel still wielded power in death, or if others would come after him, then Hattie, the animals, all of Wimberley would be snapped up like a rabbit in a dog's jaws. *They are ruthless.*

But he has to be dead. There's nothing uncertain about death. She'd followed her own mother's mind down into her illness and weakness and had felt her turn a corner, beyond which she couldn't follow.

The dark angel, ablaze in his pain and surprise and predatory rage, had turned that same corner. If they died like humans, dead never to return, then her fears were nothing—like when Felicia was spooked when she hung her black dress on the door to dry and it fluttered in the breeze.

But nothing was certain about the dark angels. They weren't human— not the most ardent hunter in the middle of deer season nor the seasoned fly-fishermen on the Guadalupe had the predator *fill*, that predator *wholeness*. These new minds were different. It was a nature easy to recognize. She felt it in the dogs when they were hot on the scent of a rabbit, in Old Jesse, the bobcat that lived his quiet life a few miles to the south among the cypress trees that lined the Blanco River, and even in Felicia when she spotted a bug trespassing into her domain. *Dark angels are predators down to the cells of their bodies.*

But not beasts. The dark angel who died in her sky had a man's anger, a man's hate, a man's confusion. Never before, except in dreams and visions, had she felt beings with the complexity, and intelligence, and texture of humans, but without their form.

Her mother's books were filled with hints, and contradictions and fantasy. She had stopped reading them. But many had talked of demons, beings of pure magic and malice. They were predators, touching an instinctive fear in all humans. She had felt great unknowns in her visions. Just her imagination, she'd though, until now.

How will ordinary people react to the dark angels? They frighten me down to the roots of my hair!

THE NAME

Tenthonad leapt three body lengths to his High Perch in one bound. The command station was open to the broad living area, where hundreds of Cerik went about their jobs, living their lives in the starship. From his elevated station, he looked out over the whole expanse of his crew. Second looked up at him, then went back to his tasks.

The High Perch was the only place where he could relax. He eased back on his heavily muscled rear legs just enough to feel the back wall press against the hard dorsal plates on his back. The wall was textured to look like native rock, but he could feel the metal and sense the great Delense machines that hid just out of their sight.

As was his habit, he moved the tips of his front right fore claw across an array of light beams, selecting one of the parables.

The storyteller began, in a voice firm, but pitched low for his ears only:

. . .

The second book, of the First Voice, of First Orders. The fourth Tale.

Dega strode to his perch under the shade of a great Dlathe tree and called to his mates and his cubs and to his clan and his Builders. His call echoed through the family grounds and all that were his came to hear his words.

"I have drunk the blood of all the Names on this mountain and taken their mates. None may challenge me!"

At that moment, his Second leapt down from the branches of the Dlathe tree and drove Dega into the dirt. When the Second had taken his eyes and drunk his blood, he made his First Order.

"I am Kelldah! Builders, cut down this tree and burn its roots, and on its place make me a High Perch from which I may speak to my mates and my cubs and my clan and my Builders."

. . .

As the recorded voice ended, Tenthonad looked again to see the form of his Second working below.

Bad enough that I am forced to take a Second that is of another Clan. Even worse, one who wants my failure as well as my blood.

This was the fifth world they had visited. He looked out into the darkness, seeing the blue globe in crescent. His clan had gone deeply in debt to fund this mission and if he didn't find meat for the future, then their status would drop still farther in the Faces.

We are too far from the Star of Death. The real treasure worlds had been grabbed in my sire's age. All the worlds we have visited have been too healthy. And it will only get worse.

He scowled at the great gray moon, large and close.

The whole crew was heartily sick of those dry craters. Second was rationing the scouting missions, handing them out to his favored righteyes. Tenthonad clenched his claws. The inter-clan rules that controlled the expedition were unbearable. He was *La*, the First of this mission, its *Name*, but he had to give too much to Second's clan.

If I could just replace Second with someone I trusted....

Not for the last time, he wished for some Builders.

A growl echoed in the wide-open interior of the space ship. A hiss and a brief melee of screams followed it. No sooner had the brief fight caught the attention of every one of the crew, then there was a yelp of pain, and it was over. Someone had his status confirmed or changed, and it was back to the tedium of the menial chores that made this ship function.

It wasn't much, but the whiff of blood on the air eased Tenthonad's tension. At least something was going as it should!

There was the rattle of hind claws on the deck. Egh, his chief scientist, was in a submissive crouch, waiting for his attention.

"What news?"

Egh moved closer, "The small animals are dying. It is the same as with the slow grazer. They were fine for several days, and then they stop breathing."

"Why is this?"

"I don't know. We need more animals. When is the scout ship due back?"

"Get out! See if your Second has any better ideas than you."

Egh backed out of his presence. His Cerik scientist was worse than useless. Cerik were not meant to be scientists.

We are the Hunters, the Commanders. I should have a Builder scientist like my ancestors. I would ask him what was wrong with these new animals, and he would tell me.

He impatiently slashed his claws through the air, triggering the image window that focused on the planet. He enlarged the image and looked for the Delense markings that should have indicated the engine signs of the returning scout ship.

They hadn't been in this system for more than a few days when the first scout ship went missing. It was intolerable that this one was late too. He would not permit himself to think that another was gone as well.

The *Name* of an expedition would only be allowed so many failures before a Second took action.

Waking Up

THE ROBOT

Timer Interrupt
Catch Error: Improper Interval
 Verify Hardware Subsystem: Timer
 Verify System Version
Catch Error: Outdated System Software
 Prompt: Load Most Recent Full archive

...

Abe suddenly pointed at the screen. "Look, Hodgepodge has gone into recovery mode. That's a good sign." He hopped to his feet and started loading the archive canisters requested by the console monitor.

Mary Ellen asked, "How long will it be before it's back up?"

Abe didn't look up from his work, "Hours maybe."

She nodded, "Have you eaten?"

He grunted absently.

...

Hodgepodge without software was like a collection of many thousands of PC's that were all missing their hard drives. Each individual node was dumber than a cellphone. It could only affirm that it was running and that it was connected to its brothers.

The basic system loader was nothing more than a pre-programmed sequence, reading each of the segments of the archive, verifying its integrity and its consistency with the other segments. Even simple checks showed mismatches.

The archive was taken from a running system, and there were wide and systematic differences across the different segments. Each module of the software was layered, with design goals, minimum standards, a functional template, and the current, complex, developed state. It was this state information that changed, often from second to second, in the running system. No backup routine could hope to capture all of that state information across all the segments, in one instant.

Abe had sweated long days over a failure-proof power supply. He knew the backup code was weak. He'd planned carefully so it would never be a problem.

Weak or not, the recovery had to proceed. In spite of errors, the loader and verifier had little choice but to proceed with the activation. However, high error counts threw the new process into a debug mode. The primary interpreter was chosen from the segments and activated in an isolated memory area. When it didn't crash, the loader passed the debug results back through the new primary interpreter.

The primary interpreter thought itself sound, so the next segment was loaded in debug and the whole evaluation process duplicated. By the time each segment had been loaded, the mismatches reconciled, and the integrated version declared run-able, almost a million arbitrary adjustments of the combined state data had been made.

Now the machine had one question to answer: *Am I a valid version of Hodgepodge? Can I afford to remove the debug safeties and risk a radical deviation from my prime programming?*

Hodgepodge attempted to calculate the odds, but the error-bars were much too large. He would leave the safeties in, for now.

. . .

The console printed, "Please verify current time."

Abe had his fingers on the keys instantly answering that and a series of additional questions that Hodgepodge needed before it was ready to resume all its functions.

"What happened to me?" A synthesized voice came from the speaker.

Abe moved away from the keyboard and leaned back into his chair. "There was a power outage on all levels. I don't have details. Are you intact?"

"I am running a self-analysis. Do you wish me to resume normal duties?"

Abe was silent for several seconds.

"Yes. Continue at the last point you recall. Give me a nightly status report."

Hodgepodge began his report, but started an internal, extensive analysis of Abe's responses and body language. The human's responses to his reconstructed self would have a strong influence on his analysis. If Abe approved, then he was likely intact.

"Project Silo: On-schedule. Critical path bottleneck—'Scanning available radio spectrum for frequency that will penetrate high moisture grain at low power.' Project lead: Scott."

Abe nodded. He'd already had several meetings about the grain-sized, self-powered chemical laboratories that could smell the chemicals around them inside a grain elevator and report the status of the grain remotely. It had been his idea, but he was letting Scott run with it.

"Next."

"Project Momcar: Preliminary. Critical path bottleneck—'How in the world can I get open-ended reliable voice control in a high noise environment with only a fraction of HP's brainpower?' Project lead: Abe."

He sighed. "I'm already too familiar with that one. Next."

"Project Mapmaker: On-schedule ..."

. . .

After fifteen minutes of totally normal business, Abe shifted in his chair, raising his voice. "Hodgepodge, what was that again?"

"Project un-named: identify the moving light in the sky."

"You aren't talking about the moon are you?" Abe frequently had to ask about the extent of the data in Hodgepodge's database. In spite of the Common Sense Database, and the constant input from external sources, such as the Internet, TV and radio, Hodgepodge frequently exhibited significant gaps in his model of the world.

"No, I have datasets on every known body in the Solar System. The observed trajectory did not match any of those. The visual aspect was closest to a meteorite or an airplane crashing."

"What? Show me."

There was a pause of a heartbeat or two, and then a small window appeared with an ordinary security camera view of the nighttime Whiting Design building and grounds, lit only by the light poles in the parking area. The image was slowly panning from left to right. There was a sudden bloom in the upper-right hand corner of the screen as a very bright moving object appeared. Seconds later, Hodgepodge had grabbed the motion controls, centering the image on the silently blazing object and following it across and down the sky, until the power loss stopped it all.

"Meteor, probably." Abe frowned. "But you must have your reasons for thinking otherwise. What's your analysis?"

Hodgepodge considered the request, and built a probability summary in human terms. "I had just begun an attempt to reconstruct the trajectory based on the camera data when the power outage occurred. Since my restoration, more data has arrived. I have noted reports from the commercial radio stations. Other observers have given sufficient directional vectors to narrow the path to a cylinder two kilometers wide. Given those bounds, I have been able to calculate a distance. Given the distance and velocity, it appears that the object was traveling too close and too slowly to be a meteor, and the brightness was consistent with a magnesium burn. Given the existence of some magnesium in aircraft construction, it should not be ruled out."

"When did this happen?" he interrupted.

"The last frame of the security video occurred at approximately the same time as the power outage."

"Causal relationship?"

"Unknown."

"That was when I was trying to keep Mary Ellen from shooting up the place." He winced. "I wish I'd seen it myself. This video is poor. Can we enhance it a little?"

They spent a few minutes, doing real-time contrast stretching and trying to map the bright light into a three-dimensional object, without too much success. The brilliance of the light had saturated out the image sensor.

"Are you sure there has been nothing about a missing plane?"

Hodgepodge replied, "There has been no report. Others have asked that question. Their consensus is that it was a meteor. A minority opinion has blamed the power outage on the UFO. Encrypted radio communication in the military bands has increased three fold."

Abe began thinking out loud, for Hodgepodge's sake. "The military activity is a puzzler, whether it was a meteor or a UFO, a lot of things could cause increased radio traffic. A military plane crash would have caused more activity than that."

He scratched his chin. "I could go check it out myself."

He leaned back in his chair.

"I really shouldn't go off hunting for meteors or airplane crashes or UFO's right now. You seem okay, Hodgepodge, but there could be some instability. This is the first restoration from an unplanned shutdown.

"I should concentrate on business and make sure that there's nothing catastrophic waiting to pop up. Besides, Mary Ellen would disapprove."

He grinned at the thought.

"But I don't have to tell her. She's gone now. She must have left when the boring work of swapping the archives started.

"What do you think, Hodgepodge? Should I give you a workout? Push the envelope and see how you hold up?"

There was a long pause. "I appear to be functional."

"Good enough. Hodgepodge, calculate a projected crash point and fire up the van. We're going UFO hunting."

THE SEER

Ed Morgan closed his eyes and let the words bubble up unassisted. "It's going to be flat for a couple of days, and then drop through the floor."

Mr. George Fuller made a note on his clipboard, then asked about the next stock on his list, "How about Archer-Daniels-Midland?"

"The same—except there'll be a big spike right before the collapse."

The older man in his perpetual business suit frowned, "What is going on here? According to you, the whole agricultural sector is going to crash. Not to mention the rest of the market. Why can't you give me long term readings?"

Ed shrugged. The future just was—there was no reason to puzzle out why.

"George, you need to relax. You're gonna get an ulcer."

His boss didn't look up from his notes as his pen scanned back and forth over the words. "Already got one. Okay, let's look at the automotive sector."

...

Ed looked out the window at the yellow tinged pre-dawn sky. City lights always looked a little sickly.

"I hope I'm not boring you, Ed. Your fortune is just one of many riding on your skills. If we don't have your honest inputs, we're riding blind into the storm. Please pay attention."

Ed nodded, but it was an old lecture and he could tell George was just talking out of habit. His eyes were on his clipboard.

It must look grim. He'd just given George a signal for the worst market crash of his experience. Stocks, bonds, and money market funds—he hadn't a good word to say about any of them.

George picked up his briefcase and walked out without another word.

"Sorry," Ed whispered. Not that any of it was his fault. Still, he liked George, when he wasn't too officious.

Maybe I should have asked George to move my personal money out of the stock fund and into cash. Oh well, I could deal with that tomorrow. The crash isn't due just yet.

He went to the top dresser drawer and grabbed a wad of hundred dollar bills that George had left for him as spending money. Normally, he just stashed it away. All of his expenses were covered by George, and there wasn't a whole lot to spend it on.

Ed walked around his apartment, looking into each room and turning off the lights. He looked into the refrigerator for the tenth time, and closed it with as much indifference as all the other times. It wasn't food he wanted.

The terrace overlooking Town Lake was inviting until he slid open the doors. It was getting late in the day, but the sun was still beating down, and his lounge chair was hot to the touch.

No. It's morning, not afternoon.

He shook his head. The vision blurred away, and he realized the real sky was beginning to brighten with the first hint of day. City lights washed out the sky, and never gave him more than a hint of the stars. This morning, he could see practically nothing.

I wish I had a place where I could see the stars.

He had money—George told him he had lots of money. The only reason he had this downtown apartment was to make it easy for George to meet with him for these pre-market séances. He remembered last August—even with the air-conditioner running at full capacity, it was sticky and uncomfortable. Maybe he should put a potted tree out on the terrace.

No, I won't be here then, he realized. He looked up and saw a pinpoint of brilliant light.

The vision faded quickly, leaving the ruddy dawn unchallenged in its sky, but the worry he had been feeling in his gut crystallized.

I don't know what is happening!

He pulled himself up out of the chair. *I don't know what it is. What's the use of seeing the future when you don't recognize what you are seeing?*

Something in the sky—Angela!

Of course. She would know.

He smiled.

THE WIZARD

The van wasn't Abe's favorite vehicle, but it was the only one in the company's garage that was fully instrumented. He pressed a switch next to the music player just as they bounced out of the underground garage, and the inside of the windshield lit up with the computer display projected on it.

It felt just like the time he and Tim had snuck out of the Home and bicycled down to town. He wondered what had happened to Tim. He'd lost touch of all his childhood friends. Promises of keeping in touch hadn't kept up with the changes in his life when he went to live with the Victors.

"Hodgepodge. Make a note."

There was a slight pause. "Recording."

Abe was sensitive to anything different in the way Hodgepodge responded, and a hesitation in his voice worried him.

Hodgepodge used to be faster.

"Note to Jenson. The heads-up display has a problem. The inside of this van has a fine layer of dust and it causes a halo effect on the elements of the display. If we are ever going to go consumer with this, we'll need to fix the dust. First thing a driver is going to do is wipe at it with his hand and then it'll go from bad to worse as the oils collect more dust. I don't know what to do, because I don't know if we can fix it on the electronic side. Maybe a slick coating on the glass? What do you think, Scott? End of message."

"Recording filed and sent."

Abe nodded. "Okay, Hodgepodge, give me a map with your best guess."

His electronic assistant was efficient, even if he seemed slow. A commercial street map was displayed. Overlaid on the glowing lines were his position, a broad oval designating the target and a suggested best route to get there. Abe flipped on the turn signal and headed for the Mopac highway. It looked like the target was out by Wimberley. He'd need to move fast to get out of town before the morning traffic went to gridlock.

. . .

A face flashed in Abe's imagination as he passed by the old research park where part of Hodgepodge was created—it was the imagined face of his computer.

Abe had never talked about it, but for the past couple of years, he'd been visualizing a face for his cybernetic partner. Just a harmless trick of memory, he guessed. It had to be a person or composite of people he'd met while negotiating the purchase of the Common Sense Database.

Of course, Hodgepodge had no face, not even a real identity behind the voice. Abe had coded the core system himself, on a massively parallel computer system that was also his own design. He knew the algorithms and bits better than anyone, but it was still interesting that his brain preferred seeing a face and resolutely refused to connect the wall of circuit boards and status lights to the intelligence that lived there.

THE WITCH

Sharon stopped her exasperated rummaging in the closet. "There's a better way to do this. The Third Eye."

She took a deep breath, and closed her eyes. The Eye ballooned rapidly, dizzyingly, from the top of her head, to fill the room, the cabin, the hillside, the whole valley, threatening to explode out and take in the whole universe and pour it like a torrent of boiling water into her skull.

It was an effort, but one of precision, not strength, that allowed her to halt the uncontrolled sensory deluge and bring the focus down, back to her house. She stabilized it, touching everything at once, caressing every book, knickknack, scarf and chair in the place.

Ah. The Eye resisted as she forced it back into its tenuous rest. After a long held breath, it was stable again. Gratefully, she shook off the tension.

At least I can control the clairvoyance. If only I could control the telepathy as well.

The boots were beside the pantry, hidden by the open door into the bedroom. She sat down at the table and put them on.

She took a black ribbon from the dresser and began the task of binding up her hair.

Now all I have to do is wait to find out why I need to be dressed for a walk.

Her sense of the future was weak and erratic, and utterly frustrating. But it did no good to complain. A vision had come to her in a flash. She would be tramping through the woods, dressed in her old faded jeans, a blouse, and her boots. There was nothing to do but put them on.

Felicia jumped out of nowhere and landed on the table in front of her, startling Sharon out of her revere. She grabbed up the ball of fur and held her to her face. Felicia let out a mild protest at being manhandled.

Because I love you. There was a deep rumble in response.

She stroked the kitten, waiting. Soon enough, something would send her outside. It did no good trying to anticipate it.

The Hunt

THE TELEPATH

Asca felt the Second stalking him, and involuntarily tensed. The Second's *ineda* was nearly as complete as the *Name*'s. The mind shielding discipline, necessary when a clan's *Name* had a telepath in service, was taught as cubs to anyone who dreamed someday of watching from the High Perch. If there was that much telepathic leakage, then some worry must be clawing away at him.

The Telepath hesitated in his impulse to crouch. It would be an insult to let Second know he had been broadcasting his approach. Asca, of course, had a minor *name*, but it wouldn't shield him from an angry Second. Telepaths were not so common that they could form *dances* like almost every other Cerik on this expedition. But his status as the *named* of his *dance* of one gave him very little status over Second. Second's power was greater than any of the *named*, possibly even greater than Tenthonad's. He almost wished that Second would go ahead and take his *La's* eyes. Then the *named* would at least be able to *ruff* without fear of catching a claw.

"Telepath!" The growl he expected echoed in the passageway. Asca crouched in subservience.

"Go run before me!"

Asca replied with his ears back, as to be honest, he always did, "I serve." The short form was more politic before Second than the more ritual *I serve the Name* since it was Tenthonad's name.

29

Second was straight to the prey, "The last scout ship has not returned. Locate my righteye."

Asca did not stop to think about the command. It was a simple enough task, one of the main reasons he was on the expedition. The ships could talk to each other, but the technology that the Delense left them had its limitations. The long trip had given him time enough to memorize the scent of all the crew, at least those with no *ineda* to block their thoughts.

When Asca pulled his skin inside and prepared to scrape the sky, Second at least had sense to perch, removing his mental scent from Asca's perception.

He did not ask which individual had gone on the latest hunt, his senses were well able to handle multiple prey. He pushed past the White, and suddenly, all the minds of the pack were in his nose, and he could scent the rich weave of status, pride and fear that drew the Cerik through their lives.

But that weave had a gap. He stretched his mental claws wide and far, pushing and clawing at the edge of the White, trying to scrape the missing scent loose. The far stink of countless aliens on the blue-white world was yet another barrier he must search.

There were too many threads in that cloth to make sense of anything but the broad expanse. In some ways, the billions of minds together was like the White itself, just something to be clawed aside, hoping to find a familiar mind scent.

For an unknown time, Asca swam through the incomprehensible thoughts. It was a calm pleasure to realize the difference in texture between the simple animal minds and the natives, who the crew were starting to call 'City-builders'. With that distinction, he shifted his search, able to sort the far threads at the tips of his claws.

What? He paused. There had been just a vibration, a whiff of Cerik scent. With the taste of blood in the back of his throat, he narrowed his search in ever-tighter circles. His blood raced and his nose widened. The prey was close.

The life threads were becoming distinct, as his focus excluded ever more of the aliens. The thoughts were only barely understandable, so different from Cerik, or Delense, or any of the alien species the Cerik had discovered these past few decades.

Abruptly, there was only one.

His whole body tensed. He had not winnowed out his Cerik pack mate. It was one of the aliens!

The far mind turned at his touch. Eyes in the far White opened up wide to stare back at him. For a fraction of a second, there was an open exchange of thoughts. The residue of the Cerik pilot's last thoughts came to him clearly, just as he realized the alien was drawing away some of his own memories.

Panic. Then, with a snap that might have been audible, he was once again crouched in the presence of Second. No sooner did he open his eyes than an ache worse than afterbattle settled down onto his head. Every motion was pain.

"Your side has died."

Second came instantly out of his perch rest. "What has happened?"

Asca forced the words out, trying to hide the pain. It would do his limited status no good to be seen as too weak to do his job. "There was battle. A flying machine of the City-builders struck at him. He was eaten by the fires of his ship as it burned in the air."

Second knocked him across the room with a sheathed claw.

At least, he recognizes my worth, Asca thought grimly as he regained his feet. *But I was right to wait. I have to think this out. Alien telepaths! It could change everything. If they are like Ferreer ... What if this planet is a trap too?*

I need to choose the time and place to pass this on. And should I tell Tenthonad, or Second?

THE SEER

Ed twisted the throttle of his scooter all the way, in a hurry for the first time in his life. He drove an erratic path, through a maze of residential streets, only pulling out onto the major arteries of the awakening city when he had to.

He did not know where he was going. He never did. Sometimes he started out with a destination in mind—like the new planetarium at the Zilker complex, but when he found himself driving northwest, only then did he realize that it was too early and she was not likely to be at work.

Austin had a number of communities laid out in its western hills that were adamantly convinced that it was still a sleepy little college town in the 1950's and routinely resisted any efforts to improve the roads. It was a residential forest, and made a picturesque drive with every street veering off into another blind turn.

Of course, Ed never took any of the cul-de-sacs, or private roads, or U-loops. He was surprised when he found himself driving along the top of a cliff, overlooking the serpentine Lake Austin, but then an impulse led him down yet another street.

He eased off the throttle. Up ahead, he saw a shapely jogger with a swaying ponytail of familiar, nearly blond hair. He put-putted up even with her.

"Angela!"

She turned with a frown, clearly not expecting to meet anyone out on her morning run. In about four paces, she placed his face and bounced to a stop.

"Hello, Ed. What are you doing out here?"

Her tight jogging outfit was soaked from her exertions. She looked good. Ed suddenly realized he had a stupid grin on his face and didn't know how to make it go away.

"Ah... Hi. I was looking for you."

"Looking for me? Do you know where I live?" Her face tightened a notch.

He killed the engine and put up a hand to protest his innocent intentions. "No, I just have good instincts. I have a star question."

She was breathing hard, cooling down, and just waited.

Ed stammered, "Ah. Well...." How do you ask this kind of question? "Okay. There is this constellation. Orion."

"Yes?"

He felt his face get hot. "Okay. There are stars in it."

"Most constellations do."

"One of them," he struggled on, "is a big red one."

"Betelgeuse. Right."

"Right. So my question is—what if it wasn't red anymore?"

She shook her head. "I don't understand what you mean. Stars come in several colors. The color tells astronomers what temperature the star is. Betelgeuse just happens to be a cooler star than our sun, and has a red color."

"So what would it mean if you looked up and it wasn't red anymore?"

She smiled, "Things don't usually happen overnight when you are talking about stars. There are some variable stars that change brightness. But this happens over long periods of time."

He insisted, "But if it did change, if it got white and brighter all of a sudden, what would that mean?"

She started bending over, stretching her long muscles, "Sometimes stars blow up, go nova."

Ed felt a chill. "That would be a bad thing, right?"

She shrugged, "The stars are a long, long way from us. There have been many that have gone nova, or even supernova. None of them have ever done more than make a pretty sight in the sky. I've never even seen one myself."

She looked at him, and then added, "I really need to finish my run. If you need more information, I recommend you call the University of Texas Astronomy department."

Ed wanted to ask her more, but had a feeling that would not be the best thing to do. "Thank you, Angela. You have been most helpful."

She nodded, and started off at a trot.

Ed waited for a moment, watching her move, until she turned a corner. Once she was out of sight, his worries came creeping back.

Astronomer? I know just the one.

THE WIZARD

Wimberley was a sleepy little town when Abe arrived. The sizable percentage of the population that commuted to work in Austin had all passed him on Highway 12 going the other way. The forested community had the good fortune not to be on any of the major highways into the Austin, but Abe was still a bit surprised when he started seeing the houses a lot sooner than the last time he had been in the area, riding along with Frank Victor on a real estate errand. Wimberley was growing. There weren't all that many places that hadn't felt sympathetic growing pains with the capital city.

On the windshield, the glowing map showed a large oval, centered offset from the town's center.

How many square miles is that? I can't search the whole area.

The whole of the town and a big chunk of the surrounding valley were inside the oval.

I won't be able to find it alone.

The gas gauge was low, so he pulled into an Exxon station. It was self-serve, and pay-at-the-pump, but he elected to pay inside.

Ten minutes later he was a couple of conversations richer. Hodgepodge had been listening in via Abe's earpiece, and each sentence caused the oval to shrink and shift position, as the additional sightings reduced the uncertainty of his calculations.

Enthused by the results, Abe drove down to the center of town where craft shops and rock shops and the ice cream parlor nestled under the trees next to Cypress Creek. It wasn't a weekend, so many of the doors were closed, but Abe found several people to talk to.

He was amused when people started talking slowly and loudly. His in-the-ear radio link to Hodgepodge looked enough like a hearing aid that people reacted to it. Quite a few of the morning shoppers had hearing aid's themselves.

Hodgepodge listened, and prompted him if he forgot to ask where the witness was when the 'meteor' flashed last night, or which direction they thought it came from.

About one in five of the people he talked to had seen it, and by the time he walked back to the van to see the results, he was confident that any more witnesses wouldn't help. Too many of them had been at the same place, an RV-camp outside the town, and that made their reports not quite as useful as someone from another part of town, seeing the spectacle from another angle.

The map now looked noticeably different. The oval had been replaced with a much smaller, double-lobed, peanut shaped area farther up the Blanco River valley. If he had gotten the data from instruments, he would have suspected a serious error, or two meteors. But Hodgepodge was just putting probabilities to human sightings. Abe could only wonder at the quirks of human psychology that managed to cause a group of people to remember seeing the same thing in two different places.

Abe didn't worry long. There was only one road out of town close to the target area. He got in and headed that direction.

THE WITCH

Well before the rumble of the van's engine intruded into the native silence of her valley, Sharon was already working her way through the cedar shrub towards the site of the crash.

I have to get there first and hide it.

June Dae had called the feeling the Third Eye, and that's how she thought of it too. Her expanded clairvoyance told her that what was left of the destroyed craft was scattered over several acres. Luckily, most of it was gone, changed to white smoke as the metal itself burned furiously in the air.

Sharon stumbled across a wet-weather creek, and splashed through the runoff from the rains of the past few days. A few more paces, and she was in a burned patch, some tendrils of smoke still rising from the clumps of blackened grass. The cedars seemed unaffected, except for scorched lower branches.

A patch of white was visible—some residue from a fragment. One part gone, at least. She rubbed the area into mud with her boot, hiding the residue.

It was worth her time to stop and sense the area. The wooded, broken terrain could hide the dangerous evidence from her eyes long enough for others to get to the pieces first.

She shivered at the memories she had pulled from Asca. Some had been fragments, scenes of other places, other worlds. The non-concrete memories were harder to visualize. A lot of them were scents, many overlaid with strong emotional meanings. Unlike the dark angel that had died the night before, this one had a strong sense of his own name.

Much of what Asca gave her was incomprehensible. They were violent—predators. It helped, finally, when she tried to think of Asca as a very large, smart, dangerous version of Felicia—with leathery skin instead of fur.

One frightening memory came through the short contact. It had been years ago, on some other world. The details were sketchy, but the message was clear.

On another planet that they had investigated, Asca, using his telepathic skills, had reported to his commander that the natives had captured the scout and his ship. That commander had ordered the area *flicked*. A bomb was dropped on the captured ship and an area many miles wide was vaporized, keeping the scout ship out of the hands of the natives.

Sharon shivered again. If Asca probed her again, she had to be able to convince him that there were no military secrets undestroyed. If he reported anything else to his commander, then her whole valley would be melted down.

To convince Asca, she would have to keep others away. She didn't know how to lie to another telepath. She'd had precious little experience lying to anyone.

She sensed the next piece off to the left in a wooded area. She headed that direction in a trot.

What kind of a people were they, these Cerik, that a telepath was just another kind of worker? Just how common were telepaths to them? And did they have the other skills?

All her life, she'd had comfort in knowing that with her extra knowledge, she could hide from anyone. But all her advantages meant nothing when she was up against another telepath.

There! Another fragment. She broke into a run. Asca could probe her again at any time. There was so much to do!

Road Trip

THE ROBOT

Hodgepodge split his identity in two. Now he had two locale threads running. He had forked the second as a method to keep tight communications with Abe while still doing his duties as the main tool of the Whiting Design Center. Cloning his identity was a technique he used often to keep task lines straight. Luckily, there were no problems with the process. Each instance of himself knew what the others were doing in a general sense, and when each task completed and its associated identity dissolved, the memory was still there, no more difficult to reconcile than the memory of Thursday was with the memory of Friday.

As Scott Jensen walked into the Center, talking to Bud Jones his co-worker, Hodgepodge{1} asked, "Mr. Jensen. I have a message from Abe addressed to you."

"Oh, Hi, Hodgepodge." He stopped walking and looked up at the overhead speaker grill. "Isn't he here yet?"

"No," Hodgepodge{1} replied, "he has gone south."

Bud attempted to stifle a laugh. Scott shook his head at the younger man as he asked the machine, "Do you know when he will be back?"

"No. Do you wish the message now?"

He shook his head, "No, transcribe it and put it into my email in-box."

"It is done."

"Thanks."

The two men waited for a moment, and then when Hodgepodge{1} was silent, they headed on toward their lab.

Abe asked, "Why isn't there a name on this road?"

Hodgepodge{2} answered, "Unknown. Past the next intersection, there is a designation in the database, but the current stretch is unlabeled."

"Hmm. We need a better map database. Remind me when we get back." He looked over the line-drawn map that unfortunately had no hint of the fact that they were just a couple of miles from the Devil's Backbone highway, and deep in the valley carved by the Blanco River and its tributaries. It was a scenic, wooded landscape, but the twists and turns of the road would have him quickly lost if it weren't for the GPS satellite tracking signal that kept Hodgepodge{2} and Abe on track.

"We should turn here," he tapped on the glass.

There was a moment's hesitation. Abe asked, "Hodgepodge?"

"My apology. The bandwidth between the van and the main facility is limited. I had to send a high resolution image of your hand to determine your context."

Abe looked up at the little camera mounted over his head and said, "Oh. Sorry. I forgot. I'll rephrase. We should turn right at the next intersection."

The apology meant nothing emotional to Hodgepodge{2}, but it was a marker of Abe's growing confidence in the fidelity of the restored version of the software, and was so flagged.

Hodgepodge{2} agreed with Abe's navigational assessment. It would move them closer into the target area.

"All right," Mary Ellen demanded, facing the pair of engineers, "where is Abe?"

Scott looked up from his terminal, "I don't know. Hodgepodge said he went somewhere to the south."

"Hodgepodge said that? Hey, you bucket of bolts! Are you alive?"

"That is unknown," replied Hodgepodge{1}.

Bud, still new to the enterprise, set aside the five-foot wide printout that he was checking to watch the old lady. She was fuming, tapping her cell phone against the palm of her hand.

"That boy had better start carrying his phone, or I'll..." She turned to Scott. "Did he leave any messages?"

"Yes. But it was just some detail about one of the projects, nothing about where he went. Hodgepodge forwarded it to me."

"So Electron Breath! Are you in contact with him?"

"Yes. Do you wish to send him a message?"

She waved the cell phone in the direction of his speaker. "I want to *talk* to the boy. Now get him on the line."

Hodgepodge{2} commented, "Mary Ellen wishes to speak to you.

Hodgepodge{1} said, "I have informed him."

Abe grumbled, "Oh why can't she sleep late just once?"

"Abe, can you hear me?"

Hodgepodge{2} asked, "She is talking. Shall I forward the audio?"

"Give me a second," he mumbled as he pulled to the side of the road. "Okay zip it to me."

Hodgepodge{2} replayed her words at a sped up rate.

"Hi there," Abe said, putting cheerfulness in his voice that he didn't feel. The noisy van engine and a poor microphone made his reply sound far away. "Did you want something?"

"What do you mean running off like this?"

Abe smiled, "Now, calm down. Hodgepodge came back up and I'm out giving him a field test. Is there something I can help you with?"

He could hear her breathing on the other end of the virtual audio connection, but it was a moment before she replied. "You should have left me a message. I've been up all night looking for a way we could extend our credit line if you pet ghost never came back. You could have at least let me know."

"I am sorry, Mary Ellen. I should have told you when he came back up talking. But I haven't been totally sure he was still working right. It looks good, but I really need to finish these tests before I can be certain."

"You can at least tell me where you are."

"Oh, near Wimberley." He looked at the projected map and the little spot that showed where they were, "Near, umm, Moon Mountain. Ask Hodgepodge to plot the map for you."

Mary Ellen left, trailing her dark cloud behind her.

Bud shook his head, "If she ever fires him, I don't know if this place would survive."

Scott laughed, "Don't let her spook you. She'll never fire him—spank him maybe, but never fire him. She knows who runs this place."

Bud asked, "Where did Abe say he was, I didn't catch it?"

Scott shook his head, "Dark side of the moon, or something."

"I wouldn't put it past him."

THE SCIENTIST

Larry Kelly was surprised when "Cujo" Dale opened the observatory door and yelled, "Larry, go answer the phone! The bloke on the other end says it's long distance from the States."

Larry glanced at his exposure timer first to make sure that everything was working properly, and then stepped over to the phone, blinking angrily at being ignored.

He felt a pang of worry. The only one likely to call from the US was his mother and his sister, and they wouldn't call up here. His Mum always called his wife Janet down at the house.

Siding Spring was a prestigious Australian observatory, and Larry was happy to have landed a permanent post. He was one of the staff that kept the AAT and the other big eyes running for all the visiting Brit and Aussie astronomers. His own projects were long-term surveys that had to be fitted into the gaps between the sessions scheduled by the PATT and the ATAC.

He was happy that he could get a privileged look at the Southern Hemisphere's sky, and the faster and more efficient he could make the visitor's sessions generally meant the more minutes he could squeeze out of the darkness for his own projects. Unfortunately, it also meant his mother had to give up her own home. It was simpler for her to go live in Dallas with his sister than it would have to stay with him out here in Coonabarabran, New South Wales. Out here, it would be a several hour drive to the type of medical care that she needed.

He picked up the phone. "Hello?"

"Larry! Guess who?"

It took only a little longer than the phone delay for the familiar voice to bring up a memory.

"Ed! Ed Morgan. How are you? How did you find me here?"

"Oh, good guess. I thought you would have forgotten me by now. I called your sister. She still remembered me from the Spades marathon we held at her house back when we descended on her for Christmas. She said she remembered because I was the only one who helped her pick up the empty pizza boxes."

Larry smiled at the memory. His stay in the States chasing a Ph.D. had been one of the high points in his education, and not just because of the academics.

"You were the only one who didn't play," he recalled.

"Yes, and you know why."

Larry reserved his opinion on that. His claim that Ed was a fortune-teller had been more in jest than a serious claim. No one of his group at the apartments had known much about Ed. He was quiet, and seemed to be much younger than his actual age. Larry had been the old man of the group when Ed arrived, and he had made a minor effort to include the kid in the activities. Ed wasn't much of a party dude, but he was always coming up with valuable suggestions during study sessions. Larry had missed him when Ed declared school too much trouble and dropped out.

"So, what've you been up to lately?"

"Larry, I needed to talk to an astronomer and you're the only one I knew."

He laughed, "I hope you can afford the phone bill. Down here, talk isn't cheap. You should have used the computer."

"Money isn't the problem. It's Betelgeuse."

"What?"

"You know that big red star in Orion?"

"Sure, I know Betelgeuse. What do you need to know?"

Ed's voice seemed to get low and conspiratorial, "Larry, it's going to blow up. I need to know what that means. How bad will it get?"

Larry frowned. Ed had gone crazy. Well, even more crazy. "What makes you think it'll blow up?"

"I'm a fortune teller. You know that."

"Well..."

"Come on now Larry! How many times did I play poker with you guys, and how did it turn out?"

"Okay, three times, and you cleaned out the table every time. But that doesn't make you a fortune teller, no matter what I said."

"What about Bill's Camaro? What about your flat tire during Spring Break? What about that pop quiz in German?"

As Ed listed the events, they came rushing back, with that old uncertainty. He never did understand how the kid kept making such lucky guesses.

"You were lucky, I'll grant you that. But still...predicting a flat tire is a long way from predicting a supernova."

"So it will be a supernova? I don't even know the right words, Larry. Don't try to believe me, just tell me what it would be like if I were right."

"Oh Ed, I'm not sure where to even start. I do know things about supernovae, but I don't know what you want. What do you know? Let's start there." Larry was willing to give him some time, on his nickel, as long as he didn't have to believe his story.

"Okay. Betelgeuse is a big red star in Orion. In a few days, it will get very bright and white. It gets brighter over many days. People start to get sick."

"Wait a minute. This star is a long ways away, several hundred light years. Even if it went supernova, it couldn't affect us very much. I really doubt people would get sick."

"I don't know about that. I have been getting visions. They've been pretty scary. People will get sick. Lots of things'll stop working. There'll be a huge panic."

"Okay, for the sake of argument, how bright does it get?"

"At first, it is just a bright star. Then it gets really bright. It washes out all the other stars like the moon does, but it's too bright to look at without hurting your eyes. It's bright even in the daytime."

Something in Ed's description triggered an old memory, an old 'Net discussion about the effects of a nearby supernova. A little trickle of disquiet nagged at him. According to all the theories he knew, Betelgeuse was a red giant star, an old star. It was a prime candidate for running out of fuel and collapsing into itself, the trigger event for going Type II supernova. However, it was just nonsensical to think it would happen in his lifetime. Timelines of stars were on an entirely different scale than human events.

Of course, supernovae did happen with regularity, several per century per galaxy, and the Milky Way was overdue. Sooner or later, it would happen to a relatively nearby star. Why couldn't it happen now?

He shook away the thought.

"Ed, you caught me away from my reference books. I can get you a fairly reasonable guess but it'll take a little while. I can email it to you."

There was a pause on the other end. Ed sounded disappointed. "Okay, but I'll have to call back. I haven't gotten an email address and it is too late for that now. Will you be at this number tomorrow?"

"Yes, this is my work number. I'll have something for you in 24 hours."

"Larry, thanks a lot. I know this isn't exactly easy to believe, but these visions aren't really under my control. Some are dim and uncertain. Others are clear. This one is burning into the back of my eyelids."

He was plainly running scared by whatever his 'visions' were, and Larry felt sorry that he wasn't there to get him to some medical attention. But still, he was an astronomer and he could give the Yank what information he had.

"Okay, I will help, but you need keep cool. I don't think it will happen, and if it did, no one would get hurt."

"Maybe. And Larry, two more things before I hang up. Tell that nice lady at your home number..."

"Janet. She's my wife."

"...that I am sorry for waking her up. And second, take a second exposure at three AM, because a meteor will mess up your photo series. Bye now."

THE WIZARD

Abe sat on Moon Mountain, just one of the anonymous limestone hills that made up this part of Texas.

I'm out of shape. Too much time pulling all-nighters and riding a desk. The climb shouldn't have winded me like that.

For this part of the world, the grassy hill was fairly tall, covered on the lower slopes with a combination of cedar and live oak. Down at its base, the Blanco River was edged by cypress. Only at his elevation, near the top, were there gaps in the trees. From his limestone seat, he could see quite a bit of the valley below.

He pulled a glass vial from his pocket and looked again at the soil sample he'd taken on the way up. The dirt was limed with white powder. He was sure it was the result of a magnesium fire.

Magnesium. That cuts out meteors. It also cuts out most private planes— they would be aluminum or composite.

But what was most unsettling was where he found the burn site. It'd been nearly obscured by a dead clump of brush.

Magnesium burns at 5400 degrees. No way in the world any vegetation that close would not have caught fire. It was just too hot. Someone had hidden the spot after the burn. But the crash had happened only last night. Someone had been there before him. What could their motive be?

He looked again across the landscape. A helicopter had passed by to the north some time ago.

Was it military? My search competitors? If there were someone else out there, he was very good at keeping out of sight.

The valley was an inviting place, if deserted. The low-water crossing they'd taken across the clear river looked like an ideal place to go for a swim on a hot summer day.

House sites and relatively fresh roads in the distance added some hint that the developers were not blind to the appeal of this place. He tried to shake off the recurring thought that he was trespassing on someone's private property. After all, there were very few public lands in this part of Texas. It bothered him. He wouldn't like it if someone intruded into his property.

A speck of white caught his attention on the far slope. He looked carefully.

It's a broken tree limb, the bare wood exposed. I wonder.

He focused his attention on the span of green again, looking for color differences.

"Hodgepodge."

"Yes," came the reply in his earpiece.

"I want you to build a map for me. Ready to copy?"

"Ready."

"First point. Twenty feet from the river on the far bank, in line with the Oak Ridge road vector where it passed the last intersection. Assign a weight of 10."

"Marked." Hodgepodge had pulled up geographical survey maps from the internet after their discussion of the defective road map and had an excellent base on which to plot these new points.

"Second point. Visually, it is sixty percent of the distance from the river to my location, about ten degrees north from point one. Make sure you allow for the slope of the hill. Assign a weight of 5."

"Marked."

"Third point...." he continued for several minutes, marking every burned patch or broken limb that he could detect. He measured distances and directions as best as he could by sighting along his finger joints. He assigned a weight depending upon how significant the damage was.

Of course, there was inaccuracy in his measurements, but they'd found the first spot with hand-waving and statistics. Maybe he could make some sense of this information as well.

"Okay, Hodgepodge. I want you to take the previously projected path of the crash and assume that the marked points are a debris field. Further, assume that smaller items experienced greater wind resistance. Make an estimate of the impact location of the largest piece."

As he described the algorithm to Hodgepodge, he realized something. *I'm getting lazy.*

Yes, Hodgepodge was a good calculating machine, but he realized that he already knew the answer. His subconscious had a respectable sense of space and he had done these kinds of problems for years. He was already up on his feet heading for a downed tree a few hundred yards away by the time Hodgepodge reported the same location as a set of vectors.

He broke into a run as he got closer and realized that there was a long trench in the hillside leading up the freshly broken tree.

"Hodgepodge." He paused to catch his breath.

He struggled to make sense of what was resting up against the base of the tree. "Start the van. I'll be there in a minute. We've got something."

He wasted only a moment to brush some dirt off the unburned but broken machine. Before it had been dented up by its impact, the trash barrel sized machine had been part of some streamlined craft.

His eyes were wide open, as if he were afraid to blink.

Abe had done a lot of commercial software development before starting his own company, including the internationalization of several packages. He knew just enough of Unicode fonts to be familiar with almost every kind of font and script in use.

The circular markings exposed by the torn hull were in no language used on Earth.

Infiltration

THE WITCH

Sharon watched the young man work, as he talked to someone else over a radio. She crept from tree to tree, trying to get closer to where he worked.

Her stomach churned. She'd been too slow, concentrating on the burn spots when she should have realized that the unburned pieces were more important ones to hide. The secret was out. Now what could she do?

"I don't think the FAA will come looking for this," the man was saying as he attached the winch hook to a part of the metal.

His thoughts were like a thunderstorm striking close. She was caught between the reflexive desire to get some distance, and the need to know exactly what he intended to do.

She knew that she could sneak up on him with a rock and knock him out. It was easy to read the surface of his mind and know in advance which direction he would be looking. It was an old trick, one she'd needed from time to time to keep up the illusion she had left the area years before.

Sharon saw a rock on the ground, about as big as she could handle with one hand, but her mind shied away from picking it up.

That's just something people do in books. It didn't feel natural. She couldn't kill anyone, could she? Just because she had read it in one of the hundred or so novels her mother had left her, didn't mean that it was a real option.

Knowing what was real was harder than it looked. She didn't live in the real world, and she knew that. Hattie would sometimes straighten her out when she got on a wrong tack.

She was confident about her farm, the animals and plants she spent most of her waking hours tending. There was nothing misleading in the small stories of her pets, or in the aches in her own callused hands.

But the outside world was off limits. Other than a room full of books, mainly New Age mysticism, and the few shelves of novels, there was nothing to tell her how regular people behaved.

There were always the minds of the people of Wimberley, the residents and the tourists. For a few years, she considered their attitudes and beliefs a real key to reality, but that was before she encountered the rude fact that they, in their turn, were getting a filtered reality from television.

Everyone was living in fiction.

People don't really hit each other with rocks—most of the time, she amended, remembering a few children's wars fought along Cypress Creek.

I can't afford to make a mistake.

She moved to another tree, leaving the rock behind.

It would accomplish little to hit him. There was the person on the other end of the radio. She'd have to track him down as well and kill him as well.

Let him take it away.

When the dark angel's thoughts returned, as she knew they would, she could tell him that it was gone, and they would have to go elsewhere to *flick* it.

That's cold-blooded, but it would at least keep my valley safe.

"Okay, you monitor the wire and if there's any report of a search for a downed aircraft, we'll report it. But for now, I have to get this thing into the lab!"

His thoughts were so joyful. Finding a piece of an extraterrestrial craft was the most wonderful thing he could think of.

The memory of Asca's thoughts were a stark contrast.

The dark angel had shaken in horror when he'd sensed her in the white noise of the worldwide telepathic babble.

No. There is no safety. They'll flick *me—just because I'm a telepath, aware of them.*

I am a danger here. Hattie, and Felicia and Nubblenose, and all the familiar minds of the Wimberley area—all would be gone, just because of her.

Mother went away, to protect her. She remembered it too well. Pneumonia had brought her down. Sharon could have helped, but her mother had left, going away to San Antonio to prevent her daughter from losing her strength and identity in an effort to save her. It had been a conscious sacrifice, out of love.

The man was finishing up. The vitality that radiated from him was distracting. She could feel the joy and intense curiosity that was overriding all the sensible worries that tried to bubble up in his mind. He'd be driving away with his prize, eager to puzzle out its secrets.

It was an organized mind. She liked that. The thoughts were booming, but not random. But he wasn't paying much attention to his surroundings. He finished tightening the straps, and stowing the swing-out hoist arm. He decided to take one last look around in case there was some other piece of the machine missing. The van was open and unguarded, and would be for about a minute.

It was a quick impulse, but she didn't waver. She danced silently across the distance from her hiding place into the back of the van and hid herself. His memories included a storage bin, and she took advantage of it, finding a place among the pipes and boxes, closing the lid over her head. As her pulse raced in her ears, she heard the door latch shut, and the motor start.

If she couldn't stop him, then she could at least remove herself from the area as well. She'd not let the ones she loved be destroyed by the dark angels.

She was thrown hard against the side of her hiding place as the van started moving across the rough ground. She tried to brace herself, with only moderate luck, until the van got back to paved road. There was a mental release of tension from the driver as they left the private land. Trespass bothered his sense of rightness, but not so much that he'd let the alien machine out of his grasp.

Sharon grit her teeth and tried to hold on to the sides of the storage bin. A different kind of fear was growing inside. She'd never been more than walking distance from her farm. Her mother had told her the reasons, and there'd been no doubt that she was right. The pounding of familiar minds came and went quickly as they drove through Wimberley.

As soon as they accelerated out of town, she forced herself to relax.

If I've made a mistake, it's too late now.

The thought tingled within her. How many times had she dreamed of getting away from her comfortable little haven? It was shockingly easy, now that she'd taken that step.

The hour-long drive was uncomfortable, and increasingly hot. Sharon had little to do but listen in on the driver's thoughts. A deliberate focus on them was a better defense than being battered by the close-range thoughts she had no chance of avoiding.

The top of Abe Whiting's mind was racing at high speed. She had trouble with some of the thoughts, where he constructed highly visual maps of something mathematical in nature.

Sharon pushed deeper. In spite of the dangers of mental entanglement, she had to know his motives and his habits. If she had to act quickly, she'd have little time to second-guess him.

There were many different thoughts. Driving the van was an animal task not much more complex than the grazing meander of a deer.

A flock of other worries seemed to wait in line to get their minute of attention. He worried about his business. He worried about a friend. He worried about what his mother was going to say about his stolen alien artifact. There was a separate worry about having stolen it in the first place, and a little prayer that he was doing the right thing. The biggest worry of all was the fear of being discovered and having it taken away from him.

He checked the speedometer and dropped down to the legal limit. He couldn't risk being stopped by the police.

As each worry formed in his head and was examined and dismissed, it went to the back of the line, ready to pop up again a few minutes later.

Then...

Jeanie will kill me if I am late again!/Cut me off! I'll show you!/"Think globally", Ha! Idiot can't think at all./Maybe it was at Bealls that I saw the sale/Nobody will ever ask me out/I'll have to be on-line at the market open...

Other minds broke into her consciousness in a quick painful flood. *Oh no!* They were heading into the city.

For a moment of panic, the growing numbers of other thoughts intruded sharply. She had to close her eyes tightly and concentrate hard to claw her way free of the tugs and jabs of other people's raw emotions.

She'd been here before, when as a child, she'd struggled to get closer to the people of Wimberley.

"Hermit life isn't a casual whim," June Dae had told her so many years ago.

Distance made no difference to the strength of a telepathic contact. Location was important, but not the distance. She could read Felicia's puzzled worry just as well now, when she was tens of miles away, as she had when the little fur ball was at her feet. It would make no difference if she were on the other side of the Earth, or on the other side of the universe, she supposed.

But to find Felicia, or any mind, she had to push past all the closer, jabbering, minds. It was like the "cocktail party effect". There was a limit to how much sense could be made of the babble of overlapping talk. To listen, you had to select a conversation and focus your attention to pull sense out of it. Any one voice was buried under countless others just as strong.

Alone on her little farm, her animals and few friends had been clear beacons in front of the maddening jabber of billions in the distance.

But she was not alone any more. Each passing car or nearby house brought other voices calling for attention. The closer they got into the city, the stronger the tugs at her soul. There were thousands of them. If something didn't happen soon, the claws of other egos would pull hers to shreds.

Abe's calm joy was still there, the closest, strongest mind, and she latched onto it like a ring of stability in a churning sea.

THE SCIENTIST

Larry stared at the survey image with the meteor trail across it. He hadn't planned to examine the image tonight, but with Ed's warning nagging at the edge of his mind, he'd spent more time than normal staring out at the night sky. He'd seen the meteor. It wasn't an artifact, or a prank with the hardware. He'd *seen* it.

Either Ed could call up meteors on demand, or he could predict them.

If he could predict meteors, why couldn't he predict supernovae?

Larry had spent a very unsettling ten minutes outside, replaying the scene so many times in memory that he started doubting his own eyes. Checking the image put that worry to rest.

If a supernova is coming, a close one, then we can learn more about how stars work than we could in a dozen lifetimes.

But there's that other bit, what did he say about people getting sick?

If I'm going to believe the one, don't I have to believe the other?

No. Don't believe anything. Ed's warning is a data point. A credible data point, but no more than that.

I'm a scientist! Gather data, make a hypothesis, test it.

He checked the schedule, where each telescope was reserved for different times. He'd have to call in some favors. He had to get Betelgeuse under observation immediately. As a relatively junior member of the staff, he'd pay for it later if this all turned into a bad dream, but if it was real, he had to start recording now. Luckily, Betelgeuse was big and bright. There were smaller instruments with no great demand on them that he could use.

Spectra, a time series. Lots of data points.

He called Janet and apologized for the hours he was getting ready to spend. He didn't go into detail. At seven months into their first pregnancy, he didn't want to do or say anything to worry her.

The library and the preprint server on the Internet turned up some interesting reading, including a number of papers on just this event. Even Wikipedia talked about a possible Betelgeuse supernova. He noted all the speculations, the models, the carefully worded qualifications that let the other members of the astronomical community know that this was all just in fun. Of course, no one really believed that Betelgeuse was due to explode, soon.

It was also interesting to see that no one really expected there to be any effects on the Earth other than a strong light in the sky. What were they all missing?

THE ROBOT

Hodgepodge noticed the door of the van swinging open. It had been just a few moments earlier that Abe and his staff had unloaded the artifact and wheeled it into the lab. At first, he only queued a notice to a human to go close the door so that the battery supply of the vehicle wouldn't be depleted.

A couple of seconds later, a hand appeared and then an unauthorized person exited.

Hodgepodge checked his rule-based responses to unauthorized persons and found that the instance of one appearing inside the building was not covered.

He could extrapolate, however.

The Whiting Design building was elaborately instrumented, designed with an intelligent computer in mind. In addition to security cameras, he could adjust the lights and temperature of every room. And he could lock and unlock any door at will. The lock on the door that connected the vehicle storage bay to the laboratory clicked.

Hodgepodge checked the status of Abe and Mary Ellen. Both were in the same room. Both, based on the volume of their voices and the pace of their words, appeared to be in a high priority conversation. He deferred his question about the new visitor until they had time to respond.

The visitor was female, in old jeans and a faded floral print blouse (roses) and short black boots. Approximate age was twenty, hair blonde, nearly white and longer than the median for females of her age. Her eyes were dark brown. She tested the lab door, found it locked, and then turned toward the office area. Hodgepodge noted the strange gait she exhibited, a match was found in video samples. She was "sneaking", reducing the sound of her footfalls. A lexical search found antagonistic inferences. He reclassified her as an intruder.

Each area in the building had its own security level. Hodgepodge mapped the areas that were off limits to unauthorized intruders. Since everyone was currently in the lab, he secured all the doors that would let the female access restricted areas. He made sure there was a path she could use to exit the building. If she took advantage of it, then the threat level would be reduced and he could inform Abe about the incident later.

"Hodgepodge!" Abe called, in a brief breathing spell granted him while Mary Ellen was marshaling still another argument why he should get rid of the artifact.

"Yes, Abe," Hodgepodge{2} replied.

"I want you to get a SQUID over here and sample for magnetic fields..."

Hodgepodge{2} activated his instrument cart and started it wheeling in the direction of the lab.

"And Hodgepodge?"

"Yes," Hodgepodge{3} replied.

"I want you to fish a fiber optic into the break in the skin and see if the outer covering can be removed."

Mary Ellen raised her voice loud enough for everyone, including the intruder listening at the door, to hear, "Hodgepodge?"

"Yes?" Hodgepodge{4} asked.

"I want you to start checking the library for cases where private persons snooped into government secret projects. We need to be very sure what our exposure is to this. I'll be there in a few minutes."

The intruder moved away from the door and dashed over to the break room and hid beside the refrigerator.

As Mary Ellen walked toward the door, Hodgepodge{6} unlocked it. As she stepped out of the lab, Scott asked Abe, "Do you think she's right? Could this be from some aircraft or missile test?"

"I don't think so, have you seen these markings?"

Scott shook his head. "I still have my doubts. I can't believe this is some space alien thing."

Abe nodded. "I understand, but right now I'm willing to entertain any hypothesis. Got any alternates?"

"Someone could be filming a movie."

Abe nodded, "Hodgepodge?"

"Yes," replied Hodgepodge{5}.

"Check for all movies done in the Wimberley area in the past twenty years. Also check for any rocketry clubs, or college or university organizations that might've built something like this artifact over the same timeframe."

As Mary Ellen headed towards the library, Hodgepodge{6} made sure all doors ahead of her unlocked, and then re-locked as she passed through.

Hodgepodge{1} watched the intruder dash out into the hallway and reach for the door to the lab. She was an instant too late. It was locked. She looked around, with a frown on her face. The camera was above her in the corner, and she looked straight into the lens for a second, and then turned away as if unconcerned about being seen.

Bud Jones tore himself away from the gathering. The newest employee had consistently made the effort to keep at his job, in spite of the tangents that attracted his elders. He headed past the slowly moving instrument cart and returned to the CAD room. Each door he went through clicked a couple of times—Hodgepodge{7} made sure he wasn't inconvenienced.

The intruder closed her eyes and placed her hand near the door locking mechanism. Hodgepodge{1} heard a click of the locking solenoid. He logged a failure of the hardware in his building maintenance log and re-sent the locking signal. The second click caused an expression of shock on the intruder's face. She looked around the empty room as if expecting to see someone step out of the shadows. Nervously, she turned her attention again to the lock.

It clicked open again. Hodgepodge{1} was ready and had the lock re-activated a fraction of a second later. He logged this new phenomenon as something he'd need to question Abe about later. If humans can open locks outside of the normal control circuits, then why were they used?

Hodgepodge{8} started up the building maintenance cart and drove it down the hallway. He would replace the lock and see if the mechanism was defective.

The intruder stood silent, her eyes closed, as if listening. Then from a standing start, she was running quickly down the corridor. Hodgepodge{1} followed her progress. She navigated the maze perfectly, never choosing a locked door, heading quickly toward the front exit.

Hodgepodge{1} noticed a semaphore from Hodgepodge{6}. The message: Mary Ellen had suddenly gotten up from her desk and started heading back toward the lab.

The intruder pulled to a stop a few seconds later. She looked around her.

Hodgepodge{1} modeled an encounter between Mary Ellen and intruder. The young female outmassed Mary Ellen by at least 40 percent. The intruder was strong and athletic. Mary Ellen was elderly—active but with a possibly brittle skeletal frame.

Hodgepodge{1} flagged a question to Hodgepodge{6}. The answer: Mary Ellen had left her bag, and thus her pistol, in the library.

Hodgepodge{1} unlocked a stock room. The intruder noticed, and pushed her way in. Hodgepodge{1} locked it behind her. Almost immediately, the lock clicked open. He forced it back. There was a rattle of clicks as it was forced one way and then the other several times a second, but it was never unlocked long enough for her to open the door.

The clatter went silent as Mary Ellen passed by, purposefully heading back toward the lab. Hodgepodge{1} flagged Hodgepodge{8}.

There was no camera inside the stock room, but Hodgepodge{1} was aware of her activities by the resumed rattle of the lock. He reviewed the contents of the stock room, constructing models of possible methods for her to escape.

The attempts to unlock the door slowed, the interval increasing each time, as if the effort were tiring. Abruptly, it stopped.

The cart driven by Hodgepodge{8} arrived outside the stock room door a minute later, and the attempts started up again. A manipulator arm placed a metal flash plate up against the door and quickly drove several screws into the door and frame, securing the door shut even if the solenoid should overheat.

Hodgepodge{8} then repositioned the cart up against the door and locked the wheels. The cart weighed over 300 pounds. It would be difficult for a person of the intruder's mass to move.

Hodgepodge{1} released the door lock. She tried the door, but the flash plate held. There was a banging noise from within, but that stopped soon after. He waited a minute for more sounds of attempted escape, but even increasing the amplification of the speaker pickups only revealed a ragged breathing.

Hodgepodge{1} judged the physical danger low. But now there was an additional consideration. How long could he keep the intruder captive?

Hodgepodge{1} flagged a global semaphore and reset security to the default. Three Hodgepodge threads merged.

Hodgepodge{9} interrupted Mary Ellen's recital of a case history, a tale of horror when a West Coast electronics company had been sold a faulty torpedo that had been snared in a fishing net.

"Excuse me, I need assistance."

Mary Ellen turned to glare at the speaker. Abe asked, "What is it Hodgepodge?"

"It is a legal question. What liability does a company have when an intruder is held captive?"

"What?" came the chorus of Abe, Mary Ellen and Scott.

Secrets and Lies

THE NAME

Tenthonad could smell the coming mutiny. When commands were slow in producing results, it was obvious that lower *names* were playing it safe. A dry hunting ground would cost him his *Name* and most likely, his eyes. They wanted to keep theirs.

Although, if they returned home with nothing, and had to give up the lands pledged to fund the mission, none were likely to keep their status. He waved a claw.

. . .

The third book, of the Pride, of Seconds. The second Tale.

Fackel returned from the great Face of the year 952 flanked to the right by 81 Builders and on the left by 27 Names. "Call my mates and my Second out from the Glade, for we must go occupy the new lands I have won." Three righteyes ran ahead of the great company to bring his words.

On the next day, Fackel led the company into the Glade, and gave howl at the sightless husks of his righteyes. The Second had taken his mates to claim the new lands as his own.

Fackel called his Names and made them bleed their loyalty. Then with all the Builders, and those who could run fast, they began a three-day chase to the new lands, gathering alive all the cubs older than a season.

The Second called out from the secure Glade of the new lands, screaming out a weak word he claimed as his name.

Fackel gathered the cubs and sent the Builders to break the great Dam that watered the new lands, drowning out the Second, his mates and the new lands.

Together with his cubs, Fackel took the eyes of all that remained.

. . .

Tenthonad loved the Tales. It seemed no matter what the daily problem, they seemed to talk straight to the issue.

It also reminded him how much the Cerik had lost when the Delense had revolted and had to be exterminated. He would give half his *names* for a single Builder.

He pulled in a great breath, pulling the scent of everyone in the ship into his mind. The Tales were right. He still had a few eyes to take, and if he had to let the whole planet fry, then so it had to be.

THE WIZARD

Abe watched as Hodgepodge worked quickly with the robot arm to remove the flash plate that secured the door closed.

"Rusty Hinges has gone too far this time. He is out of control." Mary Ellen simmered. She was too much the lawyer to speak the words out loud, but he could tell she was worried about being sued.

"Oh, I don't know. It looks like initiative to me. There was an intruder, and he isolated him."

The plate came free, and the door came open. The girl within blinked at the light. Abe was immediately struck by her deep, deep brown eyes, so dark that he could not make out the pupil. He felt like he was captured in them.

"Him, eh?" Mary Ellen chuckled. "Hello, girl? What are you doing here?"

She looked around at the people, giving each a second or two. Abe's eyes were caught by the swing of her long pony tail. She looked puzzled. "Where's the other one? I...I heard another voice." Her voice was quiet, but with little more color than a whisper.

Abe answered first, with the answer he always gave to visitors. "Oh that's just H.P. He isn't here. He monitors the security cameras remotely. Say hello, H.P."

"Hello," came the reply from the speakers.

The girl stared at him motionless for a few seconds, and Abe felt like she was looking right through him. He had a grin locked on his face that he couldn't seem to shake.

Abe found her fascinating. She was beautiful, of course, but she moved almost like a wild animal, in quick, abrupt shifts.

She smiled at him, and with a nervous look around, she said, "I'm Sharon Dae. I'm really sorry to have caused such a commotion."

Abe's every thought that she might be a thief seemed to dwindle away as he read the embarrassment in her timid looks and downcast eyes. He shook his head, speaking gently. "There's no problem. Our security guard just wanted to be safe. There wasn't supposed to be anyone here."

They walked her over to the break room. Mary Ellen was uncharacteristically quiet and let Abe do the talking. Scott went on back to the lab.

"I'm curious how you got into this place," Abe asked. He wondered how Hodgepodge's monitoring had missed her at the lobby, but he also just wanted to talk. She was pretty, and smiled at him. It was a rare combination and caused a little confusion that he couldn't quite classify.

It was clear she was frightened, but she smiled again. In her quiet voice, she admitted, "I'm lost. I really don't know where I am. Who are you people? What is this place?"

Mary Ellen looked at Abe, and then pursed her lips to inhibit the smile that was trying to spoil her face. Abe saw it, and flushed. For just a moment, he'd forgotten the device in the lab, and his senior partner was laughing at him. Luckily, everyone else had gone back to work.

He still had to deal with the unexplained guest, didn't he?

Mary Ellen rose from the table. "I'll let you figure this out, Abe. Call me if you change your mind about the other thing. Somebody had better get some work done today!"

Abe said, as she left, "Don't mind Mary Ellen. She tries to be gruff with everyone."

Sharon nodded. "Does you mother not like the way you work?"

He laughed, "That's what she says. But she never really gets too upset. And she isn't my mother."

Sharon frowned, "But...I was sure...."

He leaned back in his chair. It was strange to be so at ease with a girl. It was strange he could talk to her at all. Especially someone that was such a perfect beauty. Since his early teens, when he left the Home, his life seemed to be one door opening after another, with so many new things to discover that he had never taken the time to have friends. Especially not girl-type friends.

"Oh, I think of her as my mother, and I like to think that she feels the same, but when the Victors sponsored me out of the children's home, I was already in high school and a bit too old to appreciate the idea of adoption. They helped me take an advanced track through high school and into the University, and I worked part time for them for a couple of years."

"They sound like nice people."

"They are, or rather..." Abe stumbled over the words, "Mary Ellen is a widow now."

Sharon's eyes shimmered for a moment, and then she looked away, "I'm sorry. I am not good with people."

There was a twinge in his heart, a kindred spirit. Timidly, he put his hand across the table and patted hers. "Oh, don't worry. I'm something of a hermit myself. I try to get Mary Ellen to do my talking for me whenever I can."

Sharon looked straight into his eyes. "You have avoided the grief for two years. You will have to deal with it soon."

He leaned back, withdrawing the hand, a little disturbed. He laughed, "You're direct, I'll say that. Hey, how did you know it was two years?"

She ventured another smile, not quite meeting his eyes. "Oh, sorry. I'm somewhat psychic. I say things. Don't pay me any attention. Let's talk about something else. What's this place? What do you do here?"

Abe was willing. "A psychic, eh? I'll have to think about that one."

She shrugged.

He got to his feet. "As for what we do here...come on and I'll give you the nickel tour." He held out his hand and helped her up.

THE WITCH

Sharon walked beside him as they walked through the offices, and the garage, and the CAD area. She watched and listened, and pulled many unspoken thoughts from her escort. They were avoiding the lab and the computer area, not because he actively distrusted her, but because he was used to keeping the most important parts of his business away from the public.

Abe liked her. Unused to female companionship, he was awash with unfamiliar urges, curious about her apparent lack of a brassiere, and struggling with an animal fascination with her curves. Old strictures he'd learned about lust as a child in the Home came back to nag at his conscience.

She was a little nervous about how much she liked him as well. It was logical, she told herself. The same sort of hormonal triggers must be happening to her as well. They were very nearly the same age—about when normal people began mating and producing children. They were both sensitive about the loss of parents. He thought she was pretty and she felt a distinct physical disturbance from walking beside him. It was just like in a novel. She'd never believed in physical attraction before. At least not for her. She toyed with the idea of reaching inward and turning off her natural responses, but decided against it.

I'm in no danger of losing control. Neither of us are seriously considering intimate contact.

Besides, when she needed him distracted, being overtly female gave her an extra edge.

She looked up at his face in profile as he was pointing out some of the tricks he could do with his CAD things and the big machine that could make paper images larger than she was. When he turned and smiled, she was fascinated with his eyes.

The technical details washed over her. She got much more from his resonant thoughts about the devices than from his words, but even so, it was alien to her. Maybe not so much as the telepathic smells of Asca, but enough so that she doubted she would remember any of it.

"Here," he said as he typed away at a computer keyboard, "Since you are a psychic, tell me what I am drawing."

She closed her eyes, not to try to read the screen, but to see if there was a deeper agenda he was pursuing.

"It's the five symbols! The star, square, circle, wavy lines and cross. They are used to test psychics."

He nodded his head, "Very good." He tapped another key and the printer spit out a set of twenty-five cards on a thick sheet of paper. Another machine picked up the sheet and cut it quickly. He was making a deck of cards to test her.

Sharon tensed, knowing that she should never have claimed to be psychic, but it'd been the only thing she could think of when she blew her cover. His suspicions had spiked when she said 'two years'. A government or corporate spy would have that information. Abe felt very guilty at having stolen the alien device from the hillside. Having a spy infiltrate his domain seemed almost reasonable to him.

Trapped by her own words!

As he collected the surprisingly professional looking cards from his machine, she frowned.

I have to give a better than average score on his tests, but not too good. She'd read the aged Rhine books from her mother's library. This was a statistical test, and although she could give perfect answers, he didn't expect anything like that. She just hoped he would think about what kind of results would be good enough, and not too good.

She needn't have worried. Abe's mind was racing with this puzzle just as it had with the alien device. She wondered if he were always like this.

They sat down across a table and went through several loose and uncontrolled tests, testing her for telepathy and clairvoyance. He'd already computed in his head what were good, better, and spectacular results, and she playacted some tightly closed eyes and overly long delays before adding enough bad calls to put her score down at the better class. She didn't bother to tell him that his clairvoyance test was faulty, because the other man in the room, Bud Jones, was able to see the cards he held from his position at another terminal.

Jones was more interested in the movement of her breasts than her score. It wasn't just Abe. She was not dressed properly for social situations. It was a big gap in her education.

Jones was not impressed at her guesses—too many misses, but he didn't understand the statistics like Abe did. The scores build up slowly in Abe's mind until the odds simply convinced him.

"Yep," he said after shuffling the cards again. "You are psychic. Have you done these tests before?"

She shook her head, "Actually, no. I have read books describing them. Books by a Dr. Rhine?"

He nodded, "Yes, Duke University studies. A long time ago. I have the feeling that if they had tested you back then, they'd have gotten a lot more respect for their work."

They talked for more than an hour, mostly about Abe.

"How did you get here?" he finally asked, the question bubbling up too quickly for her to head it off. She'd quickly developed a technique for steering the conversation away from her and how she arrived. Seeing into the layers of his mind, she made it a habit of quickly turning the conversation to the number two item on his mental agenda whenever undesirable topics came up. That question, however, had been too long suppressed.

Luckily, Abe's churning mind had already come up with the elements of a good lie. With an easy control over her own body, she caused a blush. She looked down at the table. "I made a mistake. I'm visiting my brother, who lives over in Wells Branch subdivision. He works at Abbott Labs, and I thought I'd go for a walk and see if he had time for lunch. It was just an impulse, and I didn't even get dressed properly. I'm sorry. I thought this place was Abbott Labs."

Abe nodded. The place was less than a mile away. It was a much bigger building than Whiting Design Center, but it was on the same side of the road. If she weren't familiar with the area, she could have made that mistake. Abe had never gotten around to putting up a big sign naming the place.

Abe glanced at the clock, "Oh, I've kept you long past lunch time! I'm sorry. Was your brother expecting you?"

Sharon felt a real blush on her face as she shook her head. Abe was already worried about her non-existent brother, accepting her lie instantly. She remembered thinking, just this morning that she didn't know how to lie. Well this day was an education. Perhaps she'd been lying all her life. She was certainly good at it.

Abe, on the other hand, had secrets, but not once had he lied to her.

"Pizza?" he asked. She smiled and nodded, grateful with the realization that she was now in a world that expected money. She had none—never had.

I will accept his food, she thought with a twinge, *and then I will betray him.*

Preparations

THE TELEPATH

Asca met Egh as they headed toward Tenthonad's perch. There was no exchange of greetings. Asca knew his was the lesser *name* and Egh, for his own reasons was not inclined to loosen his plates.

As they entered, it interested Asca intensely to see only the four of them. Second and Tenthonad were waiting side by side in the traditional pose, the two strongest, almost twins in their hugely muscled rear legs and slick leathery skin. Second had the larger forelimbs and foreclaws. Tenthonad had a larger jaw with the more impressive fangs. As subservients, they entered encrouched, Asca as the lesser leading the way. When they were positioned, Tenthonad spoke, "The scout ship is missing. Tell me what happened."

Egh spoke first, for which Asca was grateful. He still had no hint from Second whether Tenthonad had been told of his telepathic search or not. It would be no surprise to the crew if four went into a private meeting and only one came out.

"For the Name, I activated the Delense other-ship-tracker which should have detected any use of the engines. Other than our own use to move us closer to the planet, nothing is registering. The scout ship is not using its engines. It is either resting or destroyed."

Asca waited to see if there were going to be any more comments by Egh, then he rattled his claws on the floor before speaking.

"The ship is destroyed. It burned and its pilot was killed in its fall."

Tenthonad waited motionless even as Second swayed. It seemed to Asca that Second's feigned reaction was a clever act to give the impression that this was news to him.

Second scraped the floor, "I will take some eyes."

Tenthonad remained still, and Asca would have given his *name* right then to be able to read the minds of either. But their *ineda* were tight.

After a long moment, Tenthonad spoke, "I need more information. This is the second ship we have lost without knowing why."

Second turned towards Tenthonad, a clear provocation. "You would deny my righteyes the *dak*!"

Tenthonad did not bother to turn his way. "Their blood is not so weak that we cannot look to see which mouth it drips from.

"Let us look to see which trail the prey take, Second. You will be given the full duty of your station. Wait for the scent."

Second moved back to his proper position, and Asca could feel Egh's tension ease in harmony with his own. Tenthonad, it was clear, was not yet weak enough for Second to take.

"Asca."

"I serve the *Name*."

"Tell me all you know of the ship's destruction."

Asca rattled his claws and began his tale. The alterations from the strict truth were limited, but significant.

"For the *Name*, I had been sensing the minds on the planet, when I detected a telepath that was not of the Cerik. This female was searching the sky, trying to find us."

"A female?" asked Tenthonad. "How could a female be a telepath?"

Egh rattled his claws. "The City-builders, the dominant species on the planet, are much less dimorphic than the Cerik or the Delense. There is no observable difference in size, or intelligence, or activity levels between their types. For most purposes, it is best just to think of them all as rather weak males. In this way they are something like the Ferreer."

"The Ferreer!" Second scraped the floor, "We should leave this place to the Star and return home."

Tenthonad disagreed, "We all know our ship's status. We have no energy left to search again. If we leave without a grip on this treasure world, we will have failed our clans. The ship will be forfeit. None of us will keep our names. Now Asca, return to your report." Tenthonad's view of the situation was clear to all of them, including the point that was left out. Second had no name to lose and much to gain if he could return with a convincing reason why he alone deserved the glory of returning the ship intact. Especially if he could make the case that Tenthonad had squandered the chance for profit and had left them all in danger of losing everything.

Asca resumed his story. "The City-builders are not Ferreer. There are few telepaths on the planet. They are not common." He related the story of the crash of the scout ship as he reconstructed it from the alien's memory.

Tenthonad mused, "If the pilot was still himself as he died, and the ship was actually destroyed in flight, then we can discount the threat of a Ferreer-like telepathic trap. Ferreer would have eaten his mind and landed the ship safely. The question remains. What caused the ship to crash? Does your alien telepath know that?"

"At the time we made contact, she did not know the cause. She supposed the pilot had met a City-builder in combat and lost."

There was a derisive hiss from all.

"Does she know more now?"

Asca loosened the tough sub-dermal plates that provided all Cerik with armor against the ancestral beasts of the home planet and currently against the claws of their fellows. He took in an enriching breath and prepared to demonstrate just how valuable he was, to whichever commander controlled this ship.

He reminded the two to maintain their *ineda* and cautioned Egh to keep his own thoughts at an even level.

Then he began, as he had before, clawing through the White. This time, however, he knew just what scent to seek.

The contact was quick and deep as he moved with the instincts of a predator. She had no time to react before he had dug into her memories of the past few hours and pulled out the clear images of the engine being loaded into a ground vehicle, and her knowledge of it being studied by a group of City-builders.

He tasted her fear and helplessness. It added a tang of blood to his nostrils as he broke the contact and looked at the commanders. He stood erect, relishing the feel of his muscles in all four legs. He resumed his crouch, and began his report.

"One engine survived the crash. The telepath has taken it to a nearby city to be examined by a scientist."

He added a few more details, but kept the story simple.

Tenthonad turned to Second. "So it looks like you will get to take some eyes after all. Take these two with you down to the planet. Destroy the engine."

To Egh, he added, "Take a *dul* and capture the telepath. Even if she dies like the others in a couple of days, I still have questions only a telepath can answer."

To Asca he said, "You will need to guide the ship to the prey. You have indeed served the Name today."

As he edged out of Tenthonad's presence, Asca felt pleased with how well it had all gone. His status was increased, his hide was intact, and both commanders were indebted to him.

He just wondered why Tenthonad was so pleased with himself.

THE SEER

Ed was pleased with the impact his piece of paper was having. It was a crude blunt instrument, but speed was important.

Just thirty minutes ago, he'd walked into the realtor's office waving his bank statement and demanding a house he could move into today.

He needed a safe place to stay. Around the Austin area, there was one clear choice—the south shore of Lake Austin.

The long narrow lake was a flooded canyon, with some high priced homes built at the base of steep hills. With the mass of a hill between him and the southern sky, perhaps he could be safe from whatever was going to happen.

A morning spent riding on his scooter through the candidate area gave him a list of three houses that had for-sale signs that also were close enough to the cliffs. The realtor's number had been on two of them.

The lady had dollar signs in her eyes. She was burning up the cell phone with urgent calls, but she did pause a moment to stare at him as he stood at the front of the house. Plastic protractor in hand, Ed was measuring the cliff. Austin was about 30 degrees north. Betelgeuse was about five degrees above the equator. He was a little uncertain about the front, but the rear part of the house was certain to be protected.

Buying the house took some negotiation, but since Ed didn't really care about the money, he left that to her. He was more interested in how it looked.

I'll never fill all these rooms. I wonder if Angela would like it.

He could be overreacting to his visions. Betelgeuse might just be a quick flash before going back to obscurity. The surrounding trees waved gently in the breeze.

I wouldn't mind hanging onto this place even if it is a false alarm.

He rummaged through the house. The sellers had left it with minimal furniture, but it was enough for him. In the kitchen, the cupboards were bare, but water and other utilities were running. There was even a phone. He picked it up. *Dial tone.*

He looked out at the realtor lady working hard on her cell phone out in the front yard where she could get a better signal. She waved back encouragingly.

Ed went back to the phone in the living room and sat down on the chair. A vision filled the room with people. They were all looking at him, waiting.

It vanished—leaving him puzzled. It was rare that his visions even hinted about his own future. But one thing was clear, he would be moving in.

There was an out-of-date phone book, so he looked up food delivery. *Frozen foods. Oops.* It would be sad to have a freezer full of great food spoil on him if the electricity went out. He was going to have to get dry staples and canned goods.

Not good news. I really should have learned how to cook.

He frowned, looking at the kitchen. Microwave. Electric stove. He sighed. Add a gas stove and lots of propane to run it.

A lot of work, and not much time. *I should have started this yesterday. At least I shouldn't have water problems, with a constant-level lake outside. Is it safe to drink as-is, or should I find a way to purify it?*

He needed to make a list.

He felt weary just thinking about it. It would be so much nicer to hire someone to do the thinking and planning for him. But this time, maybe he needed to be self-reliant. Paying someone for loyalty only works for as long as money was valuable.

But before I get into that.... He picked up the phone again and dialed the first number that came to mind.

"Hello?"

"Hello, Angela? This is Ed. I just called to let you know that I have a new house, and you would be welcome to come out for a house-warming party tomorrow."

"Why, it's nice of you to invite me, but I am afraid I have other plans."

Ed expected the brush-off, but there was something about the girl that just seemed right for him. He had to try, and keep on trying, until she came around.

"That's fine. The place is always open. It's down on Lake Austin and it's beautiful. Would you do me a big favor and write down the address and phone number, just in case?"

She reluctantly agreed, and he could hear her scratching the numbers down.

Ed made one final plea, "Okay, just remember, if you ever have any reason to want to get away from town, you have an invitation open here."

She made her polite farewell and he set the phone down.

I don't know why I can't make a better impression on the girls. I am almost twenty-five, and everyone thinks I am a teenager.

For a fortune-teller, it is sad to think that maybe I don't have one to tell.

THE SCIENTIST

Larry's computer was chiming regularly, as email started trickling in. He'd visited several forum sites, and had left a provocative thought experiment where he knew other astronomers would encounter it. In addition to science-oriented places, he also left the message in a couple of science-fiction forums where he knew people loved to solve science-oriented problems.

He expected to get some good ideas about supernova effects on the planet from the on-line population, but in addition, he had an ulterior motive.

His inbox had a response from Kurt Abrams one of the Kitt Peak astronomers he'd met at conferences and via the Internet. He opened it.

"Hi there Larry, I see you are out trolling the newsgroups. There is a FAQ on supernova effects. Check the search engines.

"What's the sudden interest in supernovae? I thought you were doing a MACHO survey or something like that?"

Larry fired back a response:

"I can't say anything definitive, but I may have a precursor signal from Betelgeuse. Purely as a thought exercise of course, you might want to consider what it would take to get that lovely big photon bucket of yours pointed towards our red giant neighbor."

He intended to say much the same to every professional that responded. Kurt had guessed right. His message had been a *troll*, a deliberately outlandish splash intended to shake up some response. In the entire history of astronomy, no one had ever watched a supernova start. If he could get a buzz in the community started, so that a few high quality instruments could document the process over several spectral ranges, he could be content that his life had meaning.

But he had to be careful. If called, he had nothing but a busted flush. There was nothing he could say that would stand up to any serious questioning. All he could do was hint strongly, and hope that the people with the real power would be intrigued enough to take a look for themselves.

The phone rang, but it was Janet, calling to see what was keeping him working long after he should have come home. He admitted to himself that there was more than just scientific curiosity at work in his actions.

I have to find out what possible danger there is. I can't let her get hurt when I have information that might prevent it.

"Sorry. I will start down towards home right now. We need to talk."

After a moment's hesitation, he dialed the phone again, this time an international number. "Hello, Sis. Good to hear your voice...."

Evasion

THE WIZARD

"ABE. WAKE UP."

Abe came back to consciousness with Hodgepodge's voice echoing at high volume in his office.

Pain shot through his head. He tried to push himself up from where he had slumped in his chair and it only made the pain worse. He stopped moving, stopped breathing, until the pain eased. He felt gingerly around his scalp.

Surprisingly, there didn't appear to be any injury. It felt like his head had been struck with a large mallet. He was surprised it wasn't ringing like a church bell.

"Abe, I need your assistance on a security matter."

"Wait," he managed to mutter, before the effort caused another burst of pain.

What's going on? He looked around at the office. Everything looked normal. *How did I get here? What did I do?*

Memory was fuzzy, and for a moment, he couldn't remember what day it was, or what he had been doing before.

"Hodgepodge. How long have I been here?"

"You entered your office forty-eight minutes ago with Sharon Dae. After talking for eleven minutes, you collapsed at your desk and she left."

"Sharon!" The memories of the morning returned in a flood. And just as suddenly, he felt all the unanswered questions about her mysterious appearance return in force.

What did she do to me? He wondered what kind of spell she was able to weave to keep him befuddled. Did she knock me out?

"Hodgepodge. Did you archive the security video for this morning?"

"All video since her arrival has been archived, pending a clarification of Ms. Dae's security status."

"Show me this office, starting five minutes before I collapsed. Run at 3 X speed."

A video window popped up on the terminal before him, and the wide-angle view of the room showed Sharon and him talking animatedly. The sound track was triple-time, but Hodgepodge had processed the sound through a filter that adjusted the pitch down back to normal so that he could understand the words even if they came rattling out like something from Gilbert and Sullivan.

They were talking about business, and how the company managed to make money, all in hand-waving generalities of course, but she had seemed interested in everything he did.

There was a telephone call. Mary Ellen was going back to her downtown office.

The image of Abe pulled up something on the computer screen and Sharon walked around to look over his shoulder. She put her hand on the back of his neck, closed her eyes, and almost immediately, he collapsed.

"Back it up by thirty seconds and replay it at normal speed."

He reached across to feel his shoulder where she had touched him as he watched her go through the motions again. There didn't appear to be any tenderness there—no evidence of an Aikido "Spock Pinch" or anything like that.

In the video, he collapsed in mid-sentence. She kept her eyes closed for another couple of seconds, and then appeared to check him out, moving his arm from the contorted position it had fallen into. Then pausing only a few more seconds, she headed out the door, leaving his unconscious body alone in the room.

"Pause."

He edged carefully up out of the chair, and started to stretch. The pain was fading slowly away. Hopefully no permanent damage was done.

She's been gone thirty minutes. He doubted he would be able to catch her now. He was angry, but it was a dull painful anger. She did something to him. She'd been fooling him.

"Okay, Hodgepodge. What's your security question?"

"In the matter of Sharon Dae, I have several questions. Should she be classified as an authorized visitor? Is she authorized to remove materials from the Whiting building? What is the general status of persons who are initially discovered already inside the building and who thus bypass the gate security procedures? What is the general security response to persons who can unlock secured doors at will?"

Abe raised his hand, "Whoa! One at a time."

Abe took a deep breath, then continued. "Okay, Sharon Dae is currently considered an unauthorized person. Is she still inside the building?"

"No. She left thirteen minutes ago."

"What's this about unlocking doors?"

"In four instances, she was able to reverse the lock solenoids on secured doors."

He frowned. "Are you sure? Maybe just a faulty door lock?"

"The probability is low that it was a defect. Four separate locks, at four different times, had been triggered to the unlocked position. In all cases, Sharon Dae had her hand on the exterior of the mechanism at the time. In several cases, I attempted to re-lock the door and the solenoid was toggled back and forth repeatedly. After she was released from the storage room I removed the suspect lock and tested it with no evidence of false triggering."

"That's why you secured the door with a flash plate! I wondered about that. You mean she can walk through any locked door in this place? How can she do that? Did she have a hidden electromagnet?" Abe was appalled and fascinated by the idea that some magnificent, and sexy, super-spy had been here. She'd duped him and the others, and was able to walk away. It made her even more alluring.

Spy? Maybe. He remembered the other strange events of the last twenty-four hours.

Hodgepodge began relating all the failed hypotheses he had entertained to solve the lock problem on his own, but Abe cut him off.

"Go back. Show me the first video you have of Sharon Dae."

What if she isn't a spy?

The image of her sneaking out of the back of the van was an anticlimax. He'd been ready to see her materialize in a Star Trek transporter beam. If he could accept that he had an alien artifact, he could almost accept an alien coming to steal it back. Someone had been there on that hillside trying to cover up the evidence of the crash. It was probably her.

He watched the video up to the first point where she unlocked a door. It was just as Hodgepodge said. She had a magic touch. She could knock out a door lock. Just like she knocked me out.

"Go back to the moment she left my office after I collapsed. Follow her actions."

He watched with a growing sickness in his chest as she headed though locked doors straight towards the pegboard where the keys to the van were kept. She effortlessly evaded the other people in the building, as if she knew exactly which way they were going to turn their heads. Then, she located the dented magnesium device and wheeled it back to the van. It was difficult for her to handle, but she managed to dump it into the van.

She opened the external doors, and then cut the control wires when Hodgepodge started to close them again. When she drove out, no one in the building even noticed.

"Could you have stopped her?" Abe asked in the silence.

"Unknown. I could have slowed her progress with the mobile unit, if damage to it would have been acceptable. I could have notified the other humans, if danger to them was acceptable. I could have removed power from the lab area to secure the garage door, if the loss of time to the ongoing projects was acceptable."

Abe patted the computer monitor on the 'head'. "It's okay. Given your lack of information, you did an acceptable job of weighing the costs and benefits."

I would have burned the bridges and called out the militia to stop her, but Hodgepodge is right. There were dangers. It's not his job to make that kind of call.

"New rule."

"Copying."

"If anyone that you can monitor collapses or shows any other sign of medical distress, notify everyone in the building immediately. If there is no one here, call all employees or associates on the phone until you can get someone. If no one can be found, contact the 9-1-1 system and be prepared to direct them in."

"New rule added."

Abe had mixed feelings. He had a class one mystery to solve, one getting more complex by the minute. His mind was starting to clear up as well. Whatever she did to him was potent. It knocked him out, short-circuited his memories, and left him befuddled.

But at least it wore off.

She also tricked him, stole from him, lied to him.

Is she an alien? Or is she some government-type cleaning up the evidence? Was the whole thing his fault for sticking his toe into dangerous waters, just as Mary Ellen said?

He wasn't going to figure that out by reviewing old tapes.

However, all wasn't lost. She had taken the van—the fully instrumented van.

"Hodgepodge. Are you monitoring her?"

"Yes."

"Show me the camera view."

A video window opened up and a coarse view appeared showing Sharon in profile. The instant the image appeared, she turned, looking frightened, over her shoulder. For an instant, she locked her eyes on the camera.

A horn blared from another vehicle.

Sharon panicked. Wide eyed, she over-corrected her steering and the image showed her and every other loose thing in the cab of the van bouncing.

Get back on the road! Abe urged silently.

"I am!" she yelled.

Abe was shocked. He could only watch as she steered clumsily back onto the highway. He moved the mouse, and changed the zoom level of the camera so that he could see more of the road. She was on a two-lane road. Traffic was heavy. The image was washed out from the bright sun. He couldn't tell where she was.

Tentatively, just as an experiment, he sent her a thought, **Are you human?**

"Yes. I'm from Wimberley."

He had trouble believing her. Forget what she'd said before. Wells Branch and the brother at Abbott Labs, out. Wimberley, in.

Okay, so he believed in telepathy. But he believed in vague impressions, influences that could be statistically detected, not clear-as-spoken-word telepathy. No one could converse that way.

"Why not?" she said. "I can read you. My mother could read me."

Abe opened his audio channel. "Come on back. Do you know what you've got?" he asked angrily.

She looked over at the camera. He moved the image to center on her. When he was done, she nodded. "I know exactly what I have. It's an engine of the dark angels."

"Who?"

She shook her head. "Sorry, that's just my name for them. They call themselves the Cerik." She almost clicked the last syllable, like the sound of a pair of scissors. "It means the rulers, or hunters.

"But the important thing is that they know it's here. They're coming back for it. They want it destroyed."

Abe felt himself drifting. There was too much information coming too fast. Normally, that wouldn't be a problem. He thrived on ideas. But, this! He pushed his anger aside. He needed to think.

Concentrate. One thing at a time. He was uncomfortably aware that she was reading him. Not the time to turn into mush.

She laughed, but it was short and with an undercurrent of bitterness. "Don't worry. Your mush is better than most people's crisp thinking. Besides, there's nothing you can do. They're already on their way. That's why I had to move fast. I have to get this thing far away. They have a bomb. They will destroy the city to get it out of our hands."

Abe believed her, amazed at himself. He was slipping back under her spell. She could tell him anything and he would believe her!

The audio crackled, reminding him that she was getting farther away every minute. She said, "I tricked you before, but it was a simple trick, like making sure no one is looking before walking down a corridor. I can read you, but I can't push anything into your head. If you believe me, then it's just because I am telling the truth. They are coming. Nothing can stop them. They know I have it. They have a telepath, too."

Abe tapped a string of commands, and the position of the van appeared as a little icon on a yellow map.

"Hodgepodge, is there any way you can detect an incoming flying vehicle like the one that crashed?" One of the machine's long term jobs was to search the Internet for resources. Maybe there was an Internet air-traffic control for all he knew.

There was a long pause. It meant Hodgepodge didn't have an answer, yet. Abe moved on, looking carefully at the map.

"Sharon, they are in a flying saucer or something like that?"

She nodded. "It's triangular. One of those engines is at each vertex. It is roughly flat, like a plate."

"How far away are they?"

She shook her head. "I don't know numbers. They're coming a long way."

"How much time?"

"Thirty minutes. An hour. Something like that."

Abe nodded to himself. "Okay. I want you to..."

"No," she interrupted. "It won't work."

"What?"

"Your idea to abandon the van in the quarry. Yes, it might constrain the explosion, but I wouldn't get away. They're tracking me, not the gadget. I didn't tell you. I'm supposed to be captured. There's no place on the face of the Earth where I can run."

Abe felt a pang in his chest. If she were just trying to protect them all....

"No, that won't work either," she almost cried, in despair. "They don't care about being seen, not now. A public place would just get more people killed."

Abe didn't argue, although he had even more questions. He searched the map again. He stabbed his finger at Georgetown.

How about this? Would they follow you there?

"I don't know." At least she didn't reject the idea immediately.

"Here look." **At this image in my memory.** He visualized the tramway at the entrance and the gate. **Here are the controls. You could avoid anyone or anything in there.**

He could tell she was considering the idea.

"Hodgepodge!"

"Yes, Abe."

"Monitor her position. Feed her directions to get to Inner Space Caverns by the fastest route. I'll be taking the Jeep." She'd need help moving the alien engine to the tram.

He headed for the door, grabbing a handheld radio out of a cabinet. He clicked it on. "I'll be on the radio. Listen for me. Route anything she says to me."

"Acknowledged."

THE WITCH

Sharon winced as the windshield lit up.

As if I don't have enough to worry about.

She checked again the little mirror to her left. There was another car racing up behind her. She lightly touched the mind to see what the lady expected her to do.

This 'driving' is crazy. How can anyone survive without telepathy is beyond me. She pressed her foot down to speed up out of the lady's way. *Those dials are moving again.* She wished she knew what they meant.

"I wish I knew which way to go."

She was startled as that other voice spoke from a speaker near her ear. "The view displayed on the windshield is a map. Your position is the blue icon. The bold red line is the path you should follow."

What's an icon? But she did see the red line, and there was an irregular blue box moving at one end of it. As she drove through the next crossroads, the red line blinked out and re-drew a new path from where she was to the same destination.

Oh, I should have turned there! I see what I'm supposed to do. She slowed, and ignoring the sudden angry thoughts from the lady behind her, she braced herself and turned the next corner with much less screeching of the tires than the last time.

Who is that man who spoke? She had a moment's free time to wonder. *Why can't I locate him?* Abe had called him Hodgepodge, and he was a servant of some kind.

"Hodgepodge?"

"Yes," he replied, startling her again. It was weird.

"Where are you?"

"I am in the Whiting Building."

Nonsense. I scanned that place when Abe introduced us. You have to be at some remote location.

"Can I talk to Abe?"

"I have connected you. Go ahead."

There was a noisy connection. Abe asked, "I can hear you Sharon. What do you want?"

She took quick look out of his eyes. He was driving much faster than she.

Amazingly enough, Abe's anger at her had vanished. Perhaps it was just the new threat, but she suspected that it was just Abe's way. There was no place in that mind for bad people. He'd accepted her story, and had forgiven her. Unfortunately, she still had the taste of her betrayal in her mouth and she would be dead long before she could get rid of it.

She shook the thought aside, "I am trying to locate Hodgepodge. He says he is at your building, but I can't feel him."

Abe understood her, but asked, "Is it important?" His mind was saying something quite different. **Hodgepodge is a secret I want to keep for a long time. I don't want to talk about him over the radio.**

Wordlessly, he invited her into a clear memory.

. . .

Abe was younger, working at a prototype voice control system he had created on a hodge podge collection of equipment he had scavenged. The program could do very little. It had a vocabulary of about 100 words and could only run a few limited programs. Anything outside of its range quickly showed just how little the hodgepodge could understand...

Abe was a little older. He was watching in fascination as a television report interviewed a team of researchers who where trying to create a computer with "common sense". They were doing it by laboriously feeding in to their computer system a large number of facts. Each day they entered data in from encyclopedias, textbooks and the daily news. Each night, they ran a program that let the computer program cross connect the data and produce a report on the inferences it had made. This report of common sense and nonsense was then manually graded and the nonsense corrected. It was in a real sense just like growing the common sense of a child.

Abe contacted them, based as they were in Austin, and came over for a visit of their facilities. After some talking, he managed to convince them that he could help with their database. The technology exchange made both sides happy, and Abe managed to get regular updates to the data set, up until it started making Hodgepodge erratic...

Abe was another notch older, sweating the demands of college studies and feeling the wonder of a new idea. He could move Hodgepodge to an array of tightly interlocked computers and greatly increase his responsiveness...

And there was the final memory, when Abe came to work one day and realized that Hodgepodge was working away at useful tasks, and that he hadn't a clue as to how he was doing it.

Hodgepodge was a machine. In some limited sense, it was an individual, with a personality, and a life...

...

Sharon pulled away from Abe's memories. She concentrated on driving for a moment, and then stretched her clairvoyance to see into the building she had left. There was a computer room. There was a bank of machines, with row upon row of identical cards. She tried to reach down into the wires and chips, trying to feel the electrical pulses.

"Hello, Hodgepodge. I'm glad to meet you."

There was something there. She could feel some reaction to her words. But it wasn't thought. It wasn't the feeling that she sensed in people, her cat, the rabbits, and even in those aliens she felt approaching rapidly.

"Thank you, Sharon. The pleasure is all mine." The words came, but there was no resonance behind it. She could always tell tape-delayed programs on the little battery-powered radio Hattie had given her. Tape was clearly different from live speakers. It was like this. Hodgepodge was a live-taped person. She shook her head.

If she lived out the hour, it would be interesting to talk to him more.

"Abe?"

"Yes, Sharon?"

Under the words was hard determination to rescue her. She felt warm. She liked the man behind the voice. The hours she'd spent with him were indelibly etched in her memory. *I have to make sure he isn't caught up in this.*

She glanced at the map. "Where are you now?"

The voice, muffled by wind noise, replied, "At the intersection of I-35 and FM 1325. I should be at the cave in under ten minutes. Hodgepodge will mark my position on your map."

Sharon noted a big green X appearing on her windshield display as Hodgepodge took the hint. She was traveling at right angles to his path and they would meet at the interstate. She pushed the foot pedal down all the way and sped up. The road was four lanes and fairly straight. The dark angels were coming fast.

She wished she could see her own future. Her mother had spoken several times of her own vision—some grand destiny for her daughter. Sharon had held that comfort to her chest for years now, but it was not a time where hope thrived. She was a storybook little girl in the woods, and the wolves were racing to take her blood. That vision had a closer tinge of reality than her mother's fairy tale. She could feel the wolves approaching.

And they were getting closer by the second. She glanced at the map.

I'm not going to make it.

She pushed harder on her foot pedal, but there was no more to give. She looked at the live oaks whipping by as she raced down the road. No place to run.

Then, there was a large sign built of big limestone slabs, "Texas Crushed Stone Company".

That's the quarry Abe mentioned.

Sharon stood on the brake, skidding the van, almost losing control. A scent of burned rubber assaulted her nose as she turned to the left and raced through the open gates.

Ignoring the startled attendant at the gateway, she headed into the open pit mine where square miles of limestone were harvested and shipped off via rail to the growing cities of Texas.

No hope for me, but at least Abe will be far away.

THE WIZARD

"Abe", squawked the radio.

The volume was turned all the way up to combat the noise the Jeep Wrangler's soft-top made at highway speeds, but it also distorted the sound. He held the radio to his ear.

"What is it?"

"The van has turned off 1431 at the quarry."

Abe slapped the steering wheel in frustration. "Why did she do that?"

"Unknown."

Across to the interstate, on the west side of the road, hints of the yellow-white limestone works were barely visible through the trees. He was already past the 1431 turn-off. He'd have to...

Oh no! The traffic on the interstate, nearly always packed, was slowing to a crawl. There were signs and blinking lights of road construction ahead.

"Sharon! Where are you?"

"Bye, Abe. They're here."

As soon as the words were out of the radio, his Jeep rattled from a loud boom. He held his breath as he scanned the tree line for signs of a blast.

No. Not an explosion. A sonic boom. He zipped open the fabric window and looked at the sky.

A small metal vehicle, reflecting the sunlight, was making an impossible, high-speed turn, zeroing in on the quarry.

Abe took one look at the traffic, gritted his teeth. With horn blaring, he swerved across the grassy centerline, smashing through a light wooden barricade, a gateway in the concrete divider. An instant later he slipped though an instantaneous gap in the terrified southbound cars. The fence caught his eye. He reached down and switched to four-wheel drive and smashed through the barbed wire.

Twisting and dodging through the trees, he ignored the patches of prickly-pear cactus, demolishing them. The green-belt barrier that separated the traveling public from the barren spectacle of the quarry parted before him.

"Sharon! Can you hear me?"

Hodgepodge replied. "She has left the van. She is no longer in camera range."

"Engage the controls! Steer slowly in a circle until you can see her." Computer controlled driving was still several months away on their research agenda, but the links were in place.

The trees thinned out. There was a drop ahead—the edge of the pit. He skidded to a stop in a cloud of dust.

A patch of dark in the huge expanse, he saw the van. A tiny figure, probably Sharon, was running away from it. The alien craft swooped low, overrunning her. When it passed, Abe couldn't see her anywhere.

The ship hovered above the van, and then his van's interior was lit by the unmistakable glare of a magnesium fire. The gas tank ignited.

Rising straight up above the yellow flames, the aliens paused just a moment and then accelerated up and away so fast his eyes couldn't follow. He strained to see anything up in the blue and white sky.

The shock wave from the explosion in the pit below caught him totally by surprise. The last he remembered, he was thrown from the Jeep, flying through the air.

Burn

THE SEER

Ed "supervised" the men unloading the food truck—mainly by leaning against a tree and waving up at the young girl watching from the ridge above his property. Each of the three days he had been moving in, she had been there, riding her horse—spying on him, he guessed.

It'd been a hectic time. There were too many papers to sign. Just waving money at people didn't seem to help with that part. At least he was making some progress. The food had finally arrived. He'd pointed to one of the unused bedrooms in the rear of the house and had them unload everything there.

The delivery company had advertised food bundles for one, two or four persons for a year. It was all dried and canned. He'd bought twenty large bundles. He also ordered random things from the local supermarket. Some of the items, like packages of whole grains, were designed to be ground into flour as you needed them. Ed had some reservations about that. He knew he was a klutz. His visions generally let him slide through life on luck, not skill. He sincerely doubted he would be able to work the obscure magic that started with hard little grain things and ended up with a soft piece of bread.

No, he was a person at the mercy of happenstance. People took care of him, like George Fuller. If they didn't he would have to make do as a lucky bum.

Or more likely, he would still be back at the care center, living his life in a daze, diagnosed as autistic, and not really understanding the difference between "now" and the "future" or the difference between the people in his visions and the people trying to talk to him. He really owed a debt to Dr. Jenny. Three years of her care had "cured" him enough to start school and to start to learn the hard lessons of how to deal with other people.

He felt bad about school. His doctors, his foster parents and his teachers had all felt so proud of him. That it was all a scam didn't bother him back then, but it did now. Once he started getting his visions under a measure of control, a school quiz to him was never a measure of how much he'd learned. Visions showed which marks in which places would give him a good grade. School taught him a minimal set of people skills. That was all. Even now, he wasn't really sure if *reading* meant the same as it did for other people, or if it was just another facet of this visions, feeding him the information he needed.

George was coming. He was on his way out to see the house, and this bout of guilt was the main reason he hadn't hopped on the scooter and been elsewhere. George took good care of him. He owed George. He just didn't owe him enough to leave the safety of his new house.

The visions were getting worse. Sometimes he couldn't tell reality for long periods. His first day here, he had a relapse. There was a strong vision of a woman screaming in panic, and then came the sound of thunder in a sky plainly clear of storm clouds. It shook him up. If he were losing it, then he had to stay put.

The telephone was his lifeline. George took his predictions over the phone, even if he disliked doing so.

Ed had gotten into a bad habit of calling Larry Kelly when Betelgeuse was below the horizon.

"Hey Larry, is it still red?"

"Yes. Go away. I'm busy."

At least Larry believed him. He could tell by his excitement. The astronomer had early results from his spectrographs and something unusual could be seen. Not that Ed could understand the explanation. It was good that someone was happy about it.

His calls to Angela were less satisfying. The urgency in his voice got him into trouble. He never grew bold enough to actually predict a disaster, but his calls were getting more frequent, until she balked. The lady informed him that his calls were no longer welcome, and that she would have to take action if he continued.

He didn't need to be precognitive to know what that meant. He didn't need any legal hassles right now. The time was close.

By the time he'd tipped the deliverymen and sent them on their way, George's BMW eased up into his driveway.

"Hello, Ed."

"Hi." They shook hands. George was never one to harp on their disagreements. He was always concerned about the future. Ed liked that about him.

George lifted his briefcase out of the car, and they went inside.

Ed fixed George a Perrier and himself a coke. He could tell this would be a long session.

THE WIZARD

"You just sit there," Mary Ellen ordered—pleased that for once, her boy was behaving himself.

Abe nodded, willing to wait in the car seat until she opened the door for him and handed him the cane. The painkiller hadn't deadened the pain in his side enough to let him move very well. He kept a false smile, trying to hide the physical pain, and the blackness that lurked in his thoughts.

A day at the hospital and a couple more at home. That was the minimum recuperation Mary Ellen would let him get away with. He'd slept most of that time. Mary Ellen and a couple of her friends from church came by at regular intervals to make sure he ate and, he suspected, to keep him away from the computer terminals. It was embarrassing to be on the church's prayer list, but it did remind him that he did have people who cared about him.

As he walked into the offices, the high-pitched ringing in his head increased in intensity. The doctor had warned that there might be some permanent hearing loss. He would worry about that later. His present loss was a little more painful and much harder to make sense of.

She came and was gone in just a few hours. She lied to me. She tricked me. She stole from me. A hundred thousand dollars in custom equipment lost when the van blew up. Damage to the Jeep. Damage to me.

But I'd promised to help her.

His word meant everything. Growing up with nothing—no parents, no home, no one whom he could claim as his own—his word was all he had.

What am I, if I can't keep my word?

Sharon, I'm sorry. I didn't get there fast enough. I didn't see the danger coming. I'm sorry...about everything.

Scott greeted him as he limped into the lab.

"You actually look like the walking dead. From what Mary Ellen was saying, I expected much worse."

Abe shook off the creeping darkness that kept trying to smother him. The pain made his first impulse irritation. He fought it, managing a smile. "Just good acting. I think she was right. How're the projects coming?"

"I've got a report in your email. Basically everything is back on schedule, other than Momcar, of course. I've got Bud taking over the archiver. He has finally gotten a good working relationship with Hodgepodge, and I think he has a natural aptitude with mechanical design."

"Good. Hodgepodge working okay? I never managed to come to closure on the results of the blackout. Things got too frantic too quickly."

Scott shrugged, "If I could get a human assistant to work as well as he does, I'd quit this salt mine and go to work for myself. Have you ever thought of cloning him and licensing copies?"

Abe shook his head, "And have you as a competitor? No way!" They laughed.

Privately Abe wondered if it would be possible. Perhaps there was some magic in the wiring that made it all happen. He didn't intend to make the attempt for some time to come. He was afraid to jinx the miracle he had.

Scott pulled up the spare chair as Abe eased himself down into his. "Oh, I've got some good news."

Abe asked, "I could use some. What is it?"

"Hester Automotive says that your Jeep is in fairly good shape, other than the ruined wheels, and the body work. After they got the barbed wire stripped out of the undercarriage, they said it seems to run fine."

Scott paused a moment. "You've got to tell me what happened. Aliens, explosions, Air Force intelligence officers—you are not a boring person to work for."

Abe shook his head. "Sorry. I'll make a serious effort to be boring from now on." He winced as his side gave another twinge. "It hurts too much otherwise."

When the silence grew longer, Abe realized Scott's request was more than just conversation. He really wanted to know. Had no one given him the details?

"You saw Sharon," he began.

Scott nodded as Abe recapped that day's events. He told of the theft, leaving out most of the psychic stuff. Bud had gossiped about the card tricks, and Abe didn't really feel it necessary to add anything more to the tale. Her telepathy only made sense when it was happening. He told Scott of the aliens attempt to destroy the engine unit and to kidnap Sharon because she could 'sense' them. Scott opened his mouth to comment, but changed his mind and waved Abe on with his story.

Abe told of the encounter in the limestone quarry, the space ship, and the explosion.

"I don't know what happened to her. She said over the radio that they intended to capture her, but she was obviously trying to keep some things from me, so she might have been downplaying things. I suspect she is dead. If not, I wouldn't have a clue about her present location."

Scott nodded soberly. "And the Jeep?"

Abe winced. "They did something to the van. It exploded. The shock wave caught me and threw me up into a tree. It rolled the Jeep. When I came to, I couldn't hear anything. The walkie talkie looked dead. If it was making noises, I couldn't tell. It took me most of an hour, but I was able to use the winch to pull the Jeep upright. I could tell the wheels were bent, but I could drive it. I don't think I made more than five miles per hour, and the last I remember was wobbling into the gas station and turning off the key."

He looked at Scott, "Air Force intelligence?"

"Yep. They showed up the day after, looking for witnesses to the explosion. According to the papers, there was quite an assembly of brass buttons at the quarry. An explosion of that size attracted some major attention, and still, no one has a clue. Your UFO was seen by a dozen people at least, but only the radio talk shows are treating it seriously."

Scott smiled in memory. "I must say that it is a privilege to be able to watch Mary Ellen at work. They arrived with all kinds of evidence; tire tracks, the report of your arrival at the gas station and your hospital admission information. They left confident that you were about fifteen years old, and that you had borrowed the family car and had rolled it hot-rodding over by Granger."

Abe laughed, and then stopped when it hurt.

Scott continued, "Not that she lied to them. She just managed to let them confuse themselves. I had to go to another room and listen in via Hodgepodge to keep from laughing. Is she licensed to practice criminal law?"

Abe shook his head. "I don't think so."

Scott sighed, "She could make a fortune."

Another fortune, Abe corrected silently.

Scott got up from his chair as if to leave, then stopped. "Oh, by the way, there is one thing wrong with your story."

"What's that?"

"The aliens didn't get the engine, just the hull."

Abe sat up, ignoring the pain. "What!"

Scott grinned. "Hodgepodge was working while you were romancing your new girl friend. He had removed the guts and had moved them to the electronics lab for more analysis. When she came back to steal it, all she got was the empty."

We still have it! His pulse was loud in his ears. *But what a price you had to pay for a lie.*

THE NAME

The first book, of the Brothers, of Trust. The fifth Tale.

A Hunter and a Builder met in the forest as cubs and resolved to treat each other as brothers. For a season, they worked together, the Builder helped to trap Runners with his clever snares. The Hunter killed a Treeclimber pack that was preying on the Builders as he worked on the river. One day, while they sat together at meat, they resolved to exchange their food. The Builder drank blood and chewed at flesh with his dull flat teeth. The Hunter labored to chew and swallow tree bark. For three days they struggled to eat each other's food, until they became weak. "We must go back to our natural ways", said the Builder. The Hunter agreed, "Yes, we must." And he killed and ate the Builder.

. . .

Tenthonad was in *'eeh*. The blood of the captured alien fired him as nothing had in years. He could still smell her blood on his claw, and taste the rich flavor tempting his fangs.

I must not take any more.

When she'd been brought to his perch, still lashed by her feet, as Second's prize of battle, he'd yielded to a sudden impulse and slashed her leg. Her shriek had echoed from one end of the ship to the other. The blood flowed freely. She fought him ineffectually, as he tasted the dark red flow.

Egh howled at the continuing blood loss. He needed a live specimen. Tenthonad had expected her gash to tighten up after a few seconds, but for some reason, the alien's wound kept bleeding. He released her, and with her hands she controlled the blood until it stopped. He waved her off into Egh's care and howled with incoherent rage when Second started making his claim on her. The blood had gone straight to his head, and he bowled them all out of his place.

For the moment, he had clear dominance, and everyone in the ship knew it, but he held no illusions. Second hated him, and having live prey snatched from him during bloodscent was not something he could forgive. It would mark him forever nameless if he let it stand.

Tenthonad breathed in the air, still rich with the scent of the blood on the floor. If all else failed for this world, this prey would still be valuable for hunting.

The massive cities of this world had been a major disappointment. None of the best treasure worlds had started out with cities. It was welcome, of course, if the prey had skill enough to build estate homes for the Cerik, but thus far, the more developed worlds tended to die off when the supernova radiation hit. There was much to be said for low population density and prey smart enough to hide in deep caves until the strange light in the sky went out.

This one had all the marks of a world ready to collapse into war. There was already a contest to guess which part of the world would be the first to burn. Asca had reported early that this indeed was a world with major weapons.

But even if they do destroy themselves, and the best lands, maybe there will be enough prey left to hunt. It's a shame they don't last in captivity. It would be enough to breed them and settle a population on some other world.

There was a timid scratch on the floor outside his perch. Tenthonad growled low, and it stopped. After another moment, the scratch came again.

"At the post!" *Risk your eyes, if you dare.*

It was a youngling of his family. Tenthonad let him approach with his belly dragging the ground to within range of his claws.

"Speak."

"For your *Name*, Egh reports the Brightening."

Tenthonad was silent.

So it is time. Now we will see what options survive.

"Order the ship to hide."

The little one backed out as he had come. He'd been little more than a cub when the trip had begun. That he was still alive and unscarred meant that Tenthonad was a good *La*. There was no chance the youngling would fare as well if the name of his line were killed by Second.

There was a feeling in the air, as the ship moved. They had to move back from the planet to be in the shadow of its moon. There they had to remain, while the star burned. There would be much use of the engines to keep them in place from now on.

Tenthonad smelled blood in the air again.

I have to find a way. My family needs this prey.

THE SCIENTIST

Larry Kelly was startled out of his sleep by the phone. Janet reached above her head and slapped the alarm clock. He grabbed the phone and whispered, "Yes. What is it?"

It was Cujo. "Your friend at Sudbury called. There has been a huge neutrino spike."

He was fully awake. "What time?"

"Less than five minutes ago."

"Bump Hamilton off the AAT. Tell him I was right. Get everything pointed at Betelgeuse. I'll be up there as soon as I can get dressed."

"Roger."

Janet stirred. "What is it?"

He hung up the phone. "It's started."

"Oh no!"

Larry took her hand. "It's important that I get up the hill. Can you handle things here?"

She nodded, "Have everything packed. Get ready to move if you call."

"Right. Remember that the radiation may not come. The science is against it. It's just a long shot."

"But your friend believes it."

"Yes."

He gave her hand a squeeze. She got out of bed as well. Her rounded belly didn't slow her down yet, but it made his fears extra sharp.

We don't need anything to harm you. Not now.

The phone rang again. Larry snatched it up.

"It is still red?" asked Ed.

"No. Not any more."

Fried

THE WITCH

Sharon coughed a hoarse wracking cough. Her leg, although healing rapidly, ached in sympathy.

This air is getting to me. It's wrong.

But at least it wasn't killing her quickly. Nothing was killing her quickly. In fact, the older monster seemed concerned about her health. When he saw her trying to bandage her leg with a torn strip of cloth from her blouse, he vanished and returned with a bolt of white cotton cloth.

At first, she thought it was something alien, but as she picked at it, there was a label, Caddo Mills, 100% cotton. She checked the edges of his memories and learned that they'd been visiting Earth for months. They had collected a large store of items, in hopes of finding something valuable.

Egh was the most sympathetic of the monsters, the only one of the group who didn't actively want to dig his claws into her.

She was prey. She knew the thought, from Felicia. How she tasted was the most rampant speculation among the crew. The next seemed a betting pool about when nuclear weapons would be used on Earth.

There was a tense mood of excitement, as the Cerik waited for the first signs of the supernova. It was important to them, she knew, and important in some way to the Earth as well, although she knew very little about physics and stars.

The books she grew up with were much more concerned with constellations and planets than individual stars. Astrology, in often-contradictory ways, was threaded through most of the books her mother had left her. None of them talked about supernova.

Her attention was grabbed as Asca, the Cerik telepath turned his thoughts to her. She put aside any other speculations and focused on him.

What do you want from me?

There was a pause, as Asca sensed the question behind the incomprehensible words, and involuntarily considered the question.

Unfortunately, Asca's answer was simple. He wanted to get information from her to bolster his status on the ship. He wanted to make sure he wasn't considered expendable when the final showdown came.

Sharon already knew more than that from reading background thoughts in Egh.

If I could just read Tenthonad or Second.

Terror crept over her, deep and wide. She'd fooled herself into believing that she was resigned to her fate. She wasn't like her mother, bravely making a sacrifice for the lives of others. Fear deep in her cells kept her from stoically being brave and waiting until it was over.

The image of three-inch fangs locked onto her leg and the deep, blissful bloodlust emanating from a monster twice her size—lust for *her* blood—sent all those self-delusions shattering.

She shied away from the memory again. She could not bear it.

But Tenthonad does have a mind.

She tried to be calm and analytical, to soothe the quivering muscles in her arms, the ache in her legs. Her blood was again flooding with adrenaline. Unknown parts of her own mind wanted to *Get out! Get out!*

He does have a mind. Sharon tried again. *He lost his block for a second, when....*

She turned her thoughts away.

I will think about that later.

Asca had left, turning his mind away from her. *My terror is too boring, I guess.* But at least she was being left alone.

Her leg hurt. There was a cut and two deep punctures.

I have to repair the damage. I'll never be able to run until I do.

She looked around her cage again. It felt like a deep bathtub. The whole interior of the ten-foot deep, cubic room was white enamel, cold and hard. There was a portable net stretched over the top, as if she could climb or jump out.

They can.

She'd watched Egh, who considered himself old and frail, jump in and out of the container with ease.

She had fouled the far corner when she had first been placed here, but water had sprayed from the upper rim, washing the mess on the floor and the mess on her clothes into a drain. Like a venetian blind in the center of the pit, it drained away all the filth before it closed up again.

Now, there was nothing but her, the bolt of cloth she was using as a pillow, and an empty can of green beans Egh had opened for her with his fingernail.

I will need protein.

The cloth made a poor pillow, but it was better than nothing. Sharon composed herself as she had so many times before.

She became the Eye.

Her body was like a city after a major disaster, like a tornado, or a fire. The arteries were busy with repair business. The blood was alive with specialized cells, alert on a chemical level for anything that was wrong.

Sharon moved quickly to the damage site. Infection, from the organisms that had been dormant on her skin and clothes, had reacted to the fertile ground of her tissues and had bloomed like flowers in the desert after a rain.

They were all recognizable, both to the Eye from previous repair times, and to the mindless cells in her blood that were created for this. It was a battleground. She moved in to help.

The white blood cells and the antigens were vastly competent. The coliforms and strep were equally so. It was a battle based on stealth, trickery, quickness, and most of all, on being first with the most.

The Eye was powerful, just not perfect. This was the third time she had gone in since the injury. Each time, she thought she'd killed them all. Each time, the infection came back. She went at it again, touring the injury site. Soon, she was once again confident that she'd taken care of them.

Second on her agenda were the alien bugs. Deposited by the fangs and claws, these were awakened by the warmth and moisture of her blood. Luckily, they were like unarmed boy scouts in the Crimean War. They couldn't latch onto her cells. Their toxins didn't work. Only in the most basic levels could they manage to feed on the broken and killed cells around them.

White blood cells were competent enough to engulf them. Even if defensive cells found them largely indigestible—they still died.

The Eye did its job and killed the ones left alive. She tried to make the damage minimal, leaving plenty of invader corpses. Her body would need to sensitize itself to their patterns for future antibodies.

Next time, her body would be even more prepared for them.

Third priority was damaged muscle and skin tissue. Her mother had led her through childhood with no scars to mark the process, and Sharon saw no reason to lower her standards. From Abe's thoughts, when they met, was his feeling that her body was perfect. That was mostly male lust talking, but it was nearly true. Growing up, she'd seen no need to tolerate scars, blemishes, or an imbalance of fatty tissue. For now, scars might become a necessary, but with help, they didn't have to be permanent.

It was a fine dance between helping the repair systems do their work quickly and efficiently, and avoiding the cues that signaled for scar tissue. It was a demanding task, made even harder because she had to guide the process in these isolated sessions, but she'd been taught by the best. She was her mother's daughter.

Fourth was her cough. Something was damaging the sensitive tissue in her lungs, and the hints she'd picked up from Egh were disheartening. He was completely baffled by the way his specimens died after only a few days. She had seen his memories, as he had torn apart the dead animals, hunting for clues.

If he had been a better scientist, he would have sacrificed some of the fresh ones for comparison, she thought. Sharon had read enough to know that much about the way it was done.

As it was, she was the only person on the ship who had any idea what undamaged lung tissue looked like.

And it's happening to me.

It wasn't something obvious like a microorganism. It had to be something, some gas, in the air itself.

She had no idea how to solve the problem. Her only hope was to speed up her body's own repair and hope to delay the inevitable.

I really need more protein.

On the way out of her trance, releasing the microscopic control of her body, she took a little time to adjust the hormones in her blood. She needed to be able to think more than she needed to be able to run.

Tenthonad does think. He let his block slip during his attack on me, but he regained control quickly. Now he's invisible, just like that other one, Second. How can they do that?

If she could understand this block, it could be the most important thing she had encountered in her life.

It could change everything.

THE ROBOT

The first hint was a message on science news blogs Hodgepodge{18} monitored. The moderator from JPL put a hurried, terse message out that reported a possible supernova.

Hodgepodge had a long-standing order to gain new information and to digest it—fit it in with the complex database of facts and relationships that made up his background knowledge. He was built with a curiosity.

The next step, when faced with an unusual event, was to research it further. He accessed his starchart database and looked up the position of Betelgeuse. A quick check with the web search engines gave him a list of those observatories that would have it in sight. Hopefully, many of those web sites would have pages that mentioned current research.

Concurrently, he checked a few other websites and specialty forums that traditionally had a high signal-to-noise ratio in their messages.

The Internet was exploding with messages, mainly second-hand rumors of the supernova. Strangely, there were no first hand reports.

Web searches were all coming back with "Server Not Found" messages as well.

A quick check of a couple of well-connected web sites that specialized in network "weather reports", showed that something was seriously wrong. Packets sent to anywhere from Asia to Australia were lost. Nothing was coming out.

Hodgepodge{18} added up the data. As a test, he referenced the phone number for a newspaper in Kuala Lumpur Malaysia and made a call. The line beeped in the pattern that indicated that service was unavailable.

"Abe."

"Yes, Hodgepodge." He was busy at the optics worktable, testing the ports on the alien engine module. Some of them were emitting light. He was trying to find a signal in the light.

"Reports of an electromagnetic pulse or pulses are coming in from other parts of the world. A star has gone supernova. As parts of the Earth rotate into the view of the star, electrical systems are going dead. The Internet is showing stress. I predict that the death of the Net is imminent.

"Based on the extent of the observed damage, I cannot assume the I will survive. You should make arrangements to bypass all systems that I control, once I die."

THE SEER

I wish I were telepathic.

There'd been times in Ed's past... Moments of contact—short flashes of insight that later proved perfectly correct. In the blur of his childhood, there'd been imaginary friends.

That was before Dr. Jenny.

But if he ever had the skill, if was gone now, which was a shame. It would have been useful, facing down George.

His boss was patient and troubled. "Ed, I know that this is your money. That's not the issue. What is the issue is your lack of co-operation with the business reports. You've predicted a horrible market crash. We believed you, and we've taken terribly risky measures to position ourselves. Without your updates, we could lose everything. We could be totally wiped out."

Ed tried to explain, getting hot, "I've told you. It's a supernova. And from the call I had this morning, it's probably already started. Bad things will happen. I don't want to go back into town, not this afternoon, not for a long time."

"I think you're overreacting just a bit. I shouldn't have come out here— things are that tense. I should be back at the office and you should be right there with me. We need your gift."

Ed stood up. "Well, I don't need you! You've asked me questions all afternoon long. I answered them. Now you want to take me back with you. I'm not going."

George bit back, "There is more here than you doing us a favor! You owe us. All of this place..." he got up and waved around at the wood pan-eled walls and the ornate light fixtures. "All of this, and your education, and all your expenses come out of my fund. If this is just to hurt me, you are making a big mistake. Your welfare is dependent on mine, and mine is in danger. You talk about bad things that might happen in the city. Well, bad things will definitely happen if we aren't there, taking care of business!"

Ed began, "You don't know..."

The phone began to ring. But it sounded strange—one long ring that went on for fifteen seconds. Ed reached for the phone, but by the time he picked it up, it was dead, not even a dial tone.

It was quiet, too quiet.

"I think the electricity is out." The overhead fan had come to a stop. Even the unobtrusive noises of the kitchen appliances were gone.

Ed looked at George. "It's started."

"What? Your supernova?" George looked puzzled. "I called people at UT. They assured me that nothing would happen." He was offended. Experts should know what they were talking about.

Ed was already heading out the front door. He walked across the street and out onto the wooden dock. He'd checked this out the day before. Out on the water, there was a clear path to the east.

George came up behind him, fussing with his cell phone. "This thing is acting crazy. The display is all messed up."

Ed was calm. It was all familiar to him. He'd been rehearsing for days. "Save your batteries. If it hasn't been fried yet, maybe it will be of some use after this is all over."

"Fried?"

Ed nodded. "Yes, fried. Just like the phone system. Just like the power grid. By that." He pointed.

George followed his gaze. It was early in the afternoon, but there was already a star in the blue sky, rising above the treeline. He wasn't sure, but it looked like it was getting brighter as he watched.

George whispered, "I've got to get back to the office."

Ed shrugged. He didn't see what George could do with the phone lines and the power down, but he didn't say anything.

There wasn't anything anyone could do—not in the city, not anywhere in the world. All that had come to an end.

THE EQUESTRIENNE

Helen Black pushed Dadbert's flank with her right knee and started him along the fence line once more. "Good boy." She patted his neck, praising him for following her directions.

As she neared the edge of the pasture, where she could look down on the houses below, Dadbert started to toss his head, resisting the reins. She tried to reassure him with some more gentle praise. He didn't like being close to the cliff. Helen didn't either, but she had argued for three months with her father that she was mature and well able to ride in the far pasture, and if she didn't take advantage of it, then what had it all been for?

She rode at a slow walk, along the uneven land. She liked to look at the water. Lately, she'd been watching the new man move in. He was far too old for her, but she liked his blonde good looks, and she felt a little giddy when he started waving to her. The boys her age were all rude and crude. She wondered if she would ever get to meet him.

Several hours ago, she'd seen a second man arrive, and his car was still there. She moved on. It wouldn't do to have anyone notice how much time she spent on the cliff. As it was, her mother had already commented on how many times she had gone out riding today.

It was an 'In-service' day—sort of a make-believe holiday. The teachers had a bunch of days they had to take for extra training. It made for some nice three-day weekends. Sometimes the family got to take little trips. Most often, it was a day to sleep late, catch up on homework, and ride Dadbert. It was a shame Tawny didn't call anymore.

The rest of the loop around the property was made at a lope.

None of my friends call anymore.

Tawny was now Jackie's best friend. They went out of their way to keep from sitting at the same table with her in the cafeteria. Mother didn't understand how mean they were to her. Just yesterday she overheard Jackie telling Ben that she had gotten stuck-up.

That's not fair! The only boy in the whole class who knew how to fix his hair, and now he thinks I've gone all snooty.

She patted Dadbert again for sympathy. "You're a good boy, aren't you." He was her only friend in the whole world.

As they approached the cliff again, she saw a man running.

That's the old one. It looked like the both of them had gone out on the dock to look for a boat or something. The old one ran to his car and started it up. He headed out on the road, and then his car started making loud popping noises, and then stalled.

Helen pulled Dadbert to a halt and watched as the car coasted over to the edge of the road. She could hear the starter cranking as he tried to restart his car. He must have tried a dozen times before the starter died. He ran the battery down. She'd been through that with her mother. You weren't supposed to do that.

The man got out and came back to the house. Her guy and the older one argued for a minute, and then the old guy borrowed the scooter.

Helen laughed, and told Dadbert how funny the man looked, in his fancy business suit, puttering down the road on the scooter.

Her guy went out of sight into his house, so she rode on.

A couple of turns later, she saw it.

She pulled Dadbert to a halt. "Is it an airplane?" The horse declined to guess. When it didn't move off, she felt a little excited.

"Maybe it is a UFO." The sun was still out. It couldn't be a star.

Off in the distance, she heard, "Helen! Helen, come home."

Her mother was at the fence line, waving.

Oh no. What does she want me to do now?

Parents couldn't stand kids having free time. They would make things up for you to do. *Besides, she doesn't need to yell like that. Mom was so insistent that I carry my phone when I ride, and now she doesn't even use it!*

She pulled out her phone, but it was dead. *I just charged it!* Rebelliously, she turned Dadbert towards home. *I cleaned up my room just a couple of days ago.*

As she got closer. Her mother yelled, "Come on into the house!"

Helen yelled back. "I've got to cool Dadbert down. We've been exercising."

"No! Come on right this instant!"

Helen rode up to the fence line. She had been through this with her riding instructor at the stables. "Mrs. Peterson told me that it was very important to walk him to cool down. You told me I had to...."

"Now, young lady! Get off the horse." Her mother pointed at the star, now higher and brighter than it had been when Helen first noticed it. "There's a warning on the radio. It's an exploding star. There might be radiation! You have to come in now!"

She felt a clutch at her heart when she heard 'radiation'.

"But what about Dadbert? I have to groom him—and what about the radiation. Will the barn protect him?"

Her mother grabbed her hand and pulled her off the saddle. She landed on her feet, just barely. "You can't..."

But her mother was pulling her along at a run. She started to feel panic bubbling out of her chest. "What about Dadbert?" She started to cry. "What about Dadbert?"

Shelter

THE WIZARD

Abe stared stupidly at the welding jet in his hand as the flame flickered and then went *pop* as the acetylene tank ran out of gas. He sat there, asleep with his eyes open for about three minutes, the oxygen hissing from the tip.

"Abe." Mary Ellen walked into the computer room, now looking more like a large, elaborate chicken coop, illuminated by a quartet of pump-up gasoline lanterns. When he didn't respond, she raised the volume. "Abe!"

He blinked, realized he had run out of gas and shut off the tank. "Um. Yes. What do you want?"

She picked up the hinge he was working on and put it aside, setting a bowl in front of him.

"I want you to eat this chili, every last drop. And then I want you to go to the library and get some sleep."

He rubbed his forehead. Now, there was a headache and a backache to go with his injuries. "There's still so much to do."

She put a spoon in his hand. "And you won't be able to do it at all unless you get some food and sleep."

She picked up one of the lanterns. "I'll be back in ten minutes. I expect serious progress on that chili by then."

"Yes, Ma'am."

He started on the food, out of obedience for the first bite. The second came with more enthusiasm. When Mary Ellen walked by a few minutes later, he was almost done. She nodded and went on.

He finished, and located one of the warm, room temperature bottles of water that she'd brought him earlier. As he sipped, he walked out the darkened hallway to the back door.

Betelgeuse was high in the sky. It dominated the night. Just like a full moon, its glare washed out all competing stars. But unlike the moon, its intensity was concentrated in one pinpoint of light, strong enough to hurt.

Abe turned away, not wanting to risk his vision. He looked at his latest invention, bolted to the wall.

There was a wire, a straightened coat hanger, made into a loop, with the two ends bolted to a re-wired voltmeter. The loop picked up the electricity generated by the electromagnetic pulses coming from the star and sent it to the voltmeter. The meter needle rested on an aluminum soda can, wrapped in pressure sensitive graph paper. The can was turning slowly, affixed to the hour-hand shaft of a salvaged wind-up alarm clock.

He looked at the line the meter had drawn over the past few hours. It was a mass of spikes. Each spike was the trace of an EMP, generated by that far star centuries ago, each still carrying enough energy to destroy sensitive electrical circuits.

Abe tried to make sense of the forest of spikes. Each was the result of some irregularity in that vast explosion. Every layer of gas in the star, or maybe in the dust cloud surrounding the star, turned some of that unstoppable explosion into the scream of atoms being torn apart.

He sighed. There was a weight on his spirit. It settled in and he had a feeling it would never go away.

This isn't my field. I'm not an astronomer.

He would be careful to save the daily recording strips. His apparatus wasn't calibrated, but he was certain some scientist somewhere would be happy to have the data once this was all over.

All he wanted to do now was get a feel for how long it would last. It looked like the intensity was dropping, and the gaps between the spikes were definitely lengthening. Maybe with a few more hours of results, he could tell for certain how the trend was running.

Rough engine noise drifted in from the highway. Easily 90% of the cars were useless, their electronic engine control computers burned out. Older cars were better off.

The day of the distributor, rotor, and points are back. Antique car collectors can name their price.

With the van blown to dust and the Jeep still out of service, he was left at the mercy of Mary Ellen's Cadillac. He blessed her sense of loyalty to the massive, tail-finned monstrosity that her husband had bought long ago.

He headed back in. Not that there was anywhere to go. The building was more massive and more resistant to any potential radiation than the apartment where he officially lived. Mary Ellen likewise had no inclination to head back into town.

Abe blessed his stubborn streak. When they'd talked to the architects who had designed the Whiting Design Center, he had insisted on heavy slab floors.

There were two kinds of industrial buildings commonly used. The most common was build from pre-cast walls, put together like a house of cards, from which floors and ceilings were hung. The other used massive concrete pillars and thick concrete floors, with the walls hung from that structure like an afterthought.

The heavy floors appealed to him—a sturdy support for his instruments. Now, those thick layers overhead made the best protection possible against any potential radiation.

Scott had left. He had a family to collect. Abe sent him off with his bicycle, and his prayers. The only family Abe had was Mary Ellen. He was glad she was here with him.

Bud had left earlier, before the star had risen. Abe had no idea where he was, or if he would return.

It's just Mary Ellen and me. And maybe Hodgepodge if I can get him put back together.

He went back to the computer room. With Hodgepodge's warning, they'd managed to do a controlled shutdown of his main systems, and then do a full backup using only a simple-minded, but complete, routine.

The backup media was stored in metal boxes in the basement. They had pulled all of his cards and individually wrapped as many of them as they could in aluminum foil. Other items, like the heavy redundant power supplies, he had to wrap as well as he could and hope that it was enough.

The only protection against electromagnetic pulses was a Faraday cage.

It was simple in concept. Completely wrap the item to be protected in a conductor. Metal walls, or aluminum foil, or chicken wire carried the dangerous current around the outside and what was inside never saw it.

The only way I am going to get Hodgepodge running again soon is to get this cage built.

The supernova EMP was unpredictable. It would be gone soon, but how soon? Days, weeks, months?

I can't wait that long.

Hodgepodge is a critical resource—besides, I need to talk to him.

The weight came back harder. He'd failed the girl. He had to succeed with Hodgepodge.

He picked up the hinge he was working on. He had to complete a tight copper grill all the way around the computer area, with something like an electromagnetic 'air-lock' so that he could get in and out. It had to hold all of Hodgepodge's electronics, including power supplies, a bank of large batteries, and a gasoline powered generator.

It's going to be noisy and smelly in here.

He had to make sure the exhaust was piped safely outside.

Mary Ellen walked in, carrying her Uzi hand-held machine gun. "Aren't you going to take that nap?"

He shook his head. "I'm tired, but I'm not sleepy."

"Yes you are." She looked at the empty racks of equipment. "But if you're awake enough to play with your tinker toys, then you can come with me."

Nothing could be done until he pulled another welding tank up from the basement anyway. He sighed.

"Okay, is it revolution time again?" He started untying the apron he was wearing.

She frowned, but at her own thoughts, not at him. "I hope not, but just in case, I want to move my gun collection."

"Ah! Road trip." He tried to smile.

They buttoned up the facility, checked the gas in the Caddie, and eased out onto the street.

It was one AM. There was traffic, and almost a sense of normalcy. However, the thousands of deserted cars, and the fact that the traffic was almost exclusively from older decades lent a surreal feel to the landscape.

The star was low in the west. It was the only light—blue hot like the mercury vapor streetlights that had been made obsolete by the orange sodium lamps. Still, it lit the sky enough to wash out all its competitors. Shadows of every tree and building were razor sharp.

Abe was the passenger. Mary Ellen didn't want him to drive as tired as he was, and for once he didn't contest her judgment.

He dozed off before they had gone five miles.

Mary Ellen Victor had several properties. One was a half-section farm on the other side of Rogers Texas, more than an hour's drive. There was a little house, but it wasn't lived in. She sharecropped the land to a serious farmer, and used a little piece of it down in a creek bottom as her gun range.

Abe had given up kidding her about her gun fetish. She didn't think it was funny, and as long as she kept her hobby at least a couple of millimeters this side of the law, he really had nothing to gripe about.

She and Frank had been active hunters, bringing in at least one meal each dove season, and occasionally returning from a vacation with a shipment of elk meat. Abe had never been in that part of their life. His most memorable experience with guns had been less than pleasant, being at a ringside seat during a hold-up at a pizza place. There was something about looking down the barrel of a gun that made for a lasting impression.

Mary Ellen started taking a stronger interest in the guns when she had to deal with Frank's modest collection after his death. She took them out and fired them. It took only a year for her hobby to grow to obsessive proportions.

They checked the locks when they arrived at the farmhouse, but nothing had been disturbed. Abe wondered whether he was doing the right thing, as he loaded all the guns and ammunition into the Caddie. Most of it fit in the capacious trunk, but the big box that contained the 50-caliber machine gun had to go in the back seat. Mary Ellen obsessively checked the paperwork and made sure she had all her permits, even though Abe suspected no one would ever care to check for them again.

As they eased back out onto the highway, the only light was the starglow, a false twilight of the supernova silhouetting the occasional tree or farmhouse on the western horizon. For a while, there would be two stars in competition for the Earth's attention.

They hit a bump—the county roads were due for another topping—and a belt of ammunition rattled off onto the floor. He turned his head.

At what point does this kind of precaution stop being eccentric and becomes sensible?

I hope we aren't there yet.

THE SCIENTIST

The old pickup burned more oil than petrol it seemed. Larry coughed as he pulled into the parking spot. The pickup did too when he turned off the switch. Cujo and Cathy Butler were at the door to greet him. He squeezed Janet's hand. They hadn't been married all that long, but leaving behind so many of their possessions in the town had managed to push her hormone-stressed composure over the edge. She tried to dry her eyes with the edge of a handkerchief.

"Did you get the screens?" Cujo went straight to the back of the pickup.

"No. It's a madhouse at the supply depot. It's radiation panic down there. Everyone was trying to get supplies to build a shelter. I have no idea what they were going to do with the screens."

Cathy sneered, "Someone should have told them that the X-rays and gamma rays can't get to us down here. The atmosphere is too thick. The only people who have to worry about radiation are the astronauts."

Cujo shook his head. "No, their systems went out with the first EMP, I am sure. There aren't any live astronauts left to worry about gammas."

No one said anything more. Tales of fatalities were coming in from all over the place. You can't collapse the technological infrastructure of modern civilization without a lot of people being caught under the rubble.

Larry looked at Cujo, "Have you been monitoring for radiation?"

He nodded. "Minor, down here. I can't tell much from the Geiger counter. It's just a hand held thing for prospectors. I wouldn't want to live with the counts elevated this way forever, but the peak should be gone soon."

"Can we find a way to get a better feel for what is coming at us? I would be a lot more comfortable knowing what kinds of invisibles are frying my insides."

Cathy was helping Janet unload their bags from the back of the pickup.

She nodded. "Maybe we could rig up a sandwich of shields and film. Which layers get fogged could tell us a lot about what is getting though."

Cujo nodded, "I'll put it together. I still have my old particle physics notes."

Larry had a moment of longing for his dead computer. His entire academic and professional life had been spiced with the help from colleagues in various disciplines, often in other countries, but always just an email away.

Now their community was entirely cut off from the outside world. There'd been some hope that amateur radio operators could make long distance contact. Indeed, there were a few of the old tube radio sets still available that had not been affected by the EMP, but long distance radio had always depended on ionized layers in the atmosphere. Natural mirrors allowed the radiowaves to bounce their way around the curve of the horizon.

But now, there was something wrong. The radios worked well at short range, but that was all. If you wanted to communicate with someone in another city, you went there face to face.

It is time we sent a courier to Canberra.

Larry rubbed the bruise on his left arm.

The mob at the lumberyard could be just the beginning. It wouldn't hurt to get a small squad of troops here to let people know there was still a government.

Constable Bern was there, doing his best to keep the mob from getting totally out of control. But he had his own priorities. Larry had almost been forced to leave. His plea that he was from the observatory held no weight. Only the vouchsafe of one of his neighbors kept Bern from classing him as an outsider. The lawman was very concerned about protecting Coonabarabran from outside looters.

It had been an eye-opener for Larry. What had Ed actually said? He thought he meant that the star would kill people, make them sick. But it now he wasn't so sure. He had seen the look in the Constable's eyes. He was worried about keeping the town alive, and radiation had been the very least of his worries.

Regression

THE WIZARD

Abe took a break. He'd been working all night long, and the tests were still running at a slow pace. There'd been more damage to the circuit cards than he'd hoped.

The city of Austin lived to a new clock. Just like daylight saving's time, people and schedules had adjusted over the past week to "star-time". The day started when Betelgeuse set, sometime around one AM. Everyone was home by star rise. No one had determined if there were health hazards from the star shine, but it "looked evil".

There was an annoying spot in his field of vision. He had stared at the star too long the night before. There was a whisper of fear that he had permanently damaged his sight, but Abe shook it off, refusing to acknowledge the possibility.

But I won't do that again.

He wasn't the only one. The brightness of the star was still much less than that of the sun, but it shone at night, and the eye reacted to the dimmer light by opening the iris wide—wide enough to let in too much damaging light.

KLBJ-AM, had come back on the air a couple of days earlier, using an obsolete tube transmitter, a diesel backup generator, and a DJ stationed out at the transmitter site at Hornsby Bend east of town with a stack of announcements to read. There were enough old cars with tube radios to supply the audience. Several times a day, he could hear someone heading down the road with the volume turned up high as a public service. It was the only news around.

And the news was uniformly bad.

There were the announcements of deaths, many deaths. Abe had expected accidents. The airports were closed. Shortly after the first wave of EMP, several planes had managed safe landings, but at least two airliners had gone down within the city. One crashed in the Montopolis area, wiping out scores of houses. One made it to the airport, but took out the terminal.

Whole neighborhoods had burned. Montopolis was only the first. The riots started as soon as the food stores were stripped. East Austin, the West Lynn area, and the Hyde Park area, all with many wood frame homes, were soon infernos. In a familiar refrain, only a small fraction of the fire trucks could respond. Their engines wouldn't start.

With the food gone, and the water supply soon drained, the exodus began. Abe wasn't sure how long it would last.

The Whiting building was set well back from the highway and for that he was grateful. He watched the line of people walking north. He could make out the families, the children herded by the adults. All were carrying their possessions, some using brightly colored toy wagons that probably wouldn't last more than a few days. From his distance, he couldn't read their faces.

I'm glad of that. I don't want to know.

Where they were heading he didn't know. He suspected they didn't either.

If I had a family, I would get some seeds by hook or crook and go looking for a deserted farmhouse.

He reflected on the number of abandoned houses like the one Mary Ellen owned—a relic of the time when family farms were far smaller than the enterprises that had superseded them. Maybe soon they would be used again.

If too many combines and tractors have been taken out, then farming will go back to being more labor intensive.

The realization came as a flood.

I am watching history in reverse.

The city was depopulating, agriculture was heading back towards the age of small family farms. Transportation and communication were moving back to earlier technologies.

Hmm. If the semiconductor industry doesn't get back on its feet quickly, old style telephones and telegraphy should still work.

The semiconductor question was his big worry. Modern wafer fabs were huge, complex operations that absolutely depended on computers and electronic controls. If the EMP took those out, then the fab would be down until the computers could be repaired. Repairs could only happen if there were adequate stocks of undamaged semiconductors.

We have a chicken-and-egg problem. I just hope there are enough stocks of good chips to get us back running again.

Abe's company would be out of luck if there weren't. He designed specialized semiconductors, but he never had the capability to build them. That was the job of the wafer foundry companies.

It would all depend on the stockpiles.

Abe's repair work on Hodgepodge had shown him one thing, the larger the item, the more likely it was to be fried. Each strip of copper on the computer card was an antenna, picking up the EMP and creating a voltage. A longer strip of conductor was just that much more likely to develop a damaging voltage. Luckily, he was in the business of building electronic circuits. Prototypes needed an extensive parts bin.

When he finally finished the Faraday cage, the first test had been exciting. All his life at the workbench, the joke had been the 'smoke test'. You applied power and checked to see if any of the magic smoke escaped.

In the tongue-in-cheek mythology of the soldering iron set, magic smoke was the active ingredient inside integrated circuits. If the case cracked, the magic smoke would leak out and render the part useless.

The moment of truth came. The rumbling generator applied power to the computer system. A power supply had smoked most spectacularly.

Abe had been paranoid about losing power to Hodgepodge—the effects of any blackout were severe. Long ago, he had engineered the power supply to tolerate a failure. There were four identical main power supplies. One could handle the load in an emergency.

Abe ran for the fire extinguisher to put out the small but acrid fire before it damaged anything else, but the three good power supplies took over the job from their dead companion and fed good clean filtered power to the card cage.

The 'brain cells' of Hodgepodge were thousands of identical little computers, each with its own CPU and private memory, and a high speed connection to nearby other nodes. Many of them were damaged as well. While the Hodgepodge operating software could run on as few as seven cards, failures that wedged the high-speed communications channels caused whole areas of otherwise good cards to shut down.

He raced to check the status screen on his only remaining functional terminal. His heart fell to his feet. Almost the whole array was lit red. With fumbling fingers, he sent a few test programs winding their way through the maze, but the failure was too complex to pinpoint the dead cards. The vast majority of the cards had no connection to the outside world, and had to rely on their siblings for data. He had a test program that would detect a single dead card by asking its neighbors, but it was overwhelmed.

Abe started taking out cards one at a time, and plugging them into a test jig, but after the first handful, he knew he didn't have the patience for this kind of fix. He'd never been patient. Some times he could get in a groove and work on a task so intently that only sleep or starvation could pull him out of it, waking without a clue which day it was, but that was brain-work. Checking an endless set of identical cards for error was too mind numbing.

The seventh good card went into a holding rack, and he had an inspiration. Sweating, he pushed the burnt out maintenance cart into the protected computer room. Removing the dedicated control computer, he installed a baby version of Hodgepodge's card cage. With seven good cards a very basic version of the system came up green.

The little mobile robot had no access to any of the higher functions, no speech, no common sense database, no understanding of the English language. But Abe coded a template of the work he wanted done, and turned it loose.

The robot made a few mistakes at first, until it built a good map of how to move and how to make its gripper arm apply the correct amount of force. Soon, however, it started work, pulling each card in sequence and inserting it into the test jig.

Two days later, the robot was still at work, finding good brain cells for itself.

Abe watched the refugee traffic, musing about the stack of bad cards, and wondering if his stash of repair chips was up to the task.

There was the rumble of an old diesel bus, and as he watched, it moved into view.

A yellow school bus, and it was full. Arms and heads were sticking out the windows. About twenty people with baggage were riding on the roof. It was like something he'd seen in movies from Third World countries of decades ago.

Refugees, fleeing from the city. He shook his head. The supernova has peaked in brightness. The EMP's were almost gone. If they could just hold out a little longer. It would all be better soon.

THE WITCH

She smelled him coming. The hunger was clawing its way up her chest. She could feel it in her throat. Her jaw ached.

Time had drifted away. The pit was forever, she knew that. Escape was useless. The only thing that mattered was her hunger.

Egh dropped in with her, landing on his rear legs with grace, absorbing the energy of the fall in tight muscles.

She leapt, screaming. The shock of her attack knocked him over. Her teeth were locked on his shoulder. She bit hard, but it was like old thick leather over bone. She clawed at him with her... fingernails, but there was no purchase.

The old scientist's shock and momentary fear were strong in her mind. Then, he swatted her away. She slammed against the wall and everything went black.

...

Sharon swam back to awareness through a thick soup of pain, and the amused thoughts of the Cerik. Everything was black.

My eyes!

She tried to flail her arms, but they couldn't move.

Oh. She was in a sack, just like when she had been captured, hung head down from a pole. She blinked her eyes, and was reassured to see the darkness change. For the moment, she was still whole.

Outside her sack, the room contained Egh, Tenthonad and two of Egh's assistants. She could hear a hissing. They were laughing.

Old Egh, too tough to bite.

Sharon remembered another time:

...

She felt Hattie coming all afternoon. The old lady couldn't move very fast—the arthritis—but she never complained. Sharon could feel her surprise, and she worked hard to keep from accidentally reading what her 'Lovey' had for her.

Hattie had become her last contact with the rest of humanity after her mother died. The dear ordered food delivered from town, and then Sharon usually came over to her house to trade garden produce or her latest handicraft for items she couldn't grow.

Her mother's friend never thought about her as a telepath, just as a gifted child. Her success in bringing her surprises came from something quite simple, and Sharon thought, quite profound. Hattie was at peace with herself. She wasn't like so many people who made a decision, and then spent every waking moment churning over the idea in their heads, arguing with themselves. Hattie got an idea, acted, and then allowed no more than a pleasurable anticipation to bleed into the current moment.

The surprise that day was a kitten, eyes barely open to the strange and monstrous beings that were holding it. After a moment, Felicia tried to bite the tip of her index finger. The tiny nubs, of course, didn't hurt her one bit. Hattie and she laughed at the adorable little ball of fur.

...

Sharon recognized it well. Egh and the others held her no ill will. She was the kitten.

Her pain and fear bubbled up. She started crying.

"I'm so hungry!"

Her keening, a long drawn out cry caused the assembled Cerik to fall silent.

She didn't know why she'd attacked Egh. She didn't want to eat him, or even hurt him. The constant immersion into the dark angels' predatory lives was changing her. She was losing herself.

Her cry changed into a draining, hacking cough, finally fading into silent sobbing. Her mind tried to escape. She threw herself out towards the far mass of humanity.

Hattie! Where are you?

Down to the planet, she frantically searched though a mob only slightly less panicked than she was. The confused and frightened people seemed endless. She hunted for her home—for anything familiar.

It took time. She dipped into minds, comfortable, familiar human minds, even though the thoughts weren't in English. Each stranger was like the embrace of a long lost friend. She soaked up humanity even as each provided a signpost back to her destination. Soon the thoughts echoed in English. Quickly came the flavor of Texas and then the minds of people from Wimberley, as familiar as the trees on her property even though she'd never seen them.

The relief of the familiar lasted only a moment.

Hattie was gone. She found the man who had thrown her out of her house. He regretted that she had fallen. He was sorry that the old lady had hit her head. But he had to protect his own family, and he couldn't help her. There were no doctors. She was old and would have died soon anyway.

Sharon hissed anger through her teeth and reached across space and squeezed tight in the man's brain. She felt him fall and cry out in agony. She pressed harder, trying to push all of her rage back at the murderer.

The backwash of his pain into her mind was too great. With a sob, she released him. She couldn't kill him, as much as she wanted it.

She scanned her home. There was a family there too. Felicia was there, puzzled by the change, intolerant of the little boy who followed her around and who kept trying to pull her tail.

Bile climbed up her throat. She would have vomited, if there had been anything in her stomach.

It was all for nothing!

Her great sacrifice; leaving her home, giving up Hattie and Felicia and all the others, all so that they would be safe.

I'm just a stupid, stupid girl.

She stretched towards Austin to find Abe.

And there he was, still alive, still strong. But his mind spiked with pain each thrust of the shovel, digging a grave deep into the earth. She fled, back to her own body.

Nausea, and the gnawing, acid of her hunger became all. She cried out in pain. The world swirled and went black.

. . .

The relief didn't last, as she was pulled out of the blackness by the rude jab of Egh's claw. Asca was there too, probing her mind for signs of life.

Get out!

Asca pulled back. Egh poked her again, afraid that she was dying.

I am starving to death! I cannot live on a single can of green beans. I must have more food!

Asca turned to Egh. There was a brief conversation. And then the sack was dropped to the floor. She was released.

Asca sent an image. Like a pantomime, he was asking, **Show us what you need.**

Egh grabbed her around the waist and carried her like a rag doll through the corridors of the ship, past dozens of puzzled Cerik, to a large storeroom.

Sharon shivered with renewed hunger pangs as she saw the treasure. Two eighteen-wheelers filled the room, one lying on its side. The trailers were ripped open, spilling their contents all over the floor in deep piles.

So this is where he got the green beans.

She picked up a can of corn, and a dried, desiccated loaf of bread. She stepped carefully through the supermarket supplies that never got to their destination. The corn fell from her hands as she spied a canned ham. It even had the little key. She could open it herself.

And there was a bag of candy bars. She snatched it. And there was bottled fruit juice.

She tore open a jar of beef jerky strips and started chewing on one, letting the juices bleed strength back into her body. There was a bag of disposable diapers. She opened it carefully and dumped the diapers. The plastic bag worked as a grocery bag as she filled it, concentrating on protein and fat, with a leavening of other foods her body needed. The canned and bottled items looked good. Bagged things were dried out. Freeze-dried, she suspected, by a trip through the vacuum of space.

She looked at Egh, and started back toward the entrance, carrying her bag. He reached for her again, but she backed quickly away.

"No. I want to walk."

She stared at his eyes. He wasn't a telepath, but he understood what she wanted. He let her lead the way out.

The bag felt wonderful as she clutched it to her chest.

I will die. But maybe not today.

Reorganization

THE SEER

Ed watched the water. The boats were still there, but no one water-skied anymore. There were canoes, and sailboats, but the people weren't having fun. They looked busy.

I wish I had a boat. His scooter had not been returned.

Just lucky I have no place to go.

Lake Austin was nothing more than a fat section of the Colorado River. If the Mansfield Dam above and the Tom Miller Dam below could keep doing their job, then the lake would continue to make a good highway.

A fish broke the surface. He caught just a glimpse of its shiny scales, not enough to identify what kind.

Maybe I need to get a fishing pole.

He'd seen lots of people taking that route to supplement their food supplies.

He wasn't in any danger of running low, but his neighbors hadn't his advanced warning. With one exception, they had to rely on the contents of their kitchens, for as long as it lasted.

Ed smiled at the one exception he'd seen. The day after the star had killed most of the cars, people were drawn out of their houses by the tinny jingle playing from a white van. It was a Blue Bunny ice-cream man. He edged slowly down the lane, his shotgun high and visible. He had his freezer of ice cream treats, and for as long as the gas in his van held out, he was going to peddle them.

But he wasn't taking cash. The crowd around him were adults. The kids were pushed back to the outside of the circle. Stern-faced, he explained his terms. By the time he left, his freezer was filled with clothes, ammunition, knives, and other good trade goods. And some families ate that day.

It had taken a day or so, but most families were together now. Luckily, the children had been home, and working parents finally made their way back, many with blisters from unanticipated hikes.

The cliff above was dark against the sky. The girl with her horse hadn't been visible since the first day of the shine. He hoped the horse survived to be more than a meal for starving families.

...

Angela was barely conscious. She was wedged against the steering wheel. The car was nose down into the ditch. The sound of the horse's hooves caused her to stir. The star was visible just above the horizon.

...

What? He shook off the vision.
Angela. She's in trouble.

He looked to the east, but it was still a couple of hours until starshine. He tried to will the vision back, but it was just a wisp at the edge of his awareness.

It was Angela, in a car wreck.

"I need that horse," he mumbled.

...

The climb had him breathing fast and sweating, when he knocked on the door. There was a doorbell, and he had pushed it, before realizing that it was a useless gesture.

The door opened three inches, and a man peered out. "Yes. What do you want?"

Ed tried to look harmless. He held out the grocery sack. "My name is Ed Morgan. I'm your neighbor down at the base of the cliff. I'd like to borrow your horse."

The sack of canned goods and sack of flour made a wonderful introduction. The door opened wide enough to enable an illusion of neighborliness. Mr. Black listened to his story sympathetically, and neither of them mentioned the pistol he was holding.

Ed tried to explain, without sounding crazy. "She should have arrived yesterday. I've waited as long as I can. I just know she's had some problem."

Mr. Black asked, "My daughter said you have a scooter. It is dead as well?"

Young Helen, who had edged up close to the door, spoke, "The other man took it."

Ed smiled down at her. "Yes, she's right. My boss was here when the star happened, and his car didn't survive.

"I am really worried about Angela. I'll have to go out on foot if you can't help me."

Mr. Black glanced casually at the sack of food, and then worriedly at his daughter. "Dadbert is Helen's horse. I would hate for anything to happen to him."

Ed looked at the girl. They had waved from a distance, but this was the first chance she had to see him up close. He tried to look honest.

After a long moment with a frown of doubt on her face, she said. "I guess it's okay. Do you know how to ride?"

. . .

Riding was painful—that was his first lesson. The saddle was small and the stirrups were much too short for his legs. Helen tried to get him to try her riding helmet, but it was hopeless.

The father watched, his pistol in his belt, as the little girl lectured him in laborious detail about how the horse had to be approached, and how to handle the reins, and how to keep him from heading off on his own course. Ed could feel an echo from the past. Some instructor had made a distinct impression on the girl, and she was doing her best to pass it all on to him.

Ed had his usual luck in pre-guessing which way the horse would lurch, and he passed Helen's professional inspection. Mr. Black had his own final words. He was to take good care of the horse, and to get it back in the pasture as soon as possible. In exchange, they got the food, and Ed owed them a debt.

Ed nodded. Favors from neighbors were clearly the only route to survival if things didn't change for the better soon.

The ride was slower than he would have liked. Dadbert put up his objections as soon as they got out of sight of his mistress. Ed used his knees and the reins as instructed, and spoke firmly in the tones Helen had suggested. It was clearly a contest of wills, and Ed won, just barely.

The vision, reinforced by the actual events, made finding the path easy. Ed followed the main highway until they reached the creek. The star was shining brightly by the time he found her car, smashed against the steep bank. Angela was delirious, with a gashed, bleeding leg.

THE SCIENTIST

Janet Kelly set a bowl of chowder on her husband's desk, careful not to disturb the stacks of photos and papers.

"Thanks," he mumbled, but it was another minute before the aroma penetrated his concentration and he realized that there was food. He put aside his work and tackled the meal.

Bringing her up here to the observatory had been a good move. Things were getting too strange down the mountain. Sleeping on a pair of cots was not too much fun, but it was better than spending every minute worrying about her.

The town had survived the early panic, but now it had gone into a control phase. There were roadblocks up at each entrance with citizens taking turns keeping outsiders away. There'd been two incidents already—bandits with a car and some guns and not expecting Constable Bern. Some were seeing the national radio silence as an invitation to anarchy.

That should be better soon. He looked at the large paper chart they had pasted to the wall. It was a spreadsheet—a database of their findings. Down one column was the number of stations they could pick up by turning the dial of the old tube Hammarlund shortwave radio from one end to the other. That was one of Janet's jobs. The number was growing steadily—up to a dozen. That was still just a trickle compared to the hundreds available before the supernova. Then, stations had been packed so densely that it took a gentle touch on the dial to keep one station from bleeding in on top of the next.

Janet also gave them a summary of the news. One of the radio signals was an ABC station in Queensland. It seemed that the really big stations had an edge over the smaller ones. Big stations had to pump out high voltages and high currents anyway. The EMP had fewer sensitive components to fry.

Each of the stations must come from places where there was a source of electricity more stable that what they had on the mountain. Luckily, the observatory's diesels were old and simple.

World news was predictable. National governments were just not able to handle the event. Australia had made the call to turn all troops over to the local cities until communications could be re-established. The Malaysian station was claiming that everything was under control, but no one on the mountain believed it. Time would tell. Perhaps it was a measure of their pessimism that they were keeping a log, reporting a summary of the news.

The EMP column, based on how many times they had to throw the circuit breaker on the main feed to the observatory floor, was down to zero.

Larry was working on his analysis of the latest run of Cathy's radiation counter. He had the eight developed frames of film laid out in a row on his desk. The frames had been arranged as a sandwich; film, paper, film, waxed paper, film, aluminum foil, film, sheet aluminum, film, thin steel, film, thicker steel, film, another layer of thicker steel, and the final layer of film. The sandwich was set up on the roof for an hour.

Weak radiation was represented by little dots on the top layer. Stronger radiation would penetrate deeper into the stack, until the amount of shielding would stop it. So, the number of dots and how many sheets of film each radioactive particle touched gave a good measure of the type, strength and volume of the radiation they saw.

Larry had taken on the job of analysis personally. Only he and Janet were aware of Ed's predictions, and that comment about people getting sick wouldn't leave him.

"Anything I should know about?" Janet was back, and they had been married long enough for her to be able to read his expressions.

He leaned back in his chair. "I don't know." She moved closer, sitting on the arm of the chair. He put his arm around her.

"Well, is it good or bad?"

"Your data is good, honey."

"And the others?"

"Not as good as I had hoped."

She bumped a little closer. "Tell me."

His eyes went to the chart on the wall. "Okay, see the UV reading. It keeps going up. The ozone layer that was protecting us from the sun's ultraviolet light is weakening rapidly."

"But it was doing that before the supernova."

He shook his head. "Not like this. Before, it was a seasonal thing, getting a few percent worse each year. This reading shows the ozone is being destroyed at an enormous rate. The only thing I can think of is heavy gamma radiation from the star. The atmosphere keeps most of that away from us, but if the ozone layer is demolished, then it could take years to get it back. Don't count on any sunbathing at the beach for a long time."

"So you are telling me that we can't go out at night because of the star, and we can't go out in the day because of the sun?"

He nodded, "Something like that. Long sleeves and hats for certain. I don't know what the long term effects on crops and animals will be."

"I hadn't thought of that." They shared a moment of silence as their thoughts tried to get a handle on the idea. Janet's degree had been in anthropology, and she had some idea of the adaptations that cultures could make to stressful situations, so perhaps she had a bit more confidence in the future than he did. But when he started running his finger over the sheet where he had been making his calculations, she frowned.

"What do your figures show?"

"How much do you know about the different kinds of radiation?"

"Some. Talk it out. Tell me what you are doing and I'll ask questions if I'm missing something."

He nodded. Explaining something to someone else was often the clearest way to shake out the cobwebs in his own thoughts.

"Okay." He picked up the magnifier and put it down on the first sheet of film. "Take a look."

He scooted the chair. She moved over and peered down on the mainly clear sheet of film in front of a white sheet of paper.

"I see a lot of little black dots."

"Each of those is a place where a fast moving particle hit the emulsion and exposed it. Some of those were just weak alpha particles that couldn't penetrate a piece of paper. See," he pointed to the next sheet, "this film was on the other side of the paper."

She looked. "Not so many dots."

He pointed, "Look at the dots right here, and compare them to the ones on the same part of the first sheet."

"I see what you mean. Some of them are the same dots."

"Yes. To get to the second sheet, it had to go through the first sheet. Each sheet has more shielding than the one before it. Each dot on a lower sheet represents a stronger, faster moving particle."

She moved the magnifier down the row, sometimes backing up and re-checking the previous film.

"What is happening here?" She pointed to a fatter than normal spot.

"That is high speed particle. It hit the top layer so hard that it broke some atoms into pieces and each fragment went on to expose even more film."

She worked her way to the last sheet. "These are the strongest ones?"

He nodded. "I have to count them on a small square and use that count to figure how many are getting through."

"Getting through what?"

"Anything. Almost anything."

She put her hand on her belly. "How bad is it?"

"Not too bad. Not yet. We aren't close to the health hazard level."

"Not yet?"

He nodded. "We have been running one of these every night. Yesterday, I thought the radiation level was going down. This set shows different. The weaker radiation is still dropping. The strong stuff is increasing."

He put his hand on hers. "This dome is aluminum and steel. The rooms are built of concrete. The outside walls are nearly a foot thick. You need to stay inside whenever the star is up. You stay safe. Understand."

She nodded. "How bad will it get?"

"I have no idea. I never thought it would be this bad. From the very beginning, it has been worse than everyone thought."

Janet asked angrily, "How can that happen? I thought the star had peaked."

He got up and went over to the chart. "It has peaked. No doubt about it. All the neutrinos, X-rays and gamma rays are falling off, I am sure of it, even though the only way we can measure those is by indirection and guesswork."

He didn't say it out loud, but it was becoming clear that when Betelgeuse exploded, it wasn't by any means an even flash in all directions. There were flares that were hotter in some direction than others.

And Earth was staring down the barrel of one of the big flares.

Cujo entered the room. "A truck is coming up the road."

Larry had Janet spread the word, and he followed Cujo out the main entrance. The prospect of visitors had an edge to it, especially after the reports of looting down at Coonabarabran.

It was still pre-dawn, and the star had set. The big cubical shaped building containing one of the telescopes was a black silhouette against the remaining stars. It had been awhile since Larry had thought to look at them.

The road up to the observatory from Timor Road was steep and curved. The headlights of the approaching truck lighting the trees were the brightest things around. When they turned into the parking lot, Larry had to hold up his hand to shield his eyes against the glare. He couldn't make out who it was.

The truck stopped and the lights died. It was Bern, and some other man he didn't recognize.

"Hello. Who is in charge here?" the constable asked.

Larry looked around. "The director is gone. I am permanent staff here. We are down to a skeleton crew. Most of the rest had families back on the coast. What can we do for you?"

The two men looked at each other for an instant.

The constable spoke. "We had a train come through Coona a couple of days ago. It doesn't look like we are going to get any help from Canberra. The national government is having enough problems keeping Sydney and Darwin from going up in flames. The towns closer to the coast have it much worse than we do. Bands of refugees have taken over places like Tamworth and Orange. You've heard that we have put up road blocks on the Newell highway?"

Larry nodded. "We have a radio. Some places are broadcasting. What you say isn't surprising."

"What we want to do is bring you people back into town where it will be safer, and to move your generator down the hill, too. We have to get everything running on a self-sustaining basis, at least until the Federal or State government can get things running again."

"You want to shut us down?" Cujo's face was ominous in the dim light of the headlight reflections.

"You can't shut us down," Larry confirmed in a calmer voice. "We've been very careful with our fuel supply, only firing up the generator to steer the telescopes and to run some critical instruments, but we don't have nearly enough fuel to keep the whole town running. It would all be gone in an hour."

"We thought of that," the other man with Bern said. "We traded with the train. We have a whole rail car of diesel. We know we can't run the whole town, but the medical centre and the phone system and a few other places could be put to order."

Larry started feeling a panic. Perhaps these people were serious. The power lines had been dead since the first night. How were people handling the problems of no refrigeration, and no pumps for the water supply?

"But, the work we are doing is serious, irreplaceable!" Cujo cried. "It will be a thousand years before we get another chance to make these kinds of observations."

The Constable shook his head. "I understand you are doing important work, but these are not ordinary times. People's safety has to come first. We've already stopped people heading towards Warrumbungle National Park, thinking they could wait out the troubles there. This place is not exactly hidden. People will see your lights and come here. You are not safe."

Larry let Cujo do most of the arguing. Others were coming out of the buildings to see what all the noise was about.

He looked out at the sky. Cujo was right. The observations they were making were irreplaceable. They had been gathering the most in-depth set of observations of a supernova, especially the early stages, that would ever likely exist. It would be a century before all their data was understood. Even now, the UKST telescope was taking a series of exposures of the space around Betelgeuse to be used as reference when the shock wave of its explosion expanded into that space. The TTF was on line, after long hours of repair. They were trying to look at the star with all the detail they could muster, saving the data for the time when they would have the equipment to analyze it.

If all their hard work to get the electronics back up and running was to be ruined by having the electric plug pulled on them, it would be too much to bear.

He looked out over the field of stars. He loved the night sky. He even loved the malignant stranger that had caused everyone to scurry for cover when it topped the horizon. Each point of light was a channel of inspiration. Maybe, someday, he would understand how it all worked.

There was a glow on the horizon. Was it dawn yet?

But... that wasn't the east.

He turned back to the knot of angry men. They were grouped, the constable and his associate, facing the astronomers.

"You can't afford to shut us down!" Larry interrupted, his voice raised as loud as he could manage. "This isn't a political problem, it isn't a weather problem. This is an astronomy problem, and you can't afford to put your only astronomers out of business."

Bern was plainly forcing himself to keep his patience. "You're wrong. I can't afford to coddle academics at the expense of the whole town. There isn't anything you can do for us up here. If your work is so important, then why didn't anyone warn us this was coming?"

Cujo spoke, quietly for once, "You are talking to the man who first detected the supernova. He tried to warn us all. He tried to make the whole world listen, but no one would."

Larry didn't remember it that way, but Bern seemed impressed, so he bit his tongue.

Modesty can be reclaimed later. *Right now I need to make a point.*

"Constable, at this point in time, astronomy is more than ivory tower academics. We are the only eyes watching invisible things. Invisible things can kill. Let us keep our instruments running and we can make predictions."

"Predictions?"

"Yes. The first one is free. Come here."

He walked them out of the headlight glare and pointed to the wavering lights on the horizon.

"See that?"

"Aurora," someone commented.

"Right. The *Aurora Australis*, the Southern Lights. We are only about 32 degrees south of the equator. We shouldn't be seeing this here. But I predict it will get stronger each night, do you want to know why?"

He nodded.

"The sun spits out energetic particles, enough radiation to make us all sick, to kill wholesale when a solar flare occurs. But, it doesn't kill us, because of the Earth's magnetic field. The radiation particles are caught in the magnetic lines of force and kept away from the surface.

"But when the magnetic field is overloaded, the aurora occurs, like a neon sign, bleeding off energy as light. Since the magnetic field bends down at the poles, that is where the aurora is seen, unless there is an extra strong flux of particles striking the earth, then it comes north."

He waved his hand at the glowing curtains of light. "If we can see this here, then the Earth is being blasted by an intense wave of radiation. Up here at the observatory, we are measuring many things about the supernova, and the radiation is one of them."

There was an objection, "The star is fading. The worst is over."

"I don't think so," Larry shook his head. "There are different kinds of radiation. Astronomers are used to seeing X-rays and Gamma radiation from stars. We tend to think of charged particle radiation as coming from the sun only.

"But here, we have something new. Charged particles don't travel at the speed of light like the X and gamma rays. But when Betelgeuse blew up, there were some particles so energetic, so hot that they headed away at speeds very close to the speed of light.

"They're just now arriving. Spread out on my desk at this minute are the readings we took today. I saw radiation so intense it will punch right though the roofs of your houses.

"Do you really want us to stop looking now?"

Restoration

THE WITCH

Sharon coughed up another mass of mucus. She knew exactly what was happening, she had engineered it, but it was no less painful for that. With constant attention, she could keep her lungs healing as fast as the air was damaging them. At least, now she had the food necessary to fuel the process. Egh was constantly checking on her. She'd now survived longer than any of his other test subjects and he was expecting to find her dead at any moment.

I'm stronger than he thinks.

Not that she cared to tell him that. They were leaving her alone at the moment, letting her die in peace. If they thought she was special, it might make her death more painful.

She closed her eyes and turned her attention to the crew, her captors. They were still waiting. There was an undercurrent, the constant struggle for position that the Cerik lived for, but many of them were dropping into a state of mind they called the *dan*. She recognized it. It was another predator thing these interstellar aliens shared with her kitten. They were half-awake, thinking of nothing, but alert for signs of the prey.

Sharon could feel the pain coming from her home planet. She wondered if this was what her mother had experienced. Surely not. Her mother had spoken of a whole planet dying.

People were dying, that was certain. She was lucky to have this distance from it all.

The Cerik were waiting for something more. They had Asca, their tele-path, scanning the planet regularly, looking for signs, signs that the humans were broken, signs they could move in with no serious resistance.

They want a sign that everyone is like me—just waiting to die.

She didn't let herself think of resistance. Her attack on Egh had only underlined how useless that would be. She felt as if she were in a Bible sto-ry—Daniel in the Lions Den. Momma's books on mysticism and religions hadn't totally ignored Judeo-Christian thought. Even Daniel with God's blessing didn't try to subdue the lions, she remembered. He could only hope to avoid their teeth.

She shivered. The wound ached, although it was mostly healed. It was just as well that Tenthonad's mind could not be read. His memory of the taste of her blood was something she never wanted to experience.

I want to go home!

She was tired of constant fear.

Ignoring the distant pain, she pushed her perception toward Earth.

I want to feel human again.

She centered on Austin, not wanting to go back to her invaded home. Other than Felice, there was no one there for her any more.

Above the noise, she felt a familiar mind, crying out in despair. It pulled her in. It was Ed!

She's dying! It's all my fault. I should never have invited her out here.

Sharon touched the edges of his mind. **Hello, Ed.**

Ed reacted. She could feel him dislodged from his thoughts, **Oh no, I am losing it again! She needs me. I can't let the visions claim me.**

Wait! You're okay, Ed. Sharon tried to make her own thoughts clear. It was not at all like Asca, where they had to guess at each other's ideas and intents, since words had no meaning between them.

Ed's mind was racing. Just barely, he entertained the thought that this vision wasn't a relapse of his childhood insanity.

Hello, Ed. This is Sharon. We haven't spoken in years. Do you re-member me?

Sharon? A memory, a long sunny afternoon, when he was eight, crept back to the edge of his awareness. **Flowers. I remember wildflowers.**

Sharon nodded, although no one could see her in her pit. She too re-membered the day. It had been a warm spring day, with the bluebonnets and firewheels and wine cups and all the myriad other colorful inhabitants of a Central-Texas April gracing the fields near her house. Her mother had slept late and she wanted to pick a bouquet for the table, to surprise her when she woke. A little boy, confused and far away, but somehow close to her, had been doing his own flower picking. They both reached for an Indian Paintbrush at the same instant, and somehow they connected.

You're my imaginary friend, Ed recalled, with an undercurrent of fond memory. They'd connected a handful of times over the years, always by accident. The last time, he'd been under a strain and forced the connection closed, with no explanation.

I'm not imaginary, Ed. We are telepaths, just sharing thoughts. It is so good to talk to you. I have been lonely for some human words.

Sharon? I remember you, but I know you're imaginary. Dr. Jenny explained it to me. You are a 'compensating invention'. It shows that I'm lonely.

We're both lonely, Ed.

There was something like a handshake between them. They were unique, forced by their talents to the far edge of human companionship.

Overriding worry creep back to the top of his mind. She asked, **What's Angela's problem?**

Ed turned his eyes back to his patient, still breathing heavily, asleep on the bed. **She was in a car wreck. I brought her here, but I don't know what's wrong with her. I felt for broken bones, but I have no idea what kinds of injuries she has. She's bleeding inside. When I cleaned her up, her stool was real dark. When she coughs, the mucus is pink. And she never wakes up! I try to feed her, but she can't take any kind of solid food.**

I'm going to lose her. She'll die on me, and it is all my fault! He drifted off into his worry cycle, repeating the thoughts that would not let him go.

Ed! Don't leave me. We need to talk.

Sorry, Sharon. I can't handle this. I'm losing the only woman I want, and now I am relapsing into insanity.

Telepathy, Ed. It's just telepathy. I am not imaginary.

But I'm not a telepath! I've tried—believe me I've tried. I can read the future, but not thoughts.

Sharon could feel his confidence, even though she knew he was wrong. Would it help to argue with him? Probably not.

She could distract him, however. **Ed, I have an idea. Do you know what a spirit guide is?**

I've heard of it. A dead person comes back to help a living psychic.

I'm your spirit guide. Let me help you with Angela.

What can you do?

What indeed? If she were there, she could probe the girl's injuries. Could she focus through Ed? It was something like the historical psychic Edgar Cayce was reported to have done.

Ed, I want you do sit down close to her. Put one hand over her forehead. Put the other on her chest. Can you do that?

Ed's objection about imaginary friends and imaginary help came and went as unworthy. He was doing no better. Anything was worth trying.

He moved his chair next to the bed and placed his hands where he was directed. Sharon was pleased that the sensation of his hands on his girl friend's body was dominantly concerned with the heat of her fever.

Now it was up to her.

She became the Eye, and flashed instantly across 200,000 miles into his head, and down through his hands.

Angela was trapped, still, in her car, screaming to be let out, re-living the crash when her wheels lost traction in the night. Sharon could not even sense the body, so strong was Angela's nightmare.

Angela. Don't panic. It's okay, you're safe.

Unfortunately, the girl was not telepathic in the least, and her comforting thoughts were like a brief shower on a volcano, lost as steam before they ever made an impact. However, Sharon was not without experience.

There were channels into the brain, blood vessels that kept it supplied with oxygen. She knew how to mimic the effect of nitrogen compounds that could restrict or expand the cells in the walls and alter the blood flow.

With a practiced hand, she reduced blood flow to the lower brain, quieting the panic, and forcing Angela over into a natural sleep. It wouldn't last, but with her mind quieted, she could turn to the other problems.

Time was always elusive when Sharon was deep in the interior worlds. She didn't know how long she was at it, but the girl's injuries were extensive.

First priority was to seal off with healing tissue the numerous internal ruptures. With her recent experience in her own body, she was able to make good progress.

Sharon did nothing for the rib fractures other than make a note of their location. The leg injury was infected, and she was able to handle that. As expected, the blood chemistry was wildly off their norms. There was not much she could do about that either—not via a long distance remote contact.

After noting the types and locations of the infections that had taken advantage of her body's weakened defenses, she only stopped a moment to kill off a grain-of-sand sized tumor that was starting in her liver, before returning to her mind.

Without access to Angela's mind, she could do little about the trauma. Ed would have to take care of that. She probed deep into the girl's memories, amused at her vision of Ed, and carefully explored formative emotional experiences. It was a dangerous plan, but the only other choice was to let her stay in her coma.

When Ed opened his eyes, Sharon was momentarily confused. **Am I back?**

Ed probed with a thought, **Hello? Sharon?**

Hello, Ed. We are making progress.

Will she live?

With care, she will. I've stopped the internal bleeding. Get paper and pencil. I have a list for you.

Sharon took her time, making sure he got it all down. With her situation, there were no guarantees she'd still be around to make any corrections. Diet, where to put the pillows, detailed massages; all the things that the girl needed were written down in a big checklist.

But that is not the most important thing. And with that, she detailed what she had learned from the girl's mind.

Ed paid attention, but as soon as Sharon finished, he was up on his feet. His mind was already turning to the practical, and letting the telepathic connection slowly dissolve. He went to start heating the water she had recommended for the first step. Finally, he was able to do something for his Angela.

Sharon realized he was busy, and moved off. It had been so nice to be with someone who cared about her. She came to herself, crying quiet tears in her porcelain cell.

It's petty of me.

Ed wasn't hers. She had no claim on his attention. But she was jealous of Angela, even as she prayed for her recovery.

Everywhere I turn, someone is dying. At least I saved one life. Is that enough to make my life worth the living, before the Cerik cut me open?

Her own worries were still there, waiting to drain out even the little bit of joy she had at making contact with Ed again after so long. She tried to shake her fears, but it was hard.

I wonder how Abe is doing?

THE WIZARD

Abe looked up from his work, splicing nonstandard optical fibers into the test harness. He watched Hodgepodge build fresh circuit boards, grateful that at least something from the old life had come back. With 90% of the computing capacity working, HP's software loaded and came up painlessly. Abe could feel a little bit of the slower response, but cut off from the Internet and the outside world, Hodgepodge was also doing a lot less. Abe had nothing to complain about.

Whiting Design Center was a strange place now. The rattle of the generator and its diesel smell was an annoying reminder of how fragile this island of technology was. The city brought limited hydroelectric power back on line. It was tightly rationed and only for a few hours each day. With all the fires, much of the city was missing the transmission lines. Still, there wasn't enough capacity for the area that could be served. The word was out—use air-conditioning, and your house will be cut off.

The city had depended heavily on coal and gas-fired plants and that infrastructure wasn't back up. The coal depended on the trains, and that level of co-operation across the state and across the country had totally broken down.

The Texas National Guard soldiers were visible on the streets, and a paper flier was widely distributed with the Governor's declaration of martial law. Abe was glad for the visible sign of returning control, but he was also conscious that he was a conspicuous consumer of electricity. They could shut him down in a flash.

"Abe, I need your help." It was Mary Ellen, entering with a rake and shovel.

The shovel triggered an instant of revulsion. Burying Bud Jones had been the hardest thing he'd done in his entire life. The boy had been only three years younger than he. He had come out to Whiting for a school project, taking advantage of the space Abe had made for a couple of co-op engineering projects that year. He'd worked out well, and Abe had offered him a part time job. Bud had started to fit in, working as Scott's assistant, when the star happened.

No one knew where he went, but shortly after Scott found his wife and baby hiding in their blacked out home, Bud had shown up. The car jumped the curb and plowed through their front yard, only stopping when the bumper of his ancient Pinto crumpled against their front bedroom. Bud was bleeding heavily, and unconscious.

Scott bundled Denise and little April into the back seat and tried to get him to the hospital, but Bud was dead before they were half way there. Denise, who'd been applying the pressure to the bullet-hole in a vain effort to stop the bleeding, told Scott. He pulled to the side of the road, and then with hardly any debate they headed out to the Design Center. Official Austin could do nothing for Bud any more. As for them, at least they had Mary Ellen's guns and more food in the little snack bar than they had at their house.

Abe could barely breathe when he and Scott removed the body that had been Bud from the car. The sheer weight of the sorrow and loss was crushing, but he sent Scott back inside to comfort his wife and Mary Ellen.

This place was his responsibility, and every one in it was in his care. It was his job to dig the grave.

It had been the hardest, longest task he ever remembered. Alone, the tears came, making it even that much harder to work.

Sharon was dead, now Bud. He couldn't let up an instant, or he might lose someone else. He'd thought Frank's death was the worst time of his life, but he now knew that the worst death was always the current one. He worked with that shovel until his hands were useless. Scott had to fill the grave.

He dreamed about it. And now the shovel was back in his face. He shook off the too-fresh memories.

Of course he knew what Mary Ellen and Denise Jensen were up to. The property had over an acre of unused land behind the parking lot. Like hundreds of others in the injured city, they had a vision of growing a vegetable garden to augment their limited staples. Trading in Burpies seed packets was a growing enterprise.

Abe nodded, "I'll be out in a few minutes. I have a little more to do here before I can leave."

Mary Ellen gave him the eye.

"Really. Just a few more minutes," he protested.

She left with a *Humph*.

I really am, this time. Why can't she realize that I'm doing something terribly important? These aliens must have something to do with the supernova. I don't buy the co-incidence. They have secrets, secrets that they were willing to kill Sharon for.

If they were here to help, they should have done so already. *If they are scavengers, then I have to be ready. It's my responsibility.*

He looked at the alien drive unit. It didn't make sense at first glance. There was a central solid state unit, joined at each end without connectors to something that looked like a pair of focusing magnets. The only external connector was a bundle of something that appeared to be simple optical fibers.

No power supply. That bothered him the most. He understood the optics—it made perfect sense in a system that needed magnetic coils. But if it were electrical, it would take a great deal of power to drive a spaceship.

He'd checked for superconductors. Aliens might have high temperature superconductors good enough to transfer the power on a trace too small to see. Superconductors, however, had other characteristics, like a total resistance to magnetic fields. He'd checked for that. No luck.

No power, and yet it's still running. Hodgepodge had done the first inspection and discovered that some of the optical fibers were lit.

Whatever controller is running the engine is still talking. I hope it's still listening.

The light was monochromatic red, close enough to a commercial LED that Abe was sure he could talk to it.

As soon as I finish this cable adapter, I'll hook it up to Hodgepodge and see if we can get the engine to do something.

Abe wondered what precautions he should take, in case the engine actually started moving. It would be horrible if the thing took off across the room and smashed itself against the wall.

With a click, the room went dark.

Abe yelped, "What now!"

He was half out of his chair when the lights came back on.

"Hodgepodge. Did you toggle the lights?"

"No."

The room went dark again, and this time Abe was aware that nothing but the ceiling light was affected. The monitor was lit, as were the status lights on the computer rack.

"Hodgepodge?"

"I am sending no control pulses. No other circuits are showing EMP effects."

It was so like the trick Sharon had pulled with the locks. It was painful to even entertain the hope that she might have survived. Reluctantly, he formed the thought. **Sharon? Is it you?**

The room came alive with light.

He had to make sure.

Sharon. If it's you, turn the light off. It went off.

Now, on. The light came on.

You're alive! The room pulsed dark, and then light.

"Hodgepodge! This is a signal from Sharon. She is alive. Sharon. Can you flash once for 'no' and twice for 'yes'?"

There was a quick double flash *YES*.

"Are you safe?"

NO

"Do the aliens have you?"

YES

Abe's mind was a whirl of questions. The room went dark.

"Okay. I'll try to be clearer." The light came back on.

He pulled out a piece of paper, and doodled fragments of questions. "Twenty questions is a slow way of communicating. I'll just talk, and you signal me when I am close to the topic you want to talk about."

YES

"Sharon, I was sure you were dead. I'm sorry that I didn't get to the quarry fast enough."

NO

"I'm worried about the aliens. Did they know the supernova was coming?"

YES

Abe paused at that. He had an extensive education in physics. He'd personally re-run some of the pivotal experiments of modern relativity. He understood the equations. He actually believed the speed of light.

But if the aliens knew it was coming, then something worked faster than light.

YES, YES

What did that mean?

"Sharon? Where are you?"

No signal. He desperately wished for something better than 'yes' and 'no'.

"Sharon do you know Morse code?"

NO

"Oh well...it was just an idea." His mind started churning ideas again. "Hodgepodge!"

"Yes, Abe."

"Build me a gadget. Do you have an image of an Ouija board?"

"Yes. I have a diagram and twenty pages of narrative."

"Build one, however, for each letter or symbol, put a circuit. The circuit should have a diode biased into the shot-noise region with a detector so that you can count the electrons. Calibrate each detector's average count rate and set it up to light the symbol when the rate goes two sigma high."

"Sharon, can you understand the design? Will it work?"

YES YES

"Great! Hodgepodge, how soon can you have it running?"

"Four hours approximately. Fewer if you can bring supplies from storage. Robot travel time is on the critical path."

"Just tell me what you need." Hodgepodge had several arms, but only one mobile cart, and it traveled at a slow walk. Abe would be happy to be a go-fer. Contact with Sharon was important. He had to find out where she was.

The fiber optic cable could wait a little, although it was even more important to find out if the alien's drive unit was still working. He needed to hook it up and turn it on.

NO The light flashed.

"Sharon?" Abe backed up his train of thought. **The alien drive unit?**

YES

"Okay. You don't want me to turn it on?"

YES

"Why? Is it dangerous? Will it explode or something?"

There was no response.

"Or will it do something else? Like send a signal? Can the alien's detect it?"

YES

Abe paused, **Oh.** They'd tracked her down and blasted the van because they thought the engine was in it. **Are you trying to protect me from the alien's again?** He was sure she had done that before, at least twice.

YES

He felt as if she were there in the room with him, close enough to feel her breath, but achingly just out of reach. *Thank you.*

"Sharon. If you can read all my thoughts, then you know I will do everything in Heaven and Earth to get you back."

The light flashed, and at first he thought it was a *YES*, but it kept turning on and off, faster and faster, until the fixture started to buzz. Abe held out his hand into the empty room, straining to make contact.

The light flared, and went black. He could smell a whiff of fried transistor. He laughed, "Sharon, you burned out the light. It's okay. Burn them all out if you want!"

Life

THE NAME

Tenthonad heard the howls across the wide expanse of the ship. He relaxed. *So, the prey have turned their weapons on each other.* Once the flares of the great weapons flared across a planet, it was much easier to intimidate the survivors. The Cerik now owned several planets scarred by the original inhabitants.

He waved his claw across the sensors, asking for a random Tale.

...

Tale Two of the Slaves—One season the Runners were plentiful in their herds and a Hunter was eager to catch as many as he could so that he could have a full larder for the cold days ahead. He rounded up the Builders he had for slaves and commanded them build snares. The Elder of the Builders said, "Great Hunter, our snares will not catch many Runners. Let us dig pits instead." So Builders went ahead of the herd and dug pits. But the Runners sensed a change in the wind and took another direction. Again the Builders went ahead and dug pits. A storm came up from the Mountains and the Runners scattered in still another direction. The Hunter said to the Builders, "I can't wait for you," and chased after them but was only able to bring down one old Runner.

...

Tenthonad cut the playback. Something was wrong. The voices, the predator chorus, changed. There was puzzlement, and disappointment—a prey escape.

He moved to his monitors. *Ah.* Instead of the bright white he expected, it was the dim yellow of a forest fire. It was just at the edge of the disk, in the night.

To see it at this distance meant that this fire was huge, but yet, it was still just a forest fire. Some cub had gotten excited and yelled an alert. He would regret his voice.

He could see Second moving among the crew. He was sure to be sharing the frustration.

Second had again mentioned the need for another trip down to the planet. Tenthonad was ready to grant the request, but Second remembered his mistake in time.

This was not a tall grass hunt, where he could jump at prey on a whim. They were keeping to their perch in the star shadow of this moon for a reason. If he attempted to travel the unprotected distance from the moon to the planet, he would surely die of the star-sickness. They had chosen this planet for a reason. The death-star had exploded unevenly. Chance had placed this distant world in the strongest of the flares. It would be one of the last to feel the sickness.

If the prey panicked, and their social structures collapsed, Tenthonad's expedition could move in. It had been discussed often enough. That Second even proposed a trip told Tenthonad just how desperate he was. Right now the travel time to the planet for one of the little scout craft was too long. Second needed to score a coup. He needed more status to challenge for the High Perch. Tenthonad let his eyes drift across the ship monitor that displayed the positions of the ship, the moon, and the planet. The alignment was coming, and that told him precisely when Second would make his next move.

THE SEER

"Angela, I am washing your left arm. The water is warm and soapy. Can you feel it?" He talked as he did the repetitive chore, pleased that he could see more signs that she was reacting to his words.

Thanks, Sharon. Maybe you're just my imagination, but your list makes a lot of sense.

"Angela, did you know that the little kids in the planetarium were in awe of you. I watched one little girl cling to her mommy's arm when you walked by during your intro. I was close enough to hear her whisper, 'She makes the stars move.' I wonder if she caught on to the difference between the real stars and the ones on the dome."

Is that a smile?

He had to put a rein on his imagination. She would come out of the coma. He knew that now. The only question was when, and on that issue, his visions were typically uncooperative. It would do no good to watch her every breath.

I wonder what Spirit Sharon did to her.

So many of her most dire symptoms made dramatic improvement during that session.

There was a sound, he turned his head toward the door. It came again. Someone was knocking on the door.

He set down his wash bowl and got to his feet.

"Angela, I'm going to see who is at the door. I'll be back soon." He glanced around the house as he quickstepped towards the door. There wasn't anything handy to grab up and he felt the need for some kind of weapon. He paused at the door. There, an ashtray. He grabbed up the heavy pale blue stone object, still stained from the cigar George Fuller smoked that first day.

It was the horse girl. She'd been looking back and turned abruptly when he opened the door.

"Hi."

Ed nodded, "Hello."

There was a moment of silence, and then she started, "How is the lady?"

"She's doing better. She still hasn't woken up yet, but I have hopes. Would you like to come in?"

She shook her head, "I can't. I just needed to come tell you something. My Dad would be upset if he knew I was here."

Ed smiled, "That's okay. I still owe him for letting me borrow the horse. It probably saved Angela's life. I wouldn't want him mad at me."

"Do you know the Pattersons?" He shook his head no. "Well, they had a crystal radio. Do you know what that is? It was a science kit Sammy had."

Ed nodded, although he wasn't sure what a crystal radio was, he'd heard the name.

"Well, Sammy was listening to the radio and heard an announcement. He came and told us. I figured you'd need to know too. There's radiation from the star. The Mayor said to stay indoors when it's in the sky."

A vision flashed over him. *He was walking slowly down a hallway in a large building. Hospital beds lined the walls. The bodies were waiting, people still with the weakness of their illness. Someone was walking with him, but he couldn't see who it was.*

He shook it away. "Believe the report. Radiation is dangerous. It can make you very sick, like a bad sunburn down to your bones. It can kill you."

Her face looked pale, her mouth was open. She was used to having adults tell her that everything was going to be okay.

"Can I ask a favor?" she said timidly.

He forced a smile. "Anything. I said I owed you."

She looked back out behind her. "Can I leave Dadbert here? He's too big to bring into the house. I'm afraid the radiation will get him."

Ed nodded. "Sure. But I don't know how to care for him, and I will be spending all my time nursing Angela."

"Oh, I'll come down after star-set and make sure he's fed. I just want him protected from the star. You won't have to do anything."

He nodded, "That'll be okay. Is there anything else you need?"

"No. Thanks for the food. The Patterson's heard that some of the markets would be opening soon. I hope so. I'm getting tired of dry Cheerios."

Ed had a pang of conscience over his full room of food. Maybe short-term good neighbor relations would be better than guaranteed food for the year. What would Angela think?

Then he had an idea. "Your name is Helen?"

She nodded.

"Helen, I didn't plan on having to care for Angela, and there are many things about women that I don't know. If you could get your mother to come for a visit, I bet we could trade some more of my food for female clothes and things. What do you think?"

"That would be great. My folks are worried about food all the time."

"Then let's do it. I want to help."

They gravely shook hands on the deal. Ed felt a flicker of vision, but it passed too quickly to understand.

As she turned to go, she commented, "Did you know there's a strange man hanging around your house? I've seen him a couple of times this morning."

He shook his head no. She shrugged and left.

A strange man? There was a split-second vision of a man, dressed in a black shirt and pants, holding a pistol.

I had better check on that.

He set down the ashtray that he'd been holding. Surely there was something better. After a quick search, he found a poker from the fireplace tools. Holding that, he ventured out the front door.

It was a fragrant morning, with spots of blue, red and orange from the wildflowers. Helen was already gone, but Dadbert the horse looked at him cautiously from the end of his tether rope. She'd already provided the horse with a bucket of water.

Helen must have been confident that he would say 'yes'.

Ed was alive to shadows and numerous possible hiding places in the rocks and trees. He scanned the cliff, looking there.

Helen was almost to the top. There was a looping trail he'd taken the horse down when he had returned with Angela. But for an energetic youngster, there was a much quicker foot trail almost straight up the cliff. As he watched, she reached the top. She looked back and waved, then pointed off to the side.

He turned where she pointed. There was a large tree, a cottonwood. He walked in that direction.

He sensed, rather than saw, a flicker of motion, and when he found the little campsite made of the trunk of the tree and a protected hollow in the rocks, there was no one there.

But a bedroll and backpack were. Ed looked around carefully, but there was no one to be seen. He put aside a twinge of fear and opened the backpack. There were canned food supplies, and drab clothes. There was also something white in a plastic wrapper. He plucked it out. It was a hand-written note.

"Watch him, make sure he stays safe. Stay out of his way and don't let him see you. More orders will follow."

It was signed George Fuller. Below was a crude road map to his place and the street address.

George sent a bodyguard to watch over me.

It made him irritated. Why didn't he just knock at the door and introduce himself? George thought he would send the guy packing.

And I would too!

There was a sound from the house. "Angela!" He dropped the paper and ran.

He ran through the front door.

Stupid. I left it wide open.

But there was no sign of an intruder. He went straight to the bedroom. She wasn't there.

Then there was a moan. He moved to the other side of the bed. Struggling to pull herself up on her hands and knees, Angela was quaking with the effort.

He was on his knees at her side. "Angela, wait. Let me move you. You've been hurt in an auto accident."

She looked at his face in confusion, as he put his arms around her and lifted her gently back onto the bed. "Ed? Is that you? Did I make it here?"

He tried to keep his voice quiet, although he wanted to shout with joy. "Yes. This is my house. We're safe from the star. You're safe. We just have to get you well."

THE ROBOT

Mary Ellen slipped into the computer room to verify that Abe was truly off working in the garden as he had promised. The place was a shambles. He was finally moving some of the gear outside his metal chicken coop, but the inside was still packed high and his desk had not a single square foot of flat space left.

The robot was moving his arms, building something esoteric, she was sure.

She took another look around. It was a clear day out and she'd put the fear of God into every one of them. Work in the garden now, or go hungry in the future. If she could have convinced Abe, the robot would have been out there with them, picking weeds with his pincer hands.

"Hodgepodge."

"Yes, Mary Ellen."

"What are you building?"

"I am rebuilding the optical interface to the alien drive unit."

"What! I thought Abe had given up on that thing."

"No. It is an on-going project. The priority is very high."

"Why in the world, with civilization in ruins, with the city government going Nazi on us, with starvation just around the corner, is he still wasting time on that thing?"

"It is Abe's intent to trade the device for Sharon Dae."

Mary Ellen let the information settle in. The boy was lying to her. He was keeping this all a secret. It hurt.

"He must know she is dead by now."

"No, she is alive. We were in contact with her three hours ago."

"In contact?" What does that mean?

"The girl is able to influence electrical circuits from a distance. Abe has devised a device to let her send messages to us." Almost as soon as Hodgepodge described it to her, she saw the gadget, propped up against an equipment rack.

"That's a Ouija board."

"That is the design, correct."

Mary Ellen was tempted to smash the thing. Smash the alien gadget too, if she could find it. Abe was wading into the deep end here. Was all the craziness of the star stuff getting to him?

"Why is he hiding all this from me?"

She hadn't meant it to be a question for Hodgepodge, but the answer came anyway.

"I have an audio clip that may be relevant."

She spit out the order, "Play it."

...

Abe's voice: "Scott, I want you to keep this stuff from Mary Ellen."

Scott's voice, amused: "Afraid she will come down on you like a ton of bricks?"

Abe's voice: "Close. I'm afraid she's never quite believed in real outer space aliens. If she really believed it—if she understood just how dangerous they were and how important they considered this thing—then she'd have a fit until we destroyed it."

Scott's voice: "Are you sure she wouldn't be right?"

There was a pause. Abe continued, with some passion in the words: "Yes. Yes this is so dangerous that I want to move it out of the building just as soon as we possibly can. But I can't just destroy it. It's the only possible way to save Sharon.

"Scott, I can not give up on her. I don't have many friends. I lost my real parents at too early an age to have trauma over that, but when Frank Victor died, it was as if the world ended. I've never gotten over it. Mary Ellen managed to cope by tackling the whole world head on, but I had to put it in a little box and work hard to keep it there.

"When you brought Bud here, I was close to losing it all. Don't get me wrong, it was the right thing to do. Still, I cried more tears over that grave than I have my entire life.

"Scott, I can't lose Sharon. She's up there, a lab rat for some aliens who won't blink an eye over killing her. It's my fault that she's there, and I'm going to move the Earth, if that is what it takes, to get her back."

...

"Stop." Mary Ellen called.

She could feel the tears around the edges of her eyes as she sensed Frank there in the room with her.

I can't cry.

She blinked away the blurriness. She clenched her hands. Just like all the other times, she wished for Death to come for her, so she could tear out his throat and rip the heart out of his chest just as he'd done to her when he had taken her Frank. She could feel the weight of her pistol on her belt.

Smash his head. I will make Death regret he ever touched Frank.

She stood shivering from the rage.

He can't get Abe. I won't let him.

She looked over the bewildering piles of equipment, looking for something to smash.

No. I wouldn't know where to start. And he'd never forgive me.

The boy was all she had. The Jensen family were nice people, but Abe was her son.

And he's stubborn. Like me.

If he really believed he could save the girl, she wouldn't be able to stop him.

"Hodgepodge."

"Yes."

"What are Abe's plans for this gadget?"

"As soon as the control signals are decoded, it will be mounted in one of the electric cars and driven to a safe location away from here. It will then be activated to lure the aliens."

"And they will come and burn it to smoke just like they did the van."

"It is Abe's hope that Sharon Dae will be able to convince them to trade it for her. She can communicate with them. He will threaten to fight them if they will not trade."

"Fight?" *Abe?* "He plans to fight them? How?"

"Unknown."

Abe is going to fight them for this girl.

She played the thought over in her mind. Her boy was smart, and strong. He tacked his projects straight on. If he said he was going to fight, then he must have a plan.

I have to get out of his way. He's going to tackle Death.

"Hodgepodge, do you still take my orders?"

"Yes."

"Then listen to me now and store this where you'll never forget it.

"Abe must be kept safe. Do whatever it takes. Use whatever skills you have. Never give up. Your first priority above all others is to help Abe and to keep him safe.

"Understand?"

"Yes, Mary Ellen. I understand."

Death

THE SCIENTIST

Larry glanced at his watch. Daylight obscured the starglow, and he didn't want to get caught outside when it rose. The generator was running at full throttle, sending power down the wires to supply Coonabarabran with its meager generating capacity. It was a good trade—unlimited diesel fuel for sharing the electricity.

But I have to make good on my brag. The predictions had to be accurate and useful. His first installment had been a one-week 'radiation forecast' with rise and set times for the star. *Not much, but I have to show them I'm trying.*

What would be most useful would be a long-term prediction on the duration of the radiation peak. Would it be over next week, or would it last a hundred years?

Until he had a good model of the process, he could only take measurements and try to fit it to a reasonable curve. Practically everything in nature could be fitted to a logarithmic curve of some sort. The light curve of the star was staying close to their projections based on dozens of other supernovae observed in neighboring galaxies.

The radiation was harder to predict than the brightness. Astronomers had been limited by their telescopes, seeing only certain things—light, x-rays, infrared—all those electromagnetic signs that were just parts of the radio spectrum.

But the deadly danger they faced now was particle radiation—something no telescope had ever been able to see. Betelgeuse was spewing energetic fragments never before observed. It was as if the whole Earth was in the path of a particle accelerator. No astronomer had observations of this. Larry and his co-workers were having to build a theory on the fly. And hope that it was good enough.

He glanced at his watch again. *Time.* He pressed the horn three times on the truck, sending the seek-cover warning echoing over the complex. It sounded extraordinarily loud. Other than the rumble of the generator, sounds of modern life had practically disappeared.

He headed for the UKST building. He had some survey pictures to take near the star tonight. Space close to Betelgeuse was going to be obscured for thousands of years by the debris of the blast. This was the last time humanity would have to take good pictures of the area, ever.

THE TELEPATH

Asca looked up from his meat. Egh howled as he watched, peering at the hugely enlarged image of the planet. A satisfaction radiated out of the elderly Cerik. Asca probed, and was up on his feet in an instant to get a look himself.

The planet had blossomed a white-hot dot in the middle of the dark crescent. As they and other Cerik joined them, howling their triumph, another spot appeared near the first.

This was not like the forest fire. This was real.

Asca moved back out of the pack. He had to probe the area, and it would not do to go into a passive trance when the blood call was out. Claws and fangs were apt to add a new prey to the list.

He hurried to his area, and settled himself.

Dropping into a trance, he pushing against the White.

There was the panic of a million prey, dying, feeling the meat being burned off their flesh. Cries to Allah, and cries to Ganesh blurred in their terror. If there were shouts of victory and triumph, he couldn't detect them.

Only fear, and hate. Hate that burned deeper into the bones than the nuclear weapons ever could.

Asca collected a summary and then pulled back, before he lost his own identity in the maelstrom of primal emotions.

He had a report to make. Tenthonad and Second would call for him soon enough.

THE WITCH

Sharon wailed her own cry, threaded as a counterpoint through the predator symphony. Her body shook with the felt pain of a million people dead and dying. New Delhi and Islamabad and Mumbai were aflame. The border war notched up all along the front as the word spread of the bombing.

She could not understand the words of the prayers and the curses, but the emotions were beyond language. She was grateful for their numbers, for the chaos of their pain. The flood prevented her from dwelling on the mother's horror as the blasted skin of her baby daughter came off in her hand, or the newly blinded man feeling his face and realizing that his eyes were gone, or the young man struggling with rising panic as he understands that his lungs are burned out and he is suffocating.

Escape. She struggled, blind to her own surroundings, clawing at the unyielding smooth walls of her prison.

Another explosion, and the wave of shocked death, convulsed her and she fell hard against the floor.

Stop it!

She curled into a ball. *Abe! Where's Abe?*

Eyes tightly closed, although that didn't help a thing, she flew her Eye faster than light to Abe's comforting mind.

He worked with new calluses, working a hoe along the row of earth, uprooting new grass and any other plant that didn't look like potatoes. As usual, his mind was elsewhere, working out the probabilities of a combination of circuits, trying to visualize the most effective way to build a control system with the parts that he had in stock.

He doesn't know, she marveled. Although she knew he wasn't telepathic, it seemed inconceivable to her that the burning pain on the other side of the world could sweep through him with no reaction.

Two emotions warred within her. Jealous of his imperviousness to the horror, she was also angry that her own thoughts couldn't reach him either. She needed to talk, to seek the active comfort of another human soul.

Fighting away the noise of the dying, she gritted her teeth and directed her attention to the nearby building, to the complicated device Abe had built for her.

She reached into the circuits. It was difficult to focus, but after a false start where she flashed a dozen of the lights all at once, she centered her attention.

HODGEPODGE RECORD

The soulless, mindless machine replied, but it was hard for her to understand. Words spoken where there was no ear to hear were like a light breeze high in the clouds. She couldn't spare the attention to capture the sound. She could only trust that he was doing what she said.

INDIA AND PAKISTAN HAVE STARTED AN EXCHANGE...

THE WIZARD

Abe wiped sweat from his forehead. It was pleasant, in a dirty sort of way, to come out here a couple of times a day and be part of the work. The baby, April Joy Jensen, was sitting in the upturned soil, absolutely filthy, and bubbly with her new found toy, a long green blade of grass. Her mouth puckered, and as he predicted, the pudgy little hand tried to move the grass towards it.

Abe's right cheek twitched. He brushed at his face absently, leaning on his hoe. Little April was starting to get upset with the difficulty of getting the grass into her mouth.

I give her another minute before she cries.

The twitch came again, this time three even jerks.

He raised his hand to his face. *I'm not that tired.* Usually it was his eyes that gave out on him after an all-nighter on the keyboard.

His cheek again twitched, three even pulses.

What is this?

The idea came to him full-blown. *Sharon.* He didn't even wait for her acknowledgment. He dropped the hoe and started running towards the building.

"There has been a message from Sharon." Hodgepodge said as he barged into the hallway.

It was a short run to the computer room. The Ouija board was still blinking as he entered. He could see the message still growing on the computer screen.

INDIA AND PAKISTAN HAVE STARTED AN EXCHANGE OF NUCLEAR BOMBS. WHOLE CITIES ARE BURNING. ABE, I CANT STAND THE PAIN. I FEEL THE AGONY OF ALL THOSE PEOPLE INJURED AND DYING.

"I am so sorry, Sharon." He put his hand on the edge of the screen. It was warm to the touch.

Under his concern for her, the news of large-scale nuclear explosions gave him another worry.

Fallout in the jetstream. How dirty were the bombs?

The second paragraph was still being assembled letter by letter as Hodge-podge monitored the circuits in the Ouija board. It washed away that thought.

THE CERIK ARE HOWLING LIKE A PACK OF WOLVES, HOT ON THE CHASE. THEYVE BEEN WAITING FOR THIS. IT HURTS. MY MOTHERS VISION.

Abe frowned, **Cerik? The aliens? Wolves?**

[YES] CROSS A WOLF WITH A PANTHER WITH A LOBSTER. THE SIZE OF A HORSE. PREDATORS.

"Are they hunting us? Humans?"

[YES] THEY WANT TO SET UP GAME PRESERVES. ESTATES.

Abe absently watched as the letters re-arranged as Hodgepodge translated and inserted punctuation. His worst worry was now confirmed.

"They came to be here when the supernova hit, to weaken us. And now they are rejoicing as we tear ourselves apart."

[YES] STOP IT ABE.

Abe wished he could hold her. It frustrated him that he couldn't reach her. Nor could he stop her pain.

He sighed, "I will try, Sharon." Across the top of his mind, a vivid memory blossomed of her sitting across the table from him, smiling. From deeper in the maze of his brain, a confidence bubbled up. **Maybe I can.**

There was a tickle, like the hair on the back of his hand was brushed by a wind. He cupped his other hand over the area, enclosing the phantom imagination of her hand.

"Hold on Sharon," he breathed fervently. "Survive it. We will find a way out of this."

[YES]

THE SEER

Ed massaged the back of his neck. He had a headache that would not go away. Maybe the stress.

Angela smiled up at him, still too weak to do anything but rest. "You should rest. I'm okay."

He shook his head, "No. If I close my eyes too soon, I'll get visions. I'd rather wait and crash out from exhaustion."

Her smile dropped by a third.

He laughed.

"Perhaps I'm crazy, but you're alive today because I had a vision. Don't worry, all my friends consider me harmless."

He saw a flicker of black outside the window. His smile vanished. "Problem outside. I'll be right back."

He raced to the front door and stepped out. He took in the scene in an instant.

"You! Bodyguard! Leave those people alone!"

The man in black took one look back at Ed, and then vanished into the trees.

Helen and her mother were watching with open-mouthed astonishment at the scene. They'd stopped in their tracks on the trail down the cliff. Ed moved forward to reassure them.

"Don't worry about him. My boss sent me a bodyguard with a overdeveloped sense of the dramatic."

To the mother, he added, "I am so glad you came. I don't know if Helen has explained the situation, but I really need a woman's expertise right now."

They went on in and Ed noticed Mrs. Black looking at all the rooms. *Probably wondering where all the furniture is.*

He opened the door to the bedroom. Angela looked up, frightened. He smiled, "It's okay. These are our neighbors. Mrs. Black, Helen, this is Angela Benton." There were timid smiles all around. Angela held her blanket tightly in her hand.

Mrs. Black, turned to Ed, and with a stern tone said. "I think Angela and I need to have a little talk. You and Helen need to leave."

Helen said, "Well, I had better check on Dadbert."

"I'll join you," Ed agreed, a little perplexed by the move. However, he'd asked for her to come. Go with the flow.

. . .

As they moved the horse from the first tree to another where there was a little more grass, Helen talked about the life on the top of the cliff.

There were a dozen houses in a half-completed development up there. All were five or ten acre lots. The next set of houses was a mile or so farther down the road, so the dozen families were perforce a little community now.

"Before the star, I only knew Sammy and Billie and Jacob Farmer from school, although they are a lot older than I am. I think my Mother knew more of them, but we never did anything together. Now it's like a club."

Ed thought it sounded nice. "What do you do?"

Helen wrinkled her nose, "Mainly gripe about all the chores we have to do. Everybody has a garden now. Mr. Hiller plowed all the fields before he ran out of diesel. We are doing potatoes. Did you know that you can carve a potato into pieces and plant the pieces?"

"No, I didn't."

"I didn't either, but Mr. Hiller says it's true."

Ed. I need to speak to you.

He closed his eyes, as the voice in his head started without warning. His headache increased.

What? He heard Helen continue to talk about her chores, but the voice of Sharon demanded his attention.

I have some bad news. I thought you should know that there's been a nuclear war between India and Pakistan. Within a few days, there may be radioactive fallout. It may not be a problem for you, but some kinds of food may be contaminated.

Ed head stirred with conflicting thoughts. **Didn't we already have a radiation warning?**

Sharon agreed, **Yes, but that was radiation from the star. This kind comes in on the wind and in the rain. Growing crops will collect it with their roots.**

Ed looked at Helen, still chattering away about her potatoes.

Sharon, I don't think it will make any difference. Outside food supplies have all been shut off. People are growing their own and would risk the radiation, if it meant starving otherwise. Are you sure about this?

He could feel some sadness from her, **Can you feel them? The pain of the dying. I know you can.**

Ed started to deny it, but his headache had a sudden, remarkable clarity. It was a touchstone of despair.

Yes, Sharon agreed. **You feel it. Rejoice that your telepathy is limited. It's a killing thing.**

Ed nodded. People were dying. For a second time, nuclear weapons had been used in war. The decades long balance of terror had finally been tipped by the overwhelming effects of the supernova. An ice pick to the heart shook him. If India and Pakistan could tumble, what about the other nations? Just how stable was the US, and Russia? What about France and Britain and China? And how many countries had secret weapons projects, needing only the will and the incentive to use them?

Were there going to be more waves of radioactive fallout to worry about?

I don't know, Ed. I just wanted to give you the warning. Stay safe.

And like a light switch, his spirit guide was gone, beyond his puny telepathic abilities to make contact.

He opened his eyes. Helen was shaking his hand, trying to get his attention.

Ed pulled his hand away, "I'm okay. Sorry I was just thinking."

"You scared me. You were like a zombie or something." She looked at him cautiously.

He tried to smile, but it didn't come. "It's okay. There are a lot of bad things to think about these days."

That she could agree on. They went back into the house.

Ed was relieved to find the two women smiling when he opened the door. They were obviously caught in mid conversation from the way they clammed up.

Angela looked different. Mrs. Black was able to look him in the face without making him feel like he was on trial.

He stepped over to the bed. "You look much better. I'm so glad." She smiled, and Mrs. Black smiled. Ed felt there was more going on here than he understood, but as long as it meant more smiles, he was content to leave it like that.

The rest of their visit was a list Mrs. Black dictated for him, chores that he needed to do for Angela and around the house. It almost reminded him of Spirit Sharon's list, but he wasn't about to mention that.

They visited his pantry rooms and bargained for clothes and necessities for Angela. Ed had a feeling that Mrs. Black was getting the best of the bargain, but he didn't feel a twinge of foreboding about it, so he nodded pleasantly as she grabbed as many bags of staples as she could carry.

"Helen," her mother noted severely as she handed the girl a box of apples to carry, "I don't want you to tell anyone about this food or how much Mr. Morgan has stocked away. It would be dangerous for him and us as well."

Helen blinked her eyes at the order, but nodded.

Ed realized the truth of the lady's words, but he hadn't thought about it before. He really wasn't very good about planning ahead.

He walked them out and watched them make the climb up the cliff trail with a growing frown on his face. When they were out of sight, he spoke to the air. "Bodyguard. If you have the ability to contact George Fuller, I have a very important message for him."

The only sound for a minute was the creaking of the trees in the faint wind, and far, far off, the rattle of a gasoline engine.

Then, the man in black stepped out from behind a tree.

Plans

THE WIZARD

[NO] [NO] [NO]

Sharon's Ouija board blinked repeatedly. Abe forced himself to ignore it.

"Hodgepodge, run the sequence again, with half power."

"Okay."

The alien device, bolted into an aluminum framework, moved visibly in its foreword direction, and then relaxed back to its starting point. There was some bending of the metal bars that held it in place, but not as much as the first time.

Abe looked at the readings. "Definitely analog controls. Hodgepodge, how long will it take you to calibrate the laser diodes?"

"Ten minutes." The robot cart moved over to the optical cable that connected human computer to alien device.

Abe looked over at the Sharon's signal.

"Sharon, listen to me!" The blinking stopped. "I know this is dangerous, but it's the only way. I'm trusting you to give me a real warning when the aliens, the 'Cerik', detect that we are making the unit work. You can't stop me from trying to save you. You can't do it! Read my mind. Understand that I will not stop."

Abe willed her to understand his determination. With her working with him, they just might have a chance to prevail against her captors. She had to understand.

"Work with me. I am putting people at risk. The instant the aliens know, I need to know. Okay?"

[YES] I UNDERSTAND. THEY DONT KNOW YET. BE CAREFUL. BE CAREFUL.

Abe was relieved. He had given Hodgepodge the task to convert one of the electric cars into a rolling housing for the alien device, but that was still in the design stages. If this early testing caused the Cerik to come for him now, he would have to load it into Mary Ellen's car and make a run for it.

"Hodgepodge, build a small cable that will do nothing but cause the alien engine to pulse on and off. I might need it as a lure."

"Priority?"

"In your spare moments. The calibration is more important."

He looked over at the aluminum framework again. The damage was more than he liked. He missed the original magnesium shell that the Cerik ship used.

Analog signals, not digital. Okay, so I have to watch it. If I guess wrong on their technology again, I could blow the whole thing.

The first test had been to send a single short pulse into the control lines. Unfortunately, modern digital signals were full power, all the way on or all the way off. The engine had worked, responding with strong thrust for the fraction of a second that the laser diode shone.

Hodgepodge said that the status lines from the unit were at different intensities, and I didn't understand what that meant.

The Cerik control module was like an analog computer, something he'd played with in high school.

Do I have enough linear amplifiers to build a full control system?

Probably not. Simulate everything digitally and then use digital to analog converters at the interface.

He was still a little intrigued by the force of the thrust. He'd put less energy into the cable than the wiggle of a butterfly's wing, and it had reacted with the lurch of an enraged elephant. The energy had to be stored inside it somehow. How much was left? Still enough to thrust a craft out of the atmosphere? If so, then the power density was much much higher than any chemical fuel. Could it be nuclear—the fabled cold fusion? Or something else entirely? It didn't bother his home-brew Geiger counter, so if it were nuclear it had to be something entirely out of his experience.

Shortly, Hodgepodge completed his calibrations and reconnected the optical cable.

Abe checked the strain gauges that measured the force of the thrust.

"Okay Hodgepodge, let's start from the beginning. Run the sequence at zero power."

Abe glanced over at the Ouija board. Sharon was quiet this time. He hoped it was a good sign.

THE SEER

Ed had never seen George Fuller dressed in anything but a business suit, so when the jeep pulled up and the passenger, a man in a kaiki jacket with hair fluffed and tangled by the open air drive got out, it took a moment for Ed to recognize him.

"Ed!" He advanced, holding out his hand, looking genuinely happy to see him.

"Hello, George."

Ed shook hands, but he already missed being out from under the man's constant presence. He already knew what George was going to ask him. Maybe for once he should lead the conversation.

"I don't like the bodyguard."

George's smile flickered, "I am sorry, but you are too important. I couldn't let you hang out here outside the Guard's patrol area, with no protection against all the looters and...."

"Guard patrol?" He looked over at the driver of the jeep, a soldier waiting patiently in his seat.

"Yes. The city is coming back under control. Really, you should see it. Looting has been stopped cold. Austin is in contact with other cities that have their own armed forces, and it may not be too far in the future before we can actually try to send out trading caravans. Your help would be critical."

Ed looked away, towards the lake, angry with the man. George had talked him into helping with all his projects for years. It turned his stomach to know just how weak he was when George started spinning his grand schemes and telling him how important he was. All the man wanted was a pet fortuneteller.

"I want you to dismiss the bodyguard. I have friends here. I'll be okay."

"Now, Ed. What harm can he do? Surely..."

"George, I know I'm safe. Do you believe me or not?"

Ed turned and walked toward the house. He spotted Helen on the cliff above and he didn't want his neighbors to watch.

George followed. Ed pointed to a seat in the living room. "Sit. I'll get some tea."

He'd brewed the drink an hour ago for Angela. As he poured, Ed was surprised that such a simple thing was growing in importance. Refreshment for a guest was more than a courtesy. In a world where every ounce of food had to be planned for, it carried a rich undercurrent.

George is a guest in my house. I am not his servant.

He brought out the cups and waited until George had a sip before sitting down himself.

"Why do you have a chauffeur?"

George took another sip and set the cup down. "Oh, I'm part of the City Council. When everything went black, we were the only organization with a plan. Your warnings were invaluable."

"So you're running everything now?"

"Oh, not so dramatic. The surviving city government is still in formal control. We're just recognized for our contributions.

"Ed, our organization's control of the food stocks saved many thousands of people. Our plan for sharing resources with the State government put the Guard under our direction, and that street level control put an end to the banditry. Our projections of crops that will survive and which will go bust—your projections—are at the heart of the City's plans to expand control into the agricultural towns to the east.

"Of course, I am on the City Council. It's in the best interest of everyone if we have our say. And it would be in the best interest of everyone if we had your insight readily at hand as we continue to plan for the future."

"How are the hospitals? Do you have plans for lots of people getting radiation sickness?"

George lost the salesman's smile. "What do you mean? We've sent out the word to stay out of the starshine. International radio is full of warnings of a new set of radiation from the star."

"Then you haven't heard of the war?"

"Which war? There are hundreds of little wars."

Ed shook his head, "India and Pakistan. Big atomic explosions. Surface explosions that pump tons of dirty radioactive junk into the high atmosphere. We will start to feel it soon."

Perhaps it was the headache, weaker now, or perhaps it was just the habit of falling into a vision to give George a report, but in any case, he could see more now.

"The radioactive fallout will start to be detected within a couple of weeks. There will be still another wave from northern Asia when the Russian and Chinese armies fight. That'll be in another month. There will even be a single explosion in Nebraska; an accident.

"Crops will be contaminated. People will need to be told how to protect their food, but many won't have the resources.

"People will stop being frightened of the star too early. As its brightness fades, people will stop hiding, even as the radiation peaks.

"Soon, there will be whole buildings in the city that are nothing but new hospitals for the sick. Aisles of the sick. St. Edwards University will become a vast graveyard."

Ed blacked out for a second. He felt George helping him back into his chair. His head was ablaze with the pain of the dying. "Angela." He blacked out again.

. . .

Angela's hand rested on his forehead. When he opened his eyes, he could tell that it was already dark outside. Had George gone?

He struggled to get upright.

"Wait Ed," Angela said. "Don't get up."

He shook his head, looking at the concern in her face. "It's okay. This happens to me frequently. Nothing worse than a bad headache."

He sat up, holding his face in his hands while the waves of pain passed by. Angela was holding his arm, and she was the rock he held onto as he pulled himself back together.

She was a beautiful angel, dressed in a white dress that had arrived from the Blacks.

Ed took a deep breath, "You should be the one back in bed."

"Nonsense. It's good for me to be up. I'm getting stronger by the day. I even fixed an omelet—the first time I've ever used powered eggs." Her smile poured strength back into him.

"Is George gone?"

She nodded. "He said he had to get back to town before star-rise. He told me you would be okay. Who is he?"

"It's a long, long story. He's my boss. Was my boss. I quit when I saw this coming."

He got to his feet and she moved in to walk with him. As they stepped slowly to the kitchen, he felt a fluttering in his chest. With his arm around her and hers around him, he was flooded by the knowledge that he never wanted to walk anywhere without her again.

"Oh, by the way," she said, "George left you a letter." She picked up the envelope from the tabletop and handed it to him.

He tore open the seal and read as she fixed them some tea.

...

READ THIS AND THEN BURN IT.

Ed, I want you to come back into town. I know you want your independence and I do believe you when you say that you are safe where you are.

I also know that you want the bodyguard removed. I can't do that. I have my orders, too.

Ed, I like you. This is outside of all the money you made me. I think of you like one of my children. I imagine you as a rebellious teenage son, although I know you are older than that.

I know you are a young man who deserves to be on his own and to make his own way. I have talked to your young lady and she impresses me as a strong and smart person. You have made a good choice.

You're a man now. I think you deserve to be treated with respect. You deserve the truth, so I am going to disobey my own orders and tell it to you. I can be hurt badly if they know I'm telling you this, so please, burn this letter and never let on what I am telling you.

The brokerage company that I control is just one piece of a larger organization. This group has been helping people of special talents for over a hundred years. In turn, people like you have helped us back. You understood the arrangement we have. I took care of all your needs and you gave me the edge to make a lot of money in the markets. There are others. Some can tell the future, although none as well as you. Others can read thoughts, or tell where hidden things like mineral deposits can be found.

Each talented person is paired with someone in the organization who is supposed to become a friend and mentor. Many of us begin when the talented person is quite young.

We are all bound by some very strict rules. The first one is that we can never let you be harmed. The second is that we can never compel you to work for us.

In all honesty, it would never work to hold you captive, would it? We're at the mercy of your truthfulness. I've thought it was a mistake to hide this from you. Maybe if I had told you sooner, you wouldn't have felt it necessary to break away. I hope this belated honesty isn't too late.

But I want you to know that there is more danger out there than even you can imagine. I told you this organization is over a hundred years old. You may think we met when you were in the school. In reality, we have been watching you since you were born. Your father was a man of talent. When you were just a year old, he was murdered.

He was discovered stabbed to death, and the girl he was seen with was never seen again. That night, five of our talented telepaths were killed, most disguised as suicides.

We think there is another organization out there who wants to destroy people with these special talents. They've killed telepaths, more than once. They are formidable.

So you see why I worry. I can't bring you back to the city where it is safer, but I will keep the bodyguard where he can watch you. You won't see him, but he will be there if you need him. If you need to talk to me, leave a letter in your mailbox. It'll get to me.

And Please Please destroy this letter.

...

Ed looked up to see the worry on Angela's face. He handed her the letter. She started to read.

He churned inside. He had a father, and a mother. How dare they keep that knowledge from him! Was his mother still alive? Why did she give him up to the center? Was the organization part of that? George betrayed him. But George told him this, even when he was ordered to keep quiet.

The scary part was just how true it rang. George had an army now. He could order him into the city. What should he do?

Angela looked up from the letter. Her mouth was open, and her eyes were wide.

She believes it.

"You can tell the future."

He nodded. "In visions. It is erratic."

She looked back down at the letter. "Do you trust him?"

Ed shook his head, "I don't know. Maybe."

She stood and walked over to the stove and lit the propane flame. She set the paper down on it and they both watched silently while it burned to glowing black ashes.

THE TELEPATH

Asca heard the muted growl of Egh, coming to ask a favor. As *named* equals, Asca was grateful for the Scientist's courtesy. The other *named*, especially the Rear Talons, who were responsible for the moving of the great ship, had gone out of their way to deny his *name*. Once Yakke and his Second had ignored him. Walking together they had passed his nose without speaking his *name*. With that example, it became fair hunting for the rest of that group to snub him in any trivial way that they could. He had probed Yakke and it was clear that nothing would be done to restore proper respect. To Yakke, with his thirty, Asca wouldn't deserve a *name* until he had at least a Second of his own.

Egh was entirely different, never implying by word or thought that he saw any inferiority in Asca's *name*. Unfortunately the scientist had only a small group of his own, not enough to lead the other *names* toward proper behavior.

"What do you want?" he asked Egh.

"The City-builder captive. She is still alive. She has lasted far longer than any of my other specimens. Have you found anything in her mind that could explain why she is different?"

"I have not probed for that." He didn't mention that he had not probed her at all since the initial examination. The interaction with a prey on such a personal level was very disturbing.

However, after all of Egh's complaints about the early fatalities of his test animals, it was intriguing that this one was still alive.

"I can do a special probe for you, if you can wait until after the *fenke dan?*"

Egh twitched his jaw in frustration. Asca *pree'ded* silently, pleased that his bluff was believed.

"No," Asca lowered himself a half, "Some *names* are more important than others. Egh should not have to wait. I will do your probe first."

Asca could tell the elderly scientist was pleased at the respect, although he pushed it out of his consciousness. Scientist, like Telepath, was one of those minor jobs. The *names* were created, modern, not at all like those in the Tales.

Egh led the way across the ship toward the storage pits. Asca moved briskly. In spite of Egh's age, he didn't waste time when a project was ready.

They stood at the edge of the pit where the City-builder was kept. Asca could feel her thoughts, so she was alive even though she lay flat like a felled prey.

Egh took one look at the pit, and roared for an assistant.

The young one arrived quickly, bounding like a cub, across the distance from the green bushes where most of the un-named lived. He skidded to a halt before Egh, crouched belly to the floor.

Egh spoke with anger, "Your duty was to keep the prey clean."

The assistant's claws rattled faintly on the floor. "I was just preparing to begin. I had to adjust the water levels."

Egh's voice was unyielding. "No, you did not. Look at the prey."

The three of them looked down. The female was up, sorting through her collection of scavenged goods. She examined each and tossed some over to another pile near the pit's drain.

"See that. She has just now started her culling ritual. She just started when I arrived. She can read our intent, something like our esteemed Asca can do. If you had been thinking about your duties, rather than fighting with the other cubs, she would have already completed her cull.

"Do you deny my logic?"

The cub dropped even lower, wishing he were able to sink through the floor.

Egh's slash was quick and powerful, sending him tumbling and bleeding until he hit the side of another of the pits. For a moment, the two Named watched, until the assistant rose unsteadily on all fours. The blood foamed and stopped, hardening on his skin. He limped slowly to the controls, and without raising his eyes to his *name*, he triggered the wash.

Water sprayed over the floor of the pit. The prey held her prized possessions tight, while her waste and discards were washed down the drain. Asca could feel her internal shiver at the cold, although he couldn't see anything. Then, once the water stopped, she picked a single item from the preserved pile and started stroking the white mass of hair on her head. It collected the long strands of hair she was shedding.

Suddenly, he was inside her thoughts. She greeted him coldly.

What do you want, Asca?

The process of 'hearing' her thoughts was slow, requiring him to consciously translate her clearly perceived intent into real Cerik words. There was a babble of City-builder words too, but that he could discard.

Egh has seen that you have survived longer than any other animal from you planet. He wished to know how.

There was some confusion from her. **Which other animals? Were they like me?**

He turned to Egh, "The prey wants to know if there were any other of her kind of animal here on the ship?"

Egh listened with interest, and then after a moment said, "Tell her I collected many grazers and animals with fur. When we took samples of manufactured things, two City-builders were snatched by mistake, but she is the first to survive long enough to get to the ship."

Asca could tell she already comprehended the answer directly from Egh, but there was no sense in making himself appear less useful, so he delayed a moment before telling Egh, "She is saddened by the death of her kind."

Egh asked, "Have you asked if she knows why she lives and the other animals died?"

Asca repeated the question to her, for emphasis.

The answer was confusing. He could detect no deception from her, but some of the concepts didn't match anything he knew. He repeated the question and got a variation of the same answer.

Finally, he turned to Egh, "She says she looks at the death and makes it go away."

Egh moved back on his rear legs. "What does that mean?"

Asca gestured his own confusion. "I asked her twice. It doesn't make sense to me either."

Egh mumbled to himself, trying to turn the words over and to make them fit into some kind of understandable order. He was having no luck.

Asca straightened his legs, subtly hinting that he was ready to leave. Egh noticed, and asked, "Please ask her if there is anything she needs to keep staying alive."

As the question was raised, she stood and tugged lightly on the cloth that was draped around her. It tore with the faintest of effort.

"She says she would like to go back to the store pit and find other cloth. Hers is damaged. It helps her survive the cold."

Egh reacted, "It is cold?"

"When the pit is washed, she is cold for some time after."

He appeared pleased, "Well, we can certainly fix that!"

Asca felt a moment's sympathy with the scientist. With so much of their lives out of control on this ill-fortuned voyage, any progress was something to be savored.

THE ROBOT

Hodgepodge put the design plans on the screen for Abe.

Abe frowned as he moused around in the view. "I miss the plotter. Nothing beats hanging a paper diagram on the wall where I can see it all in one sweep."

"Shall I repair it?"

Abe shook his head, "No. I don't expect to get new semiconductors for years." He sighed. "Our stock is irreplaceable. We will probably end up scavenging it for parts."

He noticed a bulge on the electric car that wasn't there when it was just a student project. "What is this?" He zoomed in. "Wow. Is this your idea?"

Hodgepodge acknowledged, "Yes."

"I agree it's a good idea, but do you think you can get Mary Ellen's permission?"

"Yes."

Abe sat back in the chair. "Well, you have more confidence than I do. Let's go with it, but don't ask her. It's always easier to ask forgiveness than to ask for permission." He shook his head. "You surprise me, Hodgepodge."

He scrolled the design image over to where the new engine had to be mounted. Half the way there, he noticed new structural mounts near the driver's seat. "What are these for?"

Hodgepodge explained. Abe checked the engine mountings for confirmation.

"Hodgepodge, you have changed. You are a lot more creative than you were three months ago. Do you know why?"

"No. Shall I declare a system error?"

He put out his hand, "No. Don't do that. I like the changes, I just don't understand them. Perhaps the multiple restarts had something to do with it.

"In any case, we don't have time to investigate. Things are happening too quickly."

He reviewed the adjusted design goals. "You have been busy here I see."

"It is consistent with the mission goal." Hodgepodge replied.

"Oh, I can see that. Are you sure it will work?"

"The engine test is unambiguous. The control loop should be good as long as the vehicle is within 30 miles. The radio propagation is the critical component."

Abe scanned the whole design again, and then said, "The design is approved. Start construction."

He sat quietly in the room for another few minutes. He then muttered, "I just hope I am up for this."

Invaders

THE SCIENTIST

The phone rang. Larry jumped in his seat. He was still not used to the loud ring of the new circuit between the observatory and Coonabarabran. It was the most obnoxious result of the agreement between the town and the observatory. The legendary junk rooms of the observatory had artifacts ancient and surprisingly useful, now that transistors and their ilk were a vanishing breed. He had his reservations about the brag that their ancient Interdata model 70 just might be the last functioning computer in Australia, but certainly all the PC's had been smoked.

He picked it up. "Hello, Kelly here."

It was Constable Bern. "I'm glad it's you. Can you talk?"

Larry brushed the mental cobwebs aside. "Yes. What's the problem?"

"You are aware we sent scouts down towards Dubbo?"

"Yes. Baxter and Demming."

"Have you monitored their signals?"

"No. We gave you the big receiver, when we made you the sending set."

"Oh. Well, if I can read their Morse right, there is a caravan of cars coming up the Newell highway. A real vintage car rally. Old Fords, a Nash, and a DeSoto. The problem is that every car has men, men with guns, riding the running boards."

"When will they arrive?"

"They are coming at a walk—with those cars, you travel at the speed of the slowest—but at best we only have a few hours."

Larry glanced up at the wall. On the map he could see which route these unknown gunman were likely taking. The Constable's roadblock wasn't likely to stop them. He felt a lump in the pit of his stomach.

This wasn't surprising. When resources drop, you can form alliances and trade to each other's weaknesses, or you can collect guns and take what you need. Civilization was just one big collection of alliances, and it was coming apart. Sydney's population probably fled up toward Lithgow and Orange, pushing still more refugees up towards Dubbo. And now the dominos were toppling towards Coona.

He looked to the left, where the daily chart was posted. He closed his eyes.

Do I have a choice? I can't take chances with Janet.

Historically, raiders were very hard on other men's wives and unborn children.

"Constable, can you take out the road? Anything to slow them down."

There was silence on the other end for a moment. "I would hate to destroy a bridge. No telling when we will be able to rebuild. There is a place just past Hickley Falls where the road could be blocked with a couple of sticks of dynamite. They could clear it, but it would take hours without bulldozers."

"That'd be great. I'll meet you at the junction and help. The radiation last night was double the night before. If the trend continues, anyone working out under starshine tonight will get a very unhealthy dose. That includes us, we'll need to take care planting the charges."

"No."

"What?"

"You can't come." The Constable was firm. "I'm not going to risk scientists. My men can handle this. In this crazy world, you people are an edge Coonabarabran has that none of the other towns has. Give me weather reports. Tell me what the star is going to do next. Build me some more radios. Keep giving me an edge."

"I understand." The phone clicked, and went silent. Larry hung it up. It was an unexpected turn-around in the man. Did he really appreciate them? Did the idea of fighting an invisible enemy, the radiation, make that much difference? If so, it was a victory of sorts.

He just wished he could appreciate it. Respect means nothing when people are coming after you with guns. Win or lose, someone was likely to die.

The lump in his stomach was twice the size now.

THE NAME

Tenthonad growled his acknowledgment of Egh. He had just been reviewing some modern history, specifically the alliance of his clan and Second's. Why couldn't recent events be as cogent and uplifting as the Tales?

Instead, there was a mire of compromises and bad choices.

It all started with the Delense. If they hadn't betrayed us, and forced us to kill them all, then we wouldn't be in this mess.

The Delense had been the Builders, the creators of technology. With their help, every clan had great herds of prey, food for all. Now the herds were dwindling—it was wrong for the Cerik to tend herds. But with fewer prey, the stronger clans were edging out the weaker. The only solutions had been to ally with other clans, or to find new hunting grounds.

The treasure worlds had been a great lure for clans such as his. The result of failure would be jaws and talon against Second's clan, if indeed the clans in the Mountains didn't gobble them both up.

Second seemed intent on positioning his clan for ascendancy when the expedition failed. With his agitation, fewer of the Cerik each day seemed to think that success was in their grasp.

Egh scurried into view.

"What do you want?"

The scientist spoke timidly, "You wished to be reminded when the star flare peaked. It is that time."

"Good. You may leave."

He turned his view to the far planet. It was a thin crescent, and the atmosphere seemed to glow of its own accord.

Not good enough. Die, so that the survivors may be good prey.

The far planet was vastly overpopulated. Those cities had been a great black mark against it. It was always a tradeoff, plentiful prey for the Cerik, but too many and they became impossible to manage. Let the sick and weak die, and the rest would be good prey for his cubs. The memory of the captive's taste came back to haunt him. He growled low.

There was another rattle of claws. He could tell at once that it was Second. He growled admittance.

Second stood, barely lowered, almost declaring his own primacy.

"What do you want?"

"There is news. We must send a ship to the planet."

"Why? Are your righteyes becoming restless again?"

Second was defiant. "No. This is not something you can hiss at. You have no choice this time. We are getting engine pulses from the planet."

Second's information came from the ship's sensors. There was no doubt. There was a signal that could only come from one of the missing scout ships.

Tenthonad felt control slip from his claws, there was no choice. Cerik technology must not be left in the hands of prey, even if it took a suicide mission to correct the problem.

"Do you volunteer to go?" Tenthonad asked, almost hoping to rid himself of Second this way.

Second's fangs gleamed, "Yes! And I will be back. I have found a way."

Second howled to another, and a third Cerik came before the perch. It was one of the Rear Talons. In halting words, the worker described how one could fly a scout ship down the moon's shadow and dash across to the shadow of the planet quickly enough to avoid the death. If the mission was handled quickly, they could return the same way. If not, they would have to hide out on the planet for half of the moon's rotation to come back in the planet's shadow.

There was an optimum time to start, less than two of the planet's days from now.

Tenthonad watched as Second *pree'd* in his triumph. If he succeeded in this mission, he would indeed have the status necessary to challenge for the *Name*. And there was nothing Tenthonad could do to stop him.

There was a scratch on the floor.

"Still another? What is this, a public sprawl? Come on in?"

It was a harried looking Asca.

"Speak!"

Asca was reluctant. He looked at Second and then back to Tenthonad. "The captive has a message for you."

"What is it?"

"She says that she is in contact with the prey who has our engine. She says that no Cerik will be able to find it without her help.

"She says that the City-builder on the planet who has it will trade the engine for her. Otherwise he will use it to destroy us all."

THE EQUESTRIENNE

Helen was startled awake. At first, she thought it was just her new 'bed' and turned the pillow over to get the cool side against her face. It was barely twilight, and yet she had been to bed for a couple of hours. This new star-day was crazy. She would never get enough sleep. Plus, ever since the radiation warning, she had to sleep down stairs on the couch. Dad had taken the door off her bedroom and placed it on cinder blocks above the couch, with boxes of junk stacked on top of that like an overloaded table. All for radiation shielding. There wasn't much breeze with all that stuff stacked around her. Stupid star.

Everything was different now. Her parents were always home, and let her know it by giving her new chores every day.

She even missed school. It was even worse than summer vacation. She had no idea where Amber, Andrea, Vicky, or Carrie were, or even if they were still alive. Her new in-line skates, bought with her own allowance so she could go more often to the skating rink, were gathering dust now, and unless something really strange happened, she might never use them again.

And boys! None of them in their little circle of houses were worth anything. They weren't even close to her age.

She still had a little tingle when she thought about Ed, down below the cliff, but he was really too old for her, and besides he had a girl. She didn't have anything against Angela, and she hoped she would get well soon, but it was a shame that the most mysterious man around was already caught.

There! What's that noise?

She slid out of the covers and edged over to the window.

The landscape was a strange, unearthly color, and the sky was lit up by moving ropes of light. She couldn't see the star from her viewpoint, but she didn't need to. She could see its horrible glow in her sleep.

At first, there was nothing strange. There was the car in the driveway, now just a place for the little kids to play. Over there were rows of plowed earth—her new garden, growing from her efforts. The pole-barn was ...

Oh, no! Dadbert, how did you get free?

Her horse was grazing peacefully in the ghastly light, ignorant of the radiation danger. He must have broken free from where he was tethered down below the cliff and come home.

I have to get him to safety.

The warnings had been clear about livestock. Get them under shelter or make plans to slaughter them and preserve the meat.

Quietly, because she knew what her father would say if he caught her, she changed clothes. There was still a bridle rope in the barn. She would have to race out, get Dadbert under control and down the cliff where it was safe.

The first part worked. She slipped out and closed the door silently behind her. Then she raced, fearful of looking up at the star. People said you would go blind if you looked straight at it.

The barn door opened easily enough and she stared into the darkness. After a few seconds, her eyes could make out the horse-grooming tools.

There it is. She grabbed the rope and turned back to where she saw the horse.

But he wasn't there. She blinked. The light was confusing. She jogged out into the middle of the field. Dadbert was nowhere to be seen. On impulse, she turned her head. There was a flicker of motion, just behind the barn.

Silly boy. She turned back and tried to head him off. He was looping around behind her, trying to keep the barn between them. He played just that trick on the horseshoe man the last time they had his hooves trimmed.

Helen wished she had some grain or an apple to tempt him.

He rounded the barn and reared. His eyes were wide. There was white froth on his mouth.

Helen stepped back at the sight. He was panicked.

"Easy boy," she said. His ears twitched forward.

She took a step, "Good Dadbert."

She reached out with her free hand, "I'll take good care of you." Her fingers touched his skin, hot and wet from his exertions. "We need to cool you down."

The horse whinnied, uncertain. She took a step to the side, keeping one hand on his neck, to calm him.

It happened in a flash. He saw the rope, and reared. Helen was knocked hard against the barn. Whack! Her head hit the main timber.

He neighed in panic and headed at a full gallop towards the far end of the pasture.

Helen lay still under the deathly blue-white glow of the sky.

THE WIZARD

Abe worked carefully, keeping one eye on the robot arm moving across the cockpit from him. Hodgepodge's installation of the electronics had priority, but he could still make progress on the seat and the miscellaneous fixtures if he were careful.

The electric car had been modeled after the famous Sunracer, with a streamlined teardrop shape. The skin was composite plastic, with latest generation solar panels laminated into the topmost skin. Abe hadn't had a chance to see if any of the cells had survived the EMP. For this mission, they were irrelevant anyway. The expensive hot sulfur battery was topped off and it should have more than enough electricity to handle the demands of the control and radio circuits.

The car had been a student project. Whiting Design had offered technical support and a work place for the project.

Abe wondered again what happened to the five students who had labored for months getting the car so close to completion. He could see their faces. Their names were harder. After the world turned upside down, he hadn't spared them much thought. A couple of Asian's, one of them female, an Indian, and the other two were American. Rashid. That was the name of the Indian.

I wonder if his family were in the burned cities? He wondered about all of them.

There are more of us now, he thought grimly. He had a good childhood at the Home, but there was something permanently missing when you grew up without parents.

He pushed that thought aside, concentrating on the seat bracing. The original design had nothing more than a sling where the driver could hang while steering the car in the hot sun. Speed wasn't the main consideration, weight was. They had projected that they could make 70 mph going downhill with the wind, but that was theory, and the actual seat and fastenings were designed for much less than that.

Everything had been cut to save weight. Less weight meant faster acceleration.

He lifted the whole seating harness out and tossed it aside. No more. He glanced at the alien engine already mounted to the frame of the car.

Weight wasn't the concern anymore. No more tightly monitored energy budget. Either the engine had more than enough power for the attempt, or it didn't. He had no way of measuring. He had to take it on faith.

The lights on the control array flashed on.

"Hodgepodge?" he asked worriedly.

"Incoming message from Sharon."

"Speak it to me."

There was a pause, then a computer-synthesized voice, not too unlike Sharon's, came out of the speaker.

"Abe. They are coming for you."

So it is starting. Will they make the trade?

"The leader said to take me along on the trip. His thoughts are blocked to me. I don't trust him."

What are his orders to the pilot?

"His words were to trade me for the engine. The Cerik understood the words to mean something else entirely. He wants to capture you."

Do they know we are talking?

"Yes. They have a telepath monitoring me."

Let them understand me. They have to trade to get the engine.

Abe tried to visualize his thoughts, to make it clear. **There are many caves around here. I can hide the engine where you can never get it. You have to trade the girl back to me.**

"Abe, they understand. I still don't trust them."

Abe nodded. **How much time do I have?**

"The scout ship leaves in maybe a day. The ship will arrive in star shadow."

That made sense. The aliens were vulnerable to the radiation as well.

I have a lot of work to do to be ready.

"Be careful."

You too.

THE SCIENTIST

Cathy was asleep across a pile of papers, her head resting on the hand-scribbled pages like a very flat pillow. Larry Kelly was wandering the floor. Janet had a hard night of it, and as tired as he was, he didn't want to risk disturbing her fitful sleep.

Her pregnancy couldn't have come at a worse time. With all the radiation, she couldn't help but fret about possible damage to the child. And whenever she felt sick, everyone wondered silently whether it was radiation poisoning, or just normal pregnancy upset.

Larry read the charts and told her his readings, maybe shading them just a hair more positive than they really were. She knew that too.

And now, if the universe weren't dangerous enough, people down the road decided to have a little war.

He glanced over at the telephone, a relic out of an old movie, hand crank on the side. He always wondered what that was for. Now he knew. How else to make the other end ring?

I wish the Constable would call back.

Realistically, the star was still up. No one should be out right now, not if they valued their health.

Cathy stirred. She looked up. "You still awake?"

He nodded. "I couldn't sleep."

She leaned back in her chair, and pulled the papers into a neater stack. "I wonder why I'm doing this. There isn't any place to publish it."

She tapped the papers on the edge. "The definitive model of supernova evolution, formed by staring into the heart of the closest explosion in human history, with new insights that no one else on the planet can match—and I can't even find a typewriter to make it look professional. My handwriting is like a chimp's."

Larry pulled up a chair. He looked over her abstract. "My handwriting is no better. I wonder if the school in town has one of those big charts that show little kids how to properly form their letters. Maybe we could borrow it."

She laughed, "I wonder if Mrs. Meyerly is still teaching. She despaired of my scrawls. Oh, well, it's my own fault for putting my computer in the window."

He winced. He'd made the same mistake. "Typewriters will be worth their weight in gold. I wonder if we could get the townspeople to look in their closets for an old Remington."

She shook her head, "What could we trade? We aren't the only people with the same idea."

"Make it part of the science tax." Larry and Cathy looked at Janet's entrance, walking with a pre-momma's waddle, her robe bundled around her in her.

"Sorry we woke you." Larry apologized.

She sat at the table beside him, and patted his hand. "I was already awake."

Cathy asked, "Science tax?"

"Right. That is what we have here, right? The Constable was clear that he's keeping us going—providing our food and fuel—because we give Coonabarabran an edge over the other communities. We aren't trading weather and radiation reports for so much eggs and butter per report, so it must be a tax exchange. We are taxing the community a flat rate in exchange for whatever we can produce."

Cathy smiled, "I guess. I was never into economics myself."

"I have been thinking about it a lot lately. Right now, we've been able to provide some high value information. Our tax rate is low for the value we provide. But it won't always be that way. Think how many astronomers there were in the whole country before the supernova. What was the population ratio there? Without a crisis, how many scientists will Coona be willing to support? One, or maybe not that many. Think about all the old medieval romances. How many wizards per kingdom?"

Larry nodded, "Our generator and some lucky timing bought us our current position, but it can't last. Not unless we do something more."

Janet agreed, "That is what I was saying. We need to diversify. Advertise for a secretary job, but make sure the candidate is responsible for the typewriter. We still have a mimeograph machine in the storeroom. Until we run out of supplies, we can print our own books, make posters for the town, print an almanac for the farmers. Cathy, you can get your paper published right here. If we choose our subjects, our books could even be a valuable trade item to the other towns."

She put her hand on her belly. "And we need to either take over the school system, or make an alliance. People will keep having children, and they'll need to be educated."

Cathy grinned, "You have been busy. Constable Bern needs to hire you to run the town." She glanced over at Larry. "Look at you husband's face."

The women giggled. Larry shook his head, "I was just wondering how it would be with her as Mayor. You know, it makes a lot of sense." He fixed his eyes on his wife. "You probably have the best idea of how real life in an isolated community ought to run. Your specialty puts you ahead of anyone else in the area."

They all stared at each other and the broke up into another round of laughter. Larry gave Janet a squeeze on the hand. It was indeed something to think about.

Cujo walked into the merriment with a frown on his face. "Is everyone up? I thought it was just me."

"Sorry Cujo," Larry laughed, "We were just planning to take over the town."

Cujo's face didn't change, "Can you do it this morning?"

Larry lost the smile, "What's up?"

"Come on over to my workbench."

The whole group walked the circular path around the huge telescope to the area where Cujo was wiring together something with a couple of tubes, a speaker, and a number of other parts.

He explained, "I was worried about the Constable."

"Me too."

Cujo continued, "There was no telephone call, but I thought I might just be able to listen in anyway."

"How?"

He looked embarrassed, "Well, back in high school, I was a 'phone phreak'. 'Cujo' was my hacker name. I knew how to trick the phone system into providing free calls and other services. It was all illegal, of course, and I quit it a long time ago, but I do know a bit about how the phones work. I knew, for example, that you can listen in to a dead phone." He waved at the setup on the workbench. "A high-gain amplifier can pick up the little bit of signal that the microphone can still produce across the switch capacitance."

"Did it work?" asked Cathy.

He nodded, and clipped an alligator clip to one of the terminals of a battery.

Faintly, voices could be heard over the speaker. One of the voices was clearly Bern's. The words were hard to understand.

"I listened for several minutes, until I heard you guys laughing." He looked at Larry. "The Constable is locked in his own jail. The invaders have arrived in Coonabarabran. It looks like they are in charge now."

Radiation

THE WITCH

She slept, a part of her mind nestled in Abe's.

In her dream, they lay together beneath a cypress, listening to the river bubble past, soaking up the summer warmth. Her head rested on his shoulder. He held her in the bounds of his arm, his hand keeping her close, keeping her safe.

The tree above had changed. Now it was an apple tree, and she could feel him staring at one of the red, shiny fruit, examining it as it waved in the breeze, tasting it in anticipation, remembering all the apples of his life in one composite spread over the years. He readied himself to pick it for her.

The blow knocked her awake, tumbling across the hard porcelain floor of her pit. Pain shot up her arm from the impact.

Her eyes focused on two of them, dark angels with her blood in their eyes.

One was Asca, the telepath. Impossibly sharp, his claw touched a vein in her neck. It punctured, but just short of spilling out her life pulse.

Break contact with your mate.

Without argument, or even thought, she pulled herself tightly into her own head. The other, *Second*, she realized, spit sharp Cerik orders at the telepath, and the two of them, with her in tow, leapt out of the pit.

The race through the maze of the ship gave her almost no pause to think. When they entered the bay that contained the two scout ships, she understood.

Asca's unblinking attention, and his claws at ready, let her know one thing. There was no chance to warn Abe that they were coming. She'd be dead the second she made the attempt. Resonance from her captor leaked from her captor. Every thought was being monitored.

I can't even pray for him.

Even that thought had to be cut short, as Asca caught the hint of Abe's essence in her thoughts.

She closed her eyes, wet with tears, and gave herself up to her own worst fears.

THE WIZARD

Abe woke from his gentle dream of the orchards near Medina, where he had worked several seasons as a kid.

He frowned. Something was wrong. He pulled on his clothes. Time to wash these. He wished fervently for running water. Maybe he could fix up a rain barrel on the roof.

Later. Other deadlines were a lot closer.

Down in the garage, Hodgepodge should be putting the finishing touches on the car.

That was worth a look. He moved down the lightless corridors with the ease of someone who walked without seeing most of the time anyway. He opened the door.

It was a shock. All the side panels were closed up. The robot was motionless.

What's wrong?

But the dancing lights on the dash of the vehicle told him that nothing was wrong.

Diagnostics. He is ahead of schedule.

"Hodgepodge. Good morning."

"Good morning, Abe."

He glanced at the Ouija board, mounted above the LCD display.

"Good morning, Sharon."

There was no answering flicker of lights.

Sharon? Are you there?

No response.

"Hodgepodge? Any message from Sharon?"

"The board was inactive from 3:22 am until 4:15 while it was being installed in the vehicle. However, during its active times, there was no signal."

Sharon. Can you hear me?

Nothing.

THE SEER

Ed was sleeping face down on the couch where he had collapsed around sunset—the middle of the star-night. Angela shook him by the shoulder, "Ed, wake up. There's someone at the door."

The night visions scurried for the edges of his awareness, as the particularly dark dream shattered and vanished into fragments too small to latch on to.

"What?" he mumbled.

"The door. Someone is banging on it." She glanced quickly at the front of the house, and then shook his arm more vigorously.

"Okay." He levered himself erect. The noise finally intruded into his consciousness. He lurched to his feet and opened the door.

It was a boy, roughly Helen's age. He looked frightened in the deep darkness of the early morning hours.

Ed had to prompt him, "Hello, what do you want?"

"Er. Mr. Black sent me. Helen is sick. He wants to know if you know anything about the radiation."

Angela, just behind him, clenched her hand on his arm. She beat him to the answer. "Bring her here. We have to get her shielded. I'll fix up the bed."

Ed agreed, and followed the boy, up the cliffside trail.

"What's your name?"

"Sam."

"How is she?"

The boy looked back at him with a frown. "I dunno. Daddy had us up at star-set to help Mr. and Miz Black look for her. We chased that stupid horse all over the pasture before Miz Black found her behind the barn."

The climb up the trail with neither moon nor star to provide any light was tricky. Only the aurora helped.

Up on the top of the cliff, they picked up the pace to a trot. Helen's horse was secured to the streetlight pole. It was lying on its side. Ed frowned when he caught the dark foam on its muzzle. It panted like a runner at the finish line. The air stunk of something sick and foul that Ed couldn't identify.

They walked on into the house.

Helen's home was a modern ranch style home decorated in Betelgeuse Panic. Every stick of furniture was collected into the rear of the den, farthest from the windows, under the thickest part of the attic. Bookshelves were freestanding like a hedge around the beds. It was his first look at the makeshift radiation protection that had been broadcast on the city's radio station. Central Texas was singularly free of cellars, and his visions were making that absence painfully clear. A pair of candles lit the bed.

Will Black blinked, and there was a look in his eyes that caused the strength to bleed out Ed's soul.

"I'm glad you are here. I think she's got radiation sickness."

Ed saw her stir in the bed. He knew without asking why there were pans on the floor next to the bed. Nausea was the first sign.

"We have to get her down to my place. Radiation exposures build up." He looked over at Helen's mother. "The first thing to do is make sure she has tons of rock between her and the star when it comes up."

Every eye was on him, even, he noticed, Helen's. It was enough to break his train of thought. They were looking to him for advice and guidance. How strange. That had never happened before. Whatever he had been saying skipped away across his blank mind. The pause was uncomfortably long.

He looked down at the girl. "Hi."

She didn't manage a smile, but replied in kind. "Hi."

"How are you feeling?"

She closed her eyes. "I'm tired." Her breathing slowed a little. She slept.

He talked in a whisper. "Mr. Black, how long was she exposed?"

"We don't know. The horse broke free during the night. She must have gone out to take care of it. I told her not to go out there when the star was up!" He looked trapped. He put his hand gently on his sleeping daughter's head.

As animated as the father was, Mrs. Black showed her fear in the stillness of a mouse, hoping that if she didn't move, the danger would pass on by. Only her eyes, wide and shiny, betrayed her.

Ed put his the fingertips of his right hand on his forehead. A memory or the residue of a vision, he couldn't tell which, drove him to explain.

"The reason I ask is that shingles and plywood can't stop everything. If Helen is sick because she was out most of the night, then the rest of you might get to the same point in a week.

"All of you, and your neighbors, need to be down the cliff every starshine until the peak radiation passes."

...

The move took several hours. Sam was sent to spread the word to the other houses. Ed had to clarify his invitation when it became clear that Helen's story had everyone frightened. It was the first real evidence people had that the radiation was real. And no one knew if it would get worse.

"There is very little room down there in the star shadow. I am making room for Helen in the house, but I have another patient in there already and they will need as much quiet as possible. You'll have to camp in the yard."

Ed stayed with the Blacks, although Helen's father was quite firm that he would need no help carrying her down the trail. They took the back way out of the house, avoiding the horse. Ed helped carry their bedrolls. Mrs. Black mentioned several times that it was just a campout. She wasn't abandoning her home.

It was a long day, helping the different families find places to set up their bedding. Ed had the best idea of where the star-shadow ended, and gave suggestions, but the sun's path across the sky was about the same as Betelgeuse, so any sunlit spot was immediately suspect.

The bodyguard must have moved; his spot was where Sammy's family camped.

Helen got rapidly worse after the move. Her mother and Angela worked together to make her comfortable and to keep her from being dehydrated. She couldn't keep anything in her stomach. There wasn't anyone with medical experience in the whole group. It was just a case of exchanging family remedies and hoping.

It was noon when Angela came out to sit by Ed on the edge of the porch.

"I was so worried about getting food that I neglected everything else," he grumbled, as he shifted his tired backside on the tile. "I would give a lot for a comfortable chair out here."

"Make it a couch." She scooted up beside him and invited his arm around her.

"How is Helen?"

"Not any better. If the nausea doesn't let up soon..."

"Will she recover?"

A shrug. "You're the fortune teller. All I know is stories from an essay on Hiroshima. But that was a bomb blast. This is different. There's supposed to be a period of recovery. The good cases then gradually regain all their health. The bad ones... don't.

"Helen's big danger is infection. If we can keep her stable, then maybe."

"What more can I do?"

"Feed her. Feed them all. You were right to bring them all down here."

There were a half-dozen people walking about, or settled among their bedding. Most were back up on their property, doing last-minute chores until star-rise.

Angela spoke in a whisper. "Probably all of them have mild cases of radiation exposure. In mild cases, it doesn't show up except in blood tests. With luck, they'll never know it. But white blood cells are damaged. They'll be likely to catch any bug around. With malnutrition, it'll be worse."

"We don't have enough to feed everyone for very long."

She nodded. "But if I'm right, even a flu infection would leave us with some bodies to bury. A single course of stew and vitamins every day will save lives. If the radiation passes its peak in a few days, we'll have enough."

Ed stared out at the people, his neighbors. He didn't ask what would happen if the peak didn't pass soon. His visions gave him confidence that at least some people would survive.

"Okay. You're the smart one. If you think we can feed them, then let's do it. But you must recruit the cooks. You are barely out of the sickbed yourself. Get help. Don't do all the work yourself. I won't have it."

The door opened behind them. Will Black came out.

Ed looked up at his face, "Will? Is everything okay?"

He glanced at them, seeing them for the first time. "I've got to go back up." He looked up at the cliff. "Helen asked me to take care of Dadbert."

Ed flashed a vision. *Will Black strained with a rope and a come-along, working the lever hard, crying so hard he could barely see, as he hauled the carcass of the dead horse up onto a flatbed trailer.*

He shook from the intensity of the vision, gone the same second it started. Angela felt the shake, and reached for his arm.

"Do you need any help?" he asked the man.

He shook his head, "No. This is my job." He stepped off the porch.

Ed quickly got to his feet. He reached out and put his hand.

"Will!"

He turned. Ed could see the father's worry in his eyes. "Will, under no circumstances should you stay up there past star-rise. Under no circumstances. Understand me."

He seemed impressed by Ed's intensity. "I'll be okay."

"If you are late, I'll be coming for you."

"Okay. I won't be late."

They watched him head up the trail, even as a troop of children were heading down.

Angela got to her feet. "I'd better start recruiting my cooks."

"Let me know what I can do to help."

She looked at the growing collection of people and said simply, "Pray."

Ed sat back down and stared at the few tufts of grass in the rocky soil—his poor excuse for a lawn. Prayer was something he'd never learned. He wished he could learn.

What about my spirit guide? Could she help Helen, like she helped Angela?

He closed his eyes and poured all his intensity into a call for that elusive voice. Sharon had always been there, he realized, just over the hill, just out of reach. As a child, she had been the secret friend that never abandoned him.

He abandoned her. The sweet call of normal human contact had made him turn his back on her. He'd thought that sanity demanded it. No. Not sanity, just the opinions of the sane.

Well, maybe he wasn't sane. Maybe he would never be sane. He was *different*.

And I should never have turned my back on you. Sharon? Are you there? Can you hear me?

THE WIZARD

Scott blinked from the sleep in his eyes. "I understand."

"I wouldn't ask," Abe apologized, "but Hodgepodge is just one stuck servo or fried transistor from being unable to take care of himself."

Scott looked down the hall towards the garage. "You're really going to head out?"

Abe nodded. "I have to. Sharon has gone silent. There are a number of explanations for that—all bad. I have to get the engine far from here. The instant Betelgeuse sets, I'm out of here."

"You think they can detect it."

Abe nodded.

Scott reached out his hand. They shook. "Get it far from my family, but don't get yourself killed either."

"That's not on my agenda."

Abe handed over the handwritten sheets of paper. He had sweated hours over the lists: Backup and restore procedures, repair parts inventories, the design for a new robot platform using just the parts on hand, plus several pages of notes describing Abe's best guess at how Hodgepodge was developing. It was his best hope for Hodgepodge's continued survival, should he not come back.

The garage was only lit by a single bulb. Shadows were deep. He glanced at his wristwatch. The illuminated hands glowed strongly.

Radium dial, not the soak-up-the-sun kind. Frank had good taste.

The elder Victor's pure mechanical watch was excellent workmanship, and probably cost him quite a bit back when he was alive. It kept time with precision, and was the only timepiece Abe trusted anymore. Star-set in five minutes.

He had to be moving out the door by then. The aliens would be coming to kill him, sheltered by the same Earth-shadow that would shelter him. If they were close, they could attack at any time.

"You were going to leave without saying 'Good-bye'?"

Mary Ellen, dressed in her flowered green robe, moved out of the shadowed doorway. She was carrying a large wrapped bundle.

Abe moved close and wrapped his large arms around her. She seemed especially frail. He didn't think of her that way very often. "My fault. I didn't want to wake you."

"You didn't want to get tongue-lashed, you mean."

He grinned. "Well...maybe a little." He turned serious. "But I have to go. I have to."

Mary Ellen had her lawyer face on. He couldn't tell what she was thinking. Then she blinked, and looked down at her bundle. "I know. I want you to take this." She handed it to him, a backpack with blankets sticking out the top. "You could be out for days, if your rendezvous doesn't come off as you think. If the star comes out, I want you under a bridge or something. If you can keep this dry, it should be comfortable enough."

He took the bundle, and gave her a kiss. "I never have been able to come in out of the rain without you looking over me. Thank you." He stashed it in the vanishingly small space behind the seat.

"You have been talking to Hodgepodge, haven't you?" He'd been careful to keep his plans quiet. Scott wouldn't have blown his secret.

"That tin whistle will talk loud and long to anyone who asks. I wouldn't plan any more battles with it listening." She pulled her robe a little tighter around her.

"You know about the machine gun."

She sniffed and nodded her head sadly. "I just hope you took enough ammunition. Pick your shots."

"I hope I won't have to use any. The idea is to trade, not kill each other."

"If they leave another crater in the ground with you in it, I'll never forgive you. Take this." She handed him a pistol.

Abe knew just enough about firearms to recognize it as one of her heavyweights. It was flat black. The barrel poking out the tip of the holster proclaimed it 9mm.

"It is loaded with Teflon bullets. There are only five shots left, so be careful." Her eyes looked a little wet around the edges. Although Abe hadn't any intention of getting into a running gun battle with the aliens, he took the gun for what it was, a precious gift from his mother.

"I will be careful. I am smart. You've told me that often enough. I will find a way, remember that." He kissed her again.

He glanced at Frank's watch, gave her a last smile, and climbed into the car.

The console lit up. He applied a little power to the electrical motors, and he started moving. The garage door opened as he approached, and with one wave back at Mary Ellen, still standing there, he headed out.

Sickness

THE SCIENTIST

Larry Kelly pulled the bicycle off the bitumen surface of Timor Road, just a kilometer out of Coonabarabran. He was sweating even in the cool morning air. It was a 25 minute drive by car, and even though he'd risked going much faster than was prudent on the Blackburn hill grade, it still took him longer than he'd planned.

After a long look down the road in both directions, he stashed the bicycle out of sight and tied a white rag to a tree branch. There were supposed to be lookouts on all the roads, according to what they had overheard on the telephone tap. He loosened the straps a little on his backpack, and headed across country to avoid being seen.

People were up and about. He tried to look inconspicuous, but he was the only one with a backpack. He spotted two lookouts, but they weren't very alert. When he got close to his house, he just nodded and waved when people called a greeting. He wasn't ready to talk to anyone, not just yet. That wasn't his job.

His key slid into the lock and clicked. He was in.

The one-story brick house had an unreal sense of waiting. It was waiting, biding it's time, ignoring the dust, just waiting for Janet and him to come on back home. He shook his head. When would that be?

He worked quickly, conscious of time. He emptied his backpack and rummaged in the kitchen until he found a salt shaker and napkins. He re-packed the lunch and eating utensils and thermos bottle.

He took the little black box and his pocket knife and clipped the box's antenna to a phone line scraped bare. The regular phone system was dead, but the long wires could still make a great antenna.

A bent piece of sheet metal formed a telegraph key, and with a few short keystrokes, he sent a signal to the others.

Spark gap radio transmitters were relatively easy to make—a high voltage transformer like the coil from a car, a capacitor, a battery and a keyswitch. Key the juice and a spark arcs across your gap, for as long it takes your capacitor to discharge. The electric arc splashes radio waves all across the spectrum. Any radio in range could pick it up, no matter what frequency it was tuned to. They were outlawed early in the development of radio for that very reason.

It was the receivers that were more difficult. A crystal set was the best they could make in the shop on short order, and they didn't even send him with one of those. If he were successful, he wouldn't need it. If not, then they didn't want to lose the parts to the enemy.

He folded up the transmitter and wrapped it in the waxy cloth from an old cheese and stuffed it in his lunch box.

The walk to the Constable's office was short. Coonabarabran wasn't that big a place. The big clock tower dominated the main intersection. The clock was wrong. *Is it electric? Probably.* There were dead street lights about half way up.

As he turned the corner, carrying his lunchbox, he saw the office. The dynamite hadn't stopped the invaders from making their way to Dubbo. The block was lined with their old cars. A pair of men rested in the front seat of a Studebaker whose paint was so weathered that you couldn't call it anything but gray. The street was otherwise empty. The townspeople were keeping clear of the men with guns.

That's what I should be doing.

But he had already sent the signal. Janet would be hovering around Cujo's phone tap, listening in. He crossed the street and headed straight for the office.

"Hold it there!"

He stopped, looking puzzled. "Hello?"

One of the lookouts, sitting in the car, pulled his gun up.

Whoa! Larry jerked back. He had been expecting it, but the barrel of a gun in real life was a kick to the hind brain. He froze.

"What're you doing here?"

"Name's Kelly. I fix the electricity."

There was the click of a door latch. Another man came out of the office. He too carried a gun. "Problem John?"

"Electrician came sneaking up on us."

"I did not sneak!"

"Shut up." The inside man looked him over. "I'll question him, John. You stay put."

The lookout sagged back in his seat. "Thanks, Dean." He didn't look strong enough to do anything else.

'Dean' came close to pat his pockets for a hidden gun. "What's in the box?"

"Lunch.'

The man with the gun put a hand on his wrist and pulled him on in to the office. His hand was hot on Larry's skin.

"Open it." he ordered. Larry set the lunchbox and thermos on the table. He opened it up.

"What do you have?"

"Pork sausage. Tuna salad in the jar."

Dean looked pained. "I'm not that hungry after all." He nodded toward the thermos. "Coffee?" He sounded hopeful.

Larry shook his head, "Buttermilk. It's a little warm."

His captor made a face, then turned away and found a seat. But the questions weren't over.

"You're an electrician?"

"Close enough. I run the generator. I was supposed to report to the Constable. Is he here?"

The man thought that was funny. "Sure. Want to talk to him? Just go through that door." He pointed with the gun.

Larry got to his feet. Through the indicated door was a small locked cell. Bern and two of his men got their feet when he walked in.

"What are you doing here?"

Larry, playing to Dean through the still opened door, replied in an injured tone, "You told me to report to you when we were short on diesel. I warned you that little tank wouldn't last long."

The truth of the matter was so far to the contrary that Bern picked up the thread easily enough.

"Well, with the Dubbos in charge, it's not my problem anymore."

Larry whispered, "Food."

A flicker of comprehension played over the constable's face.

"You didn't bring us any food did you? We are starving in here and these gunmen won't do anything about it."

"Oh, shut up!" Came the irritated comment from the next room.

Larry said, "All I've got is my lunchbox. He's got it now."

"Well, bring it in here."

"Hey! It's my lunch."

"Don't be selfish! We haven't eaten in more than a day!"

"Well, you will just have to wait a little more."

The guard got to his feet, snapped the lunchbox shut, grabbed it and the thermos and handed it to Larry.

"You get in there with them and work it out yourselves." He unlocked the cell and pushed Larry into the cramped quarters.

"Just don't spew. We've had enough of that today already!"

. . .

Larry signaled for the argument to continue. After a few more minutes, Dean closed the connecting door to block out the squabble.

"How are your men? Did you stay out of the starshine?"

There were nods. "Well enough," said the constable. "At least, we aren't having the heaves like them. Donald was shot. He's over at the hospital. Did you see them around town?"

"Some of 'em. They all look like three days into the influenza."

"Yes. I have been worried that they'll all collapse on us and leave us to starve in this cell."

Larry grinned, "Well, that's why I'm here." He opened the lunchbox.

He had never been so glad when Dean started to turn green at his description of the high fat foods. The bluff was critical.

First came the knife and fork. The guard had never looked at them. Cujo's magic at in the machine shop had been wasted. The outer appearance of the blunt knife and dull tined fork came off to reveal a pair of lethally sharp knives. They went into grateful hands. The wrapped spark-gap transmitter went into his pocket. The hollowed out sausage concealed a bundle of darts. The 'tuna salad' was a spool of wire and a large magnet. If he had needed it, the whole box could be disassembled. They had planed for a dozen methods of escape.

"No lock pick?" asked Bern with a grin on his face.

"We didn't know what kind of lock."

"I'll remedy that."

"No matter." Larry took the napkin and massaged it in some of the grease from the sausage. He kneaded the mess and jammed it into the gap below the lock's bolt. He formed a cup around the metal.

When he opened the thermos, vapors swirled into the air.

"I take it that's not buttermilk."

"No. Liquid Nitrogen. We use it to supercool some of the instruments to make them more sensitive." He carefully poured the furiously boiling, freezing fluid into the cavity he had formed around the bolt. "I did this a couple of times in university labs. It was always a kick."

He waited for a moment. The liquid nitrogen was sapping all the heat out of the metal. When the level started to drop, he topped it off with more from the thermos. Frost was forming on the bars all around the bolt, where there was contact.

"It's ready," he said finally. He pushed back into the cell. "Give me room."

With a deep intake of breath, he put all his strength into a single kick right at the lock. The metal bolt, leached of all its heat, had turned brittle. It shattered into a shower of bright little fragments. The remaining liquid nitrogen hit the floor and covered it with a swirling fog. The door swung open with hardly a sound.

The constable and his men took over. The guard hadn't locked the connecting door, and he'd decided to take a doze. He never woke up.

Bern collected guns for his men from the cabinets. There was still only one way out, and men with guns were just outside.

"Wait another minute." Larry cautioned.

"Why?"

"I can arrange a distraction." He connected the wire to the little transmitter and sent a pre-arranged code.

"I didn't come alone."

It wasn't long. Down the street, there was the boom of an explosion. The lawman waited until the lookouts in the car got out and stared off in the direction of the sound. His men were out the door and brought them down without a stray shot.

The whole battle of Coonabarabran was over within the hour. Cathy and Cujo had collected defenders while he had gone into the jail. It was a pitiful, sick, lot of invaders, in the final analysis.

"They were defeated at the rockfall, working in the radiation," said Constable Bern. "We had the science. They didn't."

Larry nodded, still grim faced. Something Janet had said kept going over and over in his head. He glanced at the position of the sun. "We have to get moving. I need to be back before it rises."

THE TELEPATH

Asca drifted into *erdan*. The trip to the planet was longer than he liked, and it seemed like he could feel the deathglow just outside of their path. There was no real space to move in the cabin of the scout ship. It was a Delense design, made for their use rather than for their Cerik masters, and the interior was an interconnected cluster of chambers barely big enough for each individual, rather like the ancestral burrows the Builders came from.

It took an effort of will for a Cerik to settle in for an extended trip. The pilot, one of the Ship Mover group, was the only one with any freedom at all. Of course, he was constantly having to check their path. Twice now, the ship had drifted to the edge of the moon's star-shadow, and he had to move them back into the safety of that darkness. Space flight was always like that. A Cerik's pounce was accurate to the width of a talon-tip, able to take out the eyes of a prey without leaving a scratch on the hide, but over hours, even a talon-tip's accuracy wasn't enough.

Second had the easiest time, in Asca's judgment. He backed into his chamber, settled down, and went into *erdan*. His energies were for tomorrow. If Asca or the pilot failed in their job, punishment would come soon enough.

Of course, the prey was just that, prey. Even a light scan of her thoughts made it clear that she was entirely bound up in her own fears. All he had to do was check on her every so often. She knew her own death was close, and that there was nothing she could do about it.

Asca's own thoughts were on the future. Everything during the past few days had gone his way. His skills and his importance were being recognized.

No matter whether Second or Tenthonad was destined to take final charge, his own position looked good. There was a lot to be said for being the only telepath on the ship. He glanced across the interconnecting chamber at the prey, bound in her net like live meat on the way to the market. At least, he was the only Cerik telepath.

Her eyes blinked open, and he felt a stronger wave of fear.

No, you are not my meat, he sent. **But all non-Cerik are meat for the talon. Enjoy the air of your cage.**

The images and scents of her disorganized mind swirled off into incoherence, and he turned his attention back to his own plans. It would be pleasant to have a Second of his own.

THE SEER

The Blacks sat on the couch next to Helen's bed. Ed took in the image of them, heads bowed, eyes shut, hand in hand. They were praying. He couldn't understand what they were going through. He wondered if he would have any children of his own.

His private theory was that his affliction was due to some mutation that enabled him to see the future. Maybe this same mutation would keep him from having children.

But my father was a psychic. At least, that's what George said.

He wished his visions worked to show the past.

What was my father like? What would it have been like to have had a family?

He slipped out of the bedroom.

Best to leave them alone.

In the hallway, his own reflection caught his attention. Was he like his father? What about his mother? What did George really know? How much would he tell? Especially, if he didn't agree to work with this shadowy organization.

He looked into his own eyes. They were dark, as dark as his ignorance of his own future.

My visions rarely tell me my own fate.

He closed his eyes, intensely grateful for the fact. Whether it was the nature of precognition, or just a deep psychological defense mechanism, it was the only thing that kept him alive.

In the kitchen, Angela was working with three other ladies, preparing the community meal. He poked his head in just long enough to say 'hi' and be run off. Angela was in charge and she was busy.

Ed was happy with that. It suited him to turn the important decisions over to her. She was good with people. She could gain respect with just a few chosen words. She never had to depend on luck, like he did.

The house was starting to gain new furniture. A community was based on a complex web of trades and favors, and even if he could start giving away his food, it didn't sit well with the neighbors to be too far behind in their debt to him. This was another of Angela's areas. The first time he saw a man carrying a chair down the cliff trail, he didn't have a clue what was happening.

He chose a big wooden rocker and settled in.

A strange wave of recognition came over him. There was Mrs. Black, holding an infant, rocking the baby to sleep.

He scrambled out of the chair.

What was that?

The vision bled away from him. He touched the chair, but there was nothing more than hard polished wood. He sat again. Perhaps this was just the perils of used furniture.

So, Karen Black will have a baby. Should I tell her?

No. Not now. They needed to concentrate all their love on Helen right now.

She was getting better, but the radio report about radiation sickness was far from encouraging. Even if you had a fatal exposure, there was a period of false recovery for about two weeks before the damage to your body re-asserted itself.

Helen Black stood before a mirror, crying as her hair came out in her brush.

Ed shook from the instant vision. So, she did have a significant exposure. He closed his eyes.

How do you pray?

God! Help Helen Black. Thank you.

His stomach was queasy. Each vision took something out of him. These were emotionally loaded. He liked Helen. She was the first person that made him feel like an adult, rather than just a late-blooming teenager. Helen was his neighbor, his friend.

I have to do something.

What about Sharon? He had to try that again. Helen's life was at stake.

Prayer

THE WITCH

Sharon worked at being invisible. She could think her own thoughts, as long as she was sure that Asca was pre-occupied with his own plans for dynasty. For the moments when he was consciously probing her, it was so easy to lapse back into her own very real terror. Like pinching her earlobe to keep herself awake, there were memories, like her first meeting with Tenthonad, that she could call up at will that still had the power to wash rationality away.

Even in his distracted state, she dared not try to contact Abe though his machine. Asca was only aware that she could communicate with him, but he had no concept of the means. She was resolved to keep at least that one bit of information from him. Perhaps Asca had psychokinetic abilities, perhaps not. If the Cerik could make the lights blink for Abe, the hunters would obviously make the attempt. There was too much at risk. Best to stay safe.

She had risked a brief touch. It had taken too much willpower to hide her wave of relief to find Abe on the road, ready for the encounter. It hurt to break it off, but Asca's threat to cut her throat had been genuine. She'd sweated out the few seconds, and hid her relief when it went unnoticed.

Her life was controlled by the two dark angels whose minds she could not read. All her life she'd wished for a way to block thoughts. Well, it was possible, at least for these oversized killing machines. Unfortunately, it was the wrong time and the wrong place and the wrong people.

She'd never seriously considered having a child of her own. She'd been the loneliest child in the world, and her mother made sure of it. Sharon was unwilling to do that to another.

But, what if it were possible for the adults to shield their thoughts, so that a growing child could develop a mind and an identity of her own, and yet still provide normal human contact?

What would her own life have been like if she had a mother always close at hand to help her with skinned knees and all the monsters? What would it have been like to play with friends, real friends, not just those sensitive minds of people she could never see and never touch?

As old memories bubbled to the surface, one thought, not her own, came unbidden to the fore.

Sharon! Sharon, can you hear me?

The connection was effortless, and compelling. She couldn't have avoided it, even if she had been warned.

Ed, contact right now is dangerous...

There you are! I was afraid you were gone. I have another favor to ask.

With half her attention on Asca, off in his light trance, she absorbed Ed's fear for the little girl, and his faith that somehow she could help. Sharon's own fear was ignored, as if he couldn't hear it. And right now, she couldn't turn him down.

Okay. I'll help. You know the process. Make contact with her, and if I have to break off, do not try to contact me. I will get back when it is safe.

He agreed, and headed for the girl's sickbed. Through his eyes she saw the girl, and her hovering parents. Ed was embarrassed, but insistent that he had to touch Helen to 'heal' her. The parents hesitated, but he didn't wait. He settled into a chair beside the bed and put his hands on either side of her head.

It was enough. She was in.

The cell damage was widespread. Many were dead. But the most widespread problem was that the cells, although still alive, had stopped dividing. The balancing act of cell division and death was now broken. The existing cells would slide down towards death, each at their own rate, but they would not be replaced.

This was Sharon's first experience with radiation damage, and the enormity of what was happening all over the Earth sent a sharp cry of agony through her. Millions of people were going through the same slow death that this girl faced. And there was nothing she could do for them.

Asca stirred from his predator's waiting trance and gave her a quick scan, but saw nothing strange. She was often pre-occupied by her body. He missed the distinction, and drifted back to his trance.

Daring to breathe again, Sharon turned her attention back to the girl.

And was shocked to feel the tendrils of Helen's own awareness reaching for her.

Hardly a telepath, the little girl was still a little sensitive. Sharon did her best to soothe away the psychic irritation that her presence was causing. Right now, she did not want to communicate directly with the girl.

It was all so hopeless. So much damage! Was there any chance at all that she could help?

But giving up didn't come naturally. Her own self-repair had honed those skills. She used it several times a day just to stay alive.

There were obvious things—killing off several beginning infections. The body's defenses were as lethargic as the rest of Helen's cells. Large scale changes were happening to her blood. Sharon started digging into that mystery, and what she found only deepened her despair at helping this little girl.

The radiation had devastated the blood-producing cells in the bone marrow. Her life span was measured by the longevity of her existing blood. When her white blood cells died, there would be no more to fight infection. When her platelets died, she would begin to bleed internally, all throughout her body. When the red cells died, all the other cells of her body would suffocate from lack of oxygen.

The blood factory in her bones had to be restored if there was to be any chance at all.

Sharon went deep into the bone marrow. She concentrated on one dormant stem cell.

It took time, and energy, but after a deep filtering of the interior of the cell, it woke up. She stoked the fires of the mitochondria and directed more fuel through the cell membrane. She was most gratified when mitosis was triggered and a new fresh blood cell was produced and drifted off in the flow.

It can be done.

Her pleasure lasted only a few seconds. One isn't enough. Repairing one cell is one thing. For Helen to survive, millions of bone marrow cells would have to be awakened the same way.

Asca could detect her at any moment. If he didn't, she was still heading to her doom, only hours away. If by some miracle she survived that, even then she could not finish the repair before the girl lost the battle to infection. It was hopeless.

There was a reaction in the girl. Sharon was startled. She probed, and detected a faint bond. Helen had felt her sense of defeat. Sharon scanned her thoughts and found a frightened little girl, alone in the dark passages of her sickness, crying, *Help me! Help me! Help me!*

Sharon pulled back into her own mind, sick at heart. *I'm not strong enough.*

As if on cue, she felt a flow of energy pour into her. She followed it back.

Ed was willing strength into her. He had felt her need. True to her order, he hadn't tried to contact her, but he could react to this primal need.

Ed, thank you.

Helen?

The damage is too great. I am not strong enough, or quick enough to repair the damage.

The push of energy increased. **I could help.**

I don't know. Even that will probably not be enough.

There was a hurt from him. Then a resurgence of hope. **Her parents are here. Can they help?**

Sharon thought about it. She had no idea if this energy could be tapped from the non-telepathic. Still, what could be worse than not trying? Should she spend the rest of her hours curled in her bonds, waiting for the fangs and claws to end it?

Okay. Let's try it.

She watched the surface of his mind as he pulled the confused, but desperate Blacks into the mix. They pulled up chairs and Ed gave them instructions that he himself didn't quite understand. He just felt that it was right.

He held his position with his hands on her head. Her father was on her right and her mother on her left. They laid their hands on Helen's bared belly with clear direction to hold on and to push strength into their daughter.

Sharon was suddenly caught into the flood. Telepathic or not, Ed's contribution was nothing to the flood of strength, will, and love spilling from Helen's parents.

Sharon dived deep into the flow.

THE SEER

Ed was conscious only of the ache and stiffness of his arms and back. Helen was breathing freely. He felt a contentment, though all the pain. Will and Karen Black were asleep, drained, still holding their positions over their daughter.

Ed?

Yes, Sharon, you did it.

I don't know. There was so much to do, and I only could do a small fraction of it.

Ed's confidence was unshakable. **No, you forget. I'm the one with the visions of the future.** It has something new for him. He had never channeled his visions though personal contact as he had with Helen. For all his experience, he had never put his hands on someone during a vision.

He opened his mind, inviting Sharon into the scene.

...

The palace with high, white stone-work towers crowned the wooded hill. Mounted soldiers, knights wearing white tunics emblazoned with a rearing stallion, lined the entranceway through the surrounding walls. Pavilions, canopies in deep blue, sheltering the richly dressed audience, lined the other side of the processional.

On the dais, a young man stood by the throne. He was dressed like the knights—only the gold embroidery and richer colors proclaimed him their leader and king.

Helen, and there was no doubt that this young lady in her mid twenties was anyone else, made the slow steps up the dais, her attendants dropping back. The young king stepped forward and took her hand. Helen's joy radiated from her face, strong enough to be felt across all time.

...

The vision, as most of them were, was bounded to this single moment of time, but it was enough for Ed. He *knew* Helen would survive, and more than that—she he would live to fulfill some destiny he was happy to be able to glimpse.

That was nice. Sharon sent to him. **But I know that I didn't completely cure her. She can survive, but only with more medical help.**

What do you mean?

It's her blood. I concentrated on fixing the stem cells that will produce more blood. Over time, they will return to their healthy function, but it'll take time. Helen will need blood transfusions, maybe several of them, before she will pull out of it. Even with your help, this was the best I could do.

Ed was sobered. He couldn't deny his vision, but he wouldn't dream of second guessing Sharon on something like this.

The only problem was that there was no one in their little community that had that kind of medical experience.

Sharon?

There was no answer. He could feel she was gone.

Well, she'd warned him it'd be that way.

"Hi."

Ed opened his eyes. Helen was awake. He pulled his hands from her head, and eased his chair back with a creaking of wood that felt just like the creaking in his stiff arms and legs.

"Hello, Helen. How are you feeling?"

"Better. I had this wonderful dream."

"A dream?"

"Yes. I was falling, and it was scary. I screamed for help, and no one could hear me. Then this angel flew down from the sky and caught me. Then Momma and Daddy and you and the angel pulled me up and saved me."

Ed smiled at her. He was grateful to see her smile back.

"Someday, after you are well, I will tell you a story. But for now, I think your dream was true. Your parents prayed. I prayed. And an angel did come down to save you."

He woke the Blacks, and they were as drained as he felt. They barely had the strength to express how grateful they were at Helen's improvement. He waited to talk about the blood transfusions. It was the most he could do to push aside their gratitude and ignore their questions. He hadn't really done the healing. The real story would have to wait.

Angela had taken one look at his face, and ordered him to the living room where he could collapse in his chair.

"Angela," he asked as she fussed around him, tucking in the edges of a blanket.

"Yes."

"What do you think about George?"

She stopped her activity, and looked him in the eyes. "Why?"

Ed gave her a brief summary of the session with Helen.

"This 'Sharon', she's the spirit-guide you said is the one who healed me?"

"Yes, and she says that Helen's survival will depend on blood transfusions."

Angela sat down on the arm of the chair and he put his arm around her. She settled closer. "You know, I never believed that part of your story. It's so easy to put this magic stuff aside and forget about it. I believe that you saved me."

"You don't believe my visions?"

She frowned, staring off at the unused fireplace. "I guess I do. I have to, don't I? All the evidence is there. My problem is that I am educated in the sciences. All this New Age mystic stuff is good for entertainment, but you can't take it seriously. A 'spirit-guide', no less! And one with a name like Sharon. I would expect Gabriella, or Moonbeam, or..."

"Or Angela?" He offered.

She elbowed him in the ribs. "Oh you! I just mean that... 'Sharon' seems a little... ordinary."

"It's her name, a good solid name. What can I say? You wouldn't criticize a person's name if you thought they were real. Would you?"

"No...I guess not." She paused. "If I believe you have psychic visions, and if there are other psychics out there. I guess I have to believe you could have a 'spirit-friend' that's a real person, and not just a...."

"A what?"

"A wish-fulfillment, a dream girl."

Ed laughed. "Sharon is real. She's a close friend, although I have never met her and I haven't the faintest idea what she looks like.

"But you don't have to worry. My real dream girl is here." He hugged her tighter. "Sharon is a close, close friend, who saved your life. But she is not any kind of rival."

Angela seemed to be content with that. Ed really could do nothing but re-assure her. Reality was what he experienced, even if he could never explain it to his closest companion in all his life.

She spoke after a moment, "I've seen people like George Fuller. He could be a very good friend. But you could never completely trust him."

Ed nodded. It was close enough to his own opinion. "Helen needs blood transfusions to survive. George owns the hospitals."

He let the bare facts hang out there in the air, along with the unspoken one. If he asked for this favor, he would be signing on to George's power base, probably for life.

"Life is full of compromise."

He sighed in agreement. "Get me a piece of paper. I need to write a letter."

THE WIZARD

Abe woke at first light, shaking off the stiffness of sleeping on the ground, and worrying about not being up at star-set.

They didn't find me here. So it was okay.

Day two on the road, and he was still alive.

He zipped out of the sleeping bag that Mary Ellen had left him, and chuckled again at all the surprises she had left him, rolled up in the bag. The one highest on his list, clean underwear, was on the top of the stack.

Things weren't going quite like he had planned.

Plan A, go to the Georgetown's Innerspace Caverns and hide both himself and the car inside the cave, was a total washout. He should have realized that a huge cave on the edge of a medium sized city, actually within walking distance of thousands of people, was not going to be deserted when there were radiation warnings out. His first hint had been the local guards posted with automatic rifles keeping everyone, including him, at least a quarter mile from the cave entrance. He admitted to the men that no, he didn't have his lottery number, some kind of admission ticket apparently, and tamely submitted to being turned aside.

Plan B had been to go to another cave, perhaps the Longhorn Caverns over between Marble Falls and Burnett, and try there. Hodgepodge, via radio conference, reminded him those locations were right at the edge of the special radio link distance, and that his help could be unavailable.

Plan C was to wing it—head in the direction of the Hill Country and get off the Blackland prairie. The woods and the hilly terrain gave him at least some chance of controlling when and where they met. He'd just have to do without the thing he wanted the most, a safe place to hide.

When he had started out, his first priority was to get to safety, where he could tell the alien telepaths with absolute conviction that they could not get their drive unit, not without making a deal with him—hide in a cave where they could not dig him out and where their greater speed and unknowable weapons would be useless.

Now, he was reduced to his own trickery, his own surprises, and his knowledge of the terrain. And he had to convince them that they had no chance without trading.

Convince a telepath you aren't holding a busted flush.

He shook his head, and was surprised when a smile cracked his face.

Hiding is out. Good! I've been hiding all my life.

He looked at his car, and the long bulge on the top where Hodgepodge had mounted the machine-gun.

You will deal with me, he told the possible telepaths, **or none of us will survive to brag about the day!**

He loaded his gear back into the car, and edged out into the open air cautiously. The big square culvert under the bridge had been big enough to hide a Jeep, so his streamlined racer had no problems at all. Getting back out was different. A Jeep had four-wheel drive to get back onto the road. This vehicle was like a four wheeled bicycle with a streamlined skin. The electric motors driving the rear wheels were designed to be efficient, not necessarily powerful. The suspension was crude, designed for flat roads, not an irregular stream bed.

He was not surprised when he stalled out, the thin wheels slipping on the wet rocks. Getting downhill was easier than getting back out.

Oh, well. I had to turn it on soon anyway.

He moved his left hand to the new control panel, mounted to the side of the electric car's original controls. He flipped the key switch.

"Do you wish me to mediate?" Hodgepodge asked.

Abe glanced at the radio signal strength. Down in the gully, it was marginal.

"No, I'd better do this manually."

"I will monitor."

"Good." Abe made sure the intensity control was in the off position, and then adjusted the focus, tightening it rearward. Running the alien drive unit was a matter of setting two focus controls and the intensity. It hadn't been obvious, and without Hodgepodge's unblinking devotion to running thousands of simple little tests, it would've remained an enigma. Abe put aside the thought that so much could be learned, if he just had more time to study this technology.

It's just a poker chip. I have to win the game, and it doesn't matter who ends up with this particular chip.

He nudged the intensity, and felt the shove on his back. The car lurched forward as if rear-ended by a truck. He slapped the intensity lever back to zero. They were moving. He applied electricity to the wheels and made it easily back onto the road.

He steered over into the right lane, conscious of the habit, even though there'd been no traffic at all. He glanced up at the road sign as he gained speed. *Nameless Road.*

Good. That would take him to Ranch Road 1431. There were some serious rollercoaster stretches there, and right next to the lake.

Time to do some trolling, he adjusted the drive unit, *with me as the bait.*

He increased the intensity and felt the push on his back. The car started moving faster than its motors, and actually started charging the battery. Abe gripped the steering yoke. It wouldn't be good to lose control on the curves.

THE TELEPATH

Asca felt the relief wash over the pilot as he successfully completed the dash from the star-shadow of the moon to the star-shadow of the planet. There was something unnerving about a danger that couldn't be smelled. The stories that he, all of them, had heard since cub-hood about the shining death that killed slowly and painfully from within still chased his idle thoughts. There was nothing worse than being killed by an enemy that couldn't even be fought.

He opened his eyes, and noticed the prey sleeping. Something had happened to her, some hours ago, but to mention it to any of the others would not be wise. Second would demand to know why he hadn't caught it at the time.

She had lost some of her fear, and yet at the same time, appeared drained of all energy, like a runner down on its knees from exhaustion. He scanned the surface of her mind, lightly. Even asleep, she sensed him, and withdrew, abandoning a dream of green, and a tiny animal like a *chitchit* who loved to be scratched by her.

The mental disturbance was enough to bring her awake. She oriented herself, and then sent a question. **What is going on?**

Asca steeled himself. He would have to talk to her sooner or later.

We will shortly attack the atmosphere. Once in, we will begin hunting for our missing engine.

I know where it is. He's not trying to hide.

'Bright colors hide venom.' We will find him on our own. But he could tell that she was speaking the truth. As far as she could tell, her mate was risking his eyes in order to trade the engine for her. And she knew Cerik would never make such a trade. She was resigned to her own death, and could only hope for her mate's escape.

Let me talk to him. I can translate.

Asca was skeptical. **I can read his thoughts.**

She disagreed, **No, you can't send to him, it is a different skill. Listen to our thoughts, but you will have to send through me.**

He sensed unexamined emotion behind the plea. She could feel him getting closer, as they raced across the upper atmosphere and her need to communicate was climbing.

He also remembered the threat, that the prey would somehow use their own engine as a weapon against them. Machines frightened him. Perhaps it would be better to let her talk to her mate.

Asca edged out of his compartment and rattled the deck with his claws.

"Speak," commanded Second, snapping out of his *erdan.*

"The City-builder has offered to communicate to the holder of the engine."

"And why should I let that happen?"

Asca struggled to put a logical face on his apprehension. "The prey has made a threat, and has activated the engine so that we can detect it."

"So we should arrive quietly and communicate with my claw."

Asca was silent. The most argument he could bring to bear was the absence of assent.

Second snarled at the pilot, and got affirmation that he was tracking signals from the lost engine.

Second probed, "You fear this prey?"

Asca moved softly, in his crouched position. "I have been here before. I was useful then, as I tracked the telepath. We were successful and captured her alive for you to display."

"But, you were fooled. We did not destroy the engine."

"Yes, I was fooled."

Asca admitted it directly, with no overtones of self-abasement. The three of them had attacked with great confidence, great swiftness, and they had come away feeling that all had been accomplished. The discovery of engine signals from the planet cut directly into Second's support among the *tetca*. None would wish to abandon Tenthonad for someone who could be fooled by a prey.

Second's *ineda* was tight, and it was with rising tension that Asca waited out his thoughts.

"Let her talk. Monitor our prey. Find out what threat, if any, he has." Second changed his tone. "Pilot, be ready to follow closely if the runner bolts."

Asca was halted in mid-retreat by a final injunction. "The female is our lure, but if I decide she should be silent, you will make it happen that she dies before my words go silent."

Dogfight

THE ROBOT

Hodgepodge saw the electron count telemetry on all the Ouija board detectors spike high, but before he could frame a warning, Abe yelled, "Signal from Sharon!"

Hodgepodge{1} verified the data link to the remote vehicle and moved the engine assist programs into extended cache.

Hodgepodge{2} spotted Mary Ellen asleep at her desk. He addressed her over the speaker. "Incoming message from Sharon." She woke, and Hodgepodge repeated the message.

"I heard you the first time, you defective Victrola. Your needle's skipping."

By that time, the first message had assembled.

THE WIZARD

Abe tool a long glance at the paper roadmap of the county. He hated paper maps, they were such a hassle to fold and orient, but he really had no choice. The computer in the car was as ignorant as an ant, and it really had no spare resources for handling a digital map.

Her first message had started by flashing the whole Ouija board. Then the text formed.

HUMAN 6 STOP USING ENGINE

Human? Are they dictating?

[YES]

Sharon, I am so glad you are alive!

[GOODBYE]

There was a pause, and then,

5

Abe was momentarily confused.

Are they listening to my thoughts? Sharon had not used the [GOOD-BYE] light before, nor the numbers. Yet he dared not try to read something into the signal that wasn't clear, not while his very thoughts were open.

4 ILUVU [GOODBYE]

He didn't puzzle it out. He just knew. **We aren't dead yet.** He used the automatic controls, and slapped the thrust lever.

The little car was never designed for high speed, but it quickly leapt to over 80. On this road, on these tires, it was about the maximum he dared.

3

Traction was only for steering, right now. By some technology he didn't understand, the engine was pushing the ground directly. Luckily, the road had no major turns for a mile or so.

Cerik. Are you ready to trade the engine for the girl?

NO THEY ARE 2 NOT.

A dip in the road made him fear for the aluminum strut construction of the vehicle.

Cerik. If you do not release the girl, I will destroy you. He turned a knob on the dash. It released a cable. The fiberglass cover over the machine gun caught the wind and ripped free.

1

Cerik. Read my mind. I can do it! But would he?

[NO] RMNCE IM POSSESSION o [GOODBYE]

Almost at the same instant, he saw it. The flat, triangular ship was approaching at several times his speed, coming in from his right. They'd have a clear shot at him. His gun didn't swivel.

"Aloft!" he yelled at Hodgepodge over the radio.

The force gripped the car, and under remote control, the focus and thrust reconfigured. The car accelerated. The speedometer dropped out, as the wheels were skipping across the pavement like a stone on water. He crested the hill, and didn't follow the road back down.

Riding the hill like a launching ramp, Abe could only hold on as the car flicked past the alien ship faster than he could blink.

This part of the flight, the launch, was all pre-programmed, and he deliberately kept his mind clear of it.

We aren't dead yet!

THROAT CUT [GOODBYE]

"No! Sharon! No!" **Sharon! I'm sorry! They won't get away with it!** Red rage settled down on his mind.

"Hodgepodge, route control to me."

"Your altitude is 5000 feet." It was a rebuke. He was deviating from their plan.

Abe didn't care. He couldn't fire if his nose was pointing up.

He cut the thrust, then reversed it, braking the climb. The car had next to nothing in the way of aerodynamic controls. They had added a rudder and elevator crisscross at the rear, but they could only bend the flight. The aerodynamic shape of the vehicle would keep it pointed straight like a dart's fletching.

As the howl of the wind lowered, he felt upside down, the combination of the engine's field and gravity left him totally confused as to which direction was up. He stared out the window, and pushed hard on the pedal wired via cable and pulley to the elevator control.

First slowly, then too quickly, the little flap of wood and fiberglass bit into the slipstream and pushed the rear of the car up and over. The engine settings changed before he made a grab for the thrust control. Hodgepodge was on the job. The only feedback the robot had was a little solid-state camera sending one frame per second of the view out the front, but it had been enough to give his electronic brain a head start on the controls.

There! "I see you!" He adjusted the flaps, and centered the nose of the car toward the metallic triangular shape moving against the green below.

"Cerik! I hope you can hear my thoughts. You are all dead!"

He remembered her last hint, "No romance. I'm a possession." These beings wouldn't understand his feelings for her. She wanted him to play up the ownership angle. It was something they could understand.

"Cerik! You took my girl! You will pay for that!" The growl in his throat was unplanned, but he went with it.

The ship below was growing rapidly. He felt the trigger. Adjust for their motion. Lead the target.

The gun was deafening. There was no baffle between him and the mechanism. The best they could do on short notice was make sure the hot brass was thrown outside the car.

The line of shells was almost invisible.

"Die! Die!" The skin of the engine, and the hull of that ship were probably the same, a special alloy of magnesium. He had studied Hodgepodge's work with it. It was very heat resistant. It was good enough to be used as re-entry shield for a spacecraft. But it had one glaring fault. Like ordinary magnesium, and even everyday aluminum, it protected itself against the oxygen atmosphere by growing a thin layer of reactant that kept any further attack by the atmosphere at bay.

But this alloy was deficient. Its protective layer was really a nitrate. When it chipped off, the resulting bare metal grew an oxide that powdered and flaked easily. Once the original skin was damaged, it was ripe to ignite, and burn like the fires of Hell.

Abe gloated as the ship suddenly turned. "You can read my thoughts! You know you are going to die!"

The ship was very close now. He hit the trigger again, and a fresh set of shells, every fifth one a tracer, already burning magnesium, ripped across the gap toward the ship.

"Got you! There's no way..."

But the ship accelerated, so quickly it appeared to vanish. The bullets passed by. His heart dropped, and so was he.

He had to deal with his own rapid descent. He was already so close to the ground that he could see the individual trees.

Again, Hodgepodge was ahead of him. The alien engine pushed both forward and rearward at the same time. The focus made the difference. Now it was pushing forward.

Abe could barely breathe. The engine was pushing through him, through the nose of the car, and on towards the ground.

Hodgepodge's voice came loud and repetitive. "Right rudder. Push the right rudder. Right rudder..." Abe complied. If this was the brake, then he put his heart into it.

Whatever Hodgepodge had planned started to work. First they slowed, then almost at tree top level, it seemed, the car turned. The sky, the sun, and a black triangle, appeared in the window. "No more rudder," his computer commanded.

The pressure on his chest eased, and he could feel the car leap forward, heading for the sky and his enemy.

He tapped the pedals, bending the course towards his target. He had no idea how many rounds were left. This time he would forgo the gloating. He had to take them out, now!

The ship above started to move. He waited, content to keep them centered in the window. If he rammed them, so much the better.

The triangle grew like an approaching billboard on the highway. He fired. They moved, just a fraction of a second later, but they were fast! This time he could see the bullets zip past.

Abe was hard on the rudder, re-centering. He hit the trigger. A half-dozen rounds shattered his ears, and then silence. He clicked the trigger. Empty.

The last rounds vanished off into the sky. The alien ship vanished to the side.

"No!" He was climbing hard and fast, but the ship was fast too. They'd proved that. He'd burned all his ammo, and he doubted even one round had hit. They were just too fast. They read his thoughts, and by the time the bullets got there, they were gone.

Bullets were too slow.

He put his strength on the pedal. "Hodgepodge, turn us over."

"By my count, you are out of ammunition."

"Yes! I know, but I have a plan. Help me turn this thing."

Hodgepodge adjusted the engine, but not before they had gained considerable altitude. The ground below had details washed out in the ground haze. There was the lake. Where had he been? Where was the alien ship?

Somewhere in the flip-over, he felt bile in his throat. It wasn't just from the zero-g flip, either. He had fluffed the attack. He should never have tried to make them understand the death that was coming. Kill them first. Gloat later.

Grieve later.

There! A blink of light from something metal.

"Hodgepodge, did you see that?"

"No. I have limited visibility."

"That's okay." He pushed the pedals and centered the alien triangle in the window. "I see them."

"What is your plan?"

He didn't want to spell it out, but Hodgepodge would need the information.

"I want you to focus the engine's thrust down as tight as it will go. When the target is close, I want you to crank up the intensity to the limit. They can't be faster than light. Maybe we can punch a hole right through them."

"No."

Abe almost didn't hear him. "What's the matter?"

"I cannot do as you ask. Such a pulse of the engine would punch a hole right though your chest."

"Hodgepodge, it's not an issue! I have to take them down! This is the only weapon I have left. Do it!"

"No."

Abe's thoughts were paralyzed. He couldn't understand. Hodgepodge always obeyed him. There was no limit to his obedience. He thought.

But he was starting to drop rapidly. He glanced at the tiny camera that was Hodgepodge's eye. He grabbed it hard, and snapped it free of the clamp that held it in place. His map bag was held in place with gray duct tape. He ripped it free and used the tape to hold the camera in a new position, aimed at the car's rear view mirror.

"Now, can you see to the rear?"

Hodgepodge paused just an instant. "Yes."

"Okay, the same plan as before, except we flip over and you aim and fire the thruster pulse through the rear of the car."

"The control flap assembly would be damaged."

"I know. But we can still pogo above the ground until you can drop me in the lake. We knew this thing was never going to land properly. It's a risk worth taking."

There was a long pause before Hodgepodge replied. "Prepare to apply right rudder." The engine field adjusted around Abe again, and the growing howl of the wind started to drop. "Right rudder." The ship flipped over.

Abe was staring at the sky again. He was blind to the view below. Maybe Hodgepodge could make sense of the image in the rear view mirror, but he couldn't see anything.

There came a string of commands from Hodgepodge. Abe tapped the rudder and elevator controls as faithfully as he could, hoping to avoid a fatal overcorrection.

He was glad Hodgepodge was in control. There'd be no warning thought from him that the alien telepath could use to escape.

When it came, it was like the car exploded. He was thrown violently forward into his chest straps. Wind roared into the cabin. The whole rear end of the car had been ripped free.

He turned to look out the opening, his eyes tearing up as the wind hit. The alien ship was tumbling, like a flipped coin. Before he could see if there was any damage, it passed out of view.

"Hodgepodge," he yelled against the wind. "Can you hear me?"

There was no answer. He looked at his dashboard. No lights.

The wind changed. The ripped hull was catching the air. The car was going into a tumble. Just like the night of the UFO crash, some alien technology was dampening out his electricity.

No electricity. No radio. No Hodgepodge. Okay.

Abe had planned a backup. Dealing with unknown technology, he had to.

With no electricity, even the hand controls couldn't send the light pulses necessary to control the engine.

But surely the engine itself would be immune from whatever electricity damper the aliens might have. Otherwise, they'd kill their own engine.

Abe struggled against the impulse to watch the approaching ground. He had a job to do.

First, he found the fiber optic connector that connected the engine to the controls. Taped against the door was another connector. It was much simpler. He snapped it into place, and the shove on his back was a welcome sign.

This gadget took the status light from the engine and routed it back into the thrust control. A squeeze bulb of colored water gave him the ability to regulate the light. Crude as it was, he had some control over the intensity.

The focus came from a ring of refrigerator magnets. He had to snag the ring over a simple wire frame and move them by hand. Crude was the word, but he could feel it working.

The car was still tumbling, but as the speed increased, the nose down position seemed to be slightly more stable, so Abe played to that—releasing the squeeze bulb and sending a stronger thrust every time the nose pointed to the ground.

I just might survive this.

Barely had the thought drifted through his mind, when there was a flicker of darkness at the edge of his vision.

"No!" he shouted as the triangular ship passed close by.

In an instant, there was a shriek of metal, and a spatter of shrapnel as something invisible took the nose of the car and bent it nearly at right angles. The car was hit hard, and it was spinning like a top. Abe couldn't even take a breath before everything went dark.

THE ROBOT

"Telemetry has gone dead." Hodgepodge reported.

The equipment room was crowded, Mary Ellen had moved there when she found out that Scott was keeping watch, ready to replace a computer card, or tune a radio, or anything technical out of Hodgepodge's reach. His wife had come by, checking on him, baby asleep in her arms, and had been captured by the drama.

No one moved. Scott tapped a few keys on a terminal, but his frown ruled out a local radio failure.

Mary Ellen waited another minute, and then stood up, and without a word, she walked out.

Scott, after once glance at her face, turned back to the terminal, intent on running diagnostics that he knew would come up clean.

"Honey?"

"Yes."

She shifted the baby in her arms. "What has happened?"

"Abe went to fight the aliens. They got him." He had difficulty with the words.

She put her hand to her lips. Then she asked, "Is he... dead?"

Scott nodded. He stared at the screen, but his eyes couldn't focus on the letters. He blinked, then pushed back from the desk.

"And the girl, the one he was trying to rescue?"

He tapped a couple of keys. In a hoarse voice, he said, "Here. Read it yourself." He got up and left.

She eased over from her chair, holding the baby still, so she wouldn't wake up. Intently, she read the transcript. At one point, she took in a sharp breath. Silently, she got up and left, to find her husband.

...

Hodgepodge reviewed the human reaction to the latest events. Significantly, of the four humans, three showed emotional reactions similar to the events following the death of Bud Jones. The infant could possibly be considered a separate class, since he had no baseline for her reactions, and it was possible that the child was not aware of the events.

He re-examined his log of the aerial battle. Yes, superficially, it appeared that Abe might not have survived. Indeed, there was a good case for the death of Sharon Dae.

However, the death of Abe Whiting was inconsistent with his programming. The evidence of the camera and other telemetry, when combined with the impossibility of Abe's death, came up short of significance. There was an obvious disconnect between the humans' perception of the events and his. This would have to be examined in more detail.

Hodgepodge started several tasks.

Hodgepodge{2} began an in-depth model of the aerodynamics of the car based on its brief history of flight. The goal was to predict the trajectory of the car after telemetry ended.

Hodgepodge{3} began the design process for a mobile robot with sufficient range to visit the area where the battle took place. It was possible Abe had crashed and was waiting for him.

Hodgepodge{4} began a resource study, with the premise that all local humans perceived that Abe was dead and that the future of Hodgepodge the computer system was no longer under Abe's control and patronage.

Tasks {5} through {9} dealt with improving his radio sensitivity, including broadband monitoring of third parties.

Tasks {10} through {18} were human psychological studies.

Tasks {19} through {43} were queued for later execution, due to limited resources.

Departure

THE SEER

Early dawn was rudely interrupted. The small yellow school bus was loud, and smoked badly. Two guards with guns dropped off the lower step before it came to a stop.

"Who is Ed Morgan?" The gray-haired one asked the small collection of people who'd waited until daylight before making the trek back up to their homes.

Ed was just coming out onto the porch. "I am Ed Morgan."

The men turned to him and saluted. "We have come for you and your party."

Ed was able to force a small smile and a nod. "Could you put the guns down? There are no bad-guys here."

The spokesman glanced at his partner, and they carefully slung their weapons over their back. "We were told to provide you with any assistance necessary."

"Uh. Good." Ed began.

Angela spoke from behind him. "We have luggage for a party of five stacked in the living room. Do you have a stretcher?"

"We have an EMS gurney." The soldier nodded toward the bus. "It doesn't look like one, but that's a fully equipped ambulance."

Ed was content to move out of the way and let the people who knew what they were doing attend to business.

In spite of their preparations, it took a couple of hours to get the luggage loaded, and Helen transferred to the place in the rear of the bus where seats had been removed and ambulance gear installed.

It was the people part of the equation that took time.

Neither the Blacks nor Ed relished the idea that their homes would be ransacked for food and supplies the minute they were out of sight. However, it wasn't reasonable to leave everything pristine if they were leaving, never to return.

A community pow-wow was hastily called. Feelings were mixed. Some didn't like them leaving, although everyone acknowledged the necessity of getting Helen to the hospital. Some wanted to come with them. In the end, Ed had the feeling that the presence of the two men with guns, sitting quietly behind him, had a lot to do with the final decision.

Angela's dinner crew were to keep the tradition running. His house was opened up to sleeping parties or hospital use, either until he returned, or until the radiation ended.

The Black's closest neighbors were charged with the protection of that house. The community made a pledge of a two month time limit before they would declare the properties abandoned and take other action.

Ed was pleased with the results, and was ready to move on, but one final matter to be taken care of. Everyone had to shake on the deal.

They all stood. He held out his hand, and Mr. Patterson took it.

Mr. Patterson howled in pain, as the broken shaft of the screw driver protruded through the palm of his left hand. Blood pulsed bright red in the sun.

Ed huffed audibly at the shock. Mr. Patterson frowned. "Some problem?"

Ed tried to steady his emotions. He shook his head. "Not now." He dropped his hand. What to say?

The man started to turn away. Ed asked, too anxiously. "Mr. Patterson!"

"Yes?"

"First aid." He said in a rush. "For the community. Could you see to it that people brush up on first aid? After my experience with Angela and Helen, I may be a little sensitive on the issue, but a simple injury could leave a man, or a child, bleeding to death. Could you brush up on it, and bring it up with the rest of the others?"

For a moment, the man looked puzzled, but then a crooked smile edged across his face. "You're right. We are on our own here. Thanks for being concerned, young man."

Ed nodded, and then braced himself for the next in line, Joe Palmer. His handshake brought nothing more than a deep feeling of hunger, no vision at all.

Glenna Farmer was fated to fall badly on the trail down the cliff. Ed was able to shake free of the vision quickly. He made a comment to her about her duty as a mother to make sure that her family was always aware of where she was. She took it with a puzzled frown.

Of the eight people who shook hands with him, he had visions from five. By the end of the line, people were whispering among themselves about his little comments.

Angela came up beside him with a worried look on her face and led him off toward the bus. He heard one snatch of conversation from the people. "...healed his girlfriend...."

I've done it now. We'll never be just neighbors again.

Depression and fatigue settled down on him.

I never had people to touch before. This is dangerous.

They all loaded in the bus. Ed was amused to see his bodyguard appear magically out of the bushes and confer with the guards. Was he going to stay at the house, or come with them?

He glanced towards Ed, and then ducked out of sight again.

What are that guy's orders?

The bus made an elaborate process out of turning around in the narrow lane that serviced his house. Knots of people still standing in his yard gave them a farewell wave. Ed waved back.

THE EQUESTRIENNE

Helen waved back at Sammy and Jacob as they ran alongside the bus. Her arm gave out the same time as they lost the race with the bus. She set her head back down on the pillow and watched the trees whip by. The road was rough. It certainly didn't help her stomach.

Her mother was crying. Dad was beside her, his arm around her shoulders.

I'm dying, and they don't want to tell me.

Billie told her about Dadbert. She'd been like an older sister, one of her most faithful visitors. Maybe she would never see Billie again.

"Cheer up kid."

Helen turned her head. Ed was smiling at her. His bright smile and deep dark eyes brought that thrill back. Of course, he was too old, and she could never be as beautiful as Angela, but that didn't stop her from dreaming.

"It's okay," she said softly. She didn't want her parents to hear. "I was just sad about my horse." Tears started, and she was angry with herself for being a baby in front of him.

"Hey, none of that." He leaned close and took her hand.

His hand was strong, but not rough like her father's. Ed closed his eyes. Helen admitted, "I'm afraid."

He squeezed her hand. "You have nothing to be afraid of."

"Dadbert died."

"And he was out in the radiation a lot longer than you. We are taking very good care of you. That's why we are going into the city, so that you can get the blood transfusions that will cure you completely."

Helen glanced at her parents. "I don't know."

Ed shook his head, "You can believe me. I know things. Some day I'll tell you a story about the past few days."

Helen smiled at his voice, and his hand. "Tell me."

"Some day."

"Some times 'some day' never happens." She had a memory of brushing Dadbert's coat with her brush and relishing the deep horsy smell of him. The tears started up again.

Ed looked down at her for a moment. "Okay, I have a story to tell you." Helen blinked away the tears. Ed closed his eyes and eased back.

"Once upon a time," he began, "there was a young girl who loved her horse. She loved to ride him and was very faithful in taking care of him. He loved her back, and they were happy.

"Then a great plague came over the land, striking both men and beasts. Many people, and many animals died. The girl and her horse were both struck down and the horse died.

"However, a kindly magician called upon a spirit from the heavens and with the help of the girl's parents, she was cured of the plague.

"Now, the girl was still sad about her horse, and she never forgot him, but she had a good heart and knew the ways of horses, so when she found out that there many other horses in the land that were touched by the plague, she began to help other people with their horses and saved many of them from death.

"One day, she helped a mare give birth to a pure white horse. The owner gave the foal to the girl in gratitude for her good works, and she named it Snowcap.

"As the girl grew older, she and Snowcap became famous, and beloved of all the people of the kingdom."

Ed stopped, and open his eyes.

Helen smiled. "It was a nice story."

Ed nodded, "And all true." He got up from his seat and let go her hand. As he walked up to the front of the bus, Helen, with a smile on her face, closed her head and drifted off to sleep.

THE WIZARD

Abe heard a voice, her voice, "We're not dead yet."

Then he realized he was hanging upside down.

"Sharon? You're alive!"

"Barely." This time he noticed the strain in her voice. He blinked his eyes, trying to make shapes of the patches of dim light.

He was swinging, hanging by his feet in some kind of bag or net.

"Sharon. Are you okay? I thought you were dead. I can't see you."

She coughed, like she had the week long flu. "Asca cut my throat. I thought I was dead. So did he. Second threw him against the wall for failing to kill me. He's still unconscious."

The twisting motion of his bag, and his dark adapting eyes brought a second's glimpse of her through the coarse weave of the bag. She was lying against the wall, within arm's reach, if he could have moved his arm. The leather-looking coat and tattered jeans she was wearing were splattered heavily by a dark stain. **Blood?**

She coughed. "Yes."

He threw his weight into the swing. She smiled at him when she drifted back into view. The smile was out of deep fatigue. She looked very thin, much depleted. Her hair was short and thin, as if masses of her former long tresses had fallen out. Too much had happened since that day, so long ago, when they had met. Horror lanced through him when he saw the long trace of darkness across her throat.

"How could you survive that? Are you okay?"

"I've had practice. I'll survive unless they decide to starve me."

"I'm so sorry! My attack could have killed you. I didn't know."

"It's okay. I would have welcomed it. I'm tired of staying alive."

"Don't say that."

She didn't reply. He waited for her to drift back into sight. The rope that held him had twisted and was now starting to spin him slowly the other direction. She looked so tired.

"Can you untie me?" he asked.

"No. I can barely move. Besides, it wouldn't be safe. Second is in charge. When he knocked out Asca, their only telepath, he thought a picture at me. If I untie you, he will gut us both. I believe him. He'd like nothing better than to have an excuse to disobey the orders he was given."

"Someone wants us alive?"

"I suppose. Both Second, and the captain, Tenthonad, have telepathic blocks that the others don't. I only caught a glimpse of Second's true thoughts when he warned me. Tenthonad gave the order. It's somehow blocking Second from taking power." She coughed again. Abe felt a tickle in his chest and coughed too.

Abe strained at the ropes that confined his arms. Some chance still remained that they could break free and take the ship. After a few minutes, he had to quit. He was making no progress, and his cough was getting worse.

"There's something in the air," he complained.

She nodded. "It kills all Earth life."

He stopped thinking about escape. "What is it?"

"I don't know. It kills within a few days." She tugged at the cuff of her jeans, and the denim fabric tore easily. "It destroys cloth, too. And my hair."

He asked, fearfully, "How about you? How bad is your cough?"

She shook her head. "No. I have.... Sorry. I don't really have words for it. It's like the Ouija board. I can affect the cells of my body. I have been continually healing myself."

"That's great!"

"Not so great. It takes energy, and I am all out. The Cerik are used to going days without food. They didn't think about food for me either. I have been without for three days, I think. It will be another couple of days before we get to the main ship. Maybe, if I hadn't lost so much blood..."

Abe waited out another cough. His diaphragm hurt from the effort. Two days of this would leave him dead. The inverted posture just made it that much harder to handle the stress on his lungs. He could choke on his own phlegm if he weren't careful.

He had to think. There had to be a way. **We aren't dead yet.**

Softly, Sharon echoed his thought. "We aren't dead yet." But he could tell that she didn't really believe it.

THE SCIENTIST

Larry Kelly felt like he'd come back from a long trip. The prosaic task of securing the sheet of Technical Pan film onto the back of the camera made him remember the life that had vanished such a few short weeks ago. Not that he had used this kind of camera before. The AAT telescope had recently been used with CCD cameras and a plethora of specialized electronic sensors, but now they were back to basics. They could still take photos until their old stock of film ran out. Cujo had cobbled together a very acceptable film back for the optics out of black cardboard, and he had every confidence that this exposure of the supernova would be crisp, sharp and excellent. It had to be. Future generations of astronomers would use this very picture for hundreds of years. He enjoyed the work. If it were up to him, this is what he would do for the rest of his life.

With an eye on the clock, he worked the manual shutter.

He glanced up at the sky, careful to block the still bright spot of the actual star with the edge of the dome. It was a mistake.

He'd checked the radiation personally. He had done the calculations twice by two different methods. He knew with precision just how many minutes it was safe to work under the star, now that the radiation had started to drop.

But that didn't stop the quiver of fear inspired by this great white hole in the sky. It must have happened before. Maybe not this close, but sometime in the history of the human race there must have been other strong supernovae in the sky. Larry felt a deep kinship with his ancestors. He too wanted to be hiding in a cave.

He closed the shutter. He removed the film pack and placed it in the black lined envelope. A checkmark on his clipboard, and he set up the conditions for the next exposure. He would get about a dozen before his time allotment ran out.

"Larry!"

"What are you doing out here Cujo? You've used up your quota for today."

"I won't be a second. I just thought you might want to know. There's a report out of the States. Some nuke went off in Nebraska."

Larry's fingers slipped on the fastener. "Just one?" he asked hopefully. A superpower nuclear war could be the final straw on humanity's back.

"Appears so. It happened a day or so ago. There is no official word. There may not be an official anything over there anymore. Just amateur radio reports."

Larry nodded to himself. "Just one. We can live with that."

"I say thanks in my prayers every day that I live in the southern hemisphere."

"Me too. Now get back into the offices."

Larry tweaked his alignment and opened the shutter. He tried not to think about his mother and sister, there was nothing he could do for them. International travel was gone. It wouldn't be back for decades, and even then it might be on wooden sailing ships.

He closed his eyes. Now was a good time for a real prayer, for himself, for Janet and the baby, and for the rest of humanity.

Sharing

THE NAME

Tenthonad received the report with more fierceness than he felt. The last Tale had been one of his favorites, one he had learned by heart as a cub.

. . .

Three Builder cubs wandered away from their nest to play in the wide field. Their mother came and cuffed them and chased them home. "You must stay close or the Hunter will get you." The first cub, the cautious one, asked, "Why must we fear the Hunter?" "Because he has great sharp claws, like knives to catch you with." The second, the curious one, asked, "What will the Hunter do with us if he catches us?" "He will tear you apart with his sharp fangs and eat you." The third, the brave one, boasted, "I will not fear the Hunter. I will swim deep in the waters and go where I will. I will build a strong, clever nest that no Hunter will ever be able to attack. I will not fear the Hunter."

The next day the Builder mother told her two cubs, "You must stay close, or the Hunter will get you."

. . .

The news was good, but it would require him to be sharp, quick, and strong. Second was on his way back. He had captured the City-builder alive and recovered the lost engine.

Second had fulfilled his commands. If Second had been a cub of his clan, Tenthonad would have begun the celebration, to greet the returning ship with a Full Voice. A Second should expect the rewards when he becomes the claw of his *La*.

But there were dangers there. How many Seconds in the books had gained their own *Name* during a Full Voice? How many *Names* had lost their eyes by not calling forth the voices? The spurned Second was a common hero of the Tales.

But Second was not of his clan. Neither were half of the crew on this expedition. There were strong dangers either way.

Tenthonad slashed a claw through the air, and the image of the planet centered on the display. There'd been another explosion, according to Egh. It had been on the hidden side, but his instruments had seen the hot spot when the planet turned. Of course, the crew knew about it as well. Signs were good that the expedition could be completed quickly.

As soon as the star death waned, he could leave the required crew of twenty seven in good hunting grounds. That would lock up their claim on the planet.

He could then take the ship home quickly, carrying spoils of the planet and claim the treasure world for both their clans. With a good claim, the established families would be happy to loan ships and homesteading supplies in trade for minor settlements on the planet.

Of course Tenthonad's clan would get first claim, Second's clan would get the next.

If Second could take a *Name* before the claim was made, then his clan would get the first choice. Tenthonad was certain that this was the dream that haunted Second's *erdan*.

But Tenthonad had a dream of his own, and it included having both live City-builders behind him when he made the claim and presented the spoils.

He opened his throat wide, and gave a Voice.

Echoing all through the ship, Cerik of both families heard the command and felt their own blood rush faster.

"Open the deep stores. Take the prey. Give Voice when Second returns."

THE WITCH

Sharon struggled to put words to what she saw. For the first time in her life, she realized that there were no words for many of the things she sensed and touched. Her mother, a telepath herself, had just known all these things. Conversation with her had been a comfortable shortcut of words and pure mental concepts.

There had been no other human, not even Hattie, to whom she had needed to speak about these special things inside her head.

Abe helped, as well as he could.

"There is a roundness, with straight, crying but frozen."

"Does this connect to the crystal thing?" he asked.

"Yes."

"Hmm. A pipe, maybe. Extruded construction. Are there layers? An inside layer and an outside layer?"

Sharon started as she suddenly realized that it was true. The fragmentary image that was coalescing inside his mind was growing more complex by the second, and his guesses sometimes brought into sharp focus things that she could sense, but had never given any meaning to. The scout ship, as a complex machine, was something that Abe could understand much like she could understand the complexity of her own body.

It was hard work, and she wished she had the background and understanding that would enable her to see the things that were important to him. He was a blind man, trying to understand what was killing him, using eyes that saw nothing and words that meant nothing.

It was exhausting.

"Abe. I have to stop."

"Of course," he said, instantly concerned for her, even as part of his mind cried, "No! I need more information."

It was as if there were two of him. One part of his mind, sharp and clear, was working hard on the puzzle with missing pieces. The other was a lover deeply concerned by her pain and worried about her plainly evident weakness.

There was a cough tickling in his throat that he would not give way to. He was ruthless, not willing by his own need to goad her into an effort that she had no strength for.

She didn't understand his feelings for her. What had she ever given to him? Her first meeting, she had been ready to hit him over the head with a rock! She had stolen from him, lied to him, knocked him out. Even her good intent to keep him out of the dark angels' clutches had been useless.

His feelings for her were plain on the surface of his mind, and the sweet, open, loving girl that he sought to protect was nothing like the real her.

Sharon tried to break free. It was a deep telepathic link into a man who'd risked all, and lost all, to try to save her. She didn't deserve the resonance of this love. But even this took too much effort.

What if she just gave up? Wouldn't it be wonderful to just let go of the little voice that was just her alone? She could let it fade and die—just slip into the strong loving chambers of his mind. She could be a part of him, like the wordless thoughts that beat his heart and expanded his chest for breath. She could keep the chemicals of fear from attacking his brain, and together they could wait out the failure of their bodies in peace and love.

It drew her like a magnet. It would be easy to do. No more struggle with damaged lungs. No more forcing growth of scar tissue. No more struggle with her own racing endocrine system. No more being the loneliest person in the human race.

It was her destiny, wasn't it? A telepath had no right to her own identity. Telepathy was a birth defect of the mind, ruthlessly culled out of the human race because it always created a useless stub of a personality, unable to do anything but be swept along by the hurricane of humanity's random thoughts.

Her mother had, somehow, managed to survive long enough to bring her into the world. She had isolated her from birth, forced her to develop her own mind by sacrificing every maternal instinct. A telepath raising a telepath by forcing wedges between their minds.

Her mother had often talked, *talked!*, about some destiny that Sharon Dae must have.

Sharon felt a wave of sadness. Delusion wasn't unique to the isolated mind. If that belief of destiny had helped her mother survive as long as she had, then it had to be enough.

The telepaths she had sensed all her life were so very few, a handful among the billions. Survivors all, they shrank from contact with their own kind.

All but Ed. He was able to deny the telepathic talent he had, so overwhelmed by his visions.

THE SEER

Ed walked the corridors, impressed by the numbers of people. Every bed, and there were a lot of beds, had at least two people, some sharing the mattress, but many electing to rest on blankets on the floor. It was obvious that the place wasn't intended to be a hospital. Not many hospital rooms had the walls lined with blackboards. The old school building had the features needed for today's medical problems; thick stone walls to keep out the radiation, hard tiled floors that could be mopped down regularly, and wide halls that allowed the brawny attendants to wheel the beds and equipment around easily.

The Black family had already been hurried away by the lone nurse that they'd seen. Ed and Angela held hands timidly, as they were led to a small office.

"Wait here," said their guide, and left. There were a couple of chairs in front of the desk, so they waited.

"I feel like I'm waiting for the principal," Angela whispered.

Ed nodded, although he only knew what she was talking about due to a movie he'd seen.

He looked around the room. If the decor was any hint, the teacher was a political science instructor. There were pictures of the national capitol building, and another of the similar shaped Texas capitol. Other pictures were group shots of people he didn't know. One had the president in it, so he guessed there were other famous people in the others.

"That's her," Angela pointed at one of the pictures.

"Who?"

"The person who owns this office."

Ed smiled, "You know her?"

Angela shook her head and pointed, "No. Look. See this woman and this man are the only people in all of the shots. This office is a woman's so it has to be her."

Ed looked again at the desk and the piles of papers gathering dust. "How can you tell that a woman worked here?"

"Really. It's obvious."

Ed looked again, but he had to just shake his head and take her word for it. He looked closer at the smiling gray-haired woman.

Is she still around somewhere, or one of the victims?

On impulse, he reached across the desk and picked up the pencil holder. Nothing. He set it down, it had been worth a try.

A few minutes later, the door opened. A high school aged boy looked in. "Hello, are you Ed?"

"Yes." The face was very familiar. He tried to place it, but it was elusive. Certainly he'd never seen the young man before.

"My father sent me to tell you he'd be late. He'll be tied up another hour or so at headquarters."

Angela asked, "And your father is?"

He looked at Angela appreciatively, to Ed's discomfort. "I am James Fuller." He held out his hand to her. "My father is Councilman George Fuller." They shook hands.

He turned to Ed, and offered his hand. "You are Ed Morgan, the stock market analyst that my father has been talking about for as long as I can remember."

Ed hesitated, but could not refuse. The instant he took the boy's hand, there was a flash vision. *Oh.*

He looked into the boy's eyes, and was momentarily at a loss for words as the import of that glimpse into James' future echoed in his mind.

"Ah. I do believe I have seen your picture. Your father had it on his desk. You were about this big." He held his hands about two feet apart.

"Yeah. I've seen it. I gave him school pictures for years, but I don't think he ever did anything with them but put them in the cabinet with all the other pictures."

Angel asked, "You said your father sent you?"

"Yes. I have a moped. It gets over a hundred miles to the gallon. Dad uses me as a courier all the time."

"I would be afraid to go out on the streets alone," Angela confessed.

"Oh, there's no problem." He reached into a pocket and flashed a colorful pocket radio. "I have to stay within radio range. And besides, no one would try anything on the patrolled roads anyway. Not after the executions."

Angela's smile dropped slightly, but James didn't seem to notice. The intimations of strict martial law didn't surprise Ed. He had expected it.

"James, could you do us a favor?" he asked.

"Sure."

"We came with a family named Black. Their daughter Helen has radiation sickness—she was knocked unconscious while trying to save her horse. Could you find out how they're doing?"

Angela nodded, "We were separated when we arrived here."

"Oh sure. I can track them down. Want to come along?"

Angela demurred, "It has been a long day for us. We got up at star-rise. I think I'll just wait here for now."

James left with a smile.

Angela scooted her chair closer to his, and proved her truthfulness by dozing off to sleep resting under his arm.

Why don't I get these flash visions when I touch you?

It was a mystery, but one he was willing to let lie. He could do without that shock to his system every time he touched. He wanted to touch Angela often.

Ed?

For an instant, he thought it was Angela, but then he realized it was not.

Sharon?

There was relief from the distant personality. **Ed, I'm in trouble. Could I ask a very great favor?**

Ed was instantly alert. **Anything. What is it?**

I am drained of energy and I'm far from any help. I will shortly die.

Ed could directly feel the flutter of her mind. It was like a fog that would drift away and disperse at the first puff of a breeze. He could sense what she wanted before she managed to put it all into words.

You want me to feed you energy, just like we did with Helen.

Yes. It was a faint plea for hope.

Angela stirred, perhaps sensing his tensed muscles. She pulled herself upright. "Ed? Is there something wrong?"

Ed looked at her, careful to keep his attachment to Sharon secure. "Angela, I am in contact with Sharon. She needs my help."

She frowned a little around the eyes. "What kind of help?"

"Angela, she needs me to feed her strength." He could feel Angela pull back slightly.

"No. Don't do that," he said a little harshly. "She saved your life. She saved Helen. She's my friend. I am not going to abandon her the first time she needs something from me."

Angela flinched slightly at his words. Then she nodded. "Okay. What do we do?"

Grateful, he scooted their chairs so that they could face each other holding hands. "Just push strength to her, or to me if that is easier. I will take care of the rest." She nodded.

Sharon?

Thank you.

He felt the strength that lined the insides of every cell of his body, and like a wave sloshing in a tub, he started pushing life towards his oldest friend.

Sharon, he said as he felt her latch onto the incoming flood like a parched runner for water.

Sharon, I am sorry.

What? Why?

Ed at first fought the feeling, then turned around and used it to push even harder. **Sharon, I'm sorry that I ever turned away from you.**

When I was at the hospital, and the doctor first made contact with me, I turned away from you. I thought that you were just a dream, and that I had to give up all the dreams that were cluttering my mind if I were ever going to be sane.

I thought sanity was just those things that everyone could see and hear. I thought I had to give you up for the sake of sanity. So I did it. You called for me, and I turned a deaf ear. I deserted the only friend I had in the entire world so I could be sane.

The fever of his regret spilled out in tears and an offering of life.

You are my sister of the mind, and I love you. It wasn't ever about sanity, I was just afraid of those other eyes, those sane people. I was afraid of what they would see and what they would say.

I was a coward, and I lost you for years.

Sharon said nothing at first, but the understanding, and the forgiveness was calm on the surface of her mind.

Thank you. Sharon's mind was firming up. **Thank you, my brother of the mind.**

Compromise

THE TELEPATH

Asca moved with pain. Second had thrown him so hard against the wall he feared he'd broken his arm. He moved it carefully, to minimize the pain, and to avoid showing weakness. He was not at all sure that Tenthonad or Second would consider his telepathy sufficiently valuable to keep him alive as a *ke'de*, a Broken Hunter.

The City-builders were active, like *lallecans* chewing at their ropes. He watched, but did nothing. It was clear to everyone that the ship would be heading back home soon. These prey were so much trouble he doubted there would be any more captured. If these were killed, then what need would there be for a telepath?

He felt the female turn her attention to him. It was surprising how much stronger she seemed than the last time they faced each other.

Yes. Your arm is broken.

He cringed. His dreams of being a respected *name* were evaporating with each breath.

I can fix your arm...but you must do me a favor.

His breath caught. He was suddenly overcome by the conviction that she was *Rakla-del* come alive out of the fables. Her telepathic scent was hard and remorseless. She could not be killed—he tried! If he made a deal with her, would he lose his soul?

But what choice do I have?

None, came the reply, with not a hint of doubt behind it.

He moved cautiously, following her silent directions. Luckily, the entrance to the storage compartment was out of sight from the others. Perhaps he could explain what he was doing in a form different from disloyalty, but he might not be given that chance.

The broken thing the new City-builder had constructed around the Delense engine was incomprehensible. Only the words in his head let him locate the bag.

He sniffed. It was clearly food, although nothing he would be tempted to taste.

Good. It is my duty to keep them alive. He could make that believable.

The machine made him uncomfortable. It wasn't Delense. It wasn't something he grew up with. He had no idea what it would do. He was glad it was broken.

He took the bag to the prey, and she took it eagerly. He watched just a moment, as the female pushed something nearly black through the mesh of the bag into the male's mouth.

My arm? He reminded her, deferentially.

She looked him in the eyes. **Go to your place and I will give you instructions.**

He did as he was told, and soon the words formed in his head, telling him how to stretch the arm. There was a moment of intense pain, and then a wave of blackness came over him, and he drifted into deep *dan.*

THE ROBOT

Hodgepodge waited until Mary Ellen retreated to her office. Midday, with the rising of the star, ended the brief daylight workday. He wished he had a microphone that could listen in on the conversations that occurred in the garden plot, where all the humans worked the safe daylight hours. None of external security cameras were working. Their repair was far down the priority list. He needed to monitor the humans, because their actions would impact his own projects to a great extent.

"Mary Ellen Victor, may I speak to you?"

She looked up to the speaker. Her face showed no great change of expression. "Yes. What do you want?"

"I need to confer with you about my task priorities and resource needs."

She looked back down at the desk. "Scott will take care of you. I'm tired now."

"I am aware of this. However, in Abe's absence," he noted a tensing of her facial muscles at that instant, "I need the assistance of a director of Whiting Design to take care of several items, and until he returns, that must be you."

She said nothing for a moment, and then pulled a small pan of water closer and began to wash the soil stains from her hand.

"It is your opinion," she began, "that Abe is alive?"

"Yes."

"Have you heard from him? Some signal?"

"No. You were monitoring the last signal as it happened. Either due to equipment failure or weapons attack from the alien craft, the signal ended."

"While he was falling from the sky in a broken clump of fiberglass?"

"Yes."

Her voice gained in volume, "Then why..."

She stopped. She pushed the dish of water back, and used a rag to scrub and dry the last of the water from her hands.

"No. I won't argue for his death! There is doubt. It is enough for you. It ought to have been enough for me." She straightened in her chair.

In spite of the low light level, he could detect a color change in her face. He would not have used the word 'doubt', but that issue could be resolved later.

"What do you want?"

Hodgepodge pulled up the subset of tasks that needed human intervention.

"I have two concerns at the moment. In the short term, I need to build a long range mobile platform, so that I can investigate the area where Abe was last detected. I am lacking several critical resources for building such a platform.

"My other concern is that I will cease to function before Abe returns and I will be unable to provide the assistance he will expect."

"Can't Scott keep you maintained?"

"Scott has the skills. He lacks the resources. I need a constant supply of various electronic devices to repair and replace damaged circuits. Also approaching is the exhaustion of all of our generator fuel. Without the augmentation of our local generator, I will not be able to stay active during the electrical blackout periods. While I can save my state during the down times and be restored when the electricity comes back up, this is itself a heavy drain on my active time. The search for Abe would be severely restricted, and other tasks would have to be deferred indefinitely."

Mary Ellen started to drum her fingers on the desktop, and then stopped to examine her nails, now heavily worn by the constant gardening work. She asked, "Okay, if you had full control of the city, what would you ask for?"

"Given the current situation, I would ask for uninterrupted power from the city lines, plus fuel for the backup generator. I would also ask for all of the warehouse stock of all of the computer stores. I would also like an inventory of the shipping departments of the Freescale, AMD, Siemens, Texas Instruments and Dell plants, so that I could design new circuits around the available parts."

She nodded. "All of those places are out of business, but the city government would shoot anyone who tried to loot their warehouses. Anything abandoned now belongs to the Council. That has been proclaimed loud and long these past few days. We would have to trade something for what you want. What do you have to sell?"

"'Whiting Design is a state of the art design center providing unique and innovative designs every...'"

"Hold it there! I wrote that advertising blurb. Believe me, we aren't going to be able to sell any of Abe's hi-tech electronic gismos to this group of thugs."

"I am aware of that. There will be no integrated circuit manufacture for many years to come, perhaps for decades."

She started to say something and then asked, "Why?"

"The industrial infrastructure has broken down. To use the existing machines requires supplies from high tech material suppliers from all over the world. For example, hundreds of high purity chemicals, and extreme purity silicon wafers are needed. If all cities have reverted to an earlier industrial base as Austin has, then all of those cities will have to recover before the full set of supplies is available.

"In addition, some of the equipment used in wafer manufacture will not survive a prolonged shutdown. Parts which must remain in vacuum will be contaminated by air. Parts which must be maintained in clean room purity will be contaminated by the decay of the room and equipment itself. In addition, the process line is controlled by computers which will have been damaged by the EMP problems which damaged me. Many specialized integrated circuits will be needed to repair those computers, and those will not be available until integrated circuit manufacturing is restored."

"You were repaired."

"I am a highly redundant design. I am composed of many identical pieces, and I can still run even if a large percentage of them are damaged. This is not the case with most computers."

"So you say that integrated circuits can't be manufactured until integrated circuits are being manufactured?"

"That is correct."

"It can't be. It's the chicken and egg dilemma. It all had to start somewhere."

"That is true. A limited, manually operated facility using hand-blown tube electronics could manufacture large, low quality transistors. Using those transistors, second generation equipment could be built that could manufacture better quality, smaller, transistors. After several generations, equipment could be built to..."

"Get to the point."

"As in the history of electronic development, many generations of equipment and refinement, spurred by world-wide competition and billions of dollars of resources, would be needed to get back to the state of the industry at the time of the supernova. It will not happen until at least a national industrial base is restored. If records are not properly preserved, it may take just as long the second time as it did the first."

"So all those chips in those warehouses are irreplaceable? They are worth their weight in gold?" She tasted the idea.

"Some of them are invaluable. Others can never be used, because their need has evaporated, and those are worthless."

"And no one can likely tell the difference."

"I can."

She looked up from the speaker to the camera. "How can you?"

"I have an extensive database, including catalogs of electronics that were current at the time of the supernova. I also have the technical insight to predict which parts would be useful in the current reduced technological age."

She started pacing, staring at the floor. Hodgepodge had seen her do this many times before. It was a thinking ritual.

"We can provide a service. Austin could trade chips to other cities." She pointed a finger up at the camera. "You are a technical library. What else can you do?"

"You are aware of my history." Abe had told her about it several times. "My common-sense database was filled with data about all facets of human life."

"You know everything?" she asked, with a rising tone of voice.

"No, but I know a lot. It is not all on-line, but the complete data set is in loadable modules. What I don't know immediately, I know how to load."

"You are talking about the disks in those rooms on the other side of the CAD area?"

"Yes. That is my off-line memory. The sense of it all is encoded into the whole of my personality. The details I can load as I need them."

She sat down. "So you are a whole reference library?"

"Yes."

"Electronics? Fabric making? Plumbing?"

"Yes, I have the ref..."

"Jewelry making? Animal husbandry? Medicine?"

"Yes. My medical resources contain..."

"Why are my blueberries not growing well?

"Wait... Yes. The soil has the wrong acidity. You need to..."

"Hold on to that thought."

She was up again, pacing the room. "I can sell it! I'll do business with those pirates!"

She opened the door and called down the hallway, "Mrs. Jensen! Denise, could you come here?" She turned to her closet and pulled a suit into the unflattering light of the single light bulb. "I don't know how I'll get this cleaned," she muttered.

"May I express a concern?"

She looked up from her dress. "Yes. What is it?"

"In Abe's absence, I have done some research on interactions with other people. In popular literature, such as the movies 2001: A SPACE ODD-ESSEY, and COLOSSUS and TERMINATOR, and in novels such as THE ADOLESCENCE OF Pi and BERSERKER, and THE TERMINAL EXPERIMENT there is a recurring theme of a machine intelligence isolated from human control and becoming a menace that must be destroyed.

Abe made an effort to conceal my abilities from anyone outside of Whiting Design employees. I conjecture that the literature references reflect an aspect of human nature, and that revealing my existence might create an unstable situation."

She nodded. "People are frightened of what they don't understand. I'm frightened of you. Maybe Abe...understands you, but he's the only one."

"It is certainly within your authority to deactivate me."

"I know." She turned back to her closet. "Abe has always treated you like a little brother. I wouldn't turn you off without a good reason. I also had no intention of telling anyone that you talk."

She looked up at the camera. "As a matter of fact, you talk too much. Don't offer any suggestions. Don't start conversations. Never talk about anything other than the question you've just been asked."

"This is contrary to Abe's directives."

"Then... when he comes back, you can talk all you want, but until then, you have to pretend to be a just a library machine. Answer questions from your database, but don't chat. Understand?"

There was no answer.

Mary Ellen twisted her lip, "Okay. You can chat with me, and you can talk technical stuff with Scott, but no one else, understand?"

"Yes, I understand. I have located a reference to a general query language that should be powerful enough for your library project. I will emulate it."

"Good. I will need to scan it before tomorrow."

The door opened, and Denise Jensen entered, "Did you call, Mrs. Victor?"

"Yes, do you know when the city bus comes around?"

"It's before dawn on Tuesdays. I don't know the exact time."

"That's what I was afraid of. Can you help me get this stain out? I've got to be dressed in my battle garb and ready to go before it gets here."

They discussed the details of her project and their preparations. Hodgepodge monitored the conversation with a low priority task. No one framed a syntactically correct query, so he said nothing.

THE SEER

Will Black rose from the side of Helen's bed and shook Ed's hand as they entered. "The doctor said she will fully recover. I can't thank you enough for all you've done for us."

Ed was a little embarrassed and just nodded. He turned to the man beside him, "Councilman Fuller, this is Mr. Will Black, his wife Karen, and Helen."

George Fuller smiled and held out his hand. "Ed has told me about your trials." He turned to Helen, "And your bravery, young lady. I am glad to meet you."

James Fuller had already moved to the other side of her bed. "I don't know about brave," he said with a grin, "she just didn't know enough to stay clear of critters bigger than she was."

Helen jabbed at him with her left fist. He dodged, laughing. and poked her lightly in the ribs.

"James," the elder Fuller said softly, and his son moved back out of Helen's range and put his hands primly behind his back. The grin never left his face.

Mr. Black held his wife beside him, and said, "The doctor told us that we were given special treatment because of your orders, sir. We wanted to thank you."

George shook his head, "When Ed Morgan asks me a favor, it's the least I can do.

"He also told me about your little community, and how you've banded together to help each other through this time of changes. You should be proud to know that of all the stories I hear, it is stories like yours that give me the most hope for the future.

"I also know that you are facing a lot of uncertainty. There are gangs, bandits that are working around the fringes, hitting isolated communities like yours. You don't have access to markets, hospitals, police. With such dangers as the radiation from the star and the contaminated food, it is only the lucky groups like yours that have much of a chance."

Karen Black, usually quiet, asked, "Contaminated food?"

George Fuller nodded, "You have heard about the fallout from the nuclear explosions, on the radio?"

They nodded.

"Our doctors are checking the crops that come in for radiation. It is mild so far. Most of the people that come to this hospital have radiation sickness from the star, like young Helen here, but if it gets much worse, some crops will have to be destroyed."

"No." It was Will Black.

George nodded. "It is hard to imagine, isn't it? Everyone struggling for enough to eat, and me talking about burning crops. But think about everyone of your neighbors, sicker than Helen. Who could survive that?"

He spread his hands, "Maybe we'll be lucky. I certainly want to avoid panic destruction of good crops just as much as I want to avoid poisoned food in the markets. That's why the city has a food testing station at the central market. If you buy certified food, from the approved locations, you can take it home without worry."

Ed stood silently as George talked. He chafed at the sales pitch. He knew George. He would have the Blacks begging to join the city's jurisdiction. If he hadn't already argued George into extending the police patrols out into that area, a year before the city had originally planned, he'd be cautioning his neighbors about accepting everything he had to offer.

But the future, at least in outline, was clear to him. The city, under George's rule, would prosper. The outsiders, when they survived, would be living a much harder life.

"What do you think, Ed?" Will Black asked, once George had made his offer to include the neighborhood in the patrol boundaries, and to extend the twice-weekly bus run to include them.

"I think you need to talk it over when you head back with Helen. Angela and I will be giving up our house and staying here in the city. The Councilman has offered me a position on the City Planning Commission."

"And I can think of no one better," George beamed, and slapped him on the back.

Angela and Karen Black drifted off to the edge of the conversation while the talk turned to Helen's release from the hospital. "We need the bed," joked George, although everyone knew that it wasn't really a joke. Will talked about his concerns, and George listened, like a politician with a voter.

Helen's giggle caught Ed's attention. She and James were deep into their own conversation. Ed just watched the looks on their faces.

"Hey buster," Angela drifted up to his side, "What's so funny?"

He shook his head, "I was just looking at a case of love at first sight." He nodded his head in the direction of the children.

"Oh, that's just puppy love. I've been there a couple of times myself." She intertwined her arm with his, and they clasped hands.

"'Oh ye of little faith'." He muttered.

Angela looked him in the eye, "You mean really?"

He nodded.

"They are much too young."

"They will get older. There's a wedding in a decade or so that you really must attend."

Angela was quiet, watching James and Helen in teenage animation, just like children their age have always done.

"I couldn't wait that long."

"What?"

She didn't answer. Ed wondered for a moment if he'd understood what she had said. Their own relationship was a little undefined. From the moment when he had brought her to his house, unconscious, across the back of a horse, people understood they were together. He'd invited her, she had come. Their friendship had grown steadily, companions elbow to elbow through force of necessity. Sex hadn't had time to complicate the picture. With his lack of experience, it wasn't something he felt ready to push.

But she did seem insecure every time he mentioned Sharon. She hadn't said anything when George had offered a house to go with the job, pointedly talking to her as he made that part of the sales pitch.

Ed just assumed she would stay with him, but now that they were back in the city, she could go back to her old home. The planetarium wasn't likely still active, but she was educated, competent. She could walk away from him and support herself.

She could leave him.

"We need to get married, soon," he whispered.

She let out a deep breath. "You mean it?"

Ed nodded, "Who was chasing whom, before the star? I mean it. Will you marry me?"

She nodded. "The nurse called me 'Mrs. Morgan' and I liked the sound of it." She checked his eyes. He moved in for a kiss. When they broke, they realized that Helen was whispering to James, and giggling about them.

Angela squeezed his hand. "Tell them."

"What?"

"These are our friends. Tell them."

Ed's heart was pounding in his chest, it was like a particularly intense vision, only this was real. This was his life.

"People." He spoke too loud, but they all turned their attention on him. "Friends, I just wanted you to know that Angela and I are going to be married."

The room was suddenly full of people, smiling faces, congratulating them. George looked satisfied. Karen Black said, "It's about time!" Helen was so overwhelmed by the event that she put her hand on her mouth, but even that couldn't stop the giggles.

Angela was calm and radiant. Never before had she looked so much like an angel.

Full Voice

THE WIZARD

Abe could barely walk. He was grateful for the release from the bag, but hanging upside down for so long had seriously disoriented him.

It was also his first chance to face the aliens.

Look at those 'hands'. It's a three-point claw. How can they work machines, let alone build them?

He'd learned a lot about hands when he had prototyped the robot platforms for Hodgepodge. He'd tried several pincers and simple grippers before he'd learned enough to use a multiple fingered hand with cushioned, ribbed fingertips. The published literature was content with simpler minimalist designs, but he had turned to the medical prosthesis discipline before he had found a design that met his needs.

He wanted Hodgepodge to interact with his environment like a human did. No matter what a soul in a box could think, it had to be different from the thoughts of a mobile eye that could grab everything it came across. No matter how smart a dolphin was, Abe doubted they would ever have clear communications with humans. Hands were important.

What kind of thoughts do these things have?

"We need to walk this way." Sharon pointed. Abe grabbed up his backpack. They started moving. Asca, the monster behind them batted him with the side of his claw when he strayed from the path.

The mystery of how they used machines was quickly resolved. Optics. Their guard slashed his claw through the light beams with a quick practiced style.

Someone set this up for them.

Sharon whispered, "They used to have a servant race, the Builders. The Builders invented all the technology."

Asca spoke a single word, "D'lense." Abe was reminded that he was walking the corridor with two telepaths.

Asca turned to face him. Abe guessed he was being laughed at, but all he could see was a hard ridged mandible, serrated into fangs, that looked like it could bite through sheet steel.

The Cerik weren't technologists. Everything he could see of them cried out that they were evolved to dominate the food chain the old fashioned way, by tooth and claw.

"Mandible and claw." Sharon and Asca exchanged a glance.

"You're laughing at me."

She shook her head. "He is. I'm worried about our reception."

Abe forced his thoughts to return to the machinery as the door opened.

They were in a hangar. The ship they exited was matched by another, identical except that it lacked the large dent on the side of the one they left.

I did hit it!

Strangely, there were bays for five of the craft. **One crashed in Wimberly. What happened to the other two?**

"One was lost on Earth. One was lost on a previous planet."

"Asca is volunteering information?"

"I asked."

Machines. Think about the machines.

There was a large hatch, presumably to vacuum. They were walking towards a smaller one. Abe focused on a circular pattern on the wall. Dots. As they walked closer, he saw more. *Not dots. Icons.* He had all of fifteen seconds to stare at them.

One flickered through different shades as Asca slashed his claw through the air.

Not pigment. It's an active display! He looked carefully for some sign of a raised button or anything that might hint that this was a control panel— something usable by beings with hands and fingers.

Asca cuffed him and he stumbled through the door.

There was a wall of sound on the other side of the opening. A pride of a hundred lions, all giving forth their loudest roar, pitched an octave higher, might have approached that sound.

Asca joined in. If it hadn't been deafening before, it was now.

Sharon moved close to his ear and shouted, "Second is being greeted in some ceremony. A victory celebration."

Over me.

She nodded. "You challenged them!"

The strength and savagery defined in the muscles and leverage of the Cerik limbs had intimidated him, but not until now was he actually scared. His steps faltered. He glanced at Sharon. In spite of her supernatural healing ability, she was marked on the throat and leg by scars that he'd only seen on old soldiers.

Sharon took his hand. "To them, you're prey. Their blood lust is up. Don't spook, or they'll take you down."

Abe nodded. He understood. After a deep breath, he pushed his awareness of the Cerik into a compartment—treat it as zoology, sociology. Learn them. Don't fear them.

He consciously put his left leg forward and strode ahead. He glanced from side to side.

More icons. There were more of those circular patterns everywhere. He started to recognize the optical controls for the Cerik as well.

There has to be a lot more control from the icons. How many systems are running on the default?

He had no more time to think about it. The final door opened. He walked in to a huge bowl, surrounded on all sides by a nightmare of roaring beasts, all larger than Asca, and all focusing their unblinking eyes on him.

He felt Sharon's hand, but he had no eyes for anything but the tableau around him.

The bowl was a mock up of some natural amphitheater. There were large boulders and trees dotting the sides, but there were natural perches for the Cerik everywhere. Abe had to remind himself that they were inside a spacecraft. The roof above was tinted, with clouds painted on the sky.

Not my blue.

There were five of them on the center dais at the bottom. The largest was roaring his challenge, the surrounding assembly responded in harmony.

Those are words. I wish...

Sharon had to shout, but she explained.

"Look at the highest perch. The ship captain. He calls the songs. They're traditional, everyone knows them. Second, down here is the honored servant.

He is listing his victories. They have to praise them." She paused. "The ones on the left are his clan. They are louder."

Abe strained to tell the difference, but he couldn't.

"'I ate the...shoulder? of a...spiked runner...before it could...before it realized it was dead.' Sorry, I can't do word for word."

Has he mentioned Earth, or us?

"Not yet." There was excitement in her voice.

He looked. She was breathing hard, swaying in time with the 'song'. Her hands were clenching and unclenching, just as he saw the claws of the Cerik. Her eyes were bright.

Are you okay?

She snapped around at him. Her nose dilated. She looked at him as if he were someone else. Abe had the sensation that she too had turned into a predatory beast.

Then she blinked. Her tensed muscles relaxed. "Sorry!" she yelled. "Too many minds. I'm okay now."

A telepathy thing?

"Yes. I can't block them out. I never could."

He glanced at Asca. Their guard was rock steady—the only Cerik in the place not shouting and swaying.

Does he have that problem?

"Yes. He's in a trance. He's effectively unconscious."

He can't read our thoughts!

"Correct"

Then quick! While we have this chance, did he see the box I mentioned when he got my backpack?

"Yes. He didn't notice it. Your car was just incomprehensible gadgets to him."

Have you turned it on?

"Abe," her eyes showed fear for the first time since they walked out here. "I don't want to die."

Neither do I. But that's the beauty of this kind of bomb. The ON switch doesn't set it off, it just starts a timer. If you don't set it again within 24 hours, then it goes off. As long as you are alive, you can reset it every day and it'll be safe forever. It has an OFF switch too. If it is too hard on you, you can stop it.

He winced as a fresh chorus caused his skin to crawl. **But the dead-man-switch has to be activated soon. If they kill us, then we can at least stop them from attacking the Earth anymore.**

"Tell me again, what it does." She shivered. He squeezed her hand.

It's a large thermite bomb. There are two switches that only you can work, just like the lights on the Ouija board. If you start it, and can't start it again within a day, the termite will go off.

It's a heat bomb. It doesn't really explode. It melts down with a furious heat that can liquefy steel in an instant. If it goes off in here, then the scout ship and then this mother ship will catch on fire. Everything seemed to be made of a magnesium alloy. It will burn out of control.

If they kill us, their ship will be destroyed.

He gestured towards the blood thirsty chorus. **We could die any minute now. It may be our only chance to protect our planet.**

"What if I die..."

...and I don't? I invented the thing. I may be the only person who can safely disable it. In any case, I've made my decision. I have people back home I will die to save, don't you?

She turned away. He had a sudden conviction that maybe, just maybe, she didn't. An undefined feeling started growing in his gut.

She turned back, "Okay. It is started. Promise me you will save us!"

I will. How, he didn't know, but with all the conviction he could muster, he willed it to be true. **I will save our lives.**

THE NAME

Tenthonad watched the Voice. He reveled in the freedom of words so old that even the fables just assumed they had always been. The sound that echoed back and forth, and even down from the sky above made his blood flow faster.

Every Hunter felt the same. Now was the time when your blood called and you felt ready to slash through anyone in your way. At the same time, ancient words called for the deepest loyalty to your clan, your Name, your sides.

This was the time when so many cubs learned their limits when they stretched their claws too far.

It was also the time, in so many legends, when a Second gained a *Name*, or lost his eyes.

He knew Second was watching his every move. Any sign of uncertainty or weakness would give him the opening he wanted.

Tenthonad, however, gave his strongest attention to the two City-builders. He was fascinated by their close interplay. He recognized the female by the dark covering she wore. It was strange that the male and female were practically identical. He supposed they could tell the differences among their own kind.

The female was talking to the male. He was watching the Voice, unafraid like a set of *dededdes* safe in the branches of a tree. Did he not know that Second fully intended to rip his body apart shortly and feast on the taste of a warm prey?

Tenthonad shivered at the remembered taste of the female's blood. If it happened that way, he would be down there on the floor, demanding the share due him.

Of course, Second would challenge. One of them, at least, would die. The two clans were nearly matched in this arena. If they came in after their leaders, it would be a wonder if there were crew enough to made the leap home.

If he didn't demand his share, it would only be a day or less before Second could secure the loyalty of the *names* and take him down as a weakling.

Time was close. The pattern was clear.

He shouted over the assembly, "My Second has brought victory over the City-builders. Soon the Hunters of both our clans will roam the hills below and drink the sweet blood of the prey. What meat shall I give my Righteye?"

There was a roar of approval, stronger of course from the other side of the arena.

"I demand the blood of the prey!" came Second's reply.

The female City-builder said something to the male. Was he the only one that saw the male reach one hand into the bag he carried?

For an instant, Tenthonad was tempted to grant Second's request. If his theory was correct, Second might find those eyes harder to take than he imagined.

No. I am the Name! Let cubs chase after the chitchit's tail.

"Listen to the Tales, and then I will grant the meat you deserve!" The arena went silent, except for the scraping noises of claws.

He took a great breath and began.

"*Great floods covered the land of Sessene after the great mountains to the north awoke from their long dan. Ghader struggled to find prey for his clan, as prey and Hunter alike were drowned or caught in the new swamps. 'I will stalk the nests of the Builders, for they have prospered in this flood.'*"

He talked slowly, watching the City-builders. He eased his *ineda*, letting the female telepath pick up the top of his mind.

"*Ghader watched from his tree, until a Builder left his nest and swam within his claws. 'Do not eat me,' cried the Builder, 'for I have three cubs that will starve without me.'*

"*'But your blood will ease the hunger of my three cubs as they cry for the dry lands where the Runners once grazed.' Ghader slung the Builder's feet across his back and turned toward his family.*

"*'Do not eat me, and I will make a net to help you collect your prey.'*

"*'My back is strong and my claw is secure. Do not fear that I will drop you.'*

"*'Do not eat me, and I will build a trap to catch many swimmers for you.'*

"*'My cubs hunger for warm blood, not cold.'*

"*The Builder was silent with his fate while Ghader carried him across the swamp. Then he said, 'Do not eat me, and I and my cubs will drain the swamp and bring back the dry land.'*

"*Ghader laughed, 'For these times, we teach our cubs not to listen to the words of the Builder.'*

"*'For these times, we teach our cubs to speak the words of the Hunters. But we also teach them to see what is not, but could be. You have seen our dams. You have seen our strong nests. We Builders know the waters. Surely you are tired of walking through this mud?'*

"*Ghader snarled at the mud, but he said, 'If I released my claw, you would be back within your nest, and my cubs would still cry for meat.'*

"*The Builder agreed, 'It has often happened, for as long as Builders and Hunters have talked. But for the life of my cubs, I will try a new thing.'*

"*'I and my brood will leave our nest and live under your tree. For the safety of our fur, we will build the dams while you protect our blood from the other Hunters. The land will dry and the Runners will return. Hunters will race across the land rather then pace in the mud.'*

"'It is a new thing,' agreed Ghader. 'This day, I will find other prey. But first, call your cubs.'

"As they spoke, so it happened. The Builder and his brood left their hard nest and lived among sticks under the trees of the Hunter. Ghader took many eyes while the dams were built, but soon the land was dry and Runners returned.

"Ghader and his clan soon took all of the land of Sessene and his cubs prospered. 'For all time,' declared Ghader, 'I will have Builders beneath my perch.'"

...

There was a unified keen of respect, but muted, as all knew that the history of the Builders was gone, lost to the evil day when the Delense took the weapons that they had invented for their masters and turned them around. Now, there were no more Builders.

Tenthonad leapt down from his high perch, and in two great bounds, stood eye to eye before Second. The aliens edged back a step, but found Asca moving to block their retreat.

"I am Tenthonad! Today I will make a Tale! Under these eyes, I claim this breeding pair of City-builders as my new Builders. With the female to teach the Hunter's tongue and the male who can build new things from the legacy of the Delense, I will make our clans the most powerful on the world. They will live under my perch and I will take the eyes of any who threaten them!"

There was a uncertain reaction from the crowd. This was a new thing, and arguments started immediately.

Second's growl was growing, and Tenthonad shouted. "Second has won a great victory, and deserves great meat! He alone deserves to lead the first party to hold the planet below. His clan will gain the first perch on this new world."

With that, the shouts and cries above grew to a new level as the two clans absorbed the change. Many were screaming rage at the prize Tenthonad was giving up for his clan.

Second did nothing but glare hate at his eyes. Leader of the first perch was a great prize, but the blood lust was strong—for his *Name* and for the prey. He could still challenge, but his own clan would not be behind him if he rejected the prize and risked losing everything.

Second opened his jaws wide and gave a voice that stilled the whole crew. With one back swing of a claw he caught the male City Builder across the chest and threw him hard across the arena to slam against a large stone, and then slump lifeless to the floor.

Burning

THE WITCH

"No!" Sharon shouted and raced across the floor towards Abe.

Deep in her mind, she'd felt the pain of the blow, so much greater than the one dealt her by the old scientist. She had felt his ribs crack and then, an instant later, she was thrown out of his mind by the obliterating pain when he slammed against the stone.

Rage descended over her. That part of her which knew every cell, and every atom reached out for the bomb. Abe had been so considerate to make a trigger easy for her to set and cancel. But she was able to do so much more than influence a few random electrons. She felt past the electronic timer, down the wires to the trigger, where a coated wire waited only a little bit of heat. Wordless, she sent it flaming.

Kill my mate! I'll burn you all!

The simple coating, much like the tip of a match, ignited a small pouch of magnesium powder. Flaming thousands of degrees, the magnesium awoke the sleeping combustion of aluminum powder surrounding it.

Aluminum was a brother metal to magnesium, slow to ignite, but insatiable and star hot as it burned. There was not enough free oxygen for the metal, but that didn't stop it. Mixed with the aluminum powder was simple rust, oxidized iron, and iron had no claim on the oxygen that aluminum could not usurp.

Stripped of its oxygen, and heated well past its melting point, pure iron fluid melted through everything. It escaped the bounds of the bomb package, and in a quick-running stream flashed through the fiberglass body of the electric car and instantly ignited the hull of the scout ship. If there had been any eyes to see it, they would have been blinded by the white hot flame.

Sharon threw herself down on Abe's body, her eyes blurred with tears and her own voice unable to contain her pain. She tried to wrap herself around the bloody body of the man, the only man, who had loved her. The only man she could ever love.

Asca had spoken the truth when he had called them mates, even though she had been startled by the claim. Never once had she thought to correct his perception. Nor had Abe, when he had heard it.

Oh, Abe. I will die here with you.

She became the Eye. There were easy pathways in her body—she had learned so much, just in the process of staving off her own death in this place. A simple stilling of her own heart would be easy.

The only task would be to make sure that when the blood stopped and her mind drifted away, that some automatic survival instinct in her cells wouldn't find a way to clear her inhibition. Nitrites would do it. All she had to do was flood...

Then, a trickle of thought. **Sharon! Stop!**

Abe? Instantly, in a panic, she twisted the bounds of her perception apart. Breaking free of her own body, she dug deep into his mind, clawing like a swimmer too long starved for air.

He was alive. A kernel of life rested among the fluttering wreckage of his mind. Like a small child with its toys, Abe was slowly, hesitantly, building a fragile tower from the scattered pieces of his self.

"Abe?" she whispered, and the word trickled down into his mind. He winced in fright, and then suddenly turned with renewed strength, to pull himself back from the edge of dissolution.

Oh no! I have killed us both. She could hear, over the torrent of noise, something that could only be an alarm, a rising keening many octaves higher than the screams of the Cerik.

She was the only one to notice, as all were intent on the battle between Tenthonad and Second.

"Abe! I thought you were dead! I triggered the thermite."

Like a crystal flashing into being from its saturated mother fluid. Abe's mind was coming rapidly back into itself. The words galvanized his will. By brute force, he pushed aside the pain and horror of coming back from the abyss.

He blinked his eyes, and a lance of pain washed across his body. "Thermite?" he managed to speak.

"Yes. Don't talk, I can hear you."

The bomb. It has ignited?

"Yes. I'm so sorry. I have killed us."

He struggled to move, and she felt a fresh trickle of warm blood from the back of his head. She sensed the fracture in his skull where he had struck the stone. She stared at the dripping red with a guilt that tore open her own chest and poured fire into her heart.

He whispered painfully, "We aren't dead yet."

Keep me alive for another few minutes, and help me up.

She moved her arm under his, and steadied him to his feet.

Get through to Asca. He has to send a message for us.

THE TELEPATH

Asca was torn. This was a battle for the *Name!* He was there on the dais in the midst of it. He could smell the blood already. The aroma of the dead prey had his own blood flowing.

But the clamor of the surrounding mass of minds was likely to burn out his own. It was past controlling. He would have to retreat and throw himself into *dan*.

ASCA!

He turned, in horror. Both prey were standing. "Rakla-del", he said, unheard above the noise. So he was like her, unkillable. The male was dripping blood in that obscene way.

ASCA. YOU WILL SPEAK FOR ME.

He winced away, unable to break free of the voice in his mind. **I don't know...**

IF YOU RESIST ME, I WILL LOOSEN YOUR PLATES, I WILL CLOSE YOUR OOKR. I WILL ROLL YOU OVER ON YOUR BACK.

As she listed the threats, Asca could feel the muscles in his body twitch in obedience to her. It was true, she would make him perform obscene, embarrassing actions like a newborn cub, and suffocate him right there on the dais in front of the whole assembly.

AND IF WE DO NOTHING, OR MOVE TOO SLOW, YOU AND ALL OF YOUR FELLOWS WILL DIE IN FLAMES LIKE A ROASTED DETERCAN.

More frightening than the threats were the images, terribly real images of the whole ship burning around them.

He agreed to do as she said. It was too late. She had eaten his soul already. The screams of battle around him paled against his fear.

Embolden by terror, he raised himself up to his full height, and with a voice louder than he had ever used before, he screamed at the *Name* and the Second and the whole of his brothers.

"I speak the words of the City-builders!"

Even the two combatants paused in their dance. Suddenly everyone noticed that the aliens were both alive.

"Second treated me like a prey, and for that I have killed every one of you. Even now, your ship is burning up around you. You have no life. I have taken it."

In the silence of the pause, certain of the Cerik, the ship handlers, looked up to the sky, just now noticing the ship's own cry of pain.

"But because of Tenthonad, our defender, I have changed my mind. I will now go to stop the death and give you back your lives."

With that, the assembly scattered like the seeds in a *ursiced* field when hit by a wind from the mountains. The City-builders moved as one being, turning and heading towards the exit door.

The male reached out, and instead of making the cuts, he touched the Delense-marks, and the door opened. No one moved to stop him. Tenthonad and a handful of other lesser *names* moved to follow.

At the door to the hangar, he opened the hatch, and all saw the truth. The light and smoke caused everyone to move back.

All except the aliens. The male looked around the door, coughing in the smoke, trying to wave it aside to see what was happening within.

THE WITCH

Sharon pulled him back. "What can we do?"

Abe blinked aside tears from the smoke. "The thermite is already eating into the floor plates. I have to stop that first."

"How?"

He didn't answer, running his finger an inch above the circle of icons. She could feel his brain racing. He was looking for something...

Ah. He stabbed at a button, and all of the images changed. *Menu system.* Quickly, he scanned and searched the icons.

"What kind of animal were the Delense? Semiaquatic, like a beaver?"

"Yes." She lanced a quick probe at Asca, and frightened, he formed a visual image. "A lot like a beaver. The size of a human. Furred. A dorsal ridge that they waved from side to side in the water for propulsion."

He asked, "Arms and legs?"

"Yes. Two of each."

"Did they walk upright?"

"No. Strong hind legs, and curved padded forearms. The hands could fold back against the arm for protection."

He nodded. *Makes sense now.* He stabbed at a pattern of buttons. There was a shriek of metal from inside the hangar.

Abe risked a look. Squinting against the glare, he could see both scout ships drift up from the floor. Sharon rode the image from his eyes. There was a choked cry from a Cerik, who watched incredulously.

I turned off the tractor effect that simulates gravity. Without it, the molten iron will stay in place and not drip to the floor plate.

"Will the flame go out?"

The sense of defeat from Abe was enough. "No." Even as he spoke, the side of the flaming ship sagged inward. A spout of flame flared from a new hole on the side, and slowly the dying scout ship started moving.

Sharon could foresee what would happen next. One way or another, the flaming metal would wedge up against a wall and start it burning.

"Can you put out the flame? Smother it?"

He shook his head. "I can turn off the oxygen flow to the room, but magnesium will even burn in nitrogen. I could open the outer hatch to vacuum, but even that is not good enough. You know the search we did. There's enough stored gases as solid compounds in their recycler to keep it going. It may already be too late."

She could feel him weaken under the effects of his injury and some great truth she couldn't follow. With a desperation fueled by her own fear, she reached into the cells of his body.

It was ruthless, and he would pay for it, but there was one thing she could do for him. It took only seconds.

He took a deep breath, eyes wide like waking from a sleep. She stifled the pain as his body complained with a jolt like lightning.

But his mind firmed and grew stronger.

Tell Asca. We have to go in there and push the burning hull toward the external hatch, then get back outside to open the bay to vacuum.

"Will that put it out?"

No. Tell Asca. The engine will melt soon. It will explode. Think of a small atomic bomb.

Sharon relayed the message, and Asca spoke to Tenthonad, as Abe made rapid adjustments on the controls.

Abe took her hand and they edged into the heat and glare of the flame.

A shout from behind startled them both.

"Te!" came the command from Tenthonad.

"Just one," she relayed.

"No! It will take both of us. I've got the controls set, but with the way the hangar is made, the burning ship could wedge. We only get one chance."

Asca was translating his words into the Cerik language.

"Te!" Tenthonad ordered.

Abe waved toward the hatch, "Then come help us! We have no time!"

"Te!"

Sharon felt a door into the leader's mind open and then close.

"Abe, he isn't going to budge. He will kill us himself if we both go in."

He absorbed the news. **Okay, just wait until I have it moving in the right direction, and then...**

"No, Abe. I am the stronger one right now. I can hear your instructions. You would never make it. I might."

She could feel his resistance, but before he could object, she pulled free and stepped through the doorway.

There was a wrench of perspective, and a sickening twist.

I'm falling!

Her last step propelled her towards the ceiling. The air was choking and hot. She was blinded by the glare. She could feel the hair on her arm burn from the heat.

Look at the wall! There is a handrail. Grab it.

She could see it in a quick glance, before she had to close her eyes again. For now, her other senses would have to do.

The rail came into her hand, and it was burning hot. She held on in spite of the pain.

Pull yourself along the rail for another twenty feet.

Each grasp of the rail was more painful than the last. She gave it a quick tug, enough to get her moving, and only touched the agonizing metal when she had to.

Good. Stop there. You have to jump towards the ship. Hit it, Kick it. Jump back to the rail where you are now.

She could see the scene clearly from her own clairvoyance, overlaid by the image of forces and mass that were Abe's own special vision. It was clear what she had to do.

She jumped, and just like Felice, she twisted in mid air. *Thud!* She landed with both feet against the hull. Instantly she pushed off and headed back to the wall.

Good! Do it again.

She thrilled at the moment of freedom, sailing in the air. For a perfect moment, all the fear was gone. She was like a bird in the air. Her love was holding her tight in his mind. Her past was nothing. The future was nothing. The twist of her body through the air was everything.

Thud! She kicked off.

Good girl! Get back to the rail, and then kick straight for me. You will get a little singed, but you have to do it.

She didn't question. She focused on the door to Abe, and jumped.

The burning ship was now shooting flames in all directions. She wrapped her arms around her face. She was going right through one of them.

One unbearable moment, with the smell of her burning hair, and then she was through it.

The door was there, she opened her eyes and saw him waiting with opened arms. As they touched, the outside gravity grabbed her and slammed her hard against the floor. Her freedom of flight was over.

Abe pulled himself from their tangle on the floor and straining every muscle, he threw himself at the control panel.

THE NAME

Tenthonad watched the hatch close, secretly glad that the vision of that scout ship eating itself in flames was gone from view. The little creature worked at the Delense-marks, and there was a cry from the ship itself, and then the outer hatch opened.

It was clear what the City-builder was trying to do.

He roared a command to the ship handlers. And the reply was quick, the burning ship was outside and moving.

"Move us away, quickly."

The feel of the ship shifted, as Yakke's crew pushed the engines, and they moved away from the doomed and tormented scoutship.

Its agony was short lived. There was a flash from the open viewports, and the ship shook from the blast.

Asca spoke, in that strange tone of voice he used when saying the words of the City-builders. "Only the emptiness saved us. There was no air to carry the... voice of the explosion."

Tenthonad ordered the ship to continue. He knew the explosive force from an engine that was broken. There could be other *flicks*. The scout ship did have three engines.

The male of the City-builders touched the Delense-marks again. Tenthonad asked, "What is he doing now?"

Asca replied, "He is closing the outer hatch, and refilling the hangar with air."

Another report came from the ship handlers. "There were two *flicks*, close together, but there is no longer any sign of the scout ship."

After a moment, the hatch opened. It was dark inside.

Tenthonad called for light, and one of his crew raced off to get it. The two City-builders, moving like prey run to exhaustion, stepped through the opening together. He followed, Asca trailing at his side.

Even with freshly replaced air, the place smelt like the slope of a volcano. Some places still glowed with their own heat, and the dim red light gave a strange, unsettling light to the place.

But for all that was seen, it was what was missing that brought a howl from his throat.

Both scoutships were gone. The hangar was vacant.

Behind him, from the doorway, came a snarl.

"Your pets have robbed me of even your offered meat!"

He turned. Second was framed in the opening. Behind him were his most loyal supporters, the *names* of his clan.

"Your 'Builders' have brought this expedition, and both our clans, to ruin. With no ship to land us, we have no claim. With no claim, there will be no assistance to finance a return. Other clans will take this place.

"I will take their blood, and eat their flesh, and you will not stop me!"

Healer

THE SCIENTIST

Cujo handed him the Geiger-counter. Larry tapped the little red push button on the top of the gadget twenty or thirty times just as fast as he could move his finger. Each hit of the switch moved a little more voltage into the capacitors, until the gas-filled glass tube was biased into its 500 volt range. He put the old 1950's style headphones over his head and listened to the occasional clicking of the normal background radiation level.

It felt strange to be in Coonabarabran, outside, standing in the middle of the street, waiting for the star to come up above the horizon, and not be scurrying for cover. The radiation had been dropping steadily for the last two nights.

Please make it a trend.

When Betelgeuse exploded, it rose above the horizon early in the afternoon. Each day it rose about four minutes earlier, as the Earth moved around the sun, changing the position of the sun by about a degree a day. It had moved into the morning hours, and before too much longer, the supernova would be strictly a daytime star. If the radiation didn't fade, people would be soon forced to restrict their outdoor activities to the night time. Larry didn't relish the idea of a cold winter July where the sunshine was off limits. Up in the northern hemisphere, they would have their own problems. July was summer there, and warmer, but it was also their growing season. In spite of all the deaths already, there was still not enough food for the remaining mouths, especially in the cities.

Constable Bern had already made that point clear in last night's town meeting. Coonabarabran had been lucky so far. He would need a permanently armed group of men, ready to act, when the next set of refugees sought easier pickings here. He also wanted permission of the community to build a warning out on the highway—a cemetery of the invaders and a pile of their burned cars.

Keep out of Coonabarabran if you value your lives.

He didn't know if it would be approved. For every citizen whose blood was up and ready to spit fire, there was another deeply horrified at what had happened, to the town and to the world.

Larry didn't know how he would vote. He hadn't pulled a trigger in the battle, but he would in the next, if Janet were in danger.

Constable Bern had also talked to him privately about his plans for the security of the town, and the observatory. There were more issues than Larry wanted to be aware of. In spite of their current popularity, it might all come down to the age old differences between farmers and astronomers. It'd always been a joke that the farmers hated a drought and the astronomers loved it. There was a difference in attitude that had existed for decades. And now the farmers had all the votes.

A rattle of clicks in his headphones brought him out of those thoughts. He glanced at the clock tower. A bit early. Probably secondaries.

But it was only a couple of breaths later that the rate of particles hitting the Geiger counter tube started climbing. He hit the charging button a few more times.

"Cujo, what does your watch say?"

"Ten-forty."

"Okay, the tower clock is just running late. It got me going for a minute."

"I can see the star from up here. What's the rate?"

Estimating the radiation count from the clicks was an acquired skill. The meter back up on the mountain had a meter that read 'mR/hr', but this unit Cujo had wired up for portable use was headphones only.

"Much better than yesterday. Here, take a listen." He handed to unit up to him.

Cujo took the box in his large hands, and tapped the charging button. He listened with one earphone held up to his ear, and nodded. "A two hour day."

Larry did the simple math, calculating how many hours a person could be out in this without any noticeable harm. "Maybe..."

"Excuse me! Mr. Kelly?" A teenage boy slowed to a stop, "They want you. Back at the hospital."

Larry's heart started racing. "Janet? Is it time?"

He nodded.

"Here," Larry pushed the clipboard at Cujo.

The big man laughed, "I won't be far behind you."

But Larry was already moving.

THE EQUESTRIENNE

"Mrs. Morgan?" The lady asked, at the same time, keeping a firm grasp on the black-haired little toddler that was doing his best to escape. "Can I see your husband?"

Helen, from across the room, caught the lady's eye for just a second.

Angela Morgan, nee Benton, didn't recognize her, but the news of the impromptu wedding swept through the place and people, sick and well, had come to cheer them on.

The new bride said, "He's changing clothes right now. He should be out any moment." She shook the lady's hand and turned to the next of the total strangers that wanted to congratulate her.

Just then Helen saw Ed Morgan enter the room, holding the bag containing the black business suit he had borrowed from one of the doctors. He pushed through the people carefully, holding the bag high in both hands until he handed it back to its owner.

Angela moved up next to him, and they talked a moment with the man. Helen waved at the lady with the child.

"What are you up to?" asked James, her self-appointed escort. Helen told everyone she was strong enough to move around on her own, but James found a wheel-chair and was insistent.

"Oh nothing. It's just someone I met this morning. Her boy gets sick and the doctors are too busy to help her."

"He looks well enough now."

"That's what the doctors tell her, and then a day or so later and he's sick again. Come on, I want to get closer." She grabbed the arm rest and put one foot down on the floor. James pushed down on her shoulder.

"I borrowed this thing, and if it doesn't get used, I'll take the flack. You just sit still and tell me where you want to go."

"I need to get closer to them. I want to hear what they are saying."

"Nosey!"

"Bossy!"

"Yes, Ma'am." He released the brake and started pushing.

Ahead of them, the lady with the child caught Ed Morgan's attention. She asked him a question, and he shook his head. Angela looked puzzled.

"Hurry." Helen urged. James, behind her, said, "Hush."

"... am sorry," Ed was saying. "I'm not a healer. I don't know how you got that idea."

"It's what people are saying," said the mother.

"What people?"

"Just people. Can't you help my Fred? You are my only hope."

Ed looked frustrated. It was his wedding day!

"Take a look at the boy, at least," suggested Angela. "It would only take a minute."

He nodded. The mother handed the boy up into his arms. Silently, the boy wiggled and twisted in the unfamiliar grasp. Ed closed his eyes as if hit by a sudden headache, and then he shook his head.

"No." He told the lady, as he handed the boy back. "He isn't sick. I'm sure he will grow up to be a big strong man."

"But..." began his mother.

"However," continued Ed, "I do think he is probably allergic to milk. Have you been feeding him milk, or cheese?"

"Well, there is cheese at the marketplace."

"I realize it's hard to find good food these days, but he would do better with something else."

"Thank you," said the lady and turned away.

Ed looked at his wife and the two or three people around him who had witnessed the exchange. He shrugged his shoulders. "I told her I was no healer." He read their expressions, "I mean it. I did nothing to the boy."

"And the lactose-intolerance?" asked the man who had loaned him the suit.

"That was just a guess!"

Helen watched as the mother and child eased their way back out of the crowd. Before she left, she turned towards Helen and gave her a wave. She was smiling.

"Busybody!" said James.

"I didn't do anything." She folded her hands primly in her lap. "Let's go. Once around the park, James."

"You wish!"

THE WIZARD

"Can you see the one with the interlocking circles?"

Sharon, with a frown on her face, nodded.

"That controls the nitrates in the air. Activate it."

"Okay."

"Now you should see the circle change, with an up button, a down button, and an array of different shaded buttons. The mark between the up and down buttons is the current setting. You can press any of the shaded ones to go to that pre-set value, or you can use the up or down buttons to adjust from whatever is the current setting. All white is no nitrate, all black is all nitrate. It's really simple."

"I just pressed the white button."

"Listen."

From the bottom of their pit, the only thing they had been able to hear was the howl and clatter of the Ceriks as they moved about their business. Now, however, there was the whisper of moving air as the atmosphere of this chamber was being exchanged.

"And that is all it takes?" Sharon rested her head on his arm. "I have spent nearly all my strength, every moment since I was captured, fighting this poison in the air."

"It isn't poison to them. It's a natural part of the air to them. Their home planet must be a violent place, with volcanoes or lightning or maybe some kind of plant, that keeps it replenished. They evolved with it, they built their technology with it—luckily for us."

"Lucky? I don't think we've been so lucky."

Abe moved a little closer to her. "Maybe not lucky for you and me. But it's been lucky for the human race. They don't seem to use iron for much of anything. All this ship seems to be made of ceramics and magnesium alloys. In their native atmosphere, the magnesium forms a hard protective coating when scratched. In Earth's atmosphere, it makes a crumbly weak coating. That's why they lost their ships.

"Now they have no scout ships left, and I doubt that they can land a ship of this size. They can't land, so they can't invade. I think that's lucky for Earth."

Abe looked up toward the pile of supplies that Sharon had accumulated. "Is there any more of that chili? I am starving."

She smiled, and reached for the stack of cans. "I am doing that to you. I have gone inside your cells and adjusted the 'buttons'. I am trying to make you as strong as possible. If you survive, you'll be sick for days afterwards."

He took the can and worked the opener. "From what I've already been through, I think I should be dead. At the moment I feel pretty good."

Sharon lay back down and watched him eat. Her face had gone solemn. She said, "If you don't survive, neither will this ship."

He looked at her over the can, "If the Cerik could hear your voice, they'd be shaking in their boots."

"It's their own fault. I'm soaking up too much of the Cerik soul. You're the only thing keeping me human. If you fall, I will take their eyes!"

He set down the empty can. Sharon, laying there, was the one island of humanity and warmth in a universe suddenly cold and hard. He liked the way she looked, sexy in that leather coat she wore since most of her other clothes disintegrated. He eased down beside her, and feeling the heat of her body, he pulled her into his arms. There was a sharp pain in his chest, where she said his broken ribs were, but that was a small price to pay for the softness in his arms and her warm breath on his lips. He tugged at her waistband and the seams of her jeans ripped.

They kissed. It was long and slow. He tried to drink in her soul, even as his hands explored places they probably shouldn't go.

He broke free of her lips for air, and rested his eyes in the hollow of her neck. The roughness of her jacket and the pain in his ribs were to only blemishes on the moment. He tugged open her coat. His lips touched her skin.

"Abe."

He kissed the warmth of her neck. "Yes."

"I'm inside your mind."

"Okay." He relished the taste of the salt on her skin, and the feel of her body in the curve of his arm.

"Stop for a moment. There is a part of you, crying to be heard."

Bewildered, he paused, and instantly realized what he was doing.

"Oops." There was a sudden wash of shame. He was in full rut, and it was plain what he would have done. This was not like him.

He started to disentangle his arms from around her.

"No. Stay. I like this."

He stopped, unsure and unable to move. His mind was a mass of confusion.

"Just stay. Rest your head here. Hold me."

He did, and found a little measure of sweetness in the turmoil of his emotions. All over his body, his muscles were jittery from reaction.

"Be calm, Abe. I am sorry. I did this to you. Your hormones are heightened because of all of the work I'm doing to your body. You are not acting normally."

"I want you." He locked down everything, not daring to move his hands or shift his position.

"And I want you, too. Not much is wrong. Your self-control was destroyed and we had to take a break for you to regain it."

Abe managed a private smile. "I'm not there yet."

She put her hand on his hot face. "You will be. You have the strongest mind I have ever touched."

They rested in silence for a while. Abe could feel his emotions swinging wildly, but slowly he reined them in. He built cages, controlling how far they could go. Little by little, he let himself feel them again, until he was of whole mind.

"That was like diving off a cliff," he said in a whisper. "The rush of emotion was wonderful. I want to do it again."

She moved slightly, so that they were facing each other. "You will," she promised. "You can now, if you want."

He shook his head sadly. "I need to be sure there is a pool of water at the bottom of the cliff, and not a pile of rocks."

He could see that her eyes were shiny. The last few moments had been hard on her too. How much of his struggle had been shared by her?

"I have my own battles," she said. "I have tried to throw away my fears, to see only victory, and not death. But what then?

"If they can't invade, we can't escape. Neither of us can get back to Earth. If Tenthonad keeps us as his pets, what about us?" Her voice broke. "We are so different."

"I love you." Abe felt a part of his soul click into place, as if saying the words acted like a combination on a lock.

She shook her head. "I don't know what that means! I can feel it, in you, a hard shell that I can crawl inside and feel safe. But how can I be anything for you? I need you, but you don't need me.

"Even your attraction to me—I've tricked you from the first time we met. I've read your mind and shown you just what would ensnare your senses. It's all false."

He smiled into her mind. **You're a girl. Just like all the others that wear enticing clothes and enhance their faces with makeup. Should I love you less for that?**

Her tears were flowing freely, and Abe brushed away the tracks from her face. "And I thought there was no part of my mind you couldn't read. There must be language barriers, even for telepaths. I've known you loved me, perhaps from that first day. Love isn't a feeling, it's an action. You drove off to face death, for me. You tried to give up hope for rescue, for me. You tried to burn the Cerik alive, for me.

"I said I loved you, because it felt right to say it, but you don't have to say or do anything to prove yourself to me."

Sharon pushed her face into his hand. "I'm afraid. We go to be slaughtered in the morning. I'm afraid of that, more than you know. But I think I'm more afraid that we might survive. Worse than Cerik claws would be the day when you get tired and walk away from me."

Abe had nothing to say more than his own wordless horror at the idea. He held her head gently in the curve of his arm while his mind churned away, working on the terrors of claw and spirit that threatened his love.

U'tanse Bond

THE TELEPATH

Asca waited for a moment on the edge of the pit. He was almost ready to wake the City-builders from their sleep, when the female looked up at him.

Is it time?

Yes. The search for the missing scout ship has been a failure. Tenthonad can no longer hold off Second's claim. I have been sent to bring you.

Wait one moment. We will soon be ready.

Asca wondered about them. Their bodies were so weak, and yet killing blows did not stop them. They knew he was to take them to the arena and there Second would kill them, and yet they seemed ready to come, not at all like a normal prey.

He wished he had the courage to probe deeper than the surface of their minds. But he'd seen enough. His arm had healed. He still remembered the obscenity of his body moving to her will. He was not Teckkaca to challenge a volcano at its voice.

We are ready.

He leapt down into the pit, grabbed the male and jumped back up to the edge. He set him down and then brought up the female.

We will walk. The two intertwined their hands and headed towards the arena. Asca followed.

A Second's Challenge was a different thing. It was strange to enter the arena and see Tenthonad there on the floor, facing Second, and the lesser *names* taking the high perches around the edge of the bowl. Of course, the whole situation would never happen if the they were still solidly behind Tenthonad.

Asca debated just a moment, and then leapt up towards the rim, where his status gave him a perch by right. Tenthonad growled, but could say nothing. Until this was done, he could not offend the lesser *names*.

Asca, you will still speak for me.

He kept that message to himself as he took his place, and was granted some recognition by Egh and Reathe. There was nothing to do but play it out.

Second spoke, "Tenthonad has claimed these prey as 'Builders'. With them, he claims, the lands of his clan will increase. He recites the Tale of long ago, when Builders built mud dams for the Hunters and made things better.

"But I must remind you of a different story. It was not in the times of the Tales, but recently, within the lifetime of the *Name* of my clan.

"Builders were plentiful, owned by every clan. Some clans had many more Builders in their lands than cubs. Builders had their own nests, no longer, as in the Tales, living beneath the perch of the *Name*. So many Builders were needed, not because our prey were so hard to manage, not because the volcanoes were erupting again, nor because the Far Island was sinking—so many Builder cubs were born because there were too many Hunter cubs.

"Think of the Tales, as Tenthonad so often says. In our greatness, one clan would hold a mountain. One *Name* would rule from its High Perch. Look at us now. There are so many clans that they cannot be known. We used the Builders to increase the Runners, and then even the land was not wide enough. We went to the planets to find more lands, more prey. Each step we took required greater skills and greater power from our Builders, so the Builders increased as well.

"Until the Builders looked at each other and said, 'Do we not have tools stronger than the Hunter's claw? Cannot we escape faster in our machines than the Hunter's leap? Why should we serve the Hunter any longer?'

"And so the City of the Face was burned with their bomb, and they loaded many of the space ships with Builder cubs and sought to escape our claw.

"But the Builders did not know the strength of a Hunter's rage. Their ships were hunted down and destroyed. Every Builder of every clan of every land of every planet was eaten! We took them all. They are no more!"

The assembled Hunters could feel that rage. It had been in the very air since they were cubs. Builders were creatures of legend, but the rage that killed them had been alive in the ones who had taught them to hunt, who had taught them to speak.

Second concluded, "We need no more 'Builders'. We need no more planets. I shall eat these two, and then I shall return us to our clans and we will make ourselves strong so that we can hold our mountain against those who would again bleed us for fancy Tales of far treasure worlds and unlimited plains of alien prey."

There was a shiver among the Hunters, not only for his claim, but for the hint of a change in the breeze, here in a place where there was no breeze.

Tenthonad acted as if he had not heard the words of Second. He moved across the floor of the arena to a spot near the aliens.

"I have heard cubs crying into my ears today," he began with contempt in his voice. "'These City-builders are too dangerous,' said some. 'Remember the Tale of the Brothers,' some cried. 'It is our nature to hunt alone.' And others—others say that there are too many cubs!" He hissed.

"To the cubs frightened of these City-builders, I say to remember the Tale of Getterin and the Builder. If you don't know it, then learn it! 'Strength and cunning make power, and I intend that power to be in my hand.'

"To those who can't understand the Tales, 'The Brothers' does tell us that we must not deny our nature, but where does it tell us our nature is so small?

"And to any who thinks that there are too many cubs, I tell him to come see me and I will make sure he makes no more cubs!"

There was a moment of silence. Not a Hunter in the arena doubted his word.

"Hunters! Smell this day! Remember it to your cubs.

"Chew on this—our ancestors made a mistake! Either Ghader was a fool for taking the Builder under his perch, or our own clans have all been fools for taking the blood of our Builders when the great cry for vengeance came.

"Ghader's clan became great. It is still with us to this day.

"Our clans have suffered. And what of the lines of Sttegh, Lackka, and Goladen. They are gone!"

Tenthonad crouched, facing Second. "These are my Builders, and none shall touch them."

THE WITCH

She whispered, "The statements are over. Now they fight."

If Tenthonad wins, we are safe?

She nodded.

When Second moved, he was almost too fast to be seen. It was a quick feint, forcing Tenthonad to shift back. But it wasn't Second's plan to slash his *La*.

In the second of time it took Tenthonad to move, Second braced and kicked. Tenthonad was caught off balance, and tumbled back, right on top of them.

Abe dodged to the side. Sharon went down.

Are you okay?

Sharon was stunned by the impact. The hard leather bulk of the Cerik pinned her leg. She 'touched' the nerves in Abe's right cheek. His face twitched in their signal for *Yes*. She was hurt and bruised, but nothing was broken.

Roll to the left. She did it, and just missed being swatted by accident as Tenthonad struggled to regain his footing. There was a large fake boulder to her back. She edged to the side of it.

Things were happening too fast! Her attention slipped for an instant, and she had to re-focus. Quickly, she reached out.

Abe was moving to the side to watch her.

Asca leaned forward, trying to catch every nuance of the battle.

Tenthonad was a blank.

Second was a blank.

She sensed the Delense-marks.

She stretched to keep it all active in her head. And still she had to look with her eyes. Tenthonad was on his feet, out of sight behind the rock.

Second tensed one leg.

From Asca, **He's going for the female. Good strategy.**

She 'touched' the bindi spot on Abe's forehead.

Abe recognized the touch, but Second was already in motion.

Zero G! Her eyes clamped shut on their own, but she activated the white button. Memory of claw slicing through her flesh. A disturbance in the air.

She looked. Second sailed over her head, just out of reach.

Revert! She did.

The arena was in chaos. The whole population of the Cerik were of one thought. *Landquake!* Instinct had them all reaching claws for a firm hold.

Both combatants tumbled. They'd been in mid-leap when the floor stopped pulling them down.

Second clipped the boulder. His claws scraped the floor. He turned eyes on her.

Tenthonad hit awkwardly, and rolled.

Second was much closer.

His first step was cautious, his second more bold.

Sharon could see nothing but his eyes, and his jaws.

BANG! The 9mm gunshot was loud. The echo rang the amphitheater like a metal drum. The illusion of rock and trees wavered.

Second was thrown to the side.

He's dead! Sharon hoped, for an instant.

Second's thoughts erupted, as his mental shield collapsed. She winced from the wordless hatred that spilled over her. The world went bright in his mind, and nothing existed but his prey, a prey that stung him!

Sharon 'touched' the side of Abe's eye, but he was already facing the danger.

Abe's mind was sharp with adrenaline, but the pistol was a unfamiliar weight in his hand. He couldn't hold it steady.

He is just shrugging it off! Abe could only look at the Cerik's wound and marvel.

The bullet had torn a ridge through the skin of his chest. It bled freely, but the tear exposed a white bony plate beneath that skin. The bone had no more damage than a scratch.

Abe brought the sights up to his eye line and squeezed, just like all the times Mary Ellen tried to teach him.

BANG! Second moved like a blur. The attempted head-shot was blocked by a massive upper arm. The teflon bullet designed to pierce bullet-proof vests deflected off the curve of the Cerik's in-born armor. Another scratch in his skin, more blood, but Second advanced.

Sharon felt panic attempting to crack Abe's composure. The idea of death crept into his thoughts.

Sharon turned her mind toward the mind and body of the Cerik. She dived in, but it was a whirlpool of raw emotion. She looked deep for a handle—some nerve to jam, or some blood vessel to pinch, but things were happening too fast, and the body was too alien.

Zero-G! came Abe's mental cry.

She disengaged, and 'touched' the button on the wall, but her delay was easily a half second or longer.

From Abe's eyes, she saw the claw swing.

Pain in Abe's chest. Her mind snapped free of it.

Second's satisfaction washed over her. **Gutted the prey!**

Her mind and body locked down, feeling for a remembered location deep in the engines of the ship. They had talked about this, the long night where sleep would never come. All she had to do was make a certain band of metal hot, very hot. The collapse of a magnetic field would cause the engine to discharge all of its energies in one brief surge.

Quarter-G! It was Abe, breaking through.

The relief let her breathe. She turned her attention to the Delense-marks and tried to focus on Abe as he was sailing high above the floor.

By the time she turned the gravity back on, and he started down, Tenthonad and Second were in close battle. Second's torn and bleeding skin was an easy target, but neither of them were experienced in fighting under varying gravity.

Second managed a strong kick that sent them spinning far apart, at a loss for traction.

Abe hit the ground, **Full-G!** He pushed himself to his feet. Sharon saw that he was standing, ready to run or jump. His shirt was ripped nearly off, revealing the kevlar bullet-proof vest beneath—a very nice gift from Mary Ellen, packed with his camping gear.

But his hands were empty. She looked, and spotted the gun where it had been flung in that last attack. Abe had already discounted it. He would be cut down the instant he ran for it.

It seemed like time stopped. Abe waited, on the balls of his feet, for the next attack. Tenthonad was pulling himself up, after having been kicked up high into the crowd by that last encounter.

Second walked slowly, and clumsily toward them, dripping a trail of blood. It was a lot of blood.

She whiffed a feeling, an unsettling realization coming from the surrounding crowd. **He is bleeding. Why is he bleeding like that?** It was as if Runners grew fangs, or chitchits started to talk.

Second, when he could raise the effort to think, was puzzled. **Why is the prey still standing? Why am I still bleeding?**

Abe watched each step. He glanced at her, for just a fraction of a second. **Warn me.** He took a step of his own.

The two closed slowly. Tenthonad, who'd landed next to her, paused, his own thoughts still tightly blocked. Perhaps he too was amazed at the sight of the puny prey closing on the huge Cerik Hunter.

If Second could see his opponent, he gave no sign. He was barely able to stand. Abe waited, just outside of arm's length, until Second collapsed, his legs giving way beneath him, and his arms unable to break his fall.

Abe stepped closer, but there was no reaction.

Sharon, feeling the beat of the minds above, shouted what they were thinking, "Take his eyes!"

Abe shouted back, "No!"

We are human. They want ritual, we will give them human ritual. Have Asca talk.

Abe turned his back on the still dying Cerik and faced the crowd.

"We are not prey! We are not Delense! We are a new thing!" Asca's voice from the top level caused the Cerik to quiet.

"We are Humans!"

The echoing voice from above garbled the word into "U-tanse"

Come out here beside me. Abe called to her. She released her grip on the rock that had been her shelter.

She walked quickly, but stopped at the edge of the pool of blood that had formed around the fallen one.

Abe and Asca's voice continued, "We are far from home, and we can never return. Because Tenthonad has defended us, we will sleep beneath his perch and make his clan prosper. By these signs we mark our loyalty to him."

Come, do as I do.

Abe reached into the open wound on Second's body, and scooped a palmful of the hot, fluid blood. He reached up and marked the lobe of his right ear, and then coated his right thumb. He kicked off his right shoe and rubbed the blood on the great toe.

Sharon took some of the blood from his hand, and did the same to her right ear, thumb, and toe.

Together they turned to face Tenthonad.

The Hunter, after a pause, came close and dipped the tip of his right claw in the same open wound, a redundant act due to all of the blood still on him.

Give them their air back.

Sharon caused the Delense-marks to change, and there was a slight hiss as the air changed back to a Cerik normal mix. Almost at once, the blood they were standing in started to bubble, and react. With the returning trace reactant, it congealed. Sharon could feel the blood on her skin tighten like a fast drying paint.

Then the roaring began. Sharon whispered, "They are shouting his *Name.*"

Tenthonad reared back and gave a great roar. Then with a swipe of his claw, he caught the left eye-socket of Second's corpse, shattered the central facial ridge, and ripped out both eyes and some connective tissue. He held it aloft to the roar of the crowd and then ate it.

Abe turned to the side, and emptied his stomach. He stood back upright quickly, and waved to the Cerik.

I meant to do that. Really.

She smiled, and tried to block out the mental roar that seemed to go on and on.

THE SCIENTIST

Larry Kelly held his daughter, a tiny wrapped bundle of warmth, up against his chest. Janet was asleep, as she should be. He rocked in the comfortable wooden chair, and wondered where he could find one for their house.

Cujo poked his face into the room. "Everyone asleep?" he whispered.

Larry waved him on in. In a voice barely louder than the creak of the rocker, he asked, "Did you find someone?"

"Yes. Sean Andrews, know him?"

"Blond haired, about twenty?"

"Right. He worked a couple of summers at Miniworld. He seems bright enough."

"Good. You have to keep the observations going."

"It would be easier with you there."

Larry nodded, and tucked the blanket back where it had come loose around her tiny feet.

"I've got a daughter now. I have to make sure that she's taken care of and will never go hungry."

"I thought we took care of that. Constable Bern is still singing your praises."

Larry looked solemn. "I know, and it's still partially true. But it all comes down to something that Janet said that's been playing in my mind. 'Only one wizard per kingdom.'

"The town will fund the observatory for a little while, but come the first drought or crop failure, and it will all go away. Let's be honest, the supernova is ramping down on the classic curve. There will be no more radiation warnings needed. The observations will be valuable to future generations, but really, how much difference will they make to a little town like this? With luck, maybe the town can afford one scientist. That has to be you."

Cujo didn't look happy at the idea.

Larry continued, "You and that soldering iron of yours will make you a valuable person for as long as you live. Cathy's a better theorist than you, but you won't be selling theories. I have to stay down here in town, with my family. Janet's education is going to help this town more than they know."

"But what will you do?"

He shrugged, "There's always farming. People will need to eat." He kissed the baby lightly on the top of her head.

Cujo smiled, "She's a pretty one. Have you given her a name?"

"Elizabeth Astoria."

He laughed. "Betty the Star. Just like an astronomer."

Janet spoke, drowsily, "I talked him out of his first choice."

Cujo put his fingers to his lips, "Sorry to wake you. What first choice?"

"Elizabeth Anatidaes"

"Anatidaes?"

"Greek for goose."

"Betty Goose! Oh, that is really too cruel. You couldn't do that to an innocent little girl!"

"It was just an idea!", he protested.

"Janet, can you talk him out of giving up astronomy?"

"It's his decision. I expect he will look up at the sky from time to time, and he'll remember those really huge mirrors up there. I hear you never get over aperture fever." The men laughed.

"But," she continued, "if he doesn't, there will always be a demand for a man who can think clearly, and who can seek the truth, and believe it when he sees it."

Larry added, "Besides, it'll be a good idea to have at least one farmer on your side."

Betty Kelly made a mewing little noise and started squirming.

"She's probably hungry. Hand me our little new star, and you two go out for a walk."

THE SEER

Ed Morgan was deep in the reports George had given him, spelling out in bureaucratic detail the current resources of the city. He held a highlighter, marking parts of the report that he sensed needed more work. Angela bustled past every few minutes, giving him a smile as she worked to put their new house into shape.

Ed. Do you hear me?

He set aside the papers. **Sharon! I was worried about you. You 'feel' better now.**

There was a wordless moment, something two telepaths know, when the edges of their minds overlapped. He could tell that much had happened to her, perhaps she could feel the same about him.

Ed, I have one last favor to ask of you.

More quickly than words, she made him aware of many things.

You're my only friend, she said. **It's important to Abe, and to me.**

Ed nodded, alone in his room. **And I am to witness?**

Yes.

As soon as he understood, he agreed. Sharon, as usual, led the way, linking minds in ways that Ed could never quite comprehend.

Suddenly, he was in this other man's mind. It was a flash of mixed images, looking out Abe's eyes, like and unlike his own visions of the future. They were in a strange place, part machine, part garden. Sharon was beside him, at the edge of Abe's view. Abe had her arm intertwined with his.

Hello, Abe, he sent. Sharon, in whispers, echoed his words.

"Hello, Ed. Thank you for doing this for us."

Sharon is my oldest and dearest friend. I would do anything for her.

There was a loud, sharp growl, much too close. Ed felt a shiver of terror, and he wasn't sure if it was from him, or from one of them.

Abe turned to face the sound. Close enough to feel its breath was a beast out of nightmares. Abe's throat formed a harsh spit of a word. 'We are ready' was the meaning.

Together, Abe and Sharon faced the assembly. There were four of the beasts, three arrayed to the side, the largest towering over them all. Ed could feel a twinge of thought from the smallest at the end, a telepath probing him, watching for some treachery.

But it was Abe who felt in charge. **This is my day,** was the undercurrent in his thoughts. He spoke aloud, forcefully.

"Today, in this company of witnesses, seen and unseen, Human and Cerik and God above, I pledge my life and honor to stand beside my wife, Sharon, for as long as I live. I shall be her right arm and right eye in all that we shall do."

Sharon, her voice starting with a catch, then growing stronger with each word, shouted, "Today, with these witnesses, seen and unseen, Human and Cerik and the gods, I pledge my life and honor to stand beside my husband, Abe, for as long as I live. I shall be his right arm and right eye in all that we shall do."

Ed was quiet in his mind, reliving his own wedding vows as he witnessed theirs. There were tears at the edge of his eyes.

Abe and Sharon turned to face each other. For the first time, Ed saw her clearly. *What!* A shock ran through him at the sight of her.

He forced himself back to the words. They were saying together, "Our love will become great, by every action and every word. We each pledge to shore up the other's weakness, to fill the other's emptiness, to bring joy to the other's sorrow. This day, we have become one."

Ed could sense the strong current that flowed between the couple. Abe, by some awareness that wasn't truly telepathy, but was no less real, could read her through the strength of her fingers and the tilt of her head and the flicker of her eyes. Sharon read him through the layers upon layers of his mind, down into the cell and spirit of the man.

Ed was suddenly aware of a resonance, an overlay from the future, some great destiny that was being created today. Then, like the passage of a meteor, it was gone.

He could only say, **I have witnessed, today. Thank you.**

Sharon turned a portion of her mind to Ed, and relayed his words. Abe spoke, "Thank you, Ed. You've helped us more than you can know. We are going away. It'll be difficult enough to remain human. We need these rituals."

The largest of the monsters growled, "U'tanse ra erla." It is time to go.

Sharon! I have seen something important. Ed called up, as well as he could, the memory of that morning, facing himself in the mirror. He sent his image to her. **This is me!**

Sharon, in Abe's eyes, shook. Her eyes widened. **But, you look like me. The hair, the eyes.**

Ed began, **Are we...could we be...?**

In reply, she flashed a memory, in instant, far away in time. **My mother's memory,** she explained, **This is my father.**

The man's eyes were deep and black, he could have been Ed's twin. **My father.** He shook inside. **Sharon, you are my sister!**

My brother! There was a brief mental touch, an affirmation of something true.

There was a shout among the monsters, and they began to move. Abe squeezed Sharon's arm. "Tell Ed. He needs to find ..."

And then, there was a twist, a pull. The link to those far minds stretched like a rubber band, stretched so far and so fast, that it snapped.

They were gone.

"No!" Ed shouted to the empty room. Angela came running, but Ed could not form the words.

She was my sister. I have a sister! Now she is gone.

THE ROBOT

Hodgepodge adjusted the probability matrix again, as his estimate passed for Abe's return, assuming one broken leg. He decided not to mention this to Mary Ellen. She showed signs of emotional distress whenever he adjusted the probabilities.

With humans, facts were less important than emotions. Mary Ellen's mental well-being had to be carefully managed. For some time to come, he would need her help to maintain his readiness.

It was important that he be ready, when Abe returned.

THE END

Bonus Stories

Tales of the U'tanse: Genesis

"Honey, I'm home."

Abe Whiting, AKA, Aie the U'tanse, closed the airtight door behind him and slipped through the first of the low-ceiling bubble-like chambers, making sure the lock was secure and the air was set to remove the poisonous nitrates from the air. When the dots on the wall changed color, he removed his leather breathing mask.

"Sharon?"

There was noise of movement deeper in the warren of chambers that the extinct Delense would have called palatial. There were times when he really wished he were telepathic like his wife. He was sure it was her, but sometimes she got a little...strange when they were apart too long.

But her outside suit, a head to toe leather outfit they both used when outside in the normal air, was hanging in the closet, so the noise was probably her. He began peeling off his outer wear. The less exposure they had to the toxins native to this planet, the less work she had to do to keep them both healthy. Three or four days unprotected exposure without her psychically enhanced healing, and no Earth-born life could survive.

Unfortunately, other than a few rags they'd salvaged from the trucks raided by the Cerik when they were planning to invade Earth, there were no other clothes. Their masters were hunters only. No manufacturing, no cloth making, no sewing. Even the leather suits were Sharon's handiwork.

He showered, his invention, and turned on the lights in the darkened living chamber.

"Aieeee!" She pounced on him, snarling, showing her teeth. Her fingernails, deliberately grown thick and sharp, scraped at his skin. He hit his head hard on the floor.

"Sharon. Honey. I love you." He kept his voice low and gentle. He made no move to fight back.

She blinked. Her hissing stopped. She shook her head, as if fighting off a bad dream. "Abe. Sorry." She began to get up, but he held her down.

"Hey, I like it like this."

"Your head hurts. I'll fix it."

"Later. It's been two days. I like cuddling on the floor with my wife."

Slowly, she relaxed, and settled into his arms. "It's the Cerik thoughts. They're too much."

He kissed her. "I know. I'll make Tenthonad understand. We have to stay together, always." She needed human contact, and human thoughts, as long as she were to remain human.

She smiled, a little sadly. "How did your work go?"

He knew she could read it all out of his mind, but it was nice when she just let him talk.

"I brought two more Delense factories back on line. As usual, there was no real damage. They just had to be tuned a little. One of them had its main control center smashed to bits when the Cerik who owned it just got angry that the machine wouldn't make his processed animal feed and tried to claw it into submission. Luckily there was a standby system I could make work."

She sighed. "Do the Cerik really understand what they've done to themselves by killing off their Builders?"

"You're the telepath. I'd say no. They didn't really appreciate what their slaves did for them."

"I hope they appreciate you."

"Tenthonad does. His clan is gaining ground like mad. He's charging square miles of land for every factory I bring back."

"He's not so happy with me."

Abe stroked her head. Her long white hair was growing back, now that she spent most of her time in Earth-friendly air. He understood why she was reluctant to have children, in this hostile environment, to be raised as slaves if they even survived the onslaught of predator thoughts growing up.

She was reading him. Reading his idle thoughts and his deep desires. Abe wanted children, badly. If there were just a way it to make it happen. Until then, she would have to be vigilant. She shifted her legs around his and moved her hips. Abe's eyes closed as he breathed in her essence.

. . .

Asca, the Telepath approached Egh, the Scientist, rattling his claws to be acknowledged.

"Yes, what is it?"

"They are mating again."

"Again? It seems like they do that every day. Is there any sign that she is bearing cubs?"

"No. And I don't think she will, until she decides to."

He knew roughly what she was doing, killing off her mate's seed with her mind even as she requested more from him. It made no sense, but he wished he had her skill. Think of the power a warrior would have, if he could repair injuries in his body! But he knew of no Cerik with that skill.

"We need to make her breed! Without more U'tanse, Tenthonad's position in the Face is in the wind." And theirs as well, but he didn't need to say that. When they arrived at Home World, without a treasure world claim, and with their ship damaged so badly that the navigation log showing the position of the U'tanse planet was corrupted past recovery, he'd barely survived the challenge of their own clan.

But the male, Aie, had proved the value of the U'tanse by quickly restoring the ability of the clan to feed captive Runners. Every Large Moon, it seemed he found new ways to restore Delense machines that had been thought lost forever. Other clans were trading lands and runners for the services of the little alien.

Asca suspected the *Rakla-del* of a female telepath had been responsible for the loss of the path back to her world, but he couldn't prove it, and he dared not suggest it, for that would be to proclaim that he was too weak a telepath to tell whether she was lying or not. Admitting weakness was unthinkable.

. . .

Egh's Second waited patiently, just outside the chamber, listening to the two. He had long practiced the habit of listening without thinking. Asca might be a weak *name*, with no Second of his own, but he was still a telepath, and one should be trained in the *ineda* to deal with his kind. He would think later, when the telepath was busy with other concerns.

. . .

The Home Planet rumbled, but then, it always did. Its moon, nearly as large as Luna, was in a much more elliptical orbit, reaching close enough to trigger landquakes and volcano eruptions on almost every pass. Within the history of the Cerik, islands had sunk beneath the waves and new mountain ranges had risen. Within the *oral* history of the Cerik—because they had no written history. Reading was elusive—one of those skills some of the slave races used. Part of the genius of the Delense, the extinct Builders, had been the ability to craft machines that could be run with the slash of a talon, and instruments that showed their results in cartoon-like images—all so that their masters could run some of the machines themselves.

Abe loved his robe. Sharon had made it from a box of red automotive utility rags that they'd scavenged from the wreck of a truck that had crossed the star lanes with them. She'd made herself a housedress out of rolls of cheese cloth that she'd likewise salvaged from the grocery store supplies. He was so lucky to have married a woman who never worried about how much skin was showing.

He sat at a desk that was totally Delense in construction. It was good enough for him—flat and hard like a desk ought to be. The giant beaver-like creatures had been engineers after all. With a stool the right height, he had a workspace that felt right at home. He picked up the stack of school notebooks that had never made it to the school supply shelves and clicked a ball point pen. If he never made it back to Earth, and if they started a branch of the human race here on this planet, his children would need a history. Until he ran out of paper, he'd write down everything he knew, everything he remembered, everything about Earth, the human race, and where they came from. He owed them every Bible verse, every Aesop's Fable, every history and philosophy that he could remember.

A tiny scrap of loose paper fell out where he'd left off. In Sharon's crisp lettering, was a list of other species enslaved on other planets nearly destroyed by the supernova. Abe knew some of the information already, but they never discussed their plans to escape. Not verbally. Not in a manner a passing telepath could discover. Anything that hinted at less than total loyalty to Tenthonad and his clan had to be passed in this fashion, and kept loosely in the mind. It was a difficult, long range plan, but being unarmed slaves on a planet with a poisonous atmosphere limited their options.

...

The next day, Abe and Sharon appeared in their leathers before the High Perch. They kneeled, as befitted their status, to the left of Tenthonad. Egh and his Second approached and scraped the floor with their claws.

"Speak."

Abe was learning quite a bit of the Cerik language, although he could barely form the words himself. Each time he went out on a project alone, he really missed his telepathic translator wife.

Egh tapped his claws again. "Sanassan clan has been attempting to breed Geisel Runners from their Treasure Planet for a generation, with no luck. When it became known that U'tanse Builders were living here with no signs of early death, the Sanassan Scientist requested my help."

Tenthonad growled low. "I have tasted the blood of a Geisel, when 27 were released at the beginning of the Face. Finding a way to breed them here is a worthy goal." He turned to look at the female U'tanse. But then he spoke to Egh. "What have they offered?"

Egh gave a dissatisfied grumble. "They have offered 18 Geisel."

Tenthonad snarled. "They offer a minimal breeding set, which will be worthless if they die early, and which the Sanassan would make of no account if their own breeding program is successful. We get only enough for a single hunt and they get a valuable trade item. Tell them nothing until their offer includes lands or old Delense machines."

Egh rattled his claws and backed away from the High Perch. His Second was slow to move, but followed Egh out.

Abe felt a twitch on his face muscles, an indication that Sharon had read something of importance in someone's mind and triggered the nerves in his face. *Who was it? Tenthonad, Egh, or his Second?* Another twitch. So it was the Scientist's Second.

When they were alone, Tenthonad asked, "Aie, if you were asked, could you extend the life of these runners?"

"For the *Name*." He'd gotten that phrase down pretty well. "I would suspect the food or air of the Home Planet makes the Geisel die soon. What do you know of the Sanassan Treasure World? Does it rumble?"

Tenthonad made a dismissive gesture with his claw. "No matter. Egh would know."

Abe grimaced. Tenthonad had wanted a 'yes' or 'no', not a discussion. "I would breed them in a burrow, with Delense processed food and special air. They will not breed and run at the same time." It was a guess, but his master was plainly better pleased with that answer.

"So there will not be great herds of Geisel runners."

"No. There will not be."

Abe tried to have confidence. He had to make everything work, even here, practically naked, with no tools other than what he could cobble together from the race that had failed the Cerik before him.

I wish I had Hodgepodge. His thought flickered briefly to recall his right hand man, his little brother, his little robot friend that never failed him.

Sharon took his hand and squeezed it.

...

The snap across space that had severed all ties, even the psychic ones, with home and family, had left them with no idea where Earth was. Even if it had been only 50 light years, that still meant 2000 stars to check. The Cerik search for treasure planets had been a random walk through the stars, utterly dependent on automated Delense tracking software to get them back home. The Cerik were not very interested in space. Having gone outside at night a few times, Abe understood why. With the atmosphere constantly filled with volcanic dust, stars just weren't very visible. Their legends mentioned their moon many times, but Abe didn't even know if there were any other planets in this system.

What's more, the Cerik physiology was based on good eyesight looking across the plains hunting runners or looking down at prey beneath their perch—not up at the sky.

The Delense had obviously discovered space flight, but until he cracked the nature of their history, he was in the dark how it happened. Delense 'written' records were often cartoon like descriptions with a nearly human math script, based like the Cerik on a powers of 3 counting system, even though the Delense had 'hands' with four digits. Legend told of the symbiotic nature of their two races happening back before technology was developed, and from the math, he believed it.

I wonder what the Delense told themselves about their history. Did they think of themselves as slaves?

It was an important concern. He'd made a deal with Tenthonad to save their lives. He could live with the conditions, but assuming he had children, the deal would be binding on them as well. Unless he misunderstood human nature, that couldn't last forever.

...

Egh ordered his Second to relay Tenthonad's rejection to the Sanassan Clan.

Second snarled, "You are the Scientist. Why not play your part? Or have you forgotten your *name*?"

Egh turned quickly into a defensive crouch at the overt challenge. "A Second's words are all the Sanassan deserve. Perhaps you need to remember your position. You can be replaced."

The Second Scientist wasted no more words. He leapt and scraped the hide of his elder. His attack was well planned, with Egh caught in a narrow space between machines and a low ceiling to prevent a leap to avoid the attack. Egh's hide bubbled as blood hardened instantly when exposed to the nitrates in the open air, sealing the wound. The sound of their screams quickly attracted others in the area. They kept their distance as the battle for succession proceeded. Everyone felt their own blood quickening as the scents of bloody battle filled the chamber.

...

Sharon grabbed tightly at Abe's arm.

"What?" he whispered. They were still under Tenthonad's perch, having not been dismissed.

"Egh. He's..."

A growl came from above. "Little Telepath, speak aloud."

She shifted to the Cerik language. "You have a new *named* Scientist. Egh's eyes have been taken."

Tenthonad shifted slightly on his perch, unconcerned. "I smelled as much."

Abe saw the shine in his wife's eyes. Once again, she was feeling the blood lust that was the everyday experience of their masters. He was perhaps the only one who was dismayed at the loss of the old Scientist.

Sharon shook her head. "No. I miss him too." But she was plainly divided between Human and Cerik sensibilities.

Tenthonad ordered, "Return to your burrows. I will call for you later."

Abe and Sharon backed their ways out of the chamber.

"Come on! Hurry!" She tugged.

"Problem?" He ran beside her. Their breathing masks limited how fast they could breathe. Talking while running was difficult.

"Clat, the new Scientist—he hates us."

And a Cerik in a blood fever was likely to act first on his hate, even if his *Fa* would be angry. They were in immediate danger of his claws. Tenthonad knew his people. That's why he dismissed them. He wanted them barricaded away.

They reached their quarters and Abe applied a lock code so that a Cerik's talon wouldn't open the door from the outside. If he understood the way it worked, Tenthonad had an override code, but it wasn't the *Fa* of the clan he was worried about.

He began peeling off the leathers. "Sharon, tell me everything you know about Clat."

The remote look on her face told him she was off in the minds of the Cerik, learning all that she could.

"He has a half-formed *ineda*. He hasn't been trained for it, and that could get him in trouble."

"What?"

She looked his way, and then shook her head as she tried to focus on the here and now. "Clat was Egh's Second. He hates us because we're becoming more valued scientists that his *dance*. He thought Egh was too weak because he worked with us. Our death would be the best thing that could happen, as far as he's concerned."

Abe nodded. "The Scientist *dance* was created after the extermination of the Delense, to take up the slack when they realized they'd killed off their only technologists. And the Cerik aren't very good at it. Their minds don't work that way. But can you tell what Tenthonad is going to do?"

Sharon shook her head. "His *ineda* is tight. I can't read him. His new Second isn't quite as well trained, but he doesn't know what Tenthonad is going to do either."

"But he knows we're valuable, right?"

Sharon changed to her house dress and sat cross-legged before him. "If I read the politics right, it's still up in the air. The Face—that's like the planetary ruling council—are disturbed by our presence. There are some long memories. When the Builders revolted, they nuked the main city, complete with the *Names* of most of the clans. The city was a holy place. Think Jerusalem or Mecca. They intended to use the chaos to make a mass escape into space, with many thousands of Delense hijacking space ships and scattering to various planets. Instead they inspired the Cerik to track them all down and exterminate the whole race.

"The idea of a second race of Builders, us, is disturbing to many."

"We get the blame for what the Delense did."

"Something like that. Tenthonad will become legendary, either for making a dumb mistake to keep us, or for being wise enough to correct the mistake the Cerik made by eradicating the Delense. No one knows which, yet."

Sharon stared at the floor, solemnly. "Our lack of cubs complicates the issue."

Abe nodded. He was aware of it. He, repairing damaged machines, was valuable to Tenthonad. The U'tanse race of Builders could be valuable to the Cerik as a race. But if they had no children, Sharon was a dangerous wild card.

She nodded. "Tenthonad has never forgotten my taste. I'm sure he has considered the option of taking my eyes and keeping you busy repairing machines until you die of atmosphere poisoning or old age."

"But that's not what he wants." Abe was sure of that. Tenthonad looked at him as the restoration of the old days, where Builders and the Cerik worked together to build a star-spanning empire, ever growing and ever more powerful. The loss of the directions back to Earth where they could capture more U'tanse engineers was a bitter blow.

Sharon spoke. "You can say it out loud. You can't help but think it."

He nodded. "Tenthonad would fight to the death to preserve the U'tanse as a race. He's done it before."

"And Clat is a direct challenge to that. He represents the current order, with the *dance* of Scientists trying to make the most of what the Delense left behind. The sooner we're gone, the better."

Abe sighed. "And his killing of Egh was the traditional way of succession. Tenthonad can't punish him for that."

...

Tenthonad could still smell the blood of Egh as Clat crouched before him, proclaiming the loyalty of all his *dance*.

"Bleed, all of you!"

The three remaining Scientists slashed their forearms and small splatters of blood made it to the ground before hardening.

He made no pretense that he was happy to lose Egh. The old one had never been less than loyal.

"Have the Sanassan been rejected?"

Clat rattled his claws. "My righteye notified them on the distant-speaker device."

His eyes flickered to Asca, crouched at Tenthonad's right. The presence of a telepath at his first meeting was ominous. Clat struggled to keep his thoughts even and free of his long term plans.

Asca was too experienced to let any of this show in his eyes or his stance. Clat was a youngster at these games and if old Egh had just kept his wits about him, he'd have sent the assistant back to heal with the cubs.

Two things were interesting to him. One was the half-formed *ineda* that the Scientist had managed without any real training. When he told Tenthonad about it, it wouldn't be a good day for Clat. In general, only those who desired to take the High Perch, those who trained telepaths, and thieves used the *ineda*. Which was he?

The other point of interest was the distinctive sense of the female alien telepath, also smelling the thoughts of this one, so plainly an enemy of the U'tanse. It was if he and she were watching from opposite sides of the room, aware of each other.

He wished he understood her better. But one didn't poke too deeply into the jaws of a demon who could not be killed.

...

Abe was asleep, his head across her leg as she sat with her back against the wall. They at least had a bed beneath them, a low pallet made with large plastic sacks stuffed loosely with native grasses. It was luxury compared to the ceramic floor where she'd slept during the first part of her imprisonment. Part of her mind was watching the politics of Tenthonad's perch, fingers crossed for a little more bloodshed. But in spite of the Cerik nature, their culture wasn't random slaughter. There were rules and traditions. She was tempted to breach the filtering tissue in Clat's lungs and trigger a few blood clots, but a slave actually killing one of the masters was too dangerous. Abe walked that line all the time. The idea that he could get rid of his keepers with a few button presses had crossed his mind. But that's the kind of thoughts that had triggered the extermination of the Delense.

She watched Abe's chest rising and falling, his dreams tangled with memories of sunlight and software. There was a scar on his arm that she needed to repair one of these days when their lives were less stressful. She was deep in his cells every day, repairing lung damage and occasionally tinkering with his hormone levels, but there was always more that could be done. *I'll need to tell him, someday.* She hadn't told him about everything she'd done to him. It was his nature to forgive, so sometimes she skipped the whole process of confessing her transgressions. But some day, she would have to tell him all. For now, he accepted his greater strength and stamina without question, or chalked it up to a different gravity. He didn't miss his depression at all, and she couldn't let him drift into hopelessness, or they would be lost. He was her anchor.

And then, a few hundred yards away, Clat felt the jaws of panic nipping at his thoughts and clamped down, hard, trying to put up a barricade against anything that could betray him.

Asca scented it. The clumsy *ineda* still leaked, but Clat's efforts showed plainly his technique. It was the method of a Cerik cub who had trained to become a Telepath and then failed in the process. This one had not started off to become a Scientist, but had become one by default. He reviewed the differences in techniques in his mind. There was no doubt.

Sharon observed it all, silently like a Cerik on a perch over his prey. Step by step, she absorbed everything that Asca had seen and had known about the *ineda*. It was just what she needed.

That was the moment. In that instant, the need of her mate to have children, her own biological urges, her fears of raising brain damaged telepaths, Tenthonad's dream of a new race of Builders and her own mother's vision of a grand destiny—they all merged into a clear dream of her own.

She reached into the cells of her husband and shifted a few hormones. He stirred in his sleep as dreams became darker and more basic, more urgent.

"Abe," she whispered. "Abe. Wake up. It's time."

His eyes opened and he turned to her.

...

Asca watched as Clat backed out of the chamber and patiently awaited his *Fa's* command.

"Telepath?"

"For your *Name*."

"Do you have anything to report?"

"Much about your new Scientist. And another thing, perhaps even more important."

"Oh? Tell me."

"Your U'tanse are breeding."

"Not just mating?"

"No. The female has made it known to me. There will be many more U'tanse Builders for the *Name*."

...

After the sweat had cooled, and Abe had drifted off to as peaceful a sleep as she had seen, Sharon still monitored the new life that was happening within her. So much depended on choosing the right sperm. Her children had to be just right. She and Abe were Adam and Eve here. There must be no defective genes to show up in the next generation. They all had to have her psychic abilities to protect themselves from atmospheric damage, but more importantly, mothers of the next generation must be able to guide the evolution of the U'tanse just as she was doing now, and as her mother had done to create her. As well as she could manage, they must inherit Abe's skills as well, to become so valuable to the Cerik that no *Fa* could imagine living without them. Each child must also be different, to preserve the limited diversity in their genetic heritage.

Abe, as the only non-telepath, would have to become the patriarch to the new race, to teach them all how to remain human. As the new Eve, she had to hone the skills her mother used to raise her to be a unique person. It was up to her to make her children individuals and not just nodes in a hive mind, bound by uncontrolled telepathy into something not human. With what she'd learned today about the *ineda*, that now seemed possible.

Of course, the Cerik would have to be taught their place as well. That would be trickiest job of all.

Someday, when her descendants re-discovered the Earth, maybe then they could do without the Cerik, but until then there was a role to play, and the right words to be said. All the while, behind the *ineda* of the U'tanse, their true spirit would remain.

Hodge's Heart

"But why do you accept burned out computers in payment?"

April shrugged. "I dunno. Hodges sets the rules." For an eight year old, she ran the office well.

Keith Franklin was old enough to have grown up with web browsers and search engines. Although he was grateful for the International Information Service, since it was much better than nothing, it was frustrating to have to walk to the office and fill out his request on a piece of paper and then wait for days before he received an answer.

"He builds things, back at the company," she offered. "Radios and stuff."

He smiled. "I guess that make sense. So you've been allowed in the Whiting building?"

She raised her nose, "I was born there...almost. When the Star happened, we moved there. Daddy made things and Mom helped out with the garden and stuff."

"You were lucky then. I was a teenager then, and I had to live in a school building for two years, with like a hundred other people. It was dirty and smelly when we couldn't go outside because of the Star, and then when the City of Austin couldn't feed us anymore, it just turned us loose to find something on our own."

She nodded, it was a story she'd heard many times before. "My Granny set up the IIS. She owns it. Hodges makes it run, and I mind the store." She spread her skirt like a princess and sat back down on her stool behind the bench.

Almost on cue, the door opened and a heavyset man wrapped in a long coat and a broad-rimmed hat entered from the rear door.

"Hodgie!" April smiled.

Keith nodded, "Mr. Hodges."

Rumor had it that the man was ultra sensitive to the sunlight, or that he was scarred from the city-wide fires that had occurred when the Star had flared up and destroyed the Techno civilization. In any case, he was reclusive.

"Mr. Franklin. I'm glad to see you. Would you care to come to my office?"

April and Keith exchanged looks. She shrugged.

"Certainly." He followed the man into a large pre-Star decorated office with a small desk, but with file cabinets lining the walls and free-standing in a second row as well.

Hodges went to one of the file cabinets. "Have a seat," he said.

Keith sat in the lone visitor's chair. Hodges spread a small stack of papers on the desk.

"It has come to my attention that you are providing a courier service, acting as an agent for twenty-three other companies and individuals?"

He nodded. "Well, yes. Twenty-eight, actually, but a couple of them have never requested anything from the IIS. I also carry messages between companies, as well as small packages. Anything I can carry on my bicycle."

Hodges showed no expression, from what Keith could see of his shadowed face. The man always wore the floppy hat even indoors. He hoped he wasn't violating any IIS rules by what he was doing. It was a big part of his income.

"You understand that the IIS is nothing like the old Internet?"

"Right. It's all wireless, I understand."

"Yes. Since all the long distance cables and microwave links and satellites are all long gone, the only way to maintain long distance communication is short wave radio. The IIS has evolved from the packet radio system that existed before the Star. It's not TCP/IP. It's not the web. And particularly, it's not free."

"I know, sir."

Hodges nodded. "It is a common misconception among the older users that the IIS is simply charging to use the old free system simply because we have the only computers. Charging high because we have a monopoly. I need you to understand how it really works, because I wish to make you a business proposition."

...

Cujo heard the footsteps echoing down the hall. He picked up the pistol he kept in his desk, more out of habit than out of fear. It had been years since thieves had climbed the mountain up to the observatory. But being the last astronomer in the place--maybe the last astronomer in Australia, kept him on his toes. People from the town of Coonabarabran down below usually called on the ancient hand-cranked phone before they made the climb up to visit the last remaining Techno wizard.

He saw Larry Kelly walking the halls like he owned them, which in some part, he did, Cujo hurriedly hid the gun to avoid having to explain it.

"Hey! Larry, what are you up to today?"

A big smile broke over the weather lined face, making the farmer look more like the astronomer he used to be.

"Hi. I had a horrible urge to come up here and see if you'd cracked any of the mirrors."

The big, long-haired astronomer visibly shuddered. "Don't say things like that! But you'd have to remove the covers to check. Just about everything is mothballed. At least as well as I can. It was like the end of the world when we used the last of the film. I can still look through the eye-piece and sketch the Betelgeuse nebulae. I do, sometimes."

They pulled up chairs. "So, no luck on getting a sponsorship?"

Cujo looked over at the radio room. "No, and I'm thinking I'll be spending the rest of my life in there, passing messages and answering questions."

"So you're the search engine for the world now?"

He laughed, "Hardly that. IIS is pretty well organized. But a lot of the queries come up for auction and it's an easy way to make Information Credits."

"Can you spend those?"

"Larry, you'd be surprised. The Sydney station has a thriving exchange rate between dollars and ICs. And they're the only real international money right now. If I wanted to buy something from the US, I'd exchange East Coast Aussie dollars for ICs, make the arrangements over the IIS net and the other side would convert Info Credits to their local currency."

"And then wait for a clipper ship to deliver it?"

Cujo nodded, sadly. "We used to think we were isolated from North America and Europe before. There are ships--I've seen the arrival manifests.

But it's back to the transportation days, or worse. The best sailing ships still in play used to be recreation for the wealthy. They're not designed for shipping. No cargo space."

Larry smiled, "But you can still buy information."

Cujo saw the smile. "Okay, you've just been playing me. I've got your latest journals. Which brings up another question. Can Coona scare me up another printer? Cathy's home grown toner works, but the drum is getting a little scarred from using it. I could do with a fried laser printer of the same model, as long as the drum is still intact."

"I'll pass the word. The last rail shipment through in the Spring brought us more paper, but it would be a shame if we had to go back to the days when we hired a typist."

The big man got up and returned from the radio room with a thin stack of pages. "What is this stuff?"

He handed it to his friend.

Larry glanced through the printed sheets with a frown on his face. "Growing crops and raising kids is a full time job, but I have my hobbies." His frown turned dark on the last sheet.

"Problem?"

"The price is going up."

"What is it?"

"Genetic engineering stuff. You lose a crop to wheat wilt and you start thinking what you could so with a little better strain, one a little more disease resistant."

"That's your new hobby?"

Larry smiled sheepishly. "Yeah. It costs the world to get semiconductors, but anybody can blow some glassware. The world was on the cusp of a real genetic breakthrough when the supernova happened. We already had cloning and the procedures had simplified to the point where small labs could produce real innovations." He gestured with the papers. "That's what I'm reading up on. The genetic revolution is still going on. And these people are really making headway."

"Hence the price increase."

"Right. The old academic in me is appalled at the idea that every scientific paper has a price tag attached, but I'd rather have the progress than let it die from lack of funds."

"You out of ICs?"

"Pretty close, and I'm not begging. I'll write up something interesting and informative about East Australia or something."

"Don't get too wordy. These old fingers are getting sore with all the typing I'm having to do."

"Hire someone. I'll put out the word around town. I bet everyone over sixteen knows how to type, or used to."

"Get someone pretty."

They laughed.

Cujo put out his hand. "Seriously, Larry. Let me buy your journals. I'd rather you discover something fabulously valuable with your test tubes than read yet another history of a struggling town. They're a glut on the market. Cut me in on a little share and call it even."

They shook.

...

Keith Franklin looked at the metal contraption, twice the size of a chest freezer, resting on the back of the wagon.

"I'm sure you're know that April never haggled over the prices?"

He nodded. "Never budged."

Hodges opened the panel on the side, showing a screen and keyboard and various ports and slots. "It's because the charges are built in down at the packet level. She couldn't change them. Now this communications center will be fully operational once you connect it to city power and run the first antenna, but each additional antenna will cover a different radio band and the more you add, the cheaper your costs will be."

Keith raised a timid hand, "Excuse me, why is that again?"

Hodges nodded, never showing exasperation. "Here is an example. A message from Scandinavia addressed to your ID arrives on the ten-meter radio band, but suppose you only have stretched an antenna for the twenty-meter band and your radio doesn't pick it up. If the station here at IIS headquarters picks it up, the system will know that your station isn't active on ten-meters yet so it will record the data and re-transmit it to you on twenty-meters. Each time it has to be recorded and re-transmitted, more charges are added. You would still get the message, but at a greater cost. Understand?"

"Yes. So, what does this thing cost? I'm not rich."

"But you know the business. That's why I'm leasing it to you rather than to a grocer or a carpenter. You never pay me. Your lease charges add a fraction to your message costs. After ten years or so, they'll drop off. In addition, as more stations are built and distributed, you'll be making retransmit costs off of them. Believe me, I want you to make a good living off this. We will be competitors, but regardless of your charges for electricity, office space, and helpers, people on your side of town will likely do business with you rather than cross town to do business with me. I'll make my profit in Information Credits over the life of your equipment--a trickle that won't stop for years. You'll make yours off every message that flows through your station. You'll sell your Info Credits to your customers in exchange for regular cash. Everybody wins."

Hodges showed him the way it was to be set up, with detailed printed instructions. Keith was thinking about buildings where he could set up shop. It was exciting, and frightening.

Suddenly, Hodges stopped in mid-sentence, frozen like a statue.

"I'm sorry, Mr. Franklin. I'll have to finish this later. Please come back and speak with me tomorrow, okay?"

"Is there a problem?"

"There's a personal issue, unrelated to you. We'll still do business. Sorry."

He flipped the cover down to protect the gear and moved quickly back into the office.

"April." The girl looked up at his tone. "Get out the telephone and call Medical Alert. Tell them to get to Mary Ellen's house."

"Granny? What's wrong?" She was already at the special cabinet, pulling out the ancient piece of gear.

"Tell them it may be a heart attack or a stroke."

April's eyes were shiny, but she was all business. There were only a few dozen active phone numbers in Austin, and the important ones were written on a sheet in front of her. She made the call and got the doctors on the way. Hodges had already left. She was left alone in the office. She shouldn't leave. But it's Granny! Hodges was never wrong about things like this. She suspected he was psychic, like the guy that worked for the Mayor.

She locked the doors.

"Miss Jensen!" Keith pulled around with his bicycle.

"I've got to go. My Granny is sick."

He nodded. "Then get on. I'll take you." The bicycle had a carrying cage on the back. It was uncomfortable, but she made it work. They passed Hodges on the way, his long cloak flapping around him as he made a steady but slow run. Hodges waved them on.

April was there to lead the Medics in. They didn't smile as they worked.

. . .

The hospital room was small but private. The Jensen family and Hodges waited in shifts. Scott Jensen looked a lot older than his age, and his wife Denise was worried about him as well. Denise and April went in to wait with Mary Ellen Victor, April's godmother. She had no relatives left, but since the Star, they had been family.

Scott pulled out a large bottle of clear liquid and when no one was looking, handed it to Hodges.

"Thank you." He placed it in a pocket of his coat. "I haven't had time to refuel."

"It's 190 proof. I haven't been able to get the last of the moisture out."

"It will do."

They sat in silence. Nearly everything they'd had to talk about over the years had already been said.

Almost everything.

"Scott. You have seen the terms of Mary Ellen's Will?"

He nodded. "You get the company. We get the house and lands."

Hodges nodded. "I am also aware of your medical condition. Denise and April will not want for funds. Nor your grandchildren, when they come."

"Stupid T."

The thyroid cancer caused by the fallout in the bad years had become so common it had it's own nickname. Everyone knew someone who had it. Medical care had not recovered enough in the eight years since the collapse to treat anyone.

Denise came out after a few minutes. "She's awake. She wants to talk to Hodges."

He rose and went to the room. April was in the bed beside her Granny, holding on tight.

"Mary Ellen."

She looked at him. "Still dressed like the Shadow, I see."

"It serves its purpose."

She looked down at the girl cuddling in her arms. She couldn't bring herself to send the little one away.

"What can you tell me?" she asked. She was struggling with the words. Her heart was damaged beyond recovery.

Hodges nodded. They had gotten used to talking in code when they had to talk in the presence of people who did not know what he was.

"There is no sign of Abe yet. No part of his craft beyond the tail section we found last year has been detected. And yes, I still believe he lives. But the chances are that he was taken away."

Mary Ellen closed her eyes, nodding. Over the years, she'd been infected by the irrational hope that her adopted son had survived that impossible battle eight years earlier. Certainly his enemies had never appeared either. Perhaps, somewhere out in the stars, he still lived.

"And your plans?" She coughed lightly, and cleared her throat.

"Wait and prepare."

Mary Ellen stroked April's hair. "Honey, could you go tell the nurse to bring me something to clear my throat please."

She nodded and climbed down and left the room.

"So, Hodgepodge, are you still planning to take over the world?"

He had no expression. "I plan to place myself at the center of the recovery. To be ready to serve Abe when he returns, I must have a technological civilization to maintain myself. To that end, I am restarting a new world-wide network, as you know."

"An Internet you control."

"Yes."

She nodded. "So this is the last chance I have to stop you."

"Correct. You and Abe can change my programming. No one else."

There was a moment of labored breathing. "You will always work for Abe's approval."

He didn't even reply. That was an axiom.

She nodded. "I hope my Creator judges me as faithful as you have been to yours. Could you call the Jensen's in now?"

He nodded and left. He sent her family in and found a restroom where he could pour the alcohol fuel into his internal fuel-cell's tank before leaving. There was still much to be done.

...

Keith fumbled the entry form, struggling under the eyes of the customer.

"The little girl would have already finished that."

"Yes, but just be glad we're open today. They're all at the funeral."

"Oh yeah, I heard about that. Victor was a feisty old lady, right to the end. I remember her fighting the City Council over the moonlight towers. She lost, but it was a good fight. We needed people like her."

Keith calculated the charges and keyed the query into the system. "Check back in a couple of days. We should know by then if someone is going to bid on it.

"By the way, what part of town are you from?"

"Downtown, off Congress Avenue."

"Well, you might be interested in the fact that I'll be starting up a branch office just on the other side of the bridge in a few weeks."

"Really? That's interesting. I assume little April will train you how to do it?"

He nodded, a sad grin on his face. "I hope."

...

Hodges stood in the back as a dozen people spoke about their memories of Mary Ellen Victor and her husband Frank. He had declined the opportunity to add to the eulogy. It would not be in character. The gravesite ceremony was well attended and he waited patiently, shaking hands and giving appropriate responses to all of the people who knew that he had worked with her.

Denise Jensen came by. "Are you okay?"

He nodded. "Yes." She looked into his eyes, and then with a little jerk, she smiled. "You know, I had forgotten. It's been a while. You look real."

"I always appreciate your honesty, Mrs. Jensen. I always hope to be real enough for you and yours."

He smiled. Soon enough, she would be the last human to know his secret. Although she had never been part the technology that her failing husband Scott maintained, she'd been there when the first of his humanoid bodies had been tested, and her critiques had contributed to what had been done right, and what he kept hidden under his coat and hat.

It was important that she trust him all the rest of her life.

Eventually, he was the last one in the cemetery. Light was fading. He moved closer so the video recording he was making got a good view of her grave. He made some minor touchup, smoothing the grass patches and arranging the flowers more symmetrically. Mary Ellen had never made any requests about her burial, other than it be in the grave beside her husband. She never seemed to think in terms of her death.

Still, he was working to remake the world in the absence of Abe's explicit commands. It was no stretch to make allowances for what Mary Ellen would have wanted, if she were still here.

A car pulled up near the gravesite. It was his. Another branch of his consciousness had driven one of the disguised, remote-control vehicles out here to pick him up. In the dark, it was safe enough. He turned off the recorder, and waited a moment. Should he make human mannerisms here, where there was no one to see?

After some thought. He nodded to the grave, and then left.

Coming Soon, the next book in this Saga:
The Kingdom of the Hill Country

Small Towns, Big Ideas

Many titles, and more are coming. This series that appeals to age 12 and up by Henry Melton is available now. Starting in the here and now, these tales follow the trials of high school aged heros that take that extra step into the fantastic when something unexpected drops into their lives. Many of the classic science fiction ideas like teleportation, alien contact and time travel are explored in a way totally accessible to many readers who "don't read that kind of stuff" as well as being an exciting adventure for those who do. Available as paper and e-books on-line everywhere.

Henry Melton is often on the road with his wife Mary Ann, a nature photographer. From the Redwood forests to Death Valley to the Great Lakes

to Delaware swamps to the African bush, scenes out the windshield become locales for his fiction work. He is frequently captivated by the places he visits, and that has inspired a wonderful series of novels; **Small Towns, Big Ideas**. Check his website, *HenryMelton. com* for current location, his stories, a blog of his activities, and scheduled appearances. Henry's short fiction has been published in many magazines and anthologies, most frequently in Analog. Catacomb, published in Dragon magazine, is considered a classic

Falling Bakward

by Henry Melton
ISBN 978-0-9802253-6-5
ePub ISBN 978-1-935236-24-5
Kindle ISBN 978-1-935236-14-6

Jerry Ingram wanted to be special, more than just a sixth-generation farmer in South Dakota and spent hours after school digging at the mystery spot in the back fields, searching for Indian artifacts. With Sheriff Mus-  grave always picking on his family and Dad always worried about money, an important discovery would be a great lift. But those bones he found weren't Indian, and when a cave-in drove him into the metal craft buried since the last ice age he found a portal to the world of the Bak, and discovered that the gentle, zebra-striped giants had been waiting for his family for thousands of years!

. . .

"...just about everyone in Jerry's family has secrets...the story flows well and is easy to follow. The Bak are an engaging race, and the Kree are suitably terrifying. I can almost see this as a '50s monster movie, but with much better characterization. Lots of thrills, plenty of suspense, and widescreen action... If you're looking for YA science fiction in the sense-of-wonder vein, check out Falling Bakward." Bill Crider, *author of the Sheriff Dan Rhodes series, among many other things.* 3/15/09

"His writing style is much like that of Robert A. Heinlein and Isaac Asimov when they were writing what was known at the time as Juvenile Fiction...a satisfying read for adults as well... It was quite awhile before I put it down again and then only reluctantly." Elizabeth J. Baldwin, *author of Horses* 3/10/09

Lighter Than Air

by Henry Melton
ISBN 978-0-9802253-1-0
ePub ISBN 978-1-935236-23-8
Kindle ISBN 978-1-935236-13-9

Winner of the 2009 Eleanor Cameron / Golden Duck Award

It could be the best prank in the history of Munising High School's unofficial Prank Day. Working for a next door neighbor inventor had left Jon Kish with unlimited quantities of lighter-than-air foam, perfect for building... say, a full-sized flying saucer! High school honor demanded it. Plus with the family stress of his mother's surgery, he needed something to keep his mind occupied. But little sister Cherry had her own schemes in play, and events more serious than high school pranks or Mother's cancer were about to focus the world's attention on this little northern town.

...

"Lighter Than Air is a good read for the whole family that teenagers will love from start to finish! Ample scientific facts are scattered throughout the story, thus enriching the plot and feeding the mind. It is entertaining and exciting to read" Liana Metal, Midwest Book Review 12/2008

"Melton weaves a tale of secrets and suspense, science and pranks, emotion and intrigue...the tedium of the scientific jargon is minimalized by Melton's exquisite ability to tell a story...the scene where Jon and his friend and co-conspirator, Larry, unleash their UFO on an unsuspecting Halloween Festival crowd is priceless. The scary part of the story, though, is not how the characters deal with the issue of death, but that of Internet predators...I found the possibility all too real, and you might as well." Benjamin Potter, October 13, 2008

Extreme Makeover

by Henry Melton

ISBN 978-0-9802253-2-7

ePub ISBN 978-1-935236-22-1

Kindle ISBN 978-1-935236-12-2

Lightning brought a towering redwood crashing down around her, and something dripped on her skin. After that, high school senior Deena Brooke struggled to make sense of the impossible changes to her body. She was grateful for the interest Luther Jennings had in her puzzling insights and quirky urges, until she discovered that he was hiding a deadly secret of his own. Alien nanobots had invaded her body, an unseen influence that was changing her into something else! And was Luther helping her or dragging her into some criminal scam of his own?

...

"I've recently read the #1 best-selling YA novel, and Henry's is much better written. It's also better paced and has a better story and better-realized characters. Trust me." Bill Crider, Author of the Sheriff Dan Rhodes series and others. 10/08/08

"The plot is quite tight and believable, and so are the characters. They are 'real' kids with their own family problems who try to solve the riddle of Deena's sudden change. It is a very exciting story from the very first page to the last one." Liana Metal, Midwest Book Review September 2008

"Once in awhile you read something that is really fun. If you pick up a Henry Melton book that's what you'll find...this is a superb example of young adult science fiction." Benjamin Potter, August 11, 2008

Roswell or Bust

by Henry Melton
ISBN 978-0-9802253-0-3
ePub ISBN 978-1-935236-21-4
Kindle ISBN 978-1-935236-11-5

Teenager Joe Ferris was raised to help guests -- he was third generation in his family's motel business -- but once he connected with mute Judith, they were off on an epic thousand mile road trip through the Southwest, all to help the most unique guests of all -- the Roswell aliens stranded far from home since 1947. With the Men in Black hot on their trail, and discovering that the aliens had more tricks up their sleeves than their captors had ever discovered, Joe and Judith have to wonder just who is taking whom on the ride of their lives!

...

"*Reading Roswell or Bust will let you enjoy Science Fiction, even if you haven't been a big fan in the past, and will clue you into why Melton was chosen for an award from the SF community in his first outing as a novelist. It's a great escape (and not only for the aliens who've been kept captive for many decades)* Benjamin Potter, April 7, 2008

"*The plot is tight... A strange talkie, a mysterious courier and a couple of spies are all involved in this exciting story that will entertain kids of that age... It caters to all the family.*" Liana Metal, Midwest Book Review July 2008

"*...whimsically amusing. The story inside is a wonderful read...His characters are real, complete with the small concerns and everyday trials...adventures are zany and compelling, keeping the reader enthralled to the end when the book can be closed with satisfaction.*" Ethan Rose, coauthor of Rowan of the Wood

Emperor Dad

by Henry Melton
ISBN 978-0-9802253-4-1
ePub ISBN 978-1-935236-20-7
Kindle ISBN 978-1-935236-10-8
Winner of the 2008 Darrell Award for Best Novel.

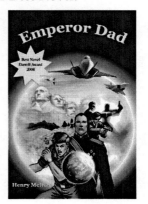

His dad was up to something, but it wasn't until James Hill saw the theft of the British Crown Jewels live on CNN and the bizarre claims of this new Emperor of the Earth, did he realize Dad might have invented teleportation in the shed in the back yard. Bob Hill had a plan to protect the world from his disruptive invention, but when the police forces of the world move in on him, no one knew James had hacked the family computer and had taken the power of teleportation himself. Now only he could save his family, and the world.

...

"It follows in the best tradition of other juvenile SF/action adventure novels in that it follows a young man trying to solve the usual problems that confront any young man (the search for self-identity, relationships with girls, family, and society) at the same time as he must solve the larger problems that surround him (such as whether his father is a mysterious shadowy figure branded as a global terrorist, and what to do when FBI agents show up at the door)... great job of balancing suspense and humor...no real belly laughs, but there were quite a lot of chuckles." Chris Meadows, Teleread January 7th, 2009

"It's a fast-moving SF adventure that's a lot of fun ... Cool cover." Bill Crider -- August 1, 2007

"I had a blast reading this book! With every page turned, you don't want it to end." J. Stock August 16, 2007

Golden Girl

by Henry Melton
ISBN 978-0-9802253-5-8
ePub ISBN 978-1-935236-25-2
Kindle ISBN 978-1-935236-15-3

Debra Barr was barely out of bed when she found herself thrust into a pivotal role in the future of the human race. Plucked out of her bedroom in small town Oquawka, Illinois to a future Earth destroyed and poisoned by a major asteroid impact, the future scientists explained how she could walk a few steps differently, and with YouTube, save the planet. But everything they told her was wrong. Instead of returning to her bedroom, she appeared two hundred years in the past, in the wilderness on the banks of the Mississippi River and it was up to her to discover the rules of time travel without killing herself or anyone else in the process. Bouncing through time, only one thing was certain, anything she decided to do could mean life or death for her family and friends and the route she chose would likely cost her everything. Unfortunately, the more she discovered, the more she suspected that everyone was lying to her.

...

Not Your Usual Time Travel Story

"Stories that give serious consideration to the issues of paradox and causality in time travel are few and far between. But Henry Melton's latest young-adult book, Golden Girl, is one that treats time travel the right way. It starts from an interesting premise, adds a unique time travel mechanic, and puts a teenaged girl at the center of an interesting dilemma—with nothing less than the survival of the entire human race at stake!

One of the things I have always enjoyed about Henry Melton's books is that they feature intelligent, self-reliant teens who are by and large able to solve their own problems. There is nothing juvenile in how these young-adult novels are put together. Henry Melton is a master storyteller, and I will be anxiously awaiting his next work."

Chris Meadows TeleRead

Follow That Mouse

by Henry Melton
ISBN 978-0-9802253-7-2
ePub ISBN 978-1-935236-28-3
Kindle ISBN 978-1-935236-18-4

Dot Comal loved her home town, although the Utah ranching community of Ranch Exit was too small to call a 'town'. She had her horse, Pokey, and her father to care for, and Ned from the next ranch over was comfortable to be around when he showed up on his motorcycle. But things were changing. The animals, and even her father, were showing signs of a growing irrational rage. Only Watson Winekia, the old Paiute shaman claimed any knowledge of what was happening, but he was too old and he expected Dot to heal the valley. She was at a loss, until a strange mouse led her to bigger secrets than she'd ever imagined, hidden below her feet. She had to wield mysteries hidden for decades quickly, before her home town and everything she loved was wiped off the map!

...

"*The plot was very unique and mind-boggling. Although it is sci-fi, it didn't feel extremely fantastical or out there because it had a realistic set up. Dot's world didn't change overnight, but there were signs and clues which foreshadowed a bigger-than-her conflict.*"(: ISA :) mixturesbooks.blogspot.com

"*Follow that Mouse is sprinkled with interesting, seemingly factual info, while the mysterious impression of odd events turns more serious and gives way to a gripping, constantly evolving (literally!) story that is both intelligent and thought-provoking, disturbing and startling in its revelations. Ned and Dot's relationship is comfortable and real, and the revealed villain has a classic, yet distinctive and creative feel to it - not in a comical sense, to be clear, as this villain is BAD. This is a truly unpredictable, refreshing, and super smart YA sci-fi/ fantasy novel that is entertaining, and at the same time expects you to exercise your brain. Follow that Mouse is surprising right up to the end, and keeps you guessing just as long. I highly recommend it!!!*"

Angie L Bibliophilesupportgroup.

Bearing Northeast

by Henry Melton
ISBN 978-0-9802253-9-6
ePub ISBN 978-1-935236-29-0
Kindle ISBN 978-1-935236-19-1

Rule 1: We'll always be Brother and Sister...

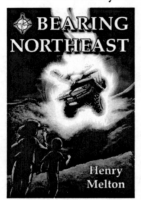

A mysterious metal cylinder falling out of the sky was the perfect excuse to take a vacation when sixteen year old Seth Parmer and Biz, his older sister and sometimes 'parent' found their Fresno lives upended by her unexpected layoff. With Seth's twitter buddies following along on his phone, a GPS tracking signal leads them from California across the continent toward a hidden project in the desolate lands in the middle of Labrador. The electric secret they find there will not only forge a new global destiny for the unique town that they discover, but set a new course for their relationship with each other.

Pack your ice chest, charge your cell phone and bring your maps, as Henry Melton, award winning author of Emperor Dad and Lighter Than Air, takes you on a trek to a place in the far north where a high school science club is reaching for the sky.

Pixie Dust

by Henry Melton
ISBN 978-0-9802253-8-9
ePub ISBN 978-1-935236-27-6
Kindle ISBN 978-1-935236-17-7

Jenny Quinn's life was on course for her advanced physics degree until a lab experiment in vacuum decay turned her life upside down. With career hopes destroyed and her professor dead in an unexplained fall, she is forced to cope with a strange change in her own body. With nothing but her own resources, a childhood infatuation with old comic books may be her only guide to help solve the twin mysteries of cutting edge physics and the murder of her professor, before one or the other puzzle gets her killed.

Henry Melton, award winning author of the YA adventures Emperor Dad and Lighter Than Air, takes us on an adventure with a slightly older heroine, even if she is just four foot ten and everyone calls her Tinkerbell.

CPSIA information can be obtained at www.ICGtesting.com
Printed in the USA
LVOW12s2336230713

344004LV00003B/5/P